D1021060

THE LAWS OF MAGIC
WORD OF HONOUR

THE LAWS OF MAGIC SERIES

Book One: Blaze of Glory

Book Two: Heart of Gold

Book Three: Word of Honour

Book Four: Time of Trial

Book Five: Moment of Truth
Available August 2010!

Book Six: Hour of Need
Coming soon!

MICHAEL PRYOR

RANDOM HOUSE AUSTRALIA

A Random House book
Published by Random House Australia Pty Ltd
Level 3, 100 Pacific Highway, North Sydney NSW 2060
www.randomhouse.com.au

First published by Random House Australia in 2008
This edition first published in 2010

Addresses for companies within the Random House Group can be found at www.randomhouse.com.au/offices.

National Library of Australia
Cataloguing-in-Publication Entry

Author: Pryor, Michael
Title: Word of honour / Michael Pryor
ISBN: 978 1 86471 864 5 (pbk.)
Series: Pryor, Michael. Laws of magic; 3
Target audience: For secondary school age
Dewey number: A823.3

Cover illustration by Jeremy Reston
Cover design by www.blacksheep-uk.com
Internal design by Mathematics
Typeset in Bembo by Midland Typesetters, Australia

10 9 8 7 6 5 4 3 2

Printed and bound by The SOS Print + Media Group

The paper this book is printed on is certified by the ©1996 Forest Stewardship Council A.C. (FSC). SOS Print + Media Group holds FSC chain of custody certification (Cert no. SGS-COC-3047).

FSC promotes environmentally responsible, socially beneficial and economically viable management of the world's forests.

For Agnes Nieuwenhuizen

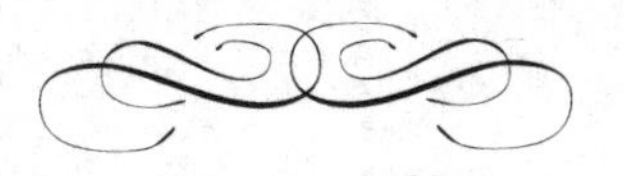

One

Aubrey Fitzwilliam was buttering toast when his father strode into the dining room. 'Ah, Aubrey. Good. I need you to help me elude the Special Services.'

Aubrey's knife hovered over the butter dish. He glanced at George, who was enjoying a large serve of bacon and eggs. His friend managed to shrug while folding half a rasher into his mouth.

'Your bodyguards?'

'What's the point of being Prime Minister if I can't nip off whenever I feel like it?' Sir Darius took a slice of Aubrey's toast. 'So I need your skills, quick smart.'

George snorted. 'These would be the skills of leaving Maidstone undetected, would they?'

'Exactly, George. Skills Aubrey has honed over the years, despite the best efforts of his parents.'

'He's got you there, old man,' George said.

Aubrey chose his words carefully. 'Without admitting that I have these alleged skills, why do you need to leave so abruptly?'

'Something has come up. I've found it tends to, when one is in charge of the country.' This time it was Sir Darius's turn to choose his words carefully. 'I need to visit Clear Haven, post-haste.'

Aubrey's curiosity – already doing a series of warm-up exercises – threw itself into an advanced callisthenic routine to make sure he paid attention to it.

He'd always wanted to visit Albion's northern naval base. While the fleet spent most of its time at Imworth in the south, Clear Haven was where much of the heavy development work was done. The best military magicians – along with eminent civilian consultants – worked at Clear Haven to produce the most effective magical weapons. The work done at Clear Haven was one of the reasons that Albion still ruled the waves, despite Holmland's efforts.

'I may be able to get you out of here unnoticed,' Aubrey said, 'but you'd have to take George and me with you.'

'Capital. I was going to ask you anyway.' Sir Darius finished the slice of toast and took another. 'Now, what do we do?'

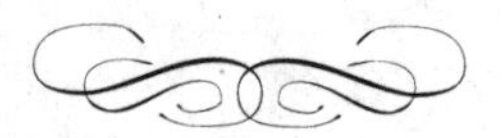

THE LANDING HAD A FINE VIEW OF THE TELEPHONE, RIGHT next to the front door. Aubrey watched as the more senior of the two bodyguards – tall, dark hair, military moustache – nodded and spoke into the mouthpiece. 'Yes, sir. Right away.'

He hung up, frowning a little, and sketched a salute to Sir Darius, who was waiting near the foot of the stairs. 'Sorry, sir, but Crowley and I have to head straight back to Lattimer Hall.'

The younger Special Services operative raised his eyebrows, but didn't say anything.

'That's quite all right, Sutcliffe,' Sir Darius said. 'I've always felt that Captain Tallis's precautions were a little overdone, two able-bodied men guarding me in my own home.'

'Tricky times, these, sir. Holmlanders and whatnot about. Can't be too careful.' Sutcliffe shifted uneasily and eyed the front door.

'You don't look happy, Sutcliffe,' Sir Darius said. 'There's no need to be concerned.'

'I know, sir. Captain Tallis said that replacements were on their way, but we shouldn't leave before they get here. That's not procedure.'

'I understand.' Sir Darius guided the two men to the door. 'But, as you say, these are tricky times. We must be flexible.'

Sir Darius stood with his back to the door once it had closed after them. He smoothed his moustache for a moment, then glanced up the stairs at Aubrey. 'Remarkable. How did you do it? Magic?'

Aubrey waited for George, who was hurrying down from upstairs. 'The magic can only achieve so much. It was George. He does a better Captain Tallis than I do.'

Aubrey didn't want to tell his father that the less magic he did at the moment, the better. His condition had been particularly unstable and magic made things worse.

'I see,' his father said. 'You've been practising imitating Captain Tallis, have you?'

'As research,' Aubrey said quickly. 'An exercise. The Law of Similarities means that it's easier to work up a spell to alter George's voice into Captain Tallis's than mine. He has a deeper timbre, and I believe Tallis spent some time in the country in his youth.'

'Country lads, both of us,' George beamed. 'Must ask him about pigs, one day.'

'I'd like to discuss this further,' Sir Darius said, 'but we must be off. I don't want to lose the opportunity.'

'One thing,' Aubrey said. 'How are you going to deal with the upshot of this little deception? Won't Tallis be furious?'

'It doesn't take much to make Tallis furious, but I take your point.' Sir Darius thought for a moment. 'This is a test,' he declared. 'A test of the capabilities of the Special Services. And it seems their methods need tightening up.'

Stubbs, the Fitzwilliam family driver, was idling the Oakleigh-Nash at the front door. The twelve-cylinder engine rumbled with the sleek power that only came from the best magically enhanced valves. 'Ormsby Square,' Sir Darius said when they'd flung the doors closed.

Stubbs accelerated smoothly and they were out of the gates into the traffic.

Sir Darius settled back into the accommodating leather seat; he gazed out of the window.

'Clive Rokeby-Taylor is joining us, isn't he?' Aubrey said suddenly.

Sir Darius turned to him. 'Your reasoning?'

'We're off to Clear Haven. Rokeby-Taylor has substantial shipbuilding concerns. And we're going to

Ormsby Square, which isn't on the way to the ornithopter port. Exclusive area. Rokeby-Taylor is its most notorious inhabitant.'

'Notorious?'

'George often mentions his name when he's trawling through the gossip columns. Gambler, racing enthusiast, attractor of scandals.'

'Number seventeen is renowned for exotic parties,' George said. 'And Rokeby-Taylor is rarely seen without a famous actress or two on his arm. Different ones each time, of course. On different arms.'

'Hmm.' Sir Darius crossed his arms. 'Clive Rokeby-Taylor and I were at school together.'

This was news to Aubrey, but he wasn't surprised – there was much about the past of both his parents that was a mystery. Not deliberately so – it was just that they had led such varied lives that minor details like this often surfaced at unexpected times. 'At Stonelea?'

'We shared rooms in our last year, then we went on to university. St Alban's College, where you two are headed.'

'You've never mentioned him.'

'We lost touch. We've been at the same functions at the same time, but I haven't actually spoken to him for ten years. Ships that pass in the night and all that.'

'He's very successful,' George said. 'Shipbuilding, electricity generation, chemical manufacture.' He caught Aubrey's look. 'I do read more than the gossip pages, you know.'

'So we *are* meeting Rokeby-Taylor?' Aubrey said to his father.

'One of his firms has been working with the Navy Board on a top secret project. He's asked me to go with him to Clear Haven on some sort of demonstration jaunt.'

'A top secret *jaunt*?'

'Clive's word, not mine. And that sums him up. Life is a jaunt to him, which is why it comes as a surprise to find him engaged in such serious matters as defence contracting.' Sir Darius frowned. 'Even though he calls this expedition a jaunt, it is serious, because of our circumstances.'

'The war,' Aubrey said simply.

'The war that we hope and pray will not happen,' Sir Darius said.

'The war that seems inevitable,' George added.

Sir Darius sighed. 'Sadly, that seems to be the case. The situation on the continent continues to worsen. Holmland ambitions, border disputes in the Goltans . . . To call the continent a powder keg is rather under-estimating affairs.'

'And how has Rokeby-Taylor come into this?' Aubrey asked.

'I authorised a special program, part of our efforts to update our fleet. This special program allocated funds for development of advanced units.'

'Magical units,' Aubrey guessed.

'Magical enhancement would be part of any innovative military development, most likely. This has been encour-aged for some time, after all. Remember Banford Park?'

Aubrey nodded. Banford Park was the research facility near Prince Albert's country residence. Aubrey and George had had several scrapes there, and it was where Dr Mordecai Tremaine had taken Sir Darius after kidnapping him.

'Rokeby-Taylor's companies have participated in this program?'

'Apparently. Always good at sniffing out money, was Clive. I had no idea of his involvement until he telephoned late last week.'

Aubrey was silent for a moment. He caught George's eye and saw the puzzlement there that he felt himself. He considered a number of indirect approaches, but then decided a frontal sortie was best. 'Sir? It seems a little odd, the Prime Minister slipping off like this after a telephone call from an old friend he hasn't spoken to for a decade.'

Sir Darius grinned. 'It does, doesn't it?' He leaned forward and rubbed his hands together. 'To tell the truth, I simply needed to do something out of the ordinary. Prime Ministership can become rather staid, even in these times. Besides, I'd heard so much about Rokeby-Taylor over the years that once we spoke, my curiosity wouldn't leave me alone until we met again.'

Something else you've handed down to me, Aubrey thought. As a family heirloom, this curiosity was a mixed blessing. It often sent him in directions that others wouldn't have noticed, but at its worst it was almost a physical itch, an acute discomfort impossible to ignore.

This time, however, it was suspicion rather than curiosity that prodded him. 'Ten years, an old friend reappearing . . . what could be more natural than wanting to meet?'

'But you're not convinced?'

'Look for the reason behind the reason, you've always advised.'

Sir Darius nodded his approval and Aubrey felt a moment of deep satisfaction. 'Very impressive, Aubrey.'

He sat back and steepled his hands. 'Would it interest you to know that the week before Rokeby-Taylor got in touch with me, both Craddock and Tallis have asked me about him?'

Tallis, Aubrey could understand. The Special Services had the responsibility for all clandestine affairs, espionage and intelligence gathering. The head of a major defence contractor would naturally be of interest to them. But Craddock? What would the Magisterium want with Rokeby-Taylor?

'Are his companies using magic at all?'

'Rokeby-Taylor has recently been hiring a number of outstandingly talented magicians.'

Snap. This sort of direction would bring any company to the Magisterium's attention. Rokeby-Taylor sounded as if he was a man to keep an eye on.

'A modern businessman, is he?' Aubrey asked. 'Working with magic like this?'

'He's always been interested in magic. He showed some talent early on. After college, he studied overseas for a few years. I heard he took some advanced magic courses, but never finished. The good life was too attractive to him.'

Aubrey found this an interesting insight into Rokeby-Taylor's character. The ability to use magic was much like the ability to do mathematics. The best magicians had natural aptitude, but it took study and discipline to achieve true competence. Aubrey had seen young people with only moderate magical ability become good magicians through dedication and hard work – and he'd seen talented boys at Stonelea squander their gifts through lack of application.

In Aubrey's view, a magician needed a number of attributes: facility with languages, strong will, adaptability, fearlessness, and an ability to deal with the unexpected. Most only had a few of these and their shortcomings usually found them out.

Still, if Rokeby-Taylor could bring magic and engineering together, good luck to him.

'He's always been in a hurry,' Sir Darius continued. 'Juggling a hundred things at once. But when he rang, he sounded positively urgent.'

Busy times, Aubrey thought. In the next month, a number of important events were imminent: a major defence-spending bill in Parliament, the birthday of the Elektor of Holmland, the Counting of the Coins – and Ophelia Hepworth's exhibition opening.

Immediately, his thoughts went to Caroline. He hoped that she was safe on his mother's Arctic expedition. For a moment, disappointment and guilt circled him like hungry ravens, but he pushed them away by imagining the multitude of things that could go wrong in the polar regions – and how he could possibly effect a miraculous rescue.

Stubbs interrupted Aubrey's musings. 'Here we are, sirs. Ormsby Square. Number seventeen, was it?'

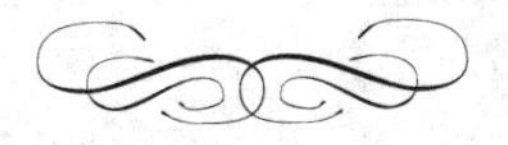

THEY WAITED FOR THEIR HOST IN THE GRAND ENTRANCE OF Rokeby-Taylor's residence. It was a magnificent round hall, full of gilt and marble, designed to impress.

'Ah, Darius! I'm glad you're here!' Clive Rokeby-Taylor appeared at the top of the wide staircase. At first,

Aubrey thought his hair was a startling white, but that was because he stood in the sunlight coming from the cupola directly above the staircase. When Rokeby-Taylor drew nearer, Aubrey saw that his hair was golden. As the industrialist came down the stairs he spread his arms wide, looking like a grain god descending to bestow the blessings of the harvest. 'It's been too long.'

'Clive.' Sir Darius shook the proffered hand. 'This is my son, Aubrey, and his good friend George Doyle. I hope you don't mind my bringing them along.'

'Not at all, not at all.' When Aubrey shook Rokeby-Taylor's hand, the grip was firm and decisive, the sort of handshake that immediately inspired confidence. Aubrey couldn't help smiling in response to Rokeby-Taylor's breezy charm. 'Aubrey. George. You're Stonelea boys, aren't you? Tell me, has the old place changed much?'

Rokeby-Taylor was only of medium height, but seemed taller because of his energy. Aubrey could easily imagine him bouncing on his toes, impatient to move if kept in one place for too long. His eager, open face made him seem younger than Sir Darius.

'I say, Clive, you're wearing green these days,' Sir Darius said, pointing to Rokeby-Taylor's tie.

Rokeby-Taylor glanced down and his brow wrinkled in what could have been irritation. It vanished in an instant, though, and he grinned sunnily. 'Many things have changed, Darius. I now wear both red and green with confidence.' He saw Aubrey and George's puzzlement. 'No secret. I'm colourblind, have been all my life. Never been able to tell the difference between red and green so I avoided both of them.' He shook his head.

'But not now. I have a man who dresses me. A whole new world, it is.'

Sir Darius cleared his throat as Rokeby-Taylor launched into a story about Stonelea and how he hid a goat under the stage of Clough Hall. 'We should go. I don't have much time.'

'Of course, Darius. But I want to hear more about the old school, you understand?' He winked at Aubrey and George. 'I've chartered an ornithopter. Shall we?'

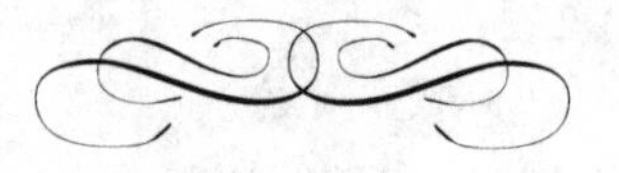

Two

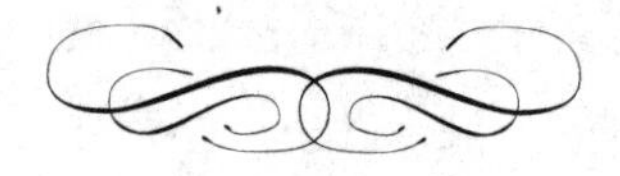

Clear Haven was a vast deepwater anchorage in the middle of the Tangasset Islands in the north of Albion. As the ornithopter swept over Bamleigh Strait, Aubrey's excitement rose. Ahead, the rocky, forbidding islands of Rothman and Hurley were separated by a wide channel – the southern access to Clear Haven.

The channel opened out before them into a wide expanse of sheltered harbour, the home of the Great Fleet of Albion. Aubrey counted more than fifty ships – battleships, destroyers, cruisers – and scores of smaller tenders, lighters and supply ships. It was a confident, almost arrogant, display of power. Aubrey hoped it would be enough for the troubled times that lay ahead.

The ornithopter tilted, banking to the left in a wide arc. The pilot eased the aircraft toward the northern island of Whiteside, where the shoreside component of the naval headquarters was situated.

Considering the short warning given by the pilot's radio contact, the welcoming party waiting at the ornithopter port was impressively large. Each man had a hand clamped to his cap to stop it blowing off in the wind created by the enormous wings.

Rokeby-Taylor craned his neck and peered out of the window. 'I've been dealing with faceless men at the Navy Board, Darius. Who's who out there?'

'Admiral Elliot's on the right,' Sir Darius said after the pilot shut down the engines. 'Admiral of the Fleet. The rest are admirals, vice admirals, rear-admirals. A few captains, but most of them are probably out there, doing the hard work of keeping their ships ready.'

'Wonderful. I'm glad they're here to see history being made.'

'There's nothing like a budget reallocation to make an admiral sit up and take notice,' Sir Darius said. 'There is a lot of money at stake here.'

'I know that, Darius, believe me. But it's still exciting, isn't it?'

George slapped a cap onto his head. 'I hope we'll get a chance to visit one of the dreadnoughts.'

'If we have time,' Sir Darius said. He smoothed his moustache with a finger, thoughtfully. 'We have other vessels to visit, first.'

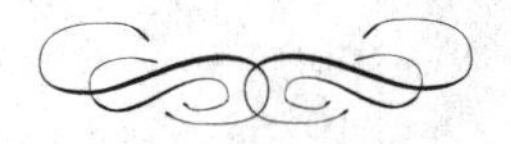

Admiral Elliot was a lanky, angular man with a close, white beard that matched his hair. His eyes were a watery blue. They looked vague and distant, but when he spoke it was with the clipped rhythm of a man accustomed to giving orders – and having them obeyed immediately.

He greeted Sir Darius and Rokeby-Taylor and took them aside. As soon as he did, a youngish-looking officer stepped forward from the gaggle of top brass and introduced himself to Aubrey and George. 'Thomas Stephens. I've been given the job of escorting you around today. Not sure if it's to keep you out of trouble or me.'

His hair was fair, cut short, but Aubrey could see that it was curly. He had a trim moustache; he was stout and of middling height.

Aubrey quickly counted the stripes on the man's sleeve. 'Captain Stephens, is it?'

Stephens spread his hands as if to suggest it was all a mystery to him. 'Apparently someone at the Admiralty got their files mixed up. Happens all the time.'

'Weren't you captain of the *Steadfast* in the Kregheim disaster?'

Stephens brushed this away. 'Fine ship, the *Steadfast*. Almost sailed herself.'

That may have been true, but Aubrey was sure that it wasn't the ship that gave the orders to steam into rebel-held Jarosevnia and rescue the Albion citizens trapped there – while being peppered by the guns in the massive fort that overlooked the city.

'And what's your current command?'

Captain Stephens grinned. 'Can't tell you right now, I'm afraid. Exciting stuff, though.' He scanned the crowd milling around Sir Darius, Rokeby-Taylor and Admiral Elliot. The officers were doing their best to look attentive while the admiral pointed out features of the base. 'A grand sailor, Admiral Elliot, can navigate the Rosscommon

Shoals on a moonless night without scraping his bottom.'

'I should hope not,' Aubrey said after some deliberation.

A dozen or so brand-new motorcars arrived. Admiral Elliot took Sir Darius and Rokeby-Taylor in the first. Captain Stephens made sure Aubrey and George were in the second, and he ordered the driver to head toward a long, nondescript building on the water's edge, just around a rocky point from the main dock area, while the other cars took the remaining officers back to the main base.

The sun was still high in the sky, even though George pointed out it was nearly four o'clock. A light breeze came onshore, carrying the smell of salt mixed with the potent tang of oil and coal. A bell rang across the water, the sound coming from one of the predatory ships that rode in the bay. Aubrey shaded his eyes against the sunlight skipping across the multitude of tiny waves. The might of Albion, the power that kept the seas free, was invested in this place. Without such a fleet, the island nation would be vulnerable in the worst way.

Which is why everyone views Holmland's naval build-up with more than a little disquiet, he thought and he counted the ships again to reassure himself.

As the party came closer to the corrugated-iron building that was their destination, Aubrey saw that one end actually projected some distance into the sea. Apart from that, it looked remarkably like a dirigible hangar – tall, with a single gable, a ridge running along its entire length. No windows. Two huge doors on the landward side, opening onto the road. A smaller door facing them.

'Is this a research facility?' he asked Admiral Elliot when they'd alighted from their vehicles.

The admiral glanced at him. Aubrey could see him weighing up whether he could afford to ignore the son of the Prime Minister or not. Eventually, he answered with some reluctance. 'It's part of it. Enclosed dock.'

'Ah. To keep away sightseers.'

Admiral Elliot worked his jaw for a moment. 'Something like that.'

Aubrey scanned the skies. They were a long way away from anywhere. Exactly who were they afraid of? Sunny skies, refreshing breeze, but suddenly the day seemed to be far more ominous than Aubrey had previously thought. He chewed at his lip. He stopped, gathered himself and reached out, using his special awareness, looking for any sign of magic, trying to get a sense of what may be going on behind the walls ahead.

He was rewarded with a palpable hit.

Heavy-duty magic was lurking behind those walls. Impressive, revolutionary stuff, if Aubrey was any judge. A derivative of spells stemming from the Law of Regression, he suspected, but exactly how that could help the navy, he had no idea.

Captain Stephens broke from the small group and hurried ahead. He unlocked the small door in the side of the facility and saluted. 'This way, Prime Minister, if you please.'

Inside, the shed was lit by electric lights suspended from the lofty ceiling. Aubrey was again reminded of the dirigible hangars in Lutetia, for the gantries, chains and heavy lifting equipment were all the same. It was apparent that serious engineering took place here. The place was quiet, but it wasn't hard to imagine it as a scene of industrial activity – hammering, welding, cutting, wrenching metal into shape.

Aubrey's sense of déjà vu had another tweak when his eyes grew accustomed to the change of light and he became more and more excited at what he saw. A long cigar shape took up most of the far end, where the shed projected into the water. Either side of the cigar shape were walkways, wooden jetties on solid piles driven into the seabed.

'Our experimental vessel, the *Electra*,' Rokeby-Taylor said. He beamed at it, as if he'd built every inch himself. 'Rokeby-Taylor Shipbuilding's finest work.'

'Ah, so this is the famous submersible,' Sir Darius said. 'At last.'

'You've heard of it?' Admiral Elliot bristled. 'This is meant to be top secret!'

'Well, I *am* the Prime Minister,' Sir Darius reminded him. 'Now, Clive, you say this is going to revolutionise naval warfare?'

'It's going to make battleships obsolete,' Rokeby-Taylor said airily. 'It's the way of the future.'

Aubrey had been admiring the size of the submersible – it was far longer than anything he'd heard of – but he winced at Rokeby-Taylor's insensitive remark.

'Obsolete?' Admiral Elliot thundered. 'Battleships? Never! Besides, these submersibles are unsporting. Hiding under water where they can't be seen? How is that fair?'

Captain Stephens coughed. 'Perhaps I should show the Prime Minister through the *Electra*?'

'That's what you're here for, Stephens,' Admiral Elliot growled. 'Take over.'

Admiral Elliot marched out of the facility without looking back. Captain Stephens apologised. 'He's a strong supporter of the submersible development program. Just don't disparage his battleships.'

'Did I do that?' Rokeby-Taylor looked crestfallen, but then he grinned. 'I won't do it again. Can't afford to have him offside. I say, Stephens, you don't know what sort of whisky old Elliot favours? I should send him a case or two, by way of apology.'

Sir Darius looked along the length of the *Electra*. 'So, Stephens, you're commanding this ship?'

'Boat,' Captain Stephens said. 'Submersibles are boats, not ships.'

'Why's that?' Aubrey asked. 'It looks big enough to be a ship.'

Stephens smiled. 'That it is, plenty big enough. One hundred and eighty feet, thirty men. But the first submersibles weren't this big, twenty, thirty years ago. Tiny things, limited range. They were called boats and it's stuck.'

'Wait until you see inside,' Rokeby-Taylor said. 'It's a masterpiece.'

Captain Stephens turned on his heel. 'This way, gentlemen.'

He took them to a gangway. Above them, a conning tower projected from the body of the submersible, twice the height of a man.

'The *Electra*, Prime Minister,' Stephens announced. 'The most advanced vessel in the Albion fleet. This boat represents the ultimate blend of science, engineering and magic. Just you wait until you see her in action.'

Aubrey grinned at Stephens's infectious enthusiam. It

was good to see someone so keen on using the latest developments. Many in the military were wary of magic; Stephens seemed eager to embrace it.

'We've had some of the best people working on it, Darius,' Rokeby-Taylor said. 'We even brought in some clever chaps from the Continent, to work on the batteries. The guidance system on the torpedoes was a collaboration job, Phelps and Ainsworth.'

'From Greythorn?' Aubrey asked. 'They were part of the research team on elemental magic.'

'This is much more important than all that theoretical stuff,' Rokeby-Taylor said. 'This is vital for the defence of the realm.'

Aubrey had a different point of view on that but he bit his tongue.

Captain Stephens strolled over the gangway. 'Double hulled, the *Electra* is,' he went on. 'The internal hull for holding pressure and the external skin shaped to let us slip through the water like a shark.'

He climbed up the ladder on the side of the conning tower. Sir Darius mounted easily; the others followed.

Aubrey was fascinated by the *Electra*. This sort of thing excited him – using magic in a careful, rational way to improve processes and materials, to break new ground, to shape new futures. The sooner all the mystical hand-waving could be left behind as an embarrassing relic of the past, the better. Magic was knowable, just as the inner workings of atoms was proving to be knowable. It was a bold world that was dawning and Aubrey was eager to be part of it.

Captain Stephens proudly showed them around. Aubrey couldn't help noticing how everything was built on a reduced scale – passageways, doors, even bunks – and he assumed the sailors selected to serve on the *Electra* would be chosen for their stature as much as anything else, the same way jockeys were.

He had a momentary vision of the narrow stairs full of colourful racing silks and he stifled a laugh.

Captain Stephens glanced sharply at him. 'Yes, you're bound to find the air a bit close down here. That's what happens when you run engines in a confined space, then pack thirty men in as well.'

'Show them the batteries, Stephens,' Rokeby-Taylor said. He turned to the others. 'It's where we have some of our most advanced magical developments.'

Captain Stephens glanced at his watch. 'It'll have to wait for a moment, sir. The officers should have come aboard and the crew is due. If you'll follow me to the wardroom.'

A long whistle sounded from above. Then the whole submersible began to echo with the noise of running feet and shouted orders. Captain Stephens glanced upward. 'We're about to get rather crowded. Let's hurry.'

The officers' wardroom was a neat, tiny area. It had a table large enough to seat four – if they didn't mind sitting shoulder to shoulder – with chairs to match. The table had a starched white cloth, but was otherwise bare. Shelves on the walls were stacked with books. A hatch opened onto the galley and Aubrey could see sailors already at work.

An officer was present. He blinked for a moment, goggled at the newcomers, and then seemed to remember what was expected of him. He rose, knocked over his chair and made what could be called a salute only by those with extremely poor eyesight.

Captain Stephens covered a smile. 'Prime Minister, Mr Rokeby-Taylor, this is Lieutenant Henry Atwood. Special Assignment.'

'Atwood,' Sir Darius said. 'We're pleased to be aboard.'

Atwood considered this. 'Sir?' His wrinkled jacket looked as if it had been only recently yanked out of a bottom drawer in lieu of anything better to wear. His cap struggled to cover a mop of black curly hair. His eyes bulged slightly and his nose was red.

'Special Assignment,' Sir Darius continued. 'You've been dragged from magical studies somewhere or other?'

'Angel College, sir. One minute I was working on transformational magic, the next I'm here.'

'Atwood is one of our specialists,' Rokeby-Taylor said. 'We needed the best, so we went out and got him.'

'I didn't have much choice,' Atwood said plaintively. 'The dean said they were closing my laboratory.'

'Quite, quite,' Rokeby-Taylor said. 'Still, the facilities at Clear Haven are first class, I'm sure. If they're not, you just let me know and I'll have something done about it right away.'

'Yes, sir.' Atwood brightened. 'Yes, sir.'

Captain Stephens saluted. 'If all is in order, sir, I'll go to the control room and take her out.'

Aubrey must have made some sound, for everyone looked at him. 'We're actually going on a cruise, in a submersible?'

Rokeby-Taylor beamed. 'It's the best way to show off this wonder. Your father has had some doubts about the project, I've heard, so I thought he needed to see it. He can't help but be impressed after the *Electra* goes through her paces.' He scratched behind his ear. 'Stephens, exactly where are we going?'

'The aim of our voyage is to head up the north-west channel, between Whiteside Island and the Glough to the west.'

'Submerged?' Aubrey asked.

'Not through the channel. Once we clear it – about half an hour or so – we're in the open sea. We'll dive, run on batteries, and we'll see what she can do. If the weather's kind, we'll surface near a speck of rock called the Widow's Sorrow, surprise the seabirds and point at the seals, if any are home.'

'Excellent,' Sir Darius said. 'I'm looking forward to it.'

'As are we all. Atwood, to your post.'

Isolated as they were in the wardroom, Aubrey nevertheless had the impression of being in the middle of furious activity. Shouts bounced along the walls, adding to the mounting vibrations; mysterious thuds and clanks made the deck shudder. Running through all of this was the muffled cursing that seemed to be the standard operating noise of seamen. Rokeby-Taylor disappeared, saying he wanted to check the battery set-up. He returned a few minutes later, red-faced and muttering about over-officious petty officers.

Soon, Sir Darius began drumming his fingers. 'Aubrey?'

'Sir?'

'You're sensing magic here?'

'Certainly. All around.'

'What sort?'

This was difficult. Describing varieties of magic to a non-magician was like describing musical scales to the tone deaf. 'Complex. Very different from anything I've experienced.'

'New?'

Aubrey spread his hands. 'It could be. I need to get closer to the source.'

'Hmm.' Sir Darius resumed his finger-drumming. 'Well, keep at it, please.' He glared at the walls of the wardroom, as if he wished he could see right through them.

Rokeby-Taylor waved a hand. 'You're interested in magic?'

'I'm going to study it at university, sir,' Aubrey said.

'Good man. You must have more talent than I had. Or more application. Fascinating stuff, magic.' He pursed his lips. 'Let me see. I might be able to remember a fire spell I was quite a dab hand at.'

'Fire on a submersible?' George said. 'Not a good idea, Mr Rokeby-Taylor.'

'Eh? I say, you're right.' He slapped himself on the forehead and laughed. 'Can't have the builder of the boat blowing it up now, can we?'

Aubrey couldn't help but join in the laughter. It was hard not to, when someone was laughing at themselves so unselfconsciously.

Rokeby-Taylor cocked an ear. 'D'you hear those engines, Darius? Most modern diesels, they are, but wait until we switch to batteries. That's where our real advances are.'

George gripped the table. 'We're moving.'

Aubrey could feel it. The sound of the diesel engines increased until it was a deep, throaty pounding, enough to set off a thousand different rattles in the wardroom alone.

After half an hour the diesel engines changed their note. They rose in pitch, turned almost to a thunder, before rumbling and then ceasing entirely. In its place was a deep hum, almost a whine, that set Aubrey's teeth on edge.

A bell rang and immediately the deck tilted beneath them.

George yelped, but caught himself before he fell off his chair. Rokeby-Taylor swayed for a second, but managed to stay upright. He looked proud of himself.

Aubrey held onto the table, his excitement rising. 'Here we go, then.'

'Interesting experience, isn't it?' Sir Darius said, raising his voice over the noise. 'Putting yourself totally in the hands of someone else.'

'Well, if we can't trust the navy,' George said, having recovered his balance, 'who can we trust?'

'I'm glad we have your confidence.' Captain Stephens appeared at the door, hands behind his back. 'The navy is here to serve, you know.'

'Shouldn't you be steering this thing?' George asked, staring.

'Lieutenant Stone, my First Mate, is at the helm. We're in good hands.'

The deck beneath their feet shifted again, then levelled. Aubrey noted how Captain Stephens altered his stance to accommodate the change in orientation, easily, without having to steady himself with a hand. It was an efficient, capable display of expertise.

'Everything running smoothly, Captain?' Sir Darius asked.

'Topnotch,' Captain Stephens said. 'I thought you might like tea once we'd reached our cruising depth.'

'Cruising depth,' Aubrey asked. 'How deep is that?'

'About ten fathoms. Deep enough to avoid enemy detection.'

'How do you find your way along when you're this deep?' George asked. 'Must be pretty murky out there.'

Captain Stephens stood back from the doorway and ushered in a steward with a tea tray. 'Pitch black. But we don't have any portholes anyway. We rely on compass headings and good charts. And we're trying out a new gadget, too.'

Rokeby-Taylor grimaced at this. 'I was saving that for a surprise.'

'Ah, more magic?' Sir Darius said.

'Partly,' Captain Stephens said. 'You should ask Atwood about it. Something to do with bouncing echoes off things. It's not working at one hundred percent efficiency as yet, but we're aiming to test it over the next few months.'

Rokeby-Taylor smiled broadly. Sir Darius glanced at him. 'What other surprises do you have for me?'

'Wait until you see the torpedo guidance system. It uses the Law of Similarities for targeting. Spectacular.'

Aubrey was alert at this but, before he could ask anything, the light overhead blinked. Then it flared a sudden blue-white before dwindling to a sickly yellow. At the same time an electrical roar came from the bow, a baleful hissing that Aubrey felt as much as heard. Suddenly, his breath was taken away as he was buffeted by a wave of complex magic. He clutched at his chest, struggling to breathe, and tried to make sense of what had struck him.

'Stay here,' Captain Stephens snapped, then bounded out of the door to the shrieking of a klaxon.

'I say,' George began, but stopped abruptly as the floor tilted again and the submersible began to plunge.

Immediately, Aubrey knew this was no controlled dive – test or not. The deck dropped away and it was suddenly like looking down the side of a tall building.

At that point, everyone scrabbled for handholds.

The klaxon continued, a harsh metallic braying that overrode a cacophony of shouting, rending and shattering. The chairs in the wardroom started to slide. Books fell from the shelves. The table was bolted to the floor, an island of solidity, but the tea service – cups, teapot, sugar bowl – crashed to the deck.

Aubrey had an awful instant where panic offered to take over; he decided that gibbering and running in circles probably wasn't going to be useful so he declined. His body had other thoughts, however. His heart accelerated, his breathing slipped straight into 'rapid and shallow' mode, his palms somehow decided that copious amounts of sweat might be useful when it came to clinging for his life, and his stomach tried to turn itself inside out in a demented effort not to be left out of the general uproar. Aubrey closed his eyes for a moment, gritted his teeth, and refused to surrender.

He clung to the table while his father wedged himself in the corner of the room. George had fetched up against the door. The walls around them shook. Deep, tortured groans came from deep in the bowels of the vessel, but these came from no human throat – they were the protests of the craft itself as its walls resisted the mounting pressure of the depths.

A colossal shock racked the submersible. Aubrey was

thrown to the deck. He lay there, alert, his mind racing, wondering what was happening.

The next moment, the *Electra* was rocked by another immense impact, much greater than the first. Aubrey was hurled against the leg of the table. He gasped as he took the blow on his shoulder and bit back a cry of pain.

Then the lights went out.

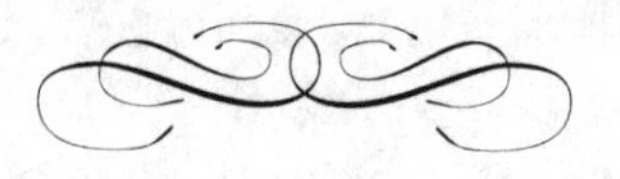

Three

AFTER A MOMENT OF INTENSE, TERRIFYING DARKNESS, the electric light flickered and came on again. Dull orange, it wavered ominously.

His heart still racing, Aubrey tried to take stock. The deck seemed to have levelled. In the corners, piles of books, broken china, chairs. He saw his father, face down, arms spread.

Fear muscled panic aside. Then Sir Darius lifted his head and scanned the room. Relief nearly turned Aubrey's muscles to rubber. 'That second thump would have been the stern hitting the sea bed,' Sir Darius said. He rose – knees bent, arms away from his side, ready for any further shocks.

Aubrey helped George up. 'I wish they'd turn off that klaxon,' he said. *It might help us hear if we're leaking or not.*

George looked around uneasily, as if he expected the walls to collapse at any second. 'What happened?'

'Clive?' Sir Darius demanded. 'What's going on?'

Rokeby-Taylor stood and straightened his jacket. He licked his lips nervously. 'I have no idea.'

'Then let's gather some information,' Sir Darius said. A stream of sailors and officers stampeded past the open doorway. Sir Darius waited, then shot out an arm and seized a collar. The young officer squawked and Sir Darius guided him into the wardroom.

He was short, about as old as Aubrey, and his dark eyes were very, very fearful.

'What's going on?' Sir Darius demanded. 'Are we in danger?'

'Sir, sorry, sir, I don't know. It's all hands to stations, so that's where I was going.'

'But what's happening?'

'The engines have stopped. Topper and Badger said there's been some sort of explosion. That's all I know. Please sir, I need to get to the torpedo bay.'

'Yes, of course,' Sir Darius said distantly. He let go of the young officer, who scampered out the door.

'What happens now?' George asked. He didn't seem to know what to do with his hands. He crossed his arms, uncrossed them, ran his fingers through his hair and finally jammed them in the pockets of his jacket. Aubrey had rarely seen his friend so anxious, but when he thought about what lay only inches away, he decided George had a right to be concerned.

'Not being an expert in submersible engineering, there's not much I can do,' Sir Darius said. 'What about you, Aubrey?'

'Now, Darius,' Rokeby-Taylor said, 'this isn't the time to panic.'

Sir Darius speared him with a look. 'Clive, your machine may have stranded us at the bottom of the sea. If you don't have any constructive advice, don't interrupt me while I talk to someone who may be able to help.'

Rokeby-Taylor opened his mouth, then shrugged. 'As you wish.'

Captain Stephens appeared at the door to the wardroom, frowning. He had a smear of grease on one cheek. 'No injuries?'

Sir Darius shook his head impatiently. 'What's going on, Captain? Are we in danger?'

'Well, we've lost our batteries and our air won't last forever.'

'That sounds like "in danger" to me,' George muttered.

'Lieutenant Atwood's been badly injured. We need someone with magical skills.'

'Aubrey is your man, then,' Sir Darius said. 'And what about you, Clive?'

'I'm rusty, but I'll see what I can do.'

'Both of you,' Captain Stephens said. 'Quickly. This way.'

George and Sir Darius went to accompany them, but Captain Stephens shook his head. 'It's a mess down there, I'm afraid. Not much room at the best of times, but now, you're better off here.'

Sir Darius nodded. 'We don't want to be nuisances. Be careful, Aubrey.'

Aubrey turned, moved by his father's concern and confidence. He sought for words, but finally settled for holding up a hand in acknowledgement before hurrying after Captain Stephens.

At first, as they struggled through the crowded passageways, Aubrey thought the submersible was in a state of chaos. Men charged pell-mell, dragging ropes and chains or carrying crates. Orders boomed off metal bulkheads. Painful hammering echoed along the walkways. But he soon realised that the expressions of the sailors were tense, not panicked. They were the faces of trained men going about their duties in extreme circumstances.

Just the sort we need if we go to war, Aubrey thought. *When we go to war.*

Aubrey was buffeted as they hurried along, but he gamely kept right at Captain Stephen's shoulder. Finally they reached a hatch.

Inside, the electric lights were sputtering. A pale, lambent glow ran across the banks of switches and dials. Steam whistled from a pinprick in a pipe to Aubrey's left. The whole room was overlaid with a throat-scratching burnt smell, while a faint magical residue set Aubrey's senses jangling.

Along one wall, metal straps hung loose on dozens of tall, narrow compartments, like doorless closets.

'The batteries.' Rokeby-Taylor pointed. His face was deathly white. 'Where are they?'

'I said we'd lost them,' Captain Stephens said. 'It's exactly what I meant.'

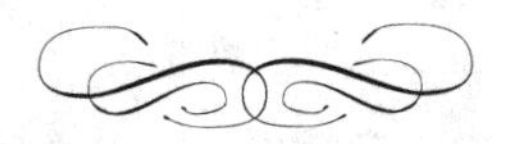

LIEUTENANT ATWOOD WAS STRETCHED OUT ON A TABLE. He had a bloody bandage wrapped around his head, and the entire left side of his uniform was scorched. He was tended by a brawny gunner's mate, who was strapping his leg with surprisingly gentle hands.

'Atwood,' Captain Stephens said, softly.

Atwood raised himself on one elbow. His gaze drifted across Aubrey's face, then rolled back again, as if he were hard to focus on. 'I never wanted to go to sea, you know,' he said in conversational tones. Then his eyelids dropped and his head fell. It was only the quick reactions of the gunner's mate that stopped his skull from bouncing on the bare metal table.

'No help there, I'm afraid,' Captain Stephens said to Aubrey and Rokeby-Taylor. 'Any suggestions?'

'I've been in a submersible for less than an hour,' Aubrey said, 'and you're asking *me* what to do?'

'I hate to say it, but it looks as though it's magic that's the problem, not the submersible,' the captain said. 'The machine is sound, but there's nothing to propel it.'

Rokeby-Taylor glanced angrily at the empty racks. 'How could they just disappear?'

Aubrey needed more information. 'Captain, what would you do if the problem weren't magic?

Captain Stephens rubbed his chin. 'The batteries power the electric motors that propel us while we're under the water. They power the pumps, too, so that means we're in real trouble.'

'Why do we need pumps? We don't seem to have sprung a leak.'

'A submersible rises and dives because of buoyancy. When we pump more water into the buoyancy tanks, we dive. When we pump water out, we rise.'

'Like a dirigible.'

'Just like a dirigible. Except when an airship loses buoyancy, it crashes to the ground. We sink to the bottom of the sea.' He touched his cheek, found grease on the end of his fingers and looked at it quizzically. 'I don't know which I'd prefer.'

Aubrey could almost feel the weight of the water outside, pressing on the thin shell of the submersible. Black, dense and cold. He shuddered.

'But what *happened* to the batteries?' he demanded. 'They couldn't just disappear.'

'That's just what happened,' Captain Stephens said. 'Atwood was fiddling with them, inspecting them, whatever he does. A flash of light, a crack like thunder that knocked me off my feet, and suddenly Atwood's on fire and the batteries are gone.'

'Impossible,' Rokeby-Taylor muttered.

'What about the diesel engines?' Aubrey asked Captain Stephens. 'Can't we run them and pump the water out?'

'Can't run diesel engines underwater. Not enough air for them and the exhaust would kill us.'

'So we need to power the pumps with no batteries.' Aubrey felt the increasing horror that comes from having only a few possible outcomes – and none of them favourable. 'Muscle power?'

'All hands to the pumps? Sorry, we left that behind when we moved from sails to steam.'

Aubrey looked up, then he had it. 'The lights. Where are they getting their power from?'

'Good thought, but pointless, I'm afraid. It's a separate battery system. Small. Nowhere near powerful enough to shift the pumps or the motors. And they won't last long.'

'I see. Just because I'm curious,' Aubrey said, 'how many submersibles have been rescued in a situation like this?'

'In the Albion fleet, or worldwide?'

'Worldwide.'

'That'd be none, then.' Captain Stephens cocked a half-smile. 'Submersiblers don't like to talk about this sort of thing, you understand.'

Rokeby-Taylor was bent over, peering into the battery racks.

'Mr Rokeby-Taylor?' Aubrey said. 'You're the expert on the *Electra*. Have you any insights?'

'Eh?' He straightened. 'Well, it was the batteries I was most interested in. Can't say I'm totally familiar with all the other aspects of the craft.'

'The batteries then. What was so special about them?'

Rokeby-Taylor reached into pocket of his jacket and pulled out a handkerchief. He swabbed at his brow. 'They were a hundred times more powerful than anything else ever invented. Spells accelerated the rate of something or other. Or decreased it.' He rubbed the bridge of his nose. 'To tell you the truth, I'm not much of a details man.'

'Can you remember anything helpful?'

'Only that we need the batteries if we're going to get out of here. Life or death, I'm afraid.'

Aubrey sighed. He hadn't really anticipated performing any major magic. His condition was fragile; it could crumble at the slightest provocation. *Like performing serious magic.*

Grimly, he turned his magical awareness inward to check his status.

His soul was nestled within his body, but it was uneasy. The golden cord that led to the portal guarding the way to the true death tugged, fitfully. It wasn't a comfortable state of affairs but Aubrey had learned to live with it, like a toothache.

He decided that he was stable enough to undertake some careful magic. And since he really didn't have any choice, he saw this as a good – and timely – thing.

He ignored the small voice in the back of his mind that wondered if he were overestimating his readiness. What else could he do?

He went to the racks where the batteries had been. Great insulated copper cables – each as thick as his wrist – drooped like overcooked noodles. There was simply nothing to connect them to.

Aubrey peered into the racks. The feeble emergency lighting made it difficult to see, but he could feel the prickling of magic on his skin. Was it just residue of whatever spell had caused the batteries to disappear, or was it something else?

Alternatives paraded in front of him. The batteries could have been transported somewhere else. That would be a major spell drawing on the Law of Displacement. Moving such bulky objects any distance at all was a highly complex task, but it was a well-established procedure. Which meant he would have detected it from a mile away, so he crossed out that possibility.

Or the batteries could simply have been destroyed. He shook his head. The residue in that case would be magical, but also physical. There were no traces of metal fragments, or pools of acid.

No. This is something esoteric, exotic, radical.

He leaned right over the restraining bar. Taking his weight on his stomach, he ran his finger across the middle of the metal plate. He examined it closely. It felt slightly gritty, but with an overtone of orange, which was his mundane senses trying to come to terms with magical remnants. He sniffed, and it smelled pointy – another sense-scrambling magical quality.

He rubbed his finger and thumb together absently; without realising it, he began to hum.

Rokeby-Taylor and Captain Stephens appeared at his shoulder. 'D'you have something?' the industrialist asked.

Aubrey started. 'Maybe. Possibly.'

'Not sounding altogether certain, then.' Captain Stephens glanced in the direction of Atwood and the gunner's mate. 'It'd be good if you did. We don't seem to have many options.'

Aubrey nodded. 'Mr Rokeby-Taylor, do you recall the Law of Dimensionality?'

Rokeby-Taylor screwed up his face. 'Dimensionality? I may have missed that lecture.'

'It's obscure stuff, usually glossed over.' Aubrey studied his thumb and forefinger. 'I have a feeling that a clever magician manipulated the batteries with a spell derived from the Law of Dimensionality. All done on a delay, of course, to go off when we were well at sea.'

'On a delay,' Rokeby-Taylor echoed. Then he narrowed his eyes. 'Manipulated the dimensions? Of the batteries?'

'Exactly. Height, width and breadth are our standard dimensions. The Law of Dimensionality states that any spell that deals with a physical object must include these aspects, to cover its physical presence.'

'Fairly obvious.'

'And that's where most people stop. But if the Law of Dimensionality is inverted, then it points the way to create spells that can *manipulate* the dimensions of objects. It's very tricky stuff, but it's possible to reduce objects to a state of having no dimensions.'

Captain Stephens stared at the racks. 'No dimensions?'

'I think the batteries have become . . . points.' Aubrey groped for an explanation. 'Imagine turning a cube until all you can see is one side – a square. In effect, you've turned a three-dimensional object into a two-dimensional object. The same thing happens if you turn a square around so you can only see one edge. A line. Two dimensions become one. These batteries have been turned, and turned again and again until three dimensions have become none.'

'If you say so.' Captain Stephens pushed back his cap and scratched his head. 'Really, I don't care if the batteries have become merry-go-rounds, as long as you can restore them.'

Aubrey thought hard. It shouldn't be difficult. The spell-caster had been arrogant, assuming that the cleverness of the magic would baffle anyone left on the submersible. In Aubrey's favour, he had the natural tendency of objects to return to their true form, reverting to their original state if given half a chance.

'Not wanting to rush you,' Captain Stephens said, 'but I'd say we only have a few hours air left.'

Aubrey's palms were sweating. He ran them along the sides of his trousers. As a possible fate, suffocating in a tin eggshell at the bottom of the sea was not high on his list of favourites.

Danaanian. The ancient Danaans were great ones for their geometry, so using their language to manipulate dimensions should work well. A few simple terms, delimiting the strictures placed on length, height and breadth, and that should do the trick. Simple – and not too taxing.

He hoped.

'Stand back,' he said to the others.

Aubrey took up a position halfway along the bank of racks. He spread his arms in a vague gesture towards his own dimensionality. He steadied himself, concentrating hard on what he was about to attempt. He felt the usual mixture of apprehension, doubt, exhilaration and excitement before finally resolving his will on the task. A deep breath, then he chanted the spell.

Each term came easily and he was pleased as each led to the next with surety. It was over in less than a minute and he added a neat final term as his signature.

Nothing happened. Aubrey cocked his head and frowned. He leaned closer to the empty racks.

And he was blown off his feet.

Even as he sailed through the air he felt a mixture of triumph and exasperation. *Air*, he thought. *I should have remembered all the air that would get displaced when the batteries reformed.*

Then he struck the bulkhead.

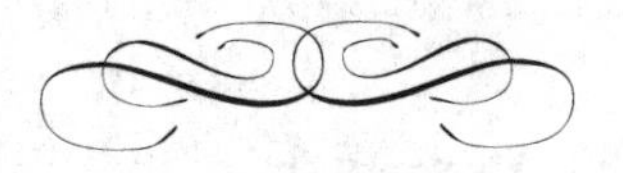

Four

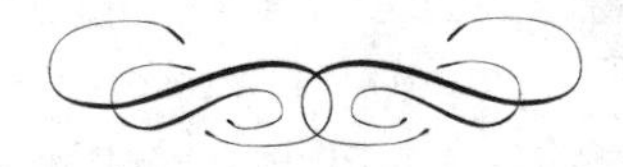

HALF AN HOUR LATER, WHEN THE KLAXON WENT OFF again in the wardroom, Aubrey slumped at the thought of another emergency. He rubbed the back of his neck and hoped that his headache would pass before his brain turned into blancmange.

It wasn't just his head, either. The magical exertion of the dimensionality spell had drained him more than he'd hoped. With resignation, he realised he had the painful internal sensation of disjuncture that meant his soul and body were not entirely united.

'What's the best way to turn that off?' he asked Rokeby-Taylor, who was stretched out on the floor of the wardroom next to where George was fascinated by *The Boiler Pressure Tolerances and Valve Assembly Maintenance Manual.*

Rokeby-Taylor, looking a little worse for wear, opened one eye. 'It's up to the captain, I'm afraid. Some of them do it just to keep the crew on their toes, I'm told.'

Aubrey looked at George, ready to hear what his friend thought, then looked again. It wasn't obvious, but he saw that while George was doing his best to appear calm and relaxed, his feet were tapping nervously – and he had a tell-tale sheen of sweat on his forehead.

George glanced up from his book and caught Aubrey's gaze. He shrugged. 'I'm a country boy,' he said, making a commendable stab at levity. 'Wobbling along at the bottom of the sea isn't my bag, old man.'

'You preferred it when we were mired on the seabed?'

'Dry land is what I'd prefer, with a nice tree to sit under.'

Sir Darius turned from the doorway, where he was once again trying to read the surging chaos of hurrying sailors. 'You look unwell, Aubrey. Surely you're not seasick.'

Sir Darius had been a champion open ocean yachtsman. He had the failing of most of those who loved the sea – he couldn't understand how someone could be upset by it.

'No, just feeling the after-effects of my head and a metal wall coming together.'

Sir Darius snorted. 'I think your heroics with the batteries deserve a little more than being ignored down here. Do you feel up to visiting the control room?'

Aubrey waved at the klaxon. 'Instead of being trapped with that? Lead away.'

It was rather like freestyle wrestling in close confines as they struggled through the narrow passageways. Shoulders, hips and elbows were essential tools as the sailors hurried from one station to another. Aubrey made sure he moved in George's wake – it made the going much easier. Rokeby-Taylor, grumbling, brought up the rear.

The control room was full of dials, levers and brass. As with the rest of the submersible, it was a model of compactness. Everything was smaller than usual – chairs, doorways, working space. Hooded lights made the place dim, and while the smell of hot oil was not as pronounced here, further away from the engine rooms, it still touched everything. Aubrey knew his clothes would stink of it.

Captain Stephens was bent nearly double. His face was pressed to an eyepiece attached to a cylinder that extended up through the conning tower. He straightened, scowling, then he saw his visitors. 'Prime Minister. I'm sorry, but we have another emergency on our hands.'

Sir Darius nodded. 'Can we help?'

Aubrey's stomach tightened at the thought of doing more magic. He had a painful lump in his throat. From dismal experience, he knew it was one of the early symptoms of his body and soul separating. Rest should stop the deterioration, but it seemed as if rest might be hard to achieve in the immediate future.

'No,' Captain Stephens said. 'Purely naval, this matter, even if it's dashed puzzling.'

Aubrey wandered over to the eyepiece and recognised it as a periscope. He remembered the toy George and he had constructed from mirrors, long ago. It had been George's father who'd showed them how to put it together, and Aubrey recalled his patience as the two young boys fumbled with glue and cardboard.

'One of our merchant ships is being attacked,' Captain Stephens continued.

Sir Darius stiffened. 'Attacked? By whom?'

Stephens pushed back his cap and rubbed his brow. 'That's the problem. It's some sort of light cruiser, but it's not flying a flag.'

Not flying an identifying flag? Aubrey couldn't believe it. Such a thing went against every international law. 'What can we do?'

'What we must,' Sir Darius said. 'Captain, can you disable the attacking ship?'

'We're armed, sir. We can do it.'

Rokeby-Taylor regained some of his earlier enthusiasm at this prospect. 'Excellent! We can use the new torpedo guidance system.'

Captain Stephens touched his jaw. 'Very well. Let's give it a go.'

He returned to the periscope then snapped out the orders to surface. The klaxon stopped and Aubrey wanted to cheer. He felt the angle of the deck beneath his feet change once more as the bow pointed upward and he wondered if mountain goats mightn't make good submersiblers, accustomed as they were to angled footing.

'Surfacing, sir!' came the cry.

'Steady as she goes,' Captain Stephens said, peering through the periscope. 'We have them stern-on. They'll have to surrender.'

'Are they still firing on the freighter?' Aubrey asked.

Stephens didn't answer immediately. 'Looks like it. The old tub is on fire,' he said eventually. 'Bad show.'

'Do they see us?' Sir Darius said.

Suddenly, the submersible lurched and the whole vessel rang like a giant gong. Aubrey managed to cling to a brass conduit, which vibrated painfully under his fingers. Rokeby-Taylor staggered backward and collided hard with a large vertical pipe. He let out a grunt of pain but George managed to grab an overhead stanchion and he held himself up as easily as a passenger on an omnibus.

From the rest of the *Electra*, shouts and breaking glass competed with the whine of the engines. The klaxon started again and it drove sharp spikes of pain into Aubrey's skull. He thought it sounded positively delighted at the opportunity to torment him again.

'Apparently they do see us,' Captain Stephens said dryly. 'Luckily, they haven't found our range yet.'

A gigantic thump sounded, then a deafening hammering on the deck over their heads. Aubrey guessed that a near miss had thrown water into the air, deluging the submersible. For a ship that was supposed to be surrendering, he decided that the cruiser was doing quite well.

'For'rd torpedo room ready,' Captain Stephens barked.

His order was repeated by a nervous midshipman into a speaking tube; he listened, then turned to his captain. 'Ready, sir.'

'Fire.'

A clang, a thump, then an instant's silence before a noise like the world's largest sigh rolled through the length of the vessel. The *Electra* shook and rolled a little.

'Torpedo away!' the midshipman reported.

Captain Stephens applied his eye to the periscope. 'We've aimed at their rudder,' he said, his voice muffled by the nearness of his face to the eyepiece. 'Let's see how this magical targeting device performs.'

Suddenly, it was as if the submersible had been slapped by an angry giant. It bucked, then plunged, and Aubrey's reflexes were tested again. He needed both hands to steady himself as the *Electra* wallowed in seas made angry.

'What happened?' Sir Darius shouted over the klaxon. Aubrey had grown to hate the noise. The thing crowed, as if it was making the most of its day in the sun.

Captain Stephens lurched back to the periscope. 'We must have hit the cruiser's ammunition store. It's gone down.'

'The freighter?'

'Damaged, sir, but still afloat.'

Sir Darius's face was grim. 'Let's see if we can rescue any survivors from the cruiser.'

SIR DARIUS, ROKEBY-TAYLOR, GEORGE AND AUBREY STOOD on the deck of the *Electra* with some of the submersible's crew.

The sailors on the freighter released boats in good form. They showed no signs of panic, even though thick black smoke was pouring from the stern of the ship, adding to the smoke from the remnants of the cruiser.

Aubrey looked in that direction and felt hollow at the destruction. No-one could have lived through that explosion. A slowly spreading oil slick was staining the surface, disrupted by gouts of air, huge eruptions of spray and an assortment of boxes, crates and floating objects that bumped about in an incongruously carefree manner.

Aubrey couldn't help but be saddened by the loss of life. How many sailors went down with the cruiser? Surely not all of them were criminals or evildoers. They must have had families, homes, loved ones.

With a bleak heart, he turned back to the freighter.

Six lifeboats pushed off. No-one was left on deck.

'We'll need to help them come alongside,' Sir Darius said. 'We shouldn't leave them to battle the swell.'

The Chief Petty Officer ran to the tower and relayed this to the control room. The diesel engines began to roar. The *Electra* was relatively good on the surface – for a submersible. She'd never win a speed or manoeuvrability contest, but the submersible doggedly ploughed through the waves.

'Ropes and grappling hooks!' Sir Darius called. Sailors at the conning tower signed their understanding and disappeared.

Up close, the freighter looked more than crippled: it looked terminal. Choking black smoke enveloped the whole bow and loud grinding noises came from below deck, as if a foundry were being wrecked by clumsy, if enthusiastic, giants.

Sailors poured out of the *Electra*'s tower with rope and hooks. Aubrey and the others moved back to allow the trained seamen to do their work.

Not standing on ceremony, deckhands pushed past and went to the other side of the submersible. With Albionite efficiency, they roped in the lifeboats. The merchant sailors were hauled aboard and stood on the deck, bewildered by the turn of events.

Aubrey stared. One of the boats was full of crates. Who would have risked their lives to load goods into a lifeboat at a time like this? The boat was overladen, to boot, and wallowed dangerously close to capsizing as it was hauled closer to the submersible.

The merchant sailors rushed to the rails with evident

concern as the last lifeboat was brought close. When the two survivors were helped out onto the submersible there was a ragged cheer.

It was then that Aubrey saw that the two survivors were female. He gripped the rail, unable to believe what he was seeing. Then he jumped up and down, hallooing wildly.

George and Rokeby-Taylor stared at him. His father, though, had seen what he'd seen. He stood there with a look of profound surprise on his face.

One of the survivors was Aubrey's mother, Lady Rose Fitzwilliam. The other was Caroline Hepworth.

THE WARDROOM WAS PACKED, AND THE CAPTAIN HAD opened it up to the corridor through an ingenious system of folding walls. Aubrey had anticipated the crush and had done his best to sit close to Caroline. By her actions, she had also anticipated it and had manoeuvred herself to keep a respectable distance. The shifting, excusing and rearranging this caused went on for some time before Sir Darius called a halt, advising those outside the wardroom to find any space they could for the journey home. The last to find a place was Rokeby-Taylor, who chattered excitedly to anyone who'd listen about how well the *Electra* had performed – simply ignoring the bizarre episode with the batteries.

Sir Darius had managed – very smoothly, Aubrey noticed – to come to Lady Rose's side. He stood with his hand on her shoulder. The look they gave each other was so full of meaning that it fascinated Aubrey. There was reproach, bafflement and relief – from both sides – and a thousand questions demanding to be asked, with an understanding that they could wait until later.

They didn't speak a word.

Caroline's hair had come loose in the chaos of fleeing the freighter, Aubrey noticed. She had a blanket around her shoulders and looked angry, as if personally affronted by the goings-on.

In all the manoeuvring in the wardroom, she hadn't directly looked at him once, whereas he found it hard to stop staring at her.

What were you doing on that freighter? he wanted to ask. *Are you all right? Why aren't you in the Arctic?*

But he knew these were really trivial excuses to avoid asking the most important question, the one that mattered most: *Have you forgiven me?*

'Coincidence?' Lady Rose said, answering her husband's initial question. She put down her cup of tea. 'Perhaps your stumbling on us was a coincidence. But the attack wasn't. They were Holmlanders and they'd been waiting for us.'

'Holmlanders?' Sir Darius said. His voice was steely and Aubrey knew he was furious. 'They flew no Holmland flag.'

'No, but I can tell a Holmland accent, even over a megaphone.'

'They hailed us,' Caroline said, fuming. 'They came alongside and hailed us. Demanded we stop and be boarded.'

'The captain would have none of that,' Lady Rose said. 'He tried to outrun them.'

'The first shell took out the bridge,' Caroline said. 'The captain was killed.'

'And then you arrived,' Lady Rose said.

'But why do you think it wasn't just opportunistic? Was the freighter carrying valuable cargo?' Aubrey asked.

'Valuable cargo?' Lady Rose said. 'Just the specimens we salvaged from our expedition. Seabirds, mostly.'

'From one disaster to another,' Caroline said. 'We were lucky to save anything at all.'

'But what were they after, then?'

Caroline looked at him for the first time. It was a look of impatience and incredulity, and it made Aubrey feel quite weak. 'Why, your mother, of course.'

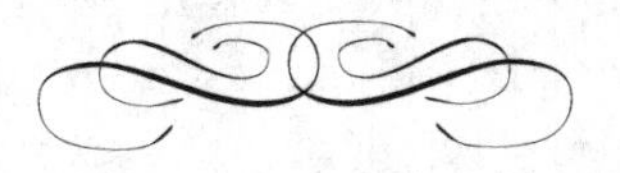

Five

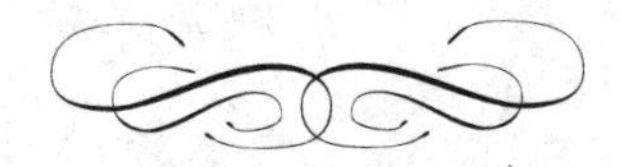

A WHOLE DAY OF APOLOGIES, ACCUSATIONS, HAND-waving, finger-pointing and promises didn't help Aubrey cope with the effects of his spell-casting exertions. As a major witness to the *Electra*'s near-disaster, instead of resting and recuperating, he joined his father in meeting after meeting. Top navy personnel, senior Magisterium operatives and embarrassed Special Service agents all wanted to document and argue over the events of the submersible's sabotage.

The word 'sabotage' was used reluctantly at first. By the end of the two days, however, all at Clear Haven used it with a certainty that chilled Aubrey. The perpetrators weren't mentioned by name, but there seemed no doubt that Holmand was responsible.

Rokeby-Taylor was noticeably absent from all of this. The moment the *Electra* had docked, he'd claimed any number of pressing engagements and hurried to his waiting ornithopter. Aubrey was impressed by this deft – if temporary – display of blame-dodging.

Rokeby-Taylor's well-oiled departure left many questions unanswered. Each meeting ended with a recommendation that development of the special submersible be halted, with continuation subject to further investigation.

Sir Darius promised Admiral Elliot that he'd take the matter up with Cabinet – and that no news of the incident would reach the public.

All throughout that long day, Aubrey tried to catch Caroline, but he was dragged from one meeting to another with barely time to catch his breath. He held out hopes for the trip back to Trinovant but Caroline snapped up the co-pilot's seat, while Aubrey was jammed in a tiny space in the rear of the ornithopter. Alone, he dozed uncomfortably all the way home, a control conduit thrumming irritatingly right near his head.

The next morning, George received a telephone call at Maidstone, asking him home, which finally gave Aubrey a chance to rest – something he needed more than anything else in the world.

The magical efforts on the submersible had jolted the hold he'd established on his soul. He was back on the wearying, painful treadmill of trying to hold himself together, and he hated it.

In this state, nothing was good. The constant threat of utter dissolution had preyed on him, haunted his days, lurked behind his successes and his everyday happiness.

He accepted that he'd made no progress; his discoveries in Lutetia had been promising, and for a brief time he'd actually felt what it was like to be cured, but ultimately it was a magical dead end in a way that went beyond punning.

His correspondence with researchers, academics and savants across the world had yielded little. Some of this was due to the guarded, theoretical nature of his inquiries, but he couldn't afford to be open. His condition was a secret that only he and George knew. He was going to keep it that way.

Part of this was simple embarrassment. He didn't want to become a laughing stock – the ambitious young magician who fell on his face. A more lofty motive was to spare his father any poor press. The Prime Minister's son a bungler on a monumental scale? What sort of a father would allow such a thing to happen?

He found rest difficult to come by. His mind kept whirring, picking up half-thoughts and poking at them, trying to tie them together. Finally he climbed out of bed, groaning when his joints felt as if someone had seeded them with ground glass.

He limped to his father's study and took Dr Tremaine's pearl from the family safe.

In the complex interweaving of plot and counterplot leading up to the attempt on the King's life, Aubrey had come into possession of the pearl that Dr Tremaine had embedded in the head of his cane. This pearl had been a present from Dr Tremaine's sister, who had died some years ago, a sister whom he loved beyond anything else.

It was roughly egg-shaped, the size of the tip of his thumb, but it wasn't smooth like most other pearls Aubrey had seen. It was creased and folded like a miniature brain.

The pearl had meant so much to Dr Tremaine, Aubrey wondered if it were a magical artefact. After probing it for some time, he provisionally decided it was what Dr Tremaine claimed – a souvenir in the true sense of the word: a remembrance, a concrete reminder of someone dear.

He put it back in the safe and returned to his room, but didn't banish it from his mind.

He was still brooding on it when Tilly, the maid, knocked at his door to say his father wanted to see him in the library.

He stood in front of the cheval mirror, and brushed his jacket and his hair, doing his best to look presentable. As long as no-one noticed the dark circles under his eyes, the sallow skin and the slight trembling of his hands, he thought he could achieve a level of presentability. Provided the standards weren't high.

He straightened his tie and he rubbed his eyes. He was tired again – naggingly, insistently tired. How could he go on like this?

The answer that came to him was simple. It was also unwelcome, almost repellent, and he realised that it had been lurking at the back of his mind for some time but he had refused to listen.

Do no more magic.

Magic was the worst sort of strain. If he renounced it, his body and soul would be much easier to keep in equilibrium. It promised an enduring, perhaps permanent, solution.

But he didn't want to do it.

He had a talent for magic. That was part of his reluctance – the natural aversion to wasting an aptitude; but it was more than that. He *enjoyed* magic. He liked being special. It was exhilarating to engage with the very stuff of the universe itself, to face challenges that required the utmost from him.

How could he give that up?

Magic was who he was. It defined him.

But even as this came to him, he resisted such a classification. He was Aubrey Fitzwilliam; he was more than a simple label!

Early on in his pursuit of magic, he'd thought it was truly possible to know everything about it, to master it in all its glory. Then he'd come to the understanding that he couldn't know it all. It had been a depressing thought. Hard on the heels of this insight came his usual response: what to do about it. In the end, he drew a diagram of the various branches of magic – including a large area categorised as 'Unknown/Yet to be established' – and circled the areas to which he wanted to dedicate himself. The challenging, the outlandish, the difficult, the mysterious held a heady allure; the well-established, the tried and true were less attractive. If he needed to know more about the Magic of Light or Thermal Magic he could consult someone.

Contemplating this now, he came to the conclusion that if he gave up the *practice* of magic, there was much to be involved with. He could still research the field. The universities were full of people who did vital work, delineating, exploring and refining spells in an abstract sense, working on crucial areas of magical theory. He could do some serious investigation into the interaction between language and magic, for instance. A universal language of magic would be a staggering breakthrough, a thoroughly worthwhile goal.

It seemed like an eminently sensible approach. Not dull in any way. Not at all.

Sir Darius stood behind the long, gilt table in the middle of the library. When Aubrey entered, he looked up from a large book. He closed it and Aubrey saw, with interest, that it was the Scholar Tan's *Deliberations on War*. It was his father's favourite, but he knew it by heart and only consulted it when wrestling with profound and knotty problems. His eye could roam over familiar words while his mind worked away.

'Ah, Aubrey. Good to see you. You've recovered from the events at Clear Haven?'

'I have, sir.' *In a way.* 'And you?'

'Quite. Thank you.'

Sir Darius contemplated the red leather cover of the book in front of him. 'Aubrey. You're seventeen now.'

For a moment, Aubrey thought he heard the appalling klaxon again. *He's stating the obvious*, he thought. *Something's very wrong.* 'Eighteen in December,' he said, carefully.

'Close the door, there's a good chap.'

Closed door. It's even worse than I thought.

By now Aubrey's imagination had conjured up a number of ghastly scenarios. A deadly disease. A scandal from the past. Blackmail. Financial mismanagement. 'What is it, sir? Is anything wrong?'

'Sit, Aubrey. There's something I need to talk to you about.'

He didn't answer the question, Aubrey thought as he perched on the edge of one of the heavy leather chairs. *It's worse than worse.*

His father took a seat on the other side of the table. Suddenly, it felt awkwardly like an interview.

Sir Darius was dressed in black. His tie was silver-grey. His shoes glowed with the sort of shine that only comes from truly dedicated – and well-paid – servants. He was every inch the modern Prime Minister.

Yet Aubrey saw that his father was immensely uncomfortable.

'Now, Aubrey. You're an only child.'

Aubrey's face fell. 'Mother isn't expecting, is she?'

'I beg your pardon?'

'I'm not going to have a baby brother. Or sister. Am I?' Aubrey pressed both his hands together and studied them. 'Well, I suppose I can live with that, if that's all that's wrong. Thousands do, I know. Have baby siblings, that is. Which I wouldn't be. Having it, that is. Him. Or her. Not it.'

Sir Darius waited until Aubrey had wound down. 'Are you finished?'

'I just wanted to reassure you, sir, that I'm happy to be an older brother. I'm aware of the responsibilities and I look forward to them.'

'I see.' A hint of a smile. 'A pity, then, that nothing of that kind is planned. And I should know, after all.'

'Of course. Sir. Yes, you would. Naturally.'

Sir Darius coughed and looked out of the window. Aubrey was grateful to follow his gaze and saw that Hobbs, the gardener, was turning the daffodils or declumping the rhododendron or some other mysterious, earthy pursuit.

After he'd sufficiently gathered himself, Sir Darius started again. 'Aubrey, you are my only heir.'

Aubrey nodded. It seemed safest not to talk.

'You would have become Duke of Brayshire after me, had I not renounced my title.'

Another nod.

'While you won't have the title, I do have something to pass on to you. I believe now is the time.'

'Now?' One word. Safe enough.

'You are a young man. You are studying at university. You are beginning to chart the course of your own life.' Sir Darius measured his words. 'Aubrey, you are a fine individual, with many gifts. Your conduct on the *Electra* was exemplary.'

Aubrey swallowed. 'Thank you, sir.'

'It is difficult, being a parent. Especially a father.'

'Sir.'

'I feared my father, Aubrey. He believed, as did all men of his generation, in discipline as the way to raise children. There was nothing gentle about him. He was fair, but stern, distant and judgemental.'

Aubrey was fascinated – and embarrassed. His father had never spoken to him this way. The old Duke of Brayshire was a dim memory to Aubrey, the grandfather who gave piggy-backs. The man must have softened in his old age. 'I . . .'

'Don't say anything, Aubrey. I realise this must be awkward for you, and talking is your first reaction in all circumstances. Listen this time, there's a good chap.'

Aubrey subsided.

'I vowed I wouldn't raise my son as my father raised his.' Sir Darius found an interesting piece of lint on his lapel. 'I dare say that's a promise that's been made more than once in history, but it was the best I could do. I may have been harsh with you, Aubrey. Difficult. It was with the best of intentions.' Sir Darius stood. 'I want you to come with me.'

'Where?'

'To the Bank of Albion.'

The landau was waiting at the front door. The weather being fine, Aubrey thought the open carriage a splendid choice, but his mind was racing. His father was being mysterious, but clumsily so. This was no clever joke or elaborate charade – there was something endearingly uncomfortable about the whole affair. It showed a side of his father that he'd rarely seen.

The driver eased the matched greys out of the gates of Maidstone. With Sir Darius sitting in reflective silence and Aubrey unwilling to spoil the moment, the carriage clip-clopped along Highton Street towards the city. The black motorcar following closely was a sign of the increased diligence of the Special Services bodyguards.

Approaching noon, the streets were busy. Sir Darius drummed his fingers impatiently on the rail until a policeman, passing on a bicycle, stopped. 'Care for some help, Prime Minister?'

'Constable, you are a veritable lifesaver. If you would.'

The policeman saluted, grinned, then proceeded to lead the carriage through intersection after intersection, with the connivance of his colleagues who were on point duty. Each of them saluted Sir Darius, who shouted his thanks as they trotted past.

'Two birds, Aubrey. One stone,' Sir Darius said abruptly as they passed the Gallery of the Arts.

Aubrey twisted this cryptic utterance around until he thought he had an answer. 'You're meeting someone at the bank?'

'Indeed.' Sir Darius took out his pocket watch. 'Clive Rokeby-Taylor. That's why I don't want to be late.'

'Meeting at the bank? Odd, isn't it?'

'Rokeby-Taylor and money were never far apart,' Sir Darius said dryly. 'Especially other people's money.'

With the help of the friendly police constable, the landau drew up right outside the Bank of Albion, with the Special Services motorcar right behind. Aubrey had never been inside the Grand Dame of Woolcroft Street, but knew the imposing edifice by sight. Grimy from city smoke, the bank still managed to look both stately and intimidating. This was an institution that was serious about money, its architecture announced, and it took such a long, steady, safe view of investment that it regarded glaciers as reckless daredevils of speed.

One of the bank's managers, grandees or high potentates marched out as Sir Darius alighted. He was stout, with a pointy beard, and a cutaway coat in a style that was forty years out of date, even though it looked as if it had been made that morning. 'Prime Minister. We have a special room ready for you.'

'Sir Norman. I wasn't expecting the chief governor to meet us.'

'It's the least we could do. I'm happy to see to your needs.'

Sir Norman gestured and a pair of doormen appeared. One stood by the carriage, the other opened the heavy, brass portal of the Bank of Albion.

The main chamber of the bank was vast. Aubrey stood

and gaped at the towering main dome and the three flanking domes. Marble, brass and dark wood, then more marble, brass and dark wood and – to top it all off – some extra marble, brass and dark wood had been used to emphasise the solidity of the bank. This was a place to do business, but it had the solemnity of a cathedral.

Pillars marked the entrance to the flanking domes – chambers for further mysterious banking business, Aubrey assumed. Loan disbursement. Fiscal calibrating. Inter-bank credit unfurling.

Under the main dome, long counters kept back a horde of clerks and tellers. The chamber was filled with a multitude of murmurs – requests, explanations, agreements – and they hovered over the hundreds of people like insubstantial moths.

Sir Norman broke the spell. 'This way, if you please.'

Sir Darius took off his hat and gloves. A uniformed doorman – of the interior variety, therefore older and more senior – materialised to take them. Aubrey hurriedly thrust his hat on him and the doorman disappeared into one of the shadowed recesses that abounded in the grand building.

'Mr Rokeby-Taylor?' Sir Darius asked.

'He's in the boardroom. I'll take you to him,' Sir Norman said. 'The other governors were to use the boardroom this morning, but they've opted to convene elsewhere.'

Clive Rokeby-Taylor had totally recovered from his brush with death. He was dressed in a dark green suit, with a jaunty sky-blue cravat. 'Darius!' he said, full of good cheer. 'Aubrey! Come in, come in. Have some tea – it's first rate!'

Rokeby-Taylor busied himself pouring tea into the bone-china cups without a trace of self-consciousness, keeping up a stream of observations about the boardroom, the tea service and the biscuits.

Eventually, he sat on the opposite side of the long boardroom table, sipped his tea and studied Sir Darius over the rim.

'What is it, Clive?' Sir Darius said. 'Why have you asked me here?'

Rokeby-Taylor glanced at Aubrey. 'Not wanting to be rude, but I think this is something between the two of us.'

'Private matters?'

'Financial matters.'

'Aubrey can stay. I trust his discretion.'

Rokeby-Taylor shrugged, then grinned. 'If you say so.'

Aubrey tried to appear as trustworthy and discreet as possible, to live up to his father's confidence. He sat up straight, laced his fingers and placed his hands on the table in front of him. As much as possible, he tried to keep his curiosity from showing on his face. Aubrey's grasp of high finance was not entirely complete, but he knew that if he was serious about politics, it was something he had to remedy.

No time like the present, he thought.

Rokeby-Taylor adjusted his cravat. 'I understand that a substantial shipbuilding contract is in the offing.'

'A bill is imminent, to be voted on in three weeks time,' Sir Darius said. 'A special allocation for six new battleships immediately, with six more to follow. This is no secret.'

'And the bill is sure to pass the Lower House? And the Lords?'

'I wouldn't have put it up if I hadn't thought it would be successful. The opposition is backing the bill. They see the situation on the Continent. I could say that there are votes in defence, but that would be cynical.'

'Quite, quite.' Rokeby-Taylor studied the ceiling for a moment. 'I don't suppose it's any secret that Rokeby-Taylor Shipbuilding is keen to get this contract.'

'The contract will be awarded by the Navy Board, after they examine all tenders. I'm sure your firm will be seriously considered.'

'And I'm sure that the Navy Board would listen to the Prime Minister.'

Aubrey had come to know his father's silences well. This was one of those where he was controlling his temper with some effort. Eventually, he touched his moustache. 'What are you suggesting, Clive?'

Rokeby-Taylor met Sir Darius's gaze and held it. 'It's been a long time, Darius. I wanted to see if you'd changed.'

'And have I?'

'Not in this respect, it seems.' Rokeby-Taylor picked up his cup and raised it to his lips.

'I'm glad,' Sir Darius said. 'If that's all, Clive, I think I should offer you some advice.'

Rokeby-Taylor set his cup down in the saucer with a clatter. 'No, actually, that's not all. I have a business proposition for you.'

'I see. Like the one you put to me a few moments ago?'

Rokeby-Taylor snorted. 'That was nothing. It never happened. And if it did it was just a joke.'

'A joke,' Sir Darius said, and Aubrey wanted to warn Rokeby-Taylor. When his father repeated someone's words like that, the ice was getting extremely thin underfoot.

But Aubrey was being discreet and trustworthy, and doing his best to appear invisible.

'A joke,' Rokeby-Taylor echoed, oblivious to the tension. 'Far more important is the chance for you to make a substantial fortune.'

'I already have a substantial fortune.'

'And so do I. But who can stop at one, eh?'

'Your proposal?'

'You become a major shareholder of Rokeby-Taylor Shipbuilding. We could use an injection of funds – a bit of a cash-flow problem at the moment, especially after that problem with the *Electra* – and you'd double your investment in six months. In the current climate. Say that you'll meet Ingles, my new financial manager. He's a wizard with things like this.'

Sir Darius stood. 'No.'

'Think carefully, Darius. This is risk-free. And it's patriotic. You'd be helping a project that will defend the nation.'

'Thank you for the tea, even though it wasn't yours.' Sir Darius smiled a chilly smile. 'But that always was your way, Clive, very free with things that didn't belong to you.'

'Wait. Before you go, I want to show you something.'

'Another opportunity?'

'Of course. No-one will ever say that Clive Rokeby-Taylor missed an opportunity. Follow me.'

He bounded out of the room. Sir Darius frowned. 'Well, Aubrey?'

'Sorry, sir, but he seems like a scoundrel.'

'No doubt about that. But is he a good-hearted scoundrel, or a black-hearted scoundrel?'

'I always thought that people generally fall somewhere in between.'

'And that is something that a politician – and especially a Prime Minister – should never forget. Shall we see what he's up to now?'

Aubrey couldn't help it. He found Rokeby-Taylor appealing, with his enthusiasms and his energy. He couldn't see how the man managed in the world of business, but his achievements were evidence that he succeeded, despite his erratic behaviour.

They found him in the main banking chamber. He stood right in the middle, under the cupola, while those more intent on their financial matters hurried past to the teller of their choice. 'Darius! Over here!' he called, unmindful of heads turning his way.

'Look up there,' he said when Sir Darius and Aubrey had joined him. 'This must appeal to you.'

He pointed. Evenly spaced around the base of the dome were a number of black boxes. They were slightly tilted, so they looked down on the great space below. Featureless, they looked to be about the size and dimensions of a small trunk.

'If I'm supposed to be impressed,' Sir Darius said, 'then I'm afraid you've failed.'

Rokeby-Taylor shook his head in mock disappointment. 'I'm sorry about that. I thought you would have been more interested in the greatest advance in magical security in the last hundred years.'

'A grand claim. What are they?'

'Magic suppressors.'

Sir Darius looked up sharply, but Aubrey couldn't help himself. 'Magic suppressors? That small?'

'Ah, I seem to have genuine interest,' Rokeby-Taylor said. 'From both of you.'

'I've heard something about them,' Sir Darius said. 'Experimental, aren't they?'

'I encourage all Rokeby-Taylor industries to be at the forefront of development. You saw that with the *Electra*.' He rubbed his hands together.

'I saw a demonstration of a magic suppressor at a Royal Society lecture last year,' Aubrey said. 'It was huge, as big as an omnibus. It didn't work properly, either.'

'I told you I have some remarkable people working for me,' Rokeby-Taylor said. He had trouble keeping a grin from his face. 'The Rokeby-Taylor Magic Suppressors are innovative in every way – size, reliability, and other details that I'm far too busy or far too stupid to understand. If they're carefully situated, they can generate an intense damping field.'

'They stop magic,' Sir Darius said.

'No magic whatsoever can be performed, undertaken or sustained within the field generated by my marvellous little boxes.'

The implications made Aubrey's head spin. 'This could be worth a fortune.'

'My thoughts precisely and I'm glad to hear it coming from someone else. A very sizeable fortune, I hope.' He gestured. 'These are the first fully operational models. All I need is some investment funds and some publicity. I put these in the bank, gratis, in order to achieve the latter.'

'And you're looking to me for the former?' Sir Darius said. 'You don't give up, do you, Clive?'

'Come this way,' Rokeby-Taylor said. 'You can see better from over here.'

He took them to the wall near the entrance, pointing out the positioning of the boxes and how they covered the entire banking chamber. A pair of uniformed guards nearby showed unfeigned interest, peering into the heights.

Aubrey automatically wanted to test the magical suppressors, and found a simple light spell springing to his lips. He bit it back. *No*, he thought, *no more magic. Not even simple stuff.*

It felt unnatural, like refusing to scratch an itch, but he was determined. It was the only way.

A scream interrupted Aubrey's thoughts and the banking murmur. Aubrey swung around to see four men emerging from one of the many doorways. One of them was struggling, held by two of the others. He called for help and the chamber underwent a transformation.

Many customers rushed directly toward the main entrance, while others fled to the walls, as far from the intruders as possible. It was a sea of humanity, surging one way then the other before clearing the centre of the chamber, leaving it stark and empty. Clerks and tellers stayed at their posts, frozen mid-count.

The intruders stumbled to the middle of the chamber, dragging their captive with them. One – the tallest – had wild, unkempt hair. He was dressed in an expensive-looking dark suit, but Aubrey could see that his boots were old and worn. He stood calmly, with a hesitant smile on his face, for all the world as if he were performing for an audience. The others were less sure of themselves and looked as if things weren't quite working out as they'd planned.

The struggling figure struck at the tall man and cried out again. Then Aubrey realised it was Sir Norman, the governor. The banker's face was an alarming shade of red.

'Stay where you are!' shouted the tallest of the three villains. He pointed at the struggling Sir Norman. 'Or I will scramble this man's brains with magic of untold power.'

Sir Norman immediately stopped his thrashing.

Uniformed guards were moving toward the intruders, a dozen or more of them closing in with steely resolve. The chief villain licked his lips nervously. 'I'm warning you,' he called. 'Step back, or I will unleash such torrents of torment that you'll be sorry you were born.'

Aubrey rolled his eyes. He had always found that the boastfulness of a magician's claims were in inverse proportion to his actual effectiveness. The guards, however, hesitated, until their grey-bearded leader stepped forward. Aubrey was reassured by the man's military bearing. 'Surrender,' he said in a sergeant-major's voice, one that had drilled more than its fair share of recruits. 'Your time is up.'

'Not until I'm escorted to the main vault, where I will melt the door with the power of a thousand suns,' the villain said. He gestured dramatically.

'Not likely,' the greybeard growled. 'At 'em, lads.'

The guards closed in. The chief villain took a step backward, then seemed to remember his role. He threw up both hands and began to chant a spell.

The guards halted their advance, knowing magic when they heard it. Aubrey listened carefully, and had to admit that the villain knew his Sumerian. Even though he hurried, he managed each syllable clearly and ended with a showy flourish of a signature. He then slammed his right fist into his left palm.

Aubrey recognised that the spell used the Law of Magnitude, with the intention of turning the fist strike into a barrage of sound. Despite the presence of the so-called magical suppressors, he felt the sudden build-up of magical power. 'Cover your ears!' he urged, and then he felt a strange, unsettling wave of magic.

Nothing happened. The chief villain gaped, stared at his hands, turned to his colleagues as if he were about to complain, then they were buried under an avalanche of guards.

'Splendid!' Rokeby-Taylor crowed over the hubbub of astonishment that filled the chamber. 'As you see, any magic is nullified by the suppressors. It doesn't matter what type, an equal and opposite effect is created and the final result is as you see.' Rokeby-Taylor beamed. 'A timely trial indeed.'

'Very timely.' Sir Darius watched thoughtfully as the struggle in the middle of the chamber proved to be short-lived. 'Most fortunate for you, Clive.'

'Well, the bank won't have any doubts about the efficacy of the devices now, will they?' Rokeby-Taylor glanced around. 'I hope some of the governors were watching.'

'Sir Norman was,' Aubrey said. That particular governor would give a good account of the magic suppressors, he was sure.

The guards separated and marched the villains out. The foiled spell-caster looked particularly affronted at his unexpected end. 'This wasn't supposed to happen!' he cried. 'I wasn't told about this!'

His protests dwindled as he was hauled out of the bank, along with his unhappy cronies, and Aubrey found himself wondering at the convenience of the attempted robbery. It was a perfect demonstration of the effectiveness of the magic suppressors, with the governors' meeting and the Prime Minister in attendance.

Very convenient.

'Your company should be flooded with orders,' Sir Darius said to Rokeby-Taylor, 'once word of this gets around.'

'I should hope so.'

'And to that end, you won't need my financial support.'

'Well, I suppose not. But I'd like to have you on board, so to speak.'

'I don't think so. Now, Aubrey, we have a matter to attend to.'

Rokeby-Taylor took Sir Darius's arm. 'Before you go, in the boardroom, you were about to offer me some advice.'

'Of course. It's just this: don't ever approach me again with anything that has the remotest hint of impropriety about it.'

Rokeby-Taylor considered this, then brightened. 'Of course not, Darius. Why would I? Now, I really must see the governors. They should be around here somewhere.'

He rushed off, slipping through the crowd that had once again populated the chamber, going about their business as though nothing had happened. The buzz of transactions, the scratching of pen on paper and the rustle and clink of money melded into a sound that was the hum of commerce.

'Will the Prime Minister be needing a room?' Sir Norman appeared at Sir Darius's elbow, looking neat and tidy, with no sign of having been a hostage in a bank robbery drama only a few minutes ago. Aubrey thought it a wonderful characteristic of the Albionite bank manager, the ability to appear unfazed by events that would necessitate most people having a good lie down.

'Of course, Sir Norman. I have another matter that needs discharging. Please bring my deposit box.'

Sir Norman straightened, enthused. 'In an instant, Prime Minister!' He cast around then pointed at one of the uniformed doorman. 'Eames.'

'Nolan, sir.'

'Nolan. Please show the Prime Minister to the Vault Room.'

The doorman ushered them briskly across the main chamber to a staircase. He took them down three flights, deep into the bowels of the bank, to a barred metal door where two guards scrutinised all three of them before using their keys in the lock.

Nolan took them along a narrow corridor. He ignored the many side doors and went directly to the door at the end.

He thumped on the solid, riveted steel and a small peephole slid open. An eye studied him for a moment, then the door was unlocked. 'I'll wait for you here, sirs,' Nolan chirped. 'Collins will take care of you until Sir Norman gets here.'

Apparently, this meant that they sat at a long mahogany table while Collins – a huge guard with a missing ear – watched them with a gaze laden with what Aubrey decided was occupational hostility.

The table wasn't quite as large as the boardroom table, but it would have seated a dozen large people with room to spare. A vase of camellias sat on one end of the table while a crystal water carafe and glasses rested on a silver tray at the other end.

The Vault Room was a misnomer. The large room actually had four massive steel doors leading to vaults. It also had a singular feature. One corner of the Vault Room was taken up by a large, irregular rock. In the austere surroundings, its gnarled and rough surface was spectacularly out of place. The walls were built around it, fitting snugly, so that it looked as if it protruded from outside.

The guard saw Aubrey's curious look. 'That's the Old Man of Albion.'

'The rock?'

'Found it when they excavated the foundations. They could have broken it up, but someone decided to leave it. Part of the bank, it is.'

Sir Darius strolled across the room and inspected it, smiling. 'It's not just any rock, is it, Collins?'

'No sir, that it isn't. It's part of the Bank of Albion. The bank's built on it, to put it another way.'

'Every governor of the Bank of Albion must take his oath while resting a hand on it,' Sir Darius said to Aubrey. 'And it's part of the Counting of the Coins.'

'That's right' Collins said. 'The King will be here in two weeks' time. He has to bless the gold of the land, as all the Kings and Queens have done, ever since ever.' Collins pointed. 'See there, that worn spot? That's where the King rests his foot while he blesses the coins and bullion. Then they're fit to go into circulation.'

'One of our nation's quaintest, and oldest, ceremonies,' Sir Darius said. 'Vitally important, of course.'

Aubrey wrinkled his brow. 'Sounds a bit silly to me.'

'In some ways, it is silly. In other ways, it's one of the ties that bind us. The rituals, great and small, are markers, items of familiarity that bring us together. Repeating something that comes from our collective history reminds us where we've come from, and who we are.'

Collins, the guard, looked at Sir Darius and nodded slowly. 'That's it, sir, right enough. The bank wouldn't be the bank without the Old Man of Albion, and the money of Albion wouldn't be the same without the Counting of the Coins. We all know it's old-fashioned, but it makes us think a bit, now and then. That's a good thing.'

'You're a lucky man,' Sir Darius said, 'being this close to part of Albion's heritage.'

'Same as you, sir, sitting in Parliament all day. Must be dozens of bits of heritage just lying around there.'

Sir Darius blinked. 'I suppose you're right. I'd never thought about that before.'

He laughed and Collins chuckled along with him.

Aubrey had seen it before, but the change in Collins from hostility to respect was another example of why his father was the leader he was. A few words, some honest understanding of what motivated people, a lack of pretension, and Sir Darius had gained another supporter. Aubrey could hear Collins in the pub tonight: 'Say what you like about the Prime Minister. I've met him, and he's straight up. Doesn't talk down, and he's willing to listen.'

One of the many goals Aubrey had set himself was to be as good a leader as his father. He couldn't do it in the same way – he had a horror of being seen as a pale imitation. He had to shape his own style. He just hadn't quite worked out what that was.

Sir Norman arrived with the deposit box. It was grey metal, the size of a small suitcase. The governor needed both arms to carry it, but the box didn't seem to be heavy. He placed it in front of Sir Darius and once the ledger had been signed, he backed out of the room, taking Collins and closing the door behind him.

Sir Darius drummed his fingers for a moment. Then he found a key in his jacket. He unlocked the box and took out a small, blue velvet bag. 'This belongs to you, Aubrey. It's time for you to have it.'

Aubrey saw that the bag was worn at one corner, and the drawstring a little frayed. He hesitated. 'Sir?'

'Take it.'

The bag was light, but lumpy. Carefully, Aubrey loosened the string. He held out his palm and shook the bag, very gently.

A deep red gemstone tumbled out and sat in his hand. It was the size of his thumbnail. 'Thank you,' Aubrey said, in his awe unable to summon anything more profound.

'It's the Brayshire Ruby. A family heirloom.'

'But shouldn't it be yours?'

'It's a Leap Legacy. It skips a generation. Your grandfather had it, now it's your turn.'

Aubrey stared at it while he tried to sort out a jumble of emotions. Mostly, he was surprised. He'd been struggling for his father's approval for so long that this tangible sign took him completely unaware. He was humbled, too, by the reality of his connection with the long history of the family that was here in his hand. And, with typical

Aubrey perverseness, he was pricked by self-doubt. Did he really deserve this?

The stone was pear-shaped. It sparkled with a fire that came from deep within, a core of ruddy light. Aubrey stroked it with the tip of his forefinger. It felt warm.

'What should I do with it?'

'That's the challenge. Your grandfather had it set in a ring, but found it too clumsy to wear, except on special occasions. Tradition says, however, you can't simply repeat what the previous holder did.'

'I'm going to have it set in a watchcase,' Aubrey said and he blinked. He hadn't consciously come to a conclusion; it had simply popped into his head fully formed. But having blurted it out, the notion seemed perfect. He was conscious of time – having too little, seeing it run away too fast, the pressing urgency of it. Perhaps having a timepiece of his own could be a way of taming it.

'A watch? Novel idea. I don't think that's been done before.' Sir Darius looked pleased. 'We'll arrange for Anderson and Sutch to send someone around. They're excellent jewellers. You can explain what you want done.'

Sir Darius sat back in his chair and steepled his fingers. He smiled.

'Was this some sort of test?' Aubrey asked.

'Only in the broadest possible sense. Each of our family heirs must go through this.'

Aubrey folded his fist over the ruby. 'You didn't.'

'Oh, but I did. I had to take possession of the Brayshire Sapphire.'

'Ah, the mysterious Brayshire Sapphire.' Aubrey had never heard of the Brayshire Sapphire.

Sir Darius snorted. 'There's nothing mysterious about it. It just made a dashed ugly cigarette case look even more hideous. I don't know what I was thinking. I've never smoked.'

Aubrey felt the gem in his hand. It was surprisingly warm. 'Thank you, sir,' he repeated.

'It's yours, Aubrey, as it was your grandfather's. It's something that's been handed down, generation after generation. It reminds you of who you are.'

Aubrey's throat was tight. He swallowed. 'Sir. I'll do my best to live up to the family name.'

'What?' Sir Darius regarded him with raised eyebrows. 'Why, you've done that already, Aubrey, a hundred times over.'

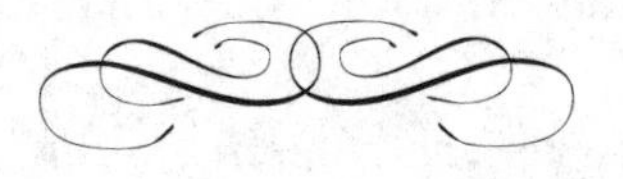

Six

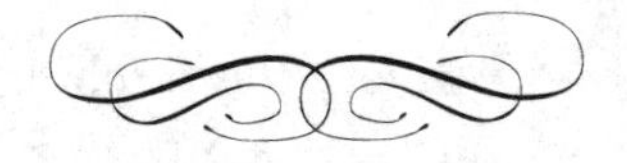

AUBREY HAD MUCH TO THINK ABOUT ON THE journey back to Maidstone, but he forgot it all when he saw the figure waiting for him at the front door.

'George! All's well at home?'

George frowned a little, then gave a slight shrug. Aubrey thought he looked tired. 'Father has an ulcer, the doctor says, and that's a miracle in itself.'

'An ulcer is a miracle?'

'No, the fact that Father actually saw a doctor.'

Sir Darius shook George's hand. 'I'm sorry to hear your father's unwell, George. Please send my regards.'

'I will, sir. He'll appreciate it.'

'And let me know if I can do anything.'

George made a face. 'Oh, sir, you know he won't have any of that. The doctor says he must stop worrying, but that's difficult right at the moment.'

Sir Darius laughed. 'Still the same stubborn William Doyle.'

Harris, the butler, had been standing silently, but at that moment he lifted his fist and coughed into it. This discreet display was followed by an infinitesimal tilt of his grey-haired head in the direction of a table next to the front door. It was piled high with dispatch boxes.

Sir Darius caught Harris's gesture, followed it, studied the tower of officialdom, and groaned. 'Aubrey. George. If you'll excuse me. I have some catching-up to do.'

He took the top three boxes. Harris took the remainder. Together, laden with the affairs of state, they started up the stairs.

Sir Darius stopped halfway. Without turning, he said, 'Aubrey. If you're not seeing the jewellers today, make sure you put the ruby in the safe.'

'Of course.' Aubrey fielded George's puzzlement cleanly and knew something that might brighten his friend's spirits. 'I'll tell you over lunch.'

A few hours later, with the afternoon fully mature and the table a picture of devastation, George sat back and picked crumbs from his chest. Aubrey thought his friend had begun the meal in a distant, abstracted mood, but he'd grown more interested as the story unfolded. Hands laced on his chest, he nodded at Aubrey. 'Magic suppressors, valuable family heirlooms, attempted bank robberies and the reappearance of Mr Clive Rokeby-Taylor. Have I missed anything?'

'No, not really.'

'Right. In that case, it sounds to me that we both need a last bit of relaxation, fun and frivolity, before we go up to Greythorn.'

'You're not anticipating any fun and frivolity at the university?'

'Not me, old man. Watch. Next week I'll have my head down in those books, the model student.'

'That's something I'm looking forward to. I *always* look forward to a miracle.'

George ignored him. 'But tonight, let's take in a show.'

Aubrey grimaced. He'd been thinking of how he could see Caroline again. Without offending her. Again. 'Why would I want to do that?'

'I've asked Caroline along.'

'A show. Splendid idea, George. What time?'

'You're sure she said she'd meet us there?'

The hansom cab ambled along the street toward the theatre district. Aubrey wished that they'd taken some more speedy form of transport. A lightning bolt, for instance.

'No, not at all.'

'What?'

'She said she'd meet *me* there. I didn't tell her that you were coming.'

'George, Caroline Hepworth isn't a fool. She'll at least suspect that you've invited me as well.'

'She still agreed to come, didn't she? What does that tell you?'

Aubrey stared at his friend without seeing him. His thoughts whirled. Caroline had left for the Arctic with the express purpose of not seeing him, the polar region being a renowned Aubrey-free environment. And yet, here she was back in Albion and after a few days she was already trying to find a way to see him. Or, at least, she wasn't going out of her way to avoid him, which was a great improvement on her project of putting thousands of miles of icecap between her and him.

'Don't jump to conclusions,' George advised. Then he slapped his forehead. 'What am I saying? You've probably leapfrogged a few dozen conclusions while you've been sitting there.'

'Perhaps,' Aubrey allowed.

'Well, don't. Sit back. Relax. Think about how you're not going to make a fool of yourself when you see her.'

'Believe me, George, I'm *always* thinking that.'

The theatre district was one of Aubrey's favourite parts of the city. While no part of Trinovant lacked life, the theatre district had cultivated its own special variety of it. Not only did the swells mix with the common folk, it appealed to Aubrey because it brought together art, magic and technology to create something wonderful – usually six evening shows a week with a matinee on Sunday. The theatre was tradition, it was story made grand, it was low farce, it was a place to find just about every expression of humanity. He loved it.

They rolled down the hill of Eastheath Street, past the Royal Theatre and the many-pillared mock classical frontage of Miller's Showcase. The streets had grown crowded and the cabby had to argue his way through the pedestrians who spilled out onto the street, waves of them promenading from theatre to theatre in search of a good night out.

They turned the corner into Harkness Street, the main theatre row. Proudly taking up the corner was the

Orient, which – to Aubrey's eye – had never looked the slightest bit oriental. The cabby saw a gap in the traffic and urged his horse forward, just as Aubrey's gaze lit on the colourful playbill outside the theatre.

He felt as if he'd been hit on the back of the head with an electric eel.

The face of Dr Mordecai Tremaine filled the playbill.

Of all the faces, the ex-Sorcerer Royal's was the last he'd expect to see on a poster advertising a light opera. The man who had plotted to kill the King, who had kidnapped Sir Darius, who had orchestrated the theft of Gallia's sacred Heart of Gold, all in order to plunge the world into war. He'd haunted Aubrey's thoughts ever since he'd disappeared from Albion.

Dr Tremaine was the greatest magician in the world. His knowledge and his bravado had led him to master arcane areas of magic that others wouldn't dare to contemplate. He achieved the difficult with casual arrogance. Hardly paying attention, he juggled spells that would drive others to distraction.

Aubrey knew that Dr Tremaine was one of Albion's greatest threats. *So why is he on a theatre poster?* he wondered.

He shook himself and twisted in his seat to see more, but a tall woman in a hat the size of an airship chose that moment to pause in front of the Orient and laugh at her companion's witticism. He grabbed George's arm. 'Did you see that?'

'I certainly did. Dreadful hat, that. Fruit *and* feathers? Appalling.'

Aubrey hissed with impatience. He hammered on the ceiling of the cab. 'Cabby! Cabby!'

The small hatch opened. The driver's eyes flicked downward for an instant, then flicked back to the swirling street ahead. 'What is it, young sir?'

'Stop here! Now!'

The driver grimaced. A ten-pound fare was vanishing in front of him, and he knew it. 'Here, sir? Can't, just yet. Hold on a mo . . .'

George leaned forward. 'Don't worry about it, driver. We have to be at the Russell by eight.'

'Eight? We'll have to get a move on, then.' He snapped a whip that looked more decorative than functional, but the cab lurched forward.

'I'll get out,' Aubrey said. He put his hand on the latch.

'You'll miss Caroline,' George said.

Aubrey froze, then let his hand drop. He sat back in his seat and noticed that his knees were trembling. 'At the Orient. The poster. It was Dr Tremaine.'

'Dr Tremaine?' George's eyebrows rose. 'Is that what this is about? I saw the poster at the Orient. That was for Arturo Spinetti, the singer.'

'Spinetti? Singer?'

'He's the talk of the town, come over from Venezia.' George crossed his arms on his chest and looked satisfied. 'You see, Aubrey, there are other sections of the newspaper apart from the politics section.'

'So it wasn't Dr Tremaine.'

George frowned. 'What a bizarre notion. Spinetti doesn't look anything like Tremaine. You know he's probably still in Holmland, constructing plots and generally making mischief. And even if he wasn't, he wouldn't plaster his face about on a poster.'

Aubrey wasn't convinced, and he had a feeling that

something was afoot here. The man he'd seen on the poster was a twin of Dr Tremaine. 'Of course.' His headache was sneaking back and he rubbed his temples wearily.

Aubrey tried to tell himself that he'd made a mistake, that was all, half-glimpsing a poster and linking it with the man who lurked in his thoughts.

He subsided, but doubt niggled at him. Dr Tremaine was brilliant, charismatic and utterly ruthless, but he was – above all – unpredictable. Not in the sense of being capricious or careless, but in the way that his motives were impossible for others to decipher. The fate of nations worried him little – his own purposes were paramount. In this world of international turmoil, he was a wild card.

Aubrey knew that Dr Tremaine was an enemy to Albion. But Aubrey was also honest enough to admit – to himself – that he had some admiration for the man. His passionate, sweeping nature, his many personal accomplishments, the gusto and swagger, as if Tremaine were a bolder, grander, more intense version of humanity.

Aubrey could see how Dr Tremaine gathered followers wherever he went. Not that he cared for them, but they were devoted to him. He was a leader, but a completely different sort of leader from Darius Fitzwilliam.

George thumped on the roof of the cab. 'That's the Russell just ahead, cabby.'

'Right you are, sir,' the cabby said with resignation. Aubrey reflected that it was part of a cabby's lot to be told things they already knew, but when they needed accurate directions to be confronted with total ignorance.

'What is this show we're seeing, George?'

'The Great Manfred. Sleight-of-hand artist.'

'A Holmlander?' Aubrey said with some astonishment.

'We're not at war yet. The Great Manfred's been on tour for over a year, the toast of the Continent.'

'I hate sleight of hand,' Aubrey grumbled. 'All their tricks are just done with magic, you know.'

The cab rolled to a halt. George bounded out. 'Ah, that's where you're wrong,' he said when Aubrey joined him on the crowded pavement. He paid the cabby, who favoured him with a grin before driving off. 'The Great Manfred gives a guarantee that every trick he performs is the result of sheer physical dexterity.'

'Impossible.'

'That's the fun of it. He does the impossible, right before your eyes, without any magic at all.'

'If this Manfred –'

'The *Great* Manfred.'

'If this Great Manfred does all that, I'll be impressed.'

The doors to the theatre were open and a crowd was trying to press through them all at once. 'Wait here,' George said. 'I'll pick up the tickets.'

Aubrey scowled. He stood on the pavement, hands in the pockets of his jacket, and studied the poster, trying not to think about Dr Tremaine.

The Great Manfred was a model Holmlander – tall, well groomed, neat pointed beard, impeccable posture. He wore a dinner jacket that had a decided shortcoming in that cards, doves and coloured scarves seemed to be exploding from its sleeves. Aubrey thought that this would be uncomfortable at best, and markedly inconvenient at worst, but it was what the illustration promised.

'Aubrey. You'll stretch your jacket out of shape like that.'

Aubrey straightened, guiltily, and whipped his hands out of his pockets. 'Hello, Caroline,' he said and all his rehearsed lines vanished from his mind. 'Hello, Caroline,' he repeated.

She stood there, cool and elegant, in the middle of the pavement. Pedestrians swirled around her as if she were an island in a raging torrent.

'I didn't think you'd be interested in sleight of hand, even when the artist is of the calibre of Manfred.'

'The *Great* Manfred,' Aubrey said.

Caroline studied him for a moment. Her face was thoughtful, but distant. His hopes of an immediate rapprochement shrivelled the longer the pause went on. 'You always did like correcting people,' she said eventually. 'Still, when you're right all of the time, it must be tempting.'

Bad start, Aubrey thought. *I've made a very bad start.* He considered his options and quickly abandoned thoughts of running away, fainting or claiming that he was, in fact, his own evil twin. 'Sorry,' he said, instead.

Caroline smiled and Aubrey took it like a hard blow to the chest. He was astonished that he didn't actually stagger back a few steps. 'Good,' she said. 'That's an improvement, anyway.'

'Improvement?'

'How quickly you were able to say sorry. When I first met you, it didn't seem to be in your vocabulary.'

'I'm aware of my shortcomings.'

'Another improvement.'

'In fact, it's hard to see past them, sometimes.'

'Oh dear. Now you're starting to sound maudlin. And that's a step backward.'

'Hmm. What about melancholic?'

'No. That sounds like someone who'd loll about under a tree and write bad poetry.'

'Brooding?'

'Ugh. If you're brooding, you belong in a chicken house.'

'Good point. Would you settle for genuinely apologetic and embarrassed for treating you so badly in Lutetia?'

'Boorish, insensitive, manipulative?'

'All that.'

'Scheming, big-headed, arrogant?'

'Yes, yes.'

She studied him. Her eyes were very dark blue and there was no-one else in the entire city. 'I can go on.'

And I'd be quite happy if you did. 'I'm sure you can.'

'I don't want to, not really.' She looked away. 'Do you know that I can't banter with anyone else like this?'

'I beg your pardon?'

'They can't keep up. Or they get confused. Or offended.'

He shrugged. 'Words. The better one can juggle them, the better off one is.'

'I agree. And I enjoy the sparring with you.'

'Ah.'

'That's why I don't think I can have anything to do with you.'

Aubrey actually looked over his shoulder. 'Are you talking to me?'

'Of course.'

'I'm sorry. I thought I was keeping up well, but that last conversational leap was a jump too far.'

'What do you mean?'

'You were saying how much you enjoyed being with me.'

'Talking to you.'

'Which usually entails being in proximity.'

She frowned, then nodded. 'Granted.'

'Which, to my mind, was sounding promising. And then you popped me on the jaw with "I can't have anything to do with you".' Aubrey put his hands behind his back and rocked on his heels for a few seconds.

Caroline looked at the sky. 'Why do I feel a sports metaphor coming on?'

'I shan't disappoint you.' He cleared his throat. 'Cricket. It's like being bowled up a series of delightful long hops and then, when you're quite expecting another, getting a searing bumper that takes your head off.'

'There. Feel better now that's out of your system?'

'Much. Thanks.'

Caroline smiled, then frowned, then settled for something in between that made Aubrey's heart ache. 'Do you see what I mean?' she said.

'About not seeing each other? No.'

'About having fun.' She put her hands together. 'But the reality is that I have other things to do in my life. Fun can wait.'

'No. Life should be fun. Life is fun.' *Even when you're balanced halfway between life and death?*

'Surely there is more to life than fun. Mindless fun.'

'Not mindless fun. Intelligent fun. Thoughtful fun. Complex, thrilling, challenging fun.'

'It sounds to me as if you're addicted to stimulus.'

Aubrey blinked. 'I suppose so. The notion had never occurred to me.' He considered it for a moment. 'There are worse flaws in a human being.'

'Do you know how many human failings can be excused that way? As long as a wicked person can find someone more wicked, he can wave his deeds away by saying, "Well, there are worse."'

Aubrey put his hands together and studied them for a time. They fitted neatly and they'd stopped trembling. 'How did we get here? Talking about the nature of good and evil?'

'We could trace back our conversational steps, if you like, but that's looking backward.'

Aubrey rubbed his chin. Where was George? 'No chaperone tonight?'

Caroline made a face. She obviously intended it to be a grimace, but Aubrey found it delightful. 'Chaperone? Please, Aubrey. We live in modern times, not the dark ages. Why should a young woman need an escort? To watch over me like a sheepdog? What an antiquated custom.'

'Of course. Ridiculous.'

'In fact, we have a speaker at the next meeting of the Eastside Suffragists on this very topic. Would you care to come?'

'Naturally,' he said automatically, as he generally did whenever Caroline requested anything. 'Perhaps we could have dinner afterwards. Or a stroll. Something.'

She frowned. 'It's a serious political meeting, Aubrey, not a rendezvous. I thought you took the cause seriously.'

'I do. I have. I shall.' *George*, Aubrey thought, *now would be a good time to appear.* He stood on tiptoes and looked through the doors of the theatre, over the heads of the people crammed into the foyer. Cigar smoke made it difficult to see, and Aubrey knew his jacket would need a good airing when he got home.

'You're looking for George?' Caroline asked.

'He's getting the tickets.' *And he's taking his time about it.*

'Really? I thought he'd come along with the sole purpose of chatting to that girl over there.'

Aubrey swivelled. Not far away, George was talking to a young blonde woman. She wore long gloves and she held a handbag so tiny that Aubrey couldn't imagine it had any use apart from providing a home for a pair of dormice.

'He's been there for some time,' Caroline said. 'And he's making sure he speaks to her mother, too.'

'That's Jane Evans. Not the mother. That's Mrs Evans. Her husband, Jane's father, is Justice Evans, the judge.'

'You know them?'

'Justice Evans is a friend of my father.' Aubrey paused. 'A proper friend, not a political friend. They knew each other in the army.'

George was nodding at something Mrs Evans had said, but Aubrey could see that it was taking him some effort to stop himself orienting on Jane. It was as if a compass point was trying to stop centring on north.

Aubrey waved. Despite George's focus, he caught the gesture. With some reluctance, he made his apologies to the Evanses and eased his way through the crowd.

'Hello, Caroline,' he said. 'Nice hat.' He rubbed his hands together. 'Cracking girl, that Jane. Dab hand at croquet.'

'You hate croquet,' Aubrey said. 'You always call it the lazy man's hockey.'

'I may have been hasty in that judgement. Time to reconsider.'

'You have the tickets?'

George looked blank for a moment, then brightened. 'Of course. Good seats, I think.' He plucked them from the inner pocket of his jacket, just as the doors opened to the auditorium.

Aubrey was decidedly ambivalent about sleight of hand. When younger, he'd desperately wanted it to be true. He wanted such deftness to be real instead of simple magic masquerading as prestidigitation. What a world it would be, if a person could make a ball vanish into thin air, just by clever manipulation and misdirection.

But with every sleight-of-hand artist he'd ever seen, the illusion didn't last. He soon saw the spells that were used to make scarves dwindle and disappear, or doves reconstitute themselves inside top hats, or pretty assistants hover in thin air, which was a great disappointment.

He settled in his seat, willing to be deceived but knowing he wouldn't be. The critical part of his brain never slept. It was always ready to squint, mutter and prod him into asking why, or how, or what.

The curtain was down. A four-piece string ensemble played in the pit – something Holmlandish, Aubrey thought, but thankfully it was something danceable rather than one of their galumphingly serious compositions.

Caroline had chosen to sit between George and him, and immediately Aubrey had the Great Armrest Issue to contend with.

In purely economic terms, he knew half the armrest was his. His ticket entitled him to it. In personal terms that could be a good thing. If he took half the armrest, and Caroline took half, his forearm – and elbow – would be close. An altogether satisfactory arrangement from his point of view as it could lead to an accidental touch or two, when he shifted position – which would be only natural.

But what if she wanted more armrest space? The courteous thing would be to concede the entire plush territory to her, for her comfort. Then he could miss out on the nearness.

The possibilities made his head spin.

In the end, he sat back, crossed his arms on his chest, and settled for simply enjoying the beguiling scent of her perfume. He made a note to himself to research perfume, so he could speak with some knowledge about it instead of the total ignorance he currently had. He imagined himself greeting her with a 'Lovely scent. *Madeleine*, isn't it? I do enjoy the floral topnotes balanced with the myrrh-like warmth.'

He settled back with a smile.

The quartet brought its playing to a conclusion. Lights dimmed and the curtains hissed back. A small square table stood alone. At the four corners of the stage stood tripods, each surmounted by featureless, black metal boxes. Aubrey's eyes opened wide, his professional interest suddenly piqued.

The boxes looked like magic suppressors.

The Great Manfred strode onto the stage to the applause of the audience. His face was grave and he did not acknowledge the plaudits. His attention was on the table.

He went and stood next to it, frowning, as if troubled. He tilted his head and, keeping the table firmly in his gaze, walked right around it. Then, with a flourish, he shook his right hand in the air above its surface. To his evident surprise, a small red ball appeared in his fingers.

Aubrey blinked. It was a simple thing to do. Any young magician learned how to materialise small objects through applying the Law of Displacement. Moving a small ball from a pocket to a hand situated hardly any distance away? Routine.

Except he'd felt no hint of magic at all.

The Great Manfred stared at the red ball, then at the table. He bent and put his left hand under the table. With a quick, precise movement, he slammed his other hand onto its surface, crushing the ball beneath his palm.

Or had he? Aubrey watched as the Great Manfred withdrew his left hand. It now had the ball in it, the ball that had apparently passed straight through the solid surface of the table.

Applause, but muted, as if the audience wasn't quite sure what it was seeing.

'Thank you, ladies and gentlemen,' the Great Manfred said, with a slight, Holmlandish bow. 'You are sceptical, which is quite correct. Magic, you are thinking. It's all done with magic.'

No it's not, Aubrey thought. *What on earth is going on here?*

The Great Manfred looked to the wings. 'Let me introduce a special guest. Professor Magnus Bromhead.'

Aubrey stiffened. He'd never have expected to find the

author of *Magical Rigour: Experimental Procedures Delineated* on the stage. It was as unexpected as bumping into an elephant in a bookshop.

The applause was polite and puzzled this time rather than sceptical. It also seemed to puzzle the grey-haired, gown-wearing don who joined the sleight-of-hand artist. He shielded his eyes from the footlights.

'Professor Bromhead,' the Great Manfred said. 'You are an expert on magic, are you not?'

'I've held the Trismegistus chair of magic at the University of Greythorn for twenty years. That's why you hired me.'

'Exactly. So you should be able to identify the devices on these tripods?'

Professor Bromhead adjusted his glasses. He harrumphed, then moved closer to the nearest tripod. 'Magic suppressors. Where'd you get 'em?'

The Great Manfred ignored the question. 'In the field generated by these devices, can any magic exist?'

'None.'

'Are you sure?'

'One way to find out. Stand back.'

The professor eyed the tripods, then moved to the very front of the stage, almost toppling into the orchestra pit. He spread his legs a little, settling his stance. Then he placed his hands together at chest height.

It was a simple light spell and Aubrey nodded in approval at the crispness of the professor's enunciation. The spell was a well-practised one, to judge by the way it rolled off his tongue. Aubrey felt the smooth build-up of magic before the professor drew back his hands and a small ball of light hovered between them.

Nervous applause tripped through the auditorium, but the professor looked up sharply. 'Watch,' he said.

Slowly, he walked backward, keeping the ball of light hovering between his hands. One step, then two, and the professor moved into the area bounded by the tripods. Aubrey felt a surge of magic, and immediately, the ball of light winked out.

Professor Bromhead dropped his hands. 'See? As soon as I stepped into this region of the stage, my magic failed, nullified by these devices. It's a sharply delineated area, determined by the placement of the boxes. Magic suppression works.'

The Great Manfred nodded. 'So you would guarantee that I can use no magic while on this stage?'

'I will. And better than that. I'll sit off in the wings and monitor for magic use each night of your show. If there's even a sniff, I'll feel it and raise a hue and cry.'

'Professor, I thank you.'

Aubrey applauded heartily as the professor left the stage. If Professor Bromhead was prepared to give his word on the truthfulness of the performance, it was good enough for him.

After that, the Great Manfred proceeded to amaze.

Aubrey was at first interested, then impressed and finally astounded. Rings linked and unlinked, ropes of colourful scarves came from nowhere, and endless numbers of eggs came from the Great Manfred's mouth.

The performer's skills were stunning. Aubrey squinted, tilted his head from side to side, but eventually had to admit to himself that he had no idea how the Holmlander was doing it.

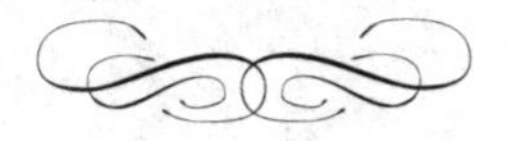

AFTERWARDS, STANDING ON THE CROWDED PAVEMENT outside the theatre, Aubrey could barely keep still. 'Incredible,' he repeated. 'Simply incredible.'

'He was very polished,' Caroline said. 'Not demonstrative, but certainly polished.'

'Oh, he was good, but I was talking about the magic suppressors. They're extraordinary.'

The notion had come to him unexpectedly. While he was trying to puzzle out the secrets of the Great Manfred's tricks, another part of his mind had apparently been gnawing away on something else.

The magic suppressors. To perform as they did, they must grapple with the nature of magic itself. Magic and anti-magic. It was a frontier area of magical research, as far as Aubrey knew, but it was immensely important for the future of rational magical theory.

Perhaps it could shed some light on death magic – and his condition.

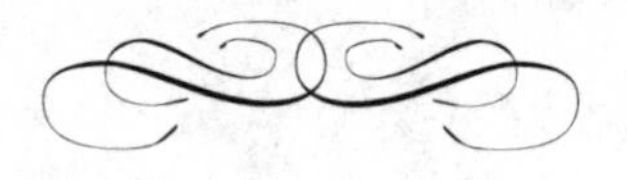

Seven

Monday morning, Greythorn. Aubrey had been to the university town many times, and had even been to the colleges, accompanying his father on one trip or another. But it was different, approaching as a student instead of a visitor.

He checked his new pocket watch to make sure they weren't late. The Brayshire Ruby had been beautifully set into the gold cover of the watch; Anderson and Sutch had done a superb job, with the internal workings as well as the decorative case.

'I'm sure I've forgotten something,' George muttered as the motor-cab rattled through the cobbled streets.

'You're bound to have,' Aubrey said. 'You can send for whatever it is.'

'Of course. Quite.' George settled back, but didn't look convinced. 'When are you planning to bump into Caroline?'

'What?'

'You know, old man, accidentally crossing paths with her, happening to be outside her lecture, something like that. Apostle's College isn't far away. Maybe your bicycle will have a flat tyre, right outside her room?'

'I have no such plans,' Aubrey said stiffly, although he had been pleased when Caroline had opted to live in college rather than stay at home with her mother in the town. He looked out of the window to see two dons arguing on a street corner, one jabbing the other with a rolled-up newspaper.

Ah, the spirited life of academic discourse, he thought.

'No?' George continued. 'Why not? I thought you'd be right onto it, opportunity and all that.'

'Caroline has her calling. She's at university to study. She doesn't want any distractions.'

'I see. How's that feel then, to be a distraction?'

'Potential distraction.' He sighed. 'I'm not going to put my foot in it again, George. Not after last time.'

'Mm. Embarrassing.'

'Embarrassment I can handle. But hurting other people, blindly? Even when I think I'm doing the right thing? Not any more.'

George pursed his lips for a while. 'Commendable, that, not wanting to hurt people.'

'I would have thought so.'

'But if it means you just don't do anything, then it's a bit limiting, what?'

'Perhaps. But better that than the alternative.'

'Are you sure?'

'Oh, definitely. I consider myself an expert in every aspect of human relationships, now.'

'Really?'

'Of course not. I'm struggling to keep my head above water.'

The motor-cab veered to one side. With a squeal of brakes, it lurched close to the kerb. 'We're here, gents,' the cabby announced. 'St Alban's College.'

THE PORTER SHOWED THEM TO THE ROOMS THEY WERE going to share. Aubrey stood at the door and took grim satisfaction in the knowledge that the quality of the rooms was a way of reinforcing their status. First-year students were the lowest of the low, and thus were put in the dingiest rooms. It wasn't anything personal, it was simply five hundred years of tradition.

Their quarters were two rooms, second floor of the northern wing, perfectly situated to catch every hint of icy wind when it rolled down from the hills, as it did with clockwork regularity in these parts.

Two beds, two wardrobes and a washstand in the bedroom; two desks with empty bookshelves in the study. It was old, it was bare, and it was going to be their home.

Aubrey skimmed his hat onto the bed. 'Wardrobes. They're spoiling us, George.'

George ambled to the window. He struggled, but eventually threw it open; fresh air edged in, as if unsure of its welcome. 'We're in the lap of luxury. Just wait until we get those trunks up here. The importance of floor space is greatly exaggerated, you know.'

Aubrey couldn't feel depressed, not here. University had beckoned for some time. Stonelea School had been as good as any in the country, but for the last two years he felt as if he'd been marking time, intellectually. His magical studies teachers had done as much for him as they could but he'd been chafing, wanting to learn more.

George groaned and smacked himself on the forehead. 'Idiot.'

'You've remembered what you forgot?'

George wiped his hand over a doleful face. 'Father gave me a book. I left it behind.'

Aubrey took this as further sign of his friend's distraction. 'It was important?'

'It was Lord Aldersham's memoirs. One of Father's favourites.'

'The newspaper magnate? Your father enjoyed that?'

'He did. And, more to the point, he knew I would.' George cursed his own forgetfulness again. He was so disconsolate Aubrey started to consider what he could do for him, but before he could think of anything, a knock came from the open door. 'Where do you want this case?' a voice asked.

'In the study,' Aubrey said, 'anywhere.'

He turned away from the window and stared at the man who was carrying one of George's suitcases. 'Commander Craddock.'

'Good morning, Fitzwilliam, Doyle. On the desk?'

Aubrey gestured, a little dazed. 'Thank you. We were on our way to get our things.'

'You'll need a few trips. Looks as if you've brought enough to last off a determined siege.'

'It was my grandmother. She insisted on helping me pack.'

'Ah, the redoubtable Duchess Maria. She is well?'

'You know perfectly well how she is,' George put in. 'That's your job, knowing about things and all.'

'Mr Doyle, you go straight to the heart of the matter, as is your wont. Now, if you'd be so kind, could you go and fetch some more of those heavy things? I need a word with your friend here.'

George raised an eyebrow. 'Aubrey?'

'I'll be fine, George. Thanks.'

George frowned, but went. Craddock waited for the sound of his footsteps on the stairs, then closed the door.

'You're being mysterious,' Aubrey said.

Craddock took off his black, broad-brimmed hat. Underneath, his hair was fine, and so blond as to be almost white. It was straight, thick and surprisingly luxurious.

'Mysterious?' he said. 'It goes with the job, rather.' He paused and took an envelope from the pocket of his long black coat.

Craddock, as head of the Magisterium, had responsibility for policing all magical affairs. It was a brief he interpreted broadly and Aubrey was convinced that he enjoyed the clandestine nature of his activities.

'I can't imagine this is a social visit,' he said.

'Quite right. I'll get to the nub of the matter.' He drew the curtains. Thin as they were, the room was plunged into half-light. 'I want to formalise your relationship with the Magisterium. I want you as an irregular operative.'

Aubrey almost smiled. Entering the service of the Magisterium had been one of the possibilities he'd considered for this year. He'd wondered how to do it – without having to ask his father for assistance. He'd put it aside, deciding instead to concentrate on his studies, and now here the opportunity was presenting itself. 'I can't. I'm studying.'

'That's one of the reasons I want you on board. You're at Greythorn, a legitimate student, studying magic. I need someone in that department and none of my operatives have been able to get in.'

'They've tried?'

'Tried, failed, been reassigned. I need you.'

'Surely I don't have the training, the skills.'

'The Magisterium takes all kinds, as long as they have magical ability. We can teach you the rest. As needed.'

It was tempting. 'What does my father say about this?'

'I haven't asked him. I'm asking you.'

That was enough. Aubrey put out his hand. 'I'm happy to help.'

'Good man. I'll be in touch, soon. Here.'

He held out the envelope he'd been cradling. 'It's from the Rector of your college. I took it from your letterbox on the way up.'

A bumping noise came from outside. Craddock opened the door to find a red-faced George battling with a huge steamer trunk. 'And here's your friend, just in time to hear about the invitation.'

George leaned on the trunk. 'Invitation?' he panted. 'That's quick. No-one knows we're here.'

Aubrey flapped the card. 'We've been invited to a ceremony, tomorrow. The awarding of degrees.'

'Ah,' Craddock said. 'The Rector likes it when the son of the Prime Minister is part of his college. Expect more of these invitations.'

Aubrey groaned and George chuckled. 'Don't laugh,

George,' Aubrey said. 'Your name's on this invitation, too, you know.'

George's groan was even louder than Aubrey's.

THE NEXT DAY WAS A WHIRL OF FACES, NAMES, PLACES AND timetables. Aubrey didn't see George until the late afternoon, a bare few hours before the ceremony was to begin.

They hurriedly dressed in their evening dress, full white tie and then their undergraduate gowns. 'Astounding stuff,' George said as he struggled with his braces. 'The Dean of History himself interviewed me, asked what sort of history I was interested in.'

'A fair question, the past being as huge as it is. It helps to narrow it down,' Aubrey said. 'Have you seen my collar studs?'

'Over there, in that box by the door. You're right, it was a fair question, on reflection, but at the time it rather took me by surprise. You see, I'm in favour of history in general, if you like. The concept of it.'

'You're saying history is a good thing. Your shoes need a shine.'

'So do yours. Cleaning kit is in that case, I think.'

'Ah, excellent.'

'Now, I didn't think I'd be getting off on the right foot if I told the Dean of History that history was a good thing. It's the sort of stuff he knows, I'd say. So I said I was interested in Classical history.'

'Why?'

'My line of reasoning is this. The further ago the period is, the less we know about it.'

'True. Mostly.'

'And the less we know about it, the more I can make up. I didn't put it exactly in those terms, you understand.'

'I'm glad.'

'So it looks like I'm studying Roman history, which I'm not altogether displeased with.'

'The Romans? They had some fine magicians in their day.' Aubrey straightened. 'There. You look acceptable.'

'And so do you. Let's go.'

The University of Greythorn and the town of Greythorn had a relationship that Aubrey thought of in biological terms. Either the university had spread through the town like weeds through a fertile field or the town had enveloped the university like a strangler fig on a jungle palm. Regardless, it was a symbiotic relationship – each depended on the other, even though they were loath to admit it.

The heart of the university was the Prescott Theatre. It was here that the great university ceremonies were held, as well as concerts and recitals. Aubrey had always admired its stately elegance – its many-pillared façade, the hexagonal dome – and he was ready to admit that Sir Robinson Hookes was at the top of his form when he built it for Lord Prescott.

The ceremony was the sort of thing that a seven-hundred-year-old institution can get very polished at. The procession, with the most senior academics from each of the colleges, made Aubrey think he'd slipped back in time. Gowns, robes, ermine, gold and silver chains, the professors, wardens, rectors, principals, masters and other big brain boxes paraded their full spectrum of colours. Aubrey amused himself by deciding which animal each of their caps looked like. He saw quite a number of moles, a few mangy cats and one outstanding badger, while organ music made the hall shake.

Soon after the raft of post-graduate degrees, he glanced at George and almost laughed aloud – which would have ruined the solemnity of the occasion. George had the glazed, stony-eyed look that he adopted when enduring ceremonial boredom. He could keep it up for hours – like an eastern mystic on a bed of nails.

When the vice-chancellor announced that the honorary degrees were about to be awarded, Aubrey nudged George, who started. 'I wasn't asleep,' he said loudly and received a few haughty looks from people nearby.

Politicians headed the list, receiving doctorates for their useful generosity to higher learning. An ex-ambassador received a doctorate of economics for working for ten years in the Antipodes. Aubrey thought that was rather rich. The ex-ambassador should have been grateful for the privilege. An archbishop picked up a doctorate of divinity, which he seemed very pleased with, almost a tick of approval.

Then the name of Arturo Spinetti was announced and Aubrey nearly leaped to his feet.

A tall figure mounted the stairs to the stage two at a time. On him, the red robes didn't look foolish – they looked dashing. His shoulders were broad, his hair long and dark. He crossed the stage with balance and grace, like the most expert of fencers. When he took the scroll from the vice-chancellor he gripped the old man's hand and grinned, fiercely.

'It's him,' Aubrey hissed to George.

'Spinetti? I know. That's what the vice-chancellor said.'

'No. It's Dr Tremaine.'

George gave Aubrey an odd look. 'Are you all right, old man?'

Aubrey didn't get a chance to answer. A magnificently whiskered gent in the seat in front of them turned and glared.

Aubrey subsided.

Spinetti (*Tremaine!*) launched into a speech of acceptance. Within a few words, the whole mood of the audience had changed. Even those who'd fallen asleep were waking and paying attention. Gone was the pained forbearance. Instead, the members of the audience began to smile and nod.

The singer charmed them. With a mixture of self-deprecation and suave aggrandisement, he spoke of his delight in accepting his doctorate. He wasn't just grateful, he made every audience member feel as if he or she were being personally thanked by someone very special.

Except Aubrey. He sat, shocked, trying to work out how Tremaine had smuggled himself into the country from Holmland, why no-one recognised him, and exactly what he was up to this time.

The new doctor finished by inviting everyone to his performances in Trinovant, promising them the time of their lives.

The Prescott Theatre had heard applause many times, but most of it was polite – especially at tedious award-giving ceremonies. The applause that the singer received was different. It echoed enough to make the windows shake; he bowed, managing to be both flamboyant and humble at the same time.

Magic, Aubrey thought frantically. *Tremaine must be using some sort of concealing magic.*

'Let's go,' he murmured to George while those around were still clapping wildly. Aubrey slipped out of his seat and hurried up the aisle towards the exit.

'What is it?' George asked once they were outside.

The wind was cool in the evening and felt good on Aubrey's brow. 'Theatre door. This way.'

George shook his head, but trotted alongside as Aubrey hurried around the curving flank of the theatre. 'Mistaken identity, old man. Granted, Spinetti looks a bit like old Dr Tremaine, but do you really think he'd front up like this? A bit blatant, isn't it?'

Aubrey stopped, suddenly, and George had to jog back to join him. 'It *is* blatant. And that's just the sort of thing he'd do.'

'You're starting to sound strange.' George rubbed his chin. 'I tell you what. Let's wait out here and see this character up close as he's leaving. I'll guarantee that you'll come to your senses.'

Aubrey found that he'd clenched his fists and that it was an effort to unclench them. 'You think I'm mad? Is that it?'

'If there's anything I've learned from my time with you, it's that if you have a bizarre notion, it should be taken seriously.'

They didn't have long to wait. The organ began again, signalling the recessional. Soon, gowned and capped academics began to spill out of the theatre entrance. They were chattering, full of high spirits, as they made their way down the stairs, a gorgeous waterfall of colour and pomp.

Aubrey grabbed George's arm. 'There he is.'

'I see him.' George frowned. 'D'you really think he looks like Dr Tremaine?'

'Looks like? George, he *is* Dr Tremaine!'

'I don't think so. Dr Tremaine is taller, for a start. And his nose is longer. Different coloured eyes, too.'

'What are you talking about?' Aubrey grabbed George's arm, hard. 'It's him, I tell you!'

'Aubrey,' George said softly, 'people are looking at us. Lower your voice.'

Aubrey blinked. He saw the concern in his friend's face and he realised he'd been on the verge of creating a scene. 'George?'

'Easy now. What would Dr Tremaine be doing here? And don't you think someone would spot him if he was stupid enough to appear? He's one of the most notorious people in the world.'

Aubrey rubbed his forehead and searched the crowd for the Dr Tremaine lookalike, but he'd gone. He let go of George's arm. 'I'm sorry. I don't know what got into me.'

'Let's head off, shall we? You're looking pale.'

Aubrey nodded. His stomach felt hollow, as if he hadn't eaten for days. 'If you say so.'

Together they slipped away from the Prescott Theatre back to St Alban's College.

Aubrey held the cup of tea in both hands. 'I don't know what came over me. I'm sorry.'

'No need to apologise. Remarkably tame occurrence,

that, compared to some of the hullabaloos we've been involved with.'

'Still, it's not the sort of thing for our first week at university. Not a good reputation enhancer.'

'Not exactly.' George munched on a biscuit. 'Protective colouration, old man, that's what's needed.'

'Protective colouration? You've been talking to Caroline, haven't you? Sounds all natural historyish to me.'

George finished his biscuit, grinned and dusted both hands together. 'Camouflage. What animals do to blend in with their surroundings so they won't get eaten.'

'I see. And how is this relevant to me? I can't see I'm in any immediate danger of being devoured.'

'No, but it might be useful to fit in, somewhat. Not arouse suspicions, if you know what I mean.'

'Ah, yes. My condition. Not drawing attention to it might be a good thing.'

'It's all well and good being the Prime Minister's son, but it might be useful to be a jolly keen member of the student population and all that entails.'

'I think I see what you're getting at. Clubs and societies?'

'Exactly. They've been touting for members. You haven't noticed?'

'I've had other things on my mind.'

'I'm surprised you haven't been press-ganged into something. They're deadly, those recruiters.'

'And what have you found yourself involved with, George?'

'I'm a Lunatic.'

'Don't be so hard on yourself.'

'Very droll. The student paper. *Luna*. I thought with my interest in journalism it could be an outlet.'

'And how did a first-year, inexperienced country boy like you manage to become a journalist on a respected publication like *Luna*?'

George waved a hand. 'Well, I mentioned that I had experience with printing presses. Especially problematic ones.'

Aubrey snorted. While wrestling with a recalcitrant printing press in the name of the Marchmaine Independence League could come under the heading of 'experience', Aubrey had filed it under 'tortures not to be repeated'. He thought he still had ink under his fingernails. 'Nothing like starting at the bottom, George. Anything else?'

'I gave the Birdwatching Society a miss. The Rationalist League sounded interesting, but a bit serious.'

'No "Lounging Around and Being Indolent Society", was there?'

George flapped his hand. 'No need for an organised club there. I can manage that on my own. I did, however, put my name down for the Cricket Club. Thought I'd put the gloves on again, a spot of wicket-keeping.'

Aubrey smiled. 'Now, that sounds like a good idea. They need players?'

'They're always looking for players, the chap behind the desk told me.'

'Splendid.' He frowned. 'Now, where did I pack my bat?'

'Oh. And there's a Musical Theatre Society. Quite active, they are, too.'

'No.'

'No?'

'No more musical theatre for me. I've had quite enough, for now. I might try picking up an instrument, though.'

'Leave the cornet to me. It requires a sensitive touch.'

'I was thinking about the violin.'

'Caroline wouldn't have mentioned she liked the violin, would she?'

'She may have talked about enjoying string quartets, but at no time has she specifically nominated the violin by name.'

George didn't look at him. He tapped his teacup with a spoon, absently. 'And Spinetti?'

Aubrey took out his pocket watch and studied the Brayshire Ruby. It was comforting, a solid reminder of his heritage and of good Albionish craft. 'He is Dr Tremaine. I'm sure of it.'

'You are?'

'Most certainly.' Aubrey put his watch away. 'I know, it makes no sense, his being here. Regardless, it is him.'

'Even if no-one else can see it.'

'George, he used to be the Sorcerer Royal. He's capable of enchantments like no-one else.'

'But why? Pretending to be a singer doesn't seem like one of his plots to take over the world.'

Aubrey slumped. 'I don't know.'

'Shouldn't you tell Craddock, then? Isn't that the sort of thing he's got you watching out for?'

'How did you know? Never mind. Craddock's another one whose motivations are opaque.' Aubrey scowled, then glanced at George. 'Are you saying that you believe me?'

George nodded. 'I'm not saying that you're never wrong, but I've learned that the unbelievable isn't what it's reputed to be.'

'I'm touched, George, and glad that you believe in me, because I was starting to doubt myself.' He stretched, then yawned. 'Tomorrow, let's go and see about doing some joining up.'

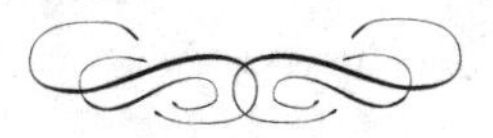

THE NEXT DAY, AUBREY TOOK GEORGE'S PROTECTIVE colouration suggestion to heart. He joined the Fencing Club, the Cricket Club and the Chess Club, as well as making enquiries about the university regiment.

He was careful not to go near the Musical Theatre Society. He knew that even if he vowed to remain a casual backstage helper, somehow he'd end up spending most of his hours there and finding himself as an understudy to someone with precarious health and uncertain commitment.

While all this was pleasant diversion – as was meeting the many and various members of the college – he quickly plunged into the serious matter of his studies. Remembering his vow not to engage in any practical magic, he'd loaded up with magical theory subjects. The denser, the better.

After his first lecture in Sub-fundamental Magic, Aubrey knew that this was the place for him. His head spun as he left the lecture theatre; he found he had to trail a hand along the stone walls of the cloisters to keep himself upright. Despite doing his preparatory reading, and despite feeling that he knew as much as anyone, he had been dazzled by the depth of reasoning, the open vistas that lay before him; he'd been impressed, too, by the remorseless, intense presentation of Professor Bromhead. The uncomfortable performer from the Great Manfred's stage show was gone. The professor was in his element – demanding, gruff, clinical in his unfolding of the mysteries of the origins of magic.

Aubrey thought this was exhilarating enough, but on the following day, the professor mentioned his protégé, Lanka Ravi.

Even in the short time Aubrey had been at the university, he had heard about the mysterious Lanka Ravi. The young genius was the prime element of any discussion around the Faculty of Magic – who was he, where was he, what was he up to?

A few things were agreed on. Some time ago, a parcel of documents had arrived unannounced on Professor Bromhead's desk. His curiosity was aroused by the stamps and the return address: it was from the Subcontinent, but he didn't recognise the name of the sender.

As the Trismegistus professor of magic at the foremost university in Albion, Professor Bromhead often received letters from the public. Mostly, these were from people with an amateur interest in magic. Obscure theories would be advanced, new laws outlined, plans suggested to overthrow established magical procedures. Almost always, these were the products of enthusiastic, but deluded, believers. Nothing ever came of them.

This time, Bromhead was ready to pen another polite letter of acknowledgement when he glanced at the topmost sheet.

Four hours later, he was still poring over the tiny,

precise handwriting. Reluctantly, he'd become convinced that this Mr Lanka Ravi had outlined at least two revolutionary magical laws, along with a supporting theoretical framework.

Professor Bromhead had trouble believing that someone so distant from modern magical discourse had derived such brilliant stuff. It sparked a frantic correspondence. After the exchange of a dozen letters, he was convinced. Lanka Ravi was a magical prodigy.

It took Professor Bromhead a year to persuade Lanka Ravi and his family, but finally the gifted isolate boarded a steamer and made his way to Albion.

Since arriving, he had been cloistered with the top brains from the Department of Experimental and Theoretical Magic, but the undergraduate speculation was constantly centred on when Lanka Ravi would give a public lecture. Bunches of magic students would congregate out of thin air, surge to a lecture theatre where Lanka Ravi's appearance was rumoured, then dissipate, morosely, when the rumour proved to be unfounded.

Of course, Aubrey was caught up in the fever. It was a giddy, thrilling time and the exotic nature of the unseen Tamil magician added to the heady atmosphere. For the rest of the week, he felt like a native scout in a canoe, swept along by rapids. By dint of furious paddling, he managed to keep from capsizing, but it was a near thing. College life, meals, socialising, meeting new and fascinating people, then lectures and tutorials and the silence of the far reaches of the library. He had his violin lessons, but gave up after a few days of furious practice, realising that expertise in some areas doesn't come overnight. He regretted it, as he enjoyed the music-making. He'd even had his fingertips temporarily hardened thanks to a neat spell cast by his violin instructor, to stop them becoming raw from pressing on the strings.

He saw George first thing in the morning, last thing at night, and at college gatherings, but since their academic leanings were so divergent, that was all.

He didn't see Caroline. They moved in different university circles. He promised himself he'd do something about this, when he had time.

The Department of Experimental and Theoretical Magic wasn't only the home of the mysterious Lanka Ravi. It was leading the way in all manner of modern magical research. Things Aubrey had only read about were being discussed and refined every day. But he soon learned that the department was made of people, the same as any other organisation. Fads, fashions, and favourites were rife. Some avenues of inquiry were seen as 'rewarding' and 'challenging', while others were yawned at, or even scorned as unworthy of serious exploration. Currently, the feverish area of speculation appeared to be the origins of magic, with many favouring the thesis that human consciousness was responsible for magic. The exact manner of this interaction was the subject of feverish discussions and exploration.

Controversy, too, was bread and butter for the department. It was a university, after all. One of the most divisive issues was military applications of magical theory. The majority of academics and students were firm patriots, and willing to countenance the notion that the army or the navy may benefit from their work. After all, their reasoning went, the alternative was worse.

However, a reasonable pacifist movement also had a presence, resisting any project that smacked of practical, war-mongering application. The result was that these people dealt with some of the most abstruse areas of magical theory – and that they walked the halls of the department building with distant, vague expressions, as if they were seeing things beyond the mundane here and now.

Only once did Aubrey hear his hero, Baron Verulam, mentioned. It was with tones of affectionate disdain, as one of the early progenitors of modern magic, but hopelessly – hopelessly – old-fashioned in these times.

Aubrey bridled at this, but bit his tongue. He needed a firmer footing before he engaged in arguments on this level.

The event, however, that caused Aubrey's studies to take a sudden sharp turn came when he was looking for George at the end of the hectic first week.

A letter arrived at their rooms from George's mother. Aubrey broke off from his studies – a little dazed, as he often was when disengaging from knotty magical theory – and immediately grabbed his jacket. He scratched his head over George's handwritten lecture timetable and went looking for his friend.

Aubrey crept into the back of the History lecture theatre and tried to spy George's sandy hair. His efforts, however, were distracted by the lecturer.

She was petite, with light brown hair, and wore rimless spectacles. Her hands were covered with rings, which flashed as she constantly gestured to emphasise one point or another.

She was passionately describing the difference between Chaldean and the Nineveh variant of the Assyrian language. 'While they are both aspects of the Babylonian,' she said, 'never, ever get them confused.' She took off her glasses. 'I did once, when I was your age. It took me a long time to live down the embarrassment.'

For the rest of the lecture, Aubrey forgot all about George. He was lost in the unfolding story of early language development in the ancient world.

When the lecture finished, Aubrey hurried down the aisle. He spotted George lingering near the exit, talking to a serious-looking girl in a green dress, and decided he'd be there for some time.

'Excuse me?' he said to the lecturer.

She was still gathering her notes at the lectern. She glanced at him. Her eyes were dark brown and Aubrey thought she was about the same age as his parents – considerably younger than any of the other dons he'd encountered.

'If you've come late,' she said, 'I'm afraid you'll have to get the notes from one of the other students.' She smiled. 'I did make a fair bit of it up as I went along, you see.'

'Er.'

'Chaldean is so intriguing, don't you think?'

'Certainly. It's perfect for most spells that require a careful timing factor.'

She looked over the top of her spectacles. 'You're not reading History.'

'No. I'm Magic.'

'Of course you are.' She slipped her papers into a case. 'So what can I do for you?'

'Ancient languages. How can I do more?'

She stood with her case in one hand and her other hand on her hip, and regarded him with amusement. 'Ancient Languages? I do a handful of lectures for you first-year Magic students in a few weeks time.'

'A handful of lectures? What if it's not enough?'

'Ah, bitten by the language bug?'

It was one way of putting it. Aubrey was thinking in more practical terms. 'The better I can handle these ancient languages, the better I can work spells.'

The lecturer put down her case and threw up her hands. She addressed the lofty ceiling. 'How long have I been waiting to hear someone say that? How long have I been saying it to those fusty Magic dons?' She dropped her gaze and smiled warmly at Aubrey. 'You'll have to give up one of your magical subjects, but I can get you into my Introduction to Ancient Languages. If you're keen.'

'Aubrey!' George said. He strolled over, looking most content with life. 'You've met Professor Mansfield, have you?'

'Mr Doyle,' Professor Mansfield said. 'You've completed all your reading on early Latin?'

George made an oddly indeterminate hand gesture – a flapping, twiddling motion. 'Not entirely, no. I've made a good dent in it, though. Fascinating.'

'I'm sure.'

'Professor Mansfield?' Aubrey said.

'Professor of Ancient Languages. And I hope you're not going to ask me how a woman my age happens to be a professor.'

'Wouldn't have dreamed of it,' Aubrey said truthfully. Knowing his mother and Caroline meant that he didn't find competent women a shock, unlike many of his contemporaries. 'I wanted to ask for a reading list.'

She smiled again, with dimples, and Aubrey was tempted to revise his age estimate downward considerably. 'Good lad. I'll get one to you. What college are you at?'

'St Alban's.'

'Name?'

'Aubrey Fitzwilliam.'

'Fitzwilliam. St Alban's.' She looked up from her notebook. 'You're not related to Rose Fitzwilliam?'

'My mother.'

She tapped her nose with her pencil, thoughtfully. 'Wish her the best from me when you see her next. Anne Mansfield. Oh, and your father.'

She picked up her case. 'See the secretary in the Languages school this afternoon.' She stopped at the door. 'We'll make all the necessary arrangements.'

When she'd gone, Aubrey was left with a feeling that he'd just complicated a life that had hitherto been marked by a distinct lack of simplicity. 'George,' he said, and he handed the letter to his friend, 'remind me never to act on impulse ever again.'

'Right you are, old man.'

George glanced at the handwriting on the envelope and frowned.

'Anything wrong?' Aubrey asked.

George didn't answer. He opened the letter and scowled as he read it.

'George?'

George sighed. He folded the letter and tucked it back in the envelope, then stared at it for a moment. 'Farming's a hard life,' he said eventually.

'A letter from home, was it? Your father is all right?'

'His health's improved, at least.' George slipped the envelope into the inner pocket of his jacket. 'You know, it's hard enough with the seasons and the crops and animals and all that. But do you know what worries farmers most?'

'No.'

'Money.'

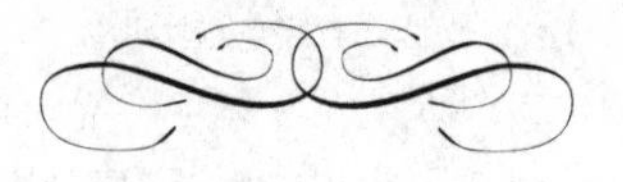

Eight

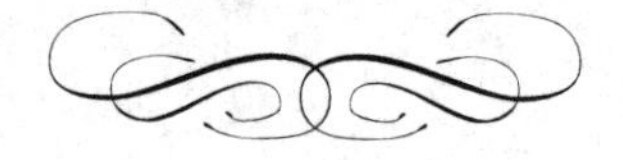

THE NEXT MORNING, AUBREY CAME BACK FROM THE bathroom, still towelling his hair. George pointed at the teapot on the desk. 'Help yourself.'

'Excellent.'

'Caroline's left a note. She was wondering if we wanted to go down to the city with her.'

Aubrey took his head from the towel and stared. 'When?

'She wants to catch the half-past nine train.'

Tea forgotten, Aubrey was at his wardrobe in an instant. Then he turned back to his friend. 'George?'

'What is it?'

'How do you know what was in the note that was left for me?'

George grinned. 'Interesting. You're assuming it was a note for you. It simply said "Room 14" on the envelope.'

'Well, when I said "for me", I actually meant "for us". Of course.'

'That makes no sense at all. You're asking me how I know what was in a note addressed to us.'

'Correct.'

'University is addling your brain. Come on, get dressed.'

CAROLINE WAS WAITING ON THE STATION PLATFORM. SHE was comparing her watch – a man's wristwatch – with the station clock. Aubrey started to catalogue her clothing for later complimenting, but gave up and enjoyed the simple fact that Caroline Hepworth would be a couturier's dream; she made all clothes look good.

He hailed her and she glanced in his direction before returning her attention to her watch. For an instant he was miffed that he was less interesting than a time-piece, but he decided that would be reading too much into things.

'Hello, Aubrey, George,' she said when she'd finished her inspection. Aubrey had the distinct impression that she was annoyed with neither the watch nor the clock, but with time in general, there being so little of it.

'Hello, Caroline,' he said. 'How's Science been?'

'Challenging. And Magic?'

'Exhilarating.'

'You're fortunate. And how's History, George?'

'Splendid. I've met some jolly interesting people.'

'Any of them male?'

'None come to mind. Unmemorable lot, History men.'

'And the Magisterium, Aubrey. Is it keeping you busy?'

Aubrey flinched, and was glad to see they were alone on the platform. 'Magisterium?'

'Commander Tallis told me that Craddock was recruiting you, temporary duty or something like that.'

'Tallis? Craddock?'

'Aubrey, you've lapsed into your parrot impersonation again, which is hardly useful. Now, why hasn't Jack Figg been able to contact you?'

'Jack –' Aubrey began, then he bit his tongue. 'He's been trying to contact me?'

'All week.'

'Ah. I've been busy.'

Caroline rolled her eyes. 'And you're the only one who's been busy?'

Aubrey had the distinct feeling that he was on a very rapid slippery dip. 'Ask George.'

'Very busy, he's been,' George said. 'Didn't even see the notes on his desk.'

'Apparently not. That's why Jack contacted me, to contact you, to contact him. If you see what I mean.'

'Perfectly,' Aubrey said faintly. He was still trying to sort out the barrage of information. '*Commander* Tallis?'

Caroline snorted. It would have been unladylike in anyone else. 'He's been promoted. To match Craddock, they say. Keeps the Special Services and the Magisterium balanced against each other.'

'You've been speaking with him?'

A whistle sounded. Caroline looked down the track. 'Right on time.' She glanced at Aubrey. 'You mightn't be the only one on special detachment, you know.'

Their gazes met. Caroline smiled, just a little, and

Aubrey immediately knew how a lump of wax felt when it's held over a candle flame.

Then, as one, they turned to look at George. He returned their regard evenly. 'Special detachment? Of course I am. Apart from my standard brief to keep an eye on you two – son of PM and daughter of one of the country's most famous artists – a representative of the Press is vital in these times. Who else can we trust if we can't trust the newspapers?'

Aubrey and Caroline burst out laughing. George couldn't keep a straight face, and the other passengers waiting on the platform stared at them with puzzlement.

The seats in the first-class compartment were roomy and comfortable. Aubrey and George were sitting opposite Caroline. Aubrey had been torn over the seating configuration. He much preferred sitting so he was facing the direction of travel – sitting with his back to the engine seemed unnatural, somehow, going backward into the future. But Caroline took the window seat – once again, Aubrey's preference – on this side of the compartment, so Aubrey had to decide whether to sit next to her – delightful – or sit opposite where he could see her without moving his head – perhaps even more delightful. The permutations were so labyrinthine that at first he stood in the middle of the compartment, unable to move until George nudged him. Aubrey let the direction of the nudge make the decision for him, and so he ended up travelling backward, but with the agreeable compensation of having Caroline in his sight the whole way.

After they'd settled into the clacketty-clack rhythm of the train, Aubrey felt as if things were resolved. Caroline still had a distance about her, but she smiled and joked merrily. If she had been a favourite cousin or a sister, all would be well, but Aubrey still harboured feelings for her that – it seemed – would go unrequited.

'So, what did Jack Figg want?' he asked, mainly to distract himself from that line of thought.

'Jack?' Caroline's chin was resting on the back of her hand as she gazed out of the window. A ghost of a reflection hovered in the glass, and Aubrey wished he were a painter. 'He wanted you, is all he'd say.'

'I hope he's not in trouble.'

'Don't be so gloomy,' George said. 'P'raps he's found the perfect solution for poverty and wants to share it with you.'

'Possibly.' It was the sort of thing Jack Figg would come up with, Aubrey decided. The plan would assume endless goodwill from everyone, plus absolute rationality to boot, where the entire population would collectively strike their foreheads and exclaim 'Of course! Why didn't we think of this before?'

And Jack would get dreadfully disappointed when flaws in his plan were pointed out to him, but it wouldn't stop him from organising, lecturing, arguing and simply badgering those around him into good works.

Jack Figg was one of the few truly humane human beings Aubrey had ever met. Aubrey did worry about him, living and working in some of the worst, most crime-ridden parts of the city, but Jack never faltered in his efforts to improve the lot of those around him.

Caroline still gazed dreamily through the window. George had unfolded one of his beloved newspapers and was immersed in the minutiae that so intrigued him. Aubrey was left alone with his thoughts.

Some time later, George nudged him. Aubrey started. 'What?'

'You were asleep.'

'No I wasn't.'

'No, of course not. You snore when you're awake, just to keep everyone on their toes.'

'And the closed eyes,' Caroline said. 'To keep out the sunlight?'

'I wasn't snoring, was I?'

'No,' Caroline said. 'Not really.'

George held the paper under Aubrey's nose. 'Like to go to a show while we're in town?'

'I don't think so. I've had enough of shows for a time.'

'Look again, old man.' George shook the newspaper significantly. 'Wouldn't you like to go to a show?'

Aubrey started to bat the newspaper aside, then his gaze landed on the advertisement in the middle of the page. 'Oh.'

'I thought so,' George said smugly.

'What on earth are you two going on about?' Caroline asked.

'Nothing,' Aubrey said.

'Nothing,' George said.

Caroline narrowed her eyes. 'Why do I suddenly feel as if I'm a headmaster? Come now, out with it.'

'Arturo Spinetti,' George said. 'Lovely tenor. Good reviews, too. "A fine repertoire, excellent control, first class presentation."'

'It doesn't sound like your sort of thing, Aubrey.'

'It's not, exactly.'

'Then what is it?'

Aubrey hesitated. Caroline's father had been killed by Dr Tremaine. Should he tell her of his suspicions? Would it be kinder to shield her until he knew more?

If she finds out later that I suspected and didn't tell her . . . 'You deserve to know.' He leaned forward and put his hands together. 'I think Dr Tremaine is back.'

All the blood ran from Caroline's face. Her eyes became diamond-hard points. 'Dr Tremaine,' she breathed in a voice that was full of such loathing, such fury that Aubrey almost felt sorry for the man.

He also thought it wise not to point out that it was Caroline who was now echoing. 'Yes. At least, I think so.' He glanced at George. 'George isn't sure.'

'Not sure?' she snapped. 'Either you saw him or you didn't.'

'I saw him. George didn't. Or George didn't think it was him.'

'Tell me everything.'

So Aubrey recounted the fiasco at the awards ceremony. When he paused, George filled in and Aubrey was grateful for his friend's impartiality. Listening to him, it didn't sound as if he were a complete raving fool.

Caroline sat silently, but Aubrey saw how the clenched hands in her lap went whiter and whiter as the story unfolded.

When Aubrey finished the account, she groped for words for a moment. 'And you weren't going to tell me this?'

He sighed. 'I considered it. But lessons learned and all that. This is the first chance I've had – we've had – to tell you.'

'I see.' She gazed out of the window again. 'This changes things. We must put it to rest once and for all. Is this Spinetti Dr Tremaine or not?'

'You really think he might be?' Aubrey asked.

'Magic, Aubrey,' she said. 'It's you who should know that just about anything can happen where magic is concerned. Some sort of disguising spell or other, I'd imagine.'

'One that I can see through but no-one else can?'

'I'll leave that for you to work out.'

Aubrey opened his mouth and then closed it again.

'Excellent.' Caroline regarded Aubrey with a steely ferocity. 'Is there anything else you're not telling me?'

Jack Figg had asked to meet at the hall in Lennox Street, the headquarters of the Society for the Preservation of Manners. The last two members of the fading society – a Miss Alwyn and her cousin Mr Renshaw – were on the Continent and had let Jack Figg have the use of the almost pristine building.

The hall was narrow, sandwiched between a barber and a boot repair shop. Jack Figg was standing on the stairs, leaning against one of the pair of fluted pillars, waiting for them in the morning sunshine.

He brightened when he saw them approach. 'Aubrey! Caroline! George! At last!'

Jack Figg was tall and thin. He stooped and his shoulders were rounded. He wore battered spectacles, a dark blue waistcoat, and a striped shirt with the sleeves rolled up. He looked harassed, but Aubrey knew it was his customary expression. Like him, Jack had many things he wanted to do with life and felt that there simply weren't enough hours in a day.

'Sorry, Jack.' Aubrey shook his friend's hand. 'Things have been hectic.'

'Saving the country again, I suppose?'

'No, not for a while, I haven't. I'm at Greythorn now, you know. Busy.'

'Ah, and how is the featherbed of the elite? Full of lotus eaters whiling their lives away?'

'Not exactly. I haven't had a lotus all the time I've been there. Have you, George? Caroline?'

'No,' George said. 'I had a good pork pie just yesterday, though.'

'Hmph,' Jack said. He stuffed his hands in the pockets of his waistcoat. 'Still, it's hardly an open institution. I don't suppose you saw many miner's sons there. Or daughters,' he hastened to add when he saw Caroline bridling.

'You know I agree with you, Jack,' Aubrey said. 'There's a long way for the country to go. We've made some progress, but some things move slowly.'

George shrugged. 'Well, here's one farmer's son who's managed to wind up at Greythorn.'

'Should be more of it, is all I'm saying,' Jack said.

'And I'm sure that's not why you've asked us here,' Aubrey said. He gazed up at the neoclassical façade of the building. The pediment was severe, looking down on the portico like a judge on the accused. 'What have you got set up in here? A soup kitchen? A workers' reading room?'

'We've got a co-operative running inside, lacemaking.'

'Jack, I didn't think you were the textiles type.'

'We've had a number of families come down from the north, turned out of their houses when the mills expanded. The old women used to make lace by hand, so I've set them up here, teaching others. Output is increasing and we've got more orders than we can fill.'

'You never cease to amaze me, Jack,' Aubrey said. 'But what's this got to do with me?'

'Nothing. The lacemakers use the auditorium, but this place has a set of offices too. Someone has asked to meet you.'

THE OFFICE HAD ONE SMALL WINDOW, AND THE GENERAL gloom this created wasn't helped by the decor. The walls were panelled with black wood, the desk and chairs were heavy and equally dark. Two large filing cabinets – in dark wood – stood like sentinels in one corner. In front of the desk, a long table stretched toward the door.

Two men and a woman looked up when Aubrey, Jack, Caroline and George entered. The men stood, tall and straight. Aubrey knew military bearing when he saw it, and suspected the origin of these strangers even before he heard them speak.

Jack addressed himself to the older of the two men. 'Count Brandt, this is Aubrey Fitzwilliam, who you've heard me talking about.'

'At last,' Count Brandt said, bowing slightly, and his accent confirmed Aubrey's suspicions. 'I get to meet your Prime Minister's son.'

Aubrey was accustomed to this sort of greeting. It ranked him somewhere between the Prime Minister's fourth assistant secretary and the Prime Minister's cuff-links. 'Count Brandt.'

While Jack introduced Caroline and George, Aubrey studied the Holmland count.

He was in his fifties, Aubrey guessed, from the grey that sprinkled his otherwise black hair and beard. Tall, powerful, but definitely starting to lose the muscularity he had once had. Too much good living? His hands were blunt, well-manicured, but Aubrey could see several scars that must have come from nasty wounds. A military background, without question, from his posture. His suit was expensive, from Maitland's, one of Old Street's finest tailors, if Aubrey was any judge.

His Albionish was excellent – precise, fluent, with a good grasp of idiom. Aubrey wondered how much time he'd spent in the country.

Brandt waited until Jack had finished his introductions and took his turn. 'These are my good friends, Mr Rudolf Bloch and Miss Anna Albers.'

Aubrey glanced at George and received a merest hint of a wink in return. 'So,' George said, 'lacemaking is popular in Holmland?'

Brandt stared at George. Bloch and Albers looked at each other, worried, and Aubrey was pleased to have them on the back foot.

'Not lacemaking?' he said, sharing another ghost wink with George. 'You must be philanthropists, then, making a large donation. I always admire Jack's ability to conjure up money.'

Jack started to talk, but Brandt held up a hand. 'No, let me explain, Mr Figg. You've been good enough to help we exiled Holmlanders settle into your country.

Now it is time for me to tell you all why I need to speak to Mr Aubrey Fitzwilliam.'

More than a little intrigued, Aubrey took his place at the table with the others. Bloch and Albers looked nervous, Bloch rubbing his hands together constantly, while Albers seemed to find it difficult to meet the gaze of anyone else in the room.

'We know of you,' Brandt began, 'Mr Fitzwilliam. Various of our members have noted your deeds, your part in several recent events.'

'Members? Is this a club?'

Bloch's and Albers's agitation increased, and Bloch mopped at his brow with a handkerchief. Brandt remained calm. 'Not a club, no. A loose association, a group of friends and like-minded Holmlanders who do not agree with the way the country is being run.'

'Which country?' Caroline said. 'Albion or Holmland?'

'Holmland, Miss Hepworth.' Brandt glanced at his colleagues. 'Please, you must understand, this is difficult.' He placed both hands, palms down, on the table in front of him. 'Some of us had to leave Holmland, unable to endure the situation. Some are still there, in positions of importance.'

'You want to overthrow the Elektor,' Aubrey said flatly.

Brandt shook his head. 'We want to restore Holmland, not destroy it. The Elektor is badly advised, easily led. We want to remove those who are steering our country toward war.'

'The Chancellor and his government?' Aubrey said.

'Just so. Once the Elektor sees how reasonable our position is, he will change his direction and all will be well.'

Bloch cleared his throat. When he spoke, it was a growl. 'If he doesn't, then –'

'Enough,' Brandt snapped. He shrugged at Aubrey. 'You must excuse us. The Chancellor's people have treated us very badly.'

Aubrey frowned. 'I still don't see how I fit in.'

'They have much to do here, Aubrey,' Jack Figg said. 'There's a sizeable Holmland community in Trinovant now. Displaced, dispossessed. Your family's work in setting up the Broad Street Clinic made me think you might be able to help.'

'Jobs,' Madam Albers said. 'Houses. Somewhere to live, our people need.'

'Of course,' Brandt said. 'This would be helpful. Vital. But it is with influence that I hope you can help most.'

This was something Aubrey was used to. 'I'm afraid I can't do much there. Father is very concerned to keep things on the up and up. No indulgences, no personal favours.'

'We understand. But if you could advise us on the proper channels, who to approach?'

'I think so. If it could help.'

'It would be greatly appreciated.'

An understanding having been reached, the conversation took a turn to the mundane. After some chat about the weather and Caroline's mother's looming exhibition, both Bloch and Albers were growing noticeably anxious and made efforts to bring the niceties to an end. Farewells were made, but as the others filed out, Count Brandt signed for Aubrey to stay. 'You have some magic, I believe?' he said softly. Caroline looked back from the corridor, frowning, but Aubrey gestured for her to go on.

'Why do you ask?'

'We have some members of our group who are well qualified, magically, but they cannot obtain positions at your universities.' He scowled. 'And your companies sneer at our Holmland degrees.'

'It's unfortunate,' Aubrey said.

'I hoped you would understand. A waste of magical talent is a sad thing. Is there any way you can help?'

Aubrey rubbed his chin. 'Let me see what I can do at Greythorn. There must be someone up there who'd be sympathetic.'

'It's important,' Brandt said. 'For our cause as well as for them.'

'I'll see what I can do.'

Brandt smiled. Aubrey knew a politician's smile when he saw one and Brandt's came straight out of the textbook. 'Thank you, Mr Fitzwilliam. I hope we meet again soon.'

A firm clasp of the hand and Brandt backed into the office, closing a door that wasn't so thick that Aubrey couldn't hear the voices immediately raised in disagreement behind it.

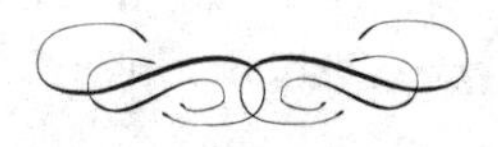

LADY ROSE WAS WAITING FOR THEM AT MAIDSTONE.

'Good,' she said as soon as they stepped through the front door. 'I need to speak to Caroline.'

Aubrey stared. 'How did you know she'd be here?'

'She rang me, of course. Yesterday.'

Then they were off, into Lady Rose's drawing room. The door shut firmly behind them.

'I wonder what that's about?' George asked.

'Probably about the specimens they brought back from the Arctic,' Aubrey asked. *Or it's about me*, he thought and he fervently hoped it was the former.

Aubrey and George went to the library, where George was happy with a selection of newspapers. Aubrey flitted from one book to another, never settling on one for long, trying to distract the part of his mind that was wondering about what was going on between his mother and Caroline.

It was nearly an hour later – when the stack of discarded books by Aubrey's armchair was threatening to topple and do serious damage to a nearby potted palm – that Caroline appeared.

Aubrey sprang to his feet. 'Are you all right?'

'All right? Why wouldn't I be?'

'Of course. Naturally.' Aubrey tried to think of a tactful way of finding out what had gone on behind closed doors.

George looked up from his newspaper. 'What were you and Lady Rose talking about, Caroline? Anything important?'

Sometimes, Aubrey realised, a direct approach was best.

'Not really, George,' she said. 'Just about the attempt on Lady Rose's life while we were on our expedition.'

For an instant, Aubrey wondered if he'd swapped lives with someone in a play. 'I beg your pardon?'

'Your mother. Lady Rose. Someone tried to shoot her. That's why our expedition was cut short.'

Astonishment and incredulity combined to overwhelm Aubrey with a totally new sensation: astondulity. 'Why didn't she tell me?'

'She didn't want to bother you, apparently.'

An instant later, Aubrey was through the doorway, down the hall and knocking on the drawing room. 'Mother?'

The door opened. Lady Rose stood there, composed, regal, sardonic. 'Aubrey. That took nearly ten seconds longer than I expected. Are you getting slow in your old age?'

'Mother.' Aubrey struggled for words. 'Are you all right?'

She stood back and ushered him into her domain, a room that sported a riotous collection of her findings over the years. 'Isn't it a bit late to be asking that? It happened a month ago.'

'But you were shot at!'

'It's not the first time I've been shot at and probably won't be the last. You can't go on expedition to some of the places I've been without being shot at. In fact, it's a sign of respect in many areas.'

Aubrey sat heavily on a sofa. A large, ceremonial mask took up the space next to him. It looked as stunned as he felt. 'Why didn't you tell me?'

'Your father and I thought it best not to worry you. Not with your setting yourself up at St Alban's.'

Aubrey thought this over for a moment. 'So you thought you knew best, where I'm concerned.'

'Now, Aubrey, I know where you're headed. Your shameless manipulation of Caroline was an altogether different matter.'

'How?'

'You're not her parent.'

'So it's all right to manoeuvre someone around, as long as he or she is your offspring?'

'I wouldn't put it as bluntly as that.'

'I see. And my behaviour isn't simply because I come from a long line of arch-manipulators?'

Lady Rose pursed her lips. 'You *are* your father's son, aren't you? Look where we've got to from where we started. When you stepped through the door, you were concerned and sympathetic over my brush with death, and now you're all nettled and feeling aggrieved.'

Aubrey considered this. 'You're correct. Let's get back to your expedition. But I reserve the right to return to feeling aggrieved later.'

'If you must.'

'You were shot at.'

'It missed.'

'I gathered that. Where? Why? How?'

'In St Ivan's, our last provisioning port before we headed north. I was supervising the loading of a bale of reindeer skins.'

'It was definitely you he was after?'

'Oh yes. He called my name. When I looked around, he fired.'

'And then?'

'Well, after Caroline and I disarmed him, he ran off. We chased him, of course, but he knew the woods better than we did and he escaped.'

'Why did you cancel the expedition? That doesn't sound like you.'

'If it were just me, I would have pressed on. But I had others to think about. One attempt, I could pass off as an error, or madness. Twice, however, is rather hard to ignore.'

'You were shot at again?'

'No, no, not shot at. But the incident was undeniably hostile. That evening. We were still berthed, but fully provisioned by that time. I took my customary stroll on deck after supper. A figure came out of the shadows – burly, stinking of fish – and brandished a large knife.'

'Caroline was there?'

'Appeared, disarmed him and I rendered him unconscious.'

'I could have warned him that he'd have been better off with a rifle,' Aubrey mused, 'rather than risking coming to close quarters with you two. You handed him over to local authorities?'

'In St Ivan's? There are no local authorities in St Ivan's.' Lady Rose actually looked discomforted for a moment. 'It meant we had to take matters into our own hands, as it were. We tied him to a chair and asked him questions. The captain helped, but had to go away after a while.'

'Weak stomach?'

'Nothing so crude as that, Aubrey, thank you. He went to find some of the more prominent citizens of St Ivan's. Or less disreputable citizens, anyway. They confirmed the identity of our assailant as a renowned local layabout and ne'er-do-well. Which is quite an accomplishment in St Ivan's, it being a sort of haven for layabouts and ne'er-do-wells. They tended to believe his story about not knowing the man who paid him. They pointed out that several strangers from the south had been in St Ivan's in the weeks prior to our arrival, leaving just before our steamer pulled in.'

'Interesting. How far south, I wonder?'

'I did ask, Aubrey. Really, sometimes you seem to think no-one else is capable of clear thinking.'

'Sorry, Mother.'

'To most St Ivanians, "south" is a rather nebulous term, meaning pretty much the whole world – seeing as there isn't much that's north of St Ivan's. One of the prominent citizens – the one with two peg legs – ventured that he recognised the accent of the strangers.'

'Distinctive, was it?'

'Holmlandish usually is.'

Aubrey sat back, laced his hands on his chest and gazed at the ceiling. 'And how angry was Father when you told him that Holmland has tried to assassinate you?'

'Extremely. He went still, and when he spoke, his voice was very, very soft.'

'Ah. That angry.'

'He immediately called in Commander Tallis. I had to repeat the whole story.'

'Tallis's reaction?'

Lady Rose smiled, a little. 'He was upset. He kept using words like "underhand" and "unsporting".'

'Yes, he would.' Aubrey was puzzled. An extraordinary plot, and it showed how far Holmland's espionage services reached. The death of the Prime Minister's wife in the polar regions would be a shock, but not totally unexpected, frontier wildernesses being what they were. The taint of suspicion would hardly fall on Holmland. The result would be a distraught, perhaps unmanned, Prime Minister, as the couple were famed for their closeness.

A distraught Prime Minister of Albion? Aubrey thought. *One whose decision-making may be compromised? What an excellent opportunity to declare war.*

He grew angrier and angrier as he considered the

implications. Firstly, he could see what Tallis was outraged about. This sort of action was different from the past. Clandestine action against non-participants? Where would it end?

He also realised that this may well have very personal implications.

'Yes, Aubrey,' his mother said, and he realised she'd been watching his face closely. 'It seems as if we live in very different times now.'

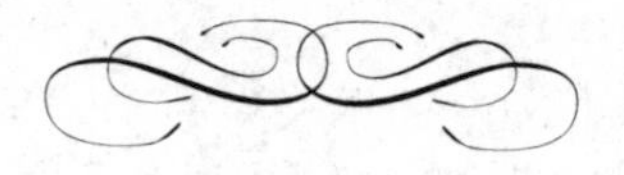

Nine

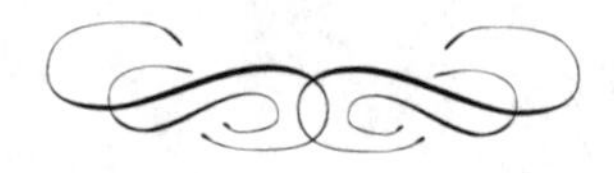

JUST BEFORE THEY LEFT, AUBREY'S FATHER HAD ARRIVED home and, after sharing a significant look with Stubbs, their driver, insisted that they take the Oakleigh-Nash to the theatre. Stubbs had been part of Sir Darius's army company, a drill sergeant whose particular skills in both armed and unarmed combat had proved useful in civilian life.

As they edged through the traffic, Aubrey sat his hat on his lap and turned to Caroline. 'Why didn't you tell me about my mother?'

She smiled. A little challengingly, he thought. 'Why, Aubrey, what a direct question! For a change, you simply asked instead of going round and round in circles.'

'Well, it's important.'

'She asked me not to, that's why.'

'And you happened to mention it back at Maidstone because she was ready to tell me, and she knew that if you dropped it into conversation I'd burst in on her and demand to know what went on?'

'Yes, something like that.'

He crossed his arms on his chest. 'I hate being predictable.'

'Never mind. I'm sure you'll make up for it by doing something frightfully capricious any minute now.'

'I should hope so.' Aubrey turned his hat over in his hands. 'I would like to have seen the expression on the face of that would-be assassin when you took to him.'

She shrugged. 'I felt sorry for him, eventually. Not very bright at all. Brutish, easily led, cruel. What sort of life is that?'

'I'm going to write a review of the show,' George announced.

Aubrey and Caroline both stared at him.

'Apropos of nothing at all?' Aubrey said.

'Actually, I've been waiting to get a word in edgewise. It's dashed difficult when you two get up and running.'

'For *Luna*?' Caroline asked.

'That's the idea. While I'm happy to help out with the printing press, I think actually writing something could be a useful step towards real journalism.'

'Did you write one for the Great Manfred's show?'

'I scratched out something, but Cedric Westerfold fancies himself as a critic, ran up a review and shot it in.'

'Westerfold?' Aubrey asked.

'You know. Short, loud, nose like an anteater.'

'Ah. Tries to sport a monocle but it keeps falling out?'

'That's the one. I have him in mind as my journalistic nemesis. It's handy to have one of those, I understand, trading barbs in the press, striving to outdo each other in the witticism department.'

Aubrey had trouble imagining it. 'I look forward to reading all about it.'

Caroline opened a window. 'Traffic's not moving at all. The street's choked.'

'Time to walk, then,' Aubrey said.

Stubbs turned around, frowning. 'I'm not sure that's a good idea, sir.'

'It's not that far, Stubbs. We can manage.'

'It's not that, sir –'

Aubrey had already leaped out of the car. He squeezed around a delivery truck and raced around to Caroline's door.

'We'll catch a cab home,' Aubrey said to the unhappy-looking Stubbs, then he joined Caroline and George on the pavement.

Pedestrians swirled and surged. Hawkers, pedlars and barrow boys added to the confusion by touting their wares, blocking the flow and diverting people onto the street, which was, fortunately, still choked with traffic that was barely inching along. The entire city seemed to be converging on the Orient Theatre.

'They're all wanting to see Spinetti,' George said over the chatter around them. 'He's popular, if nothing else.'

They joined a long queue that was snaking its way along the pavement towards the box office. It moved along well, and soon they reached the laneway that ran alongside the theatre. Aubrey glanced in that direction, trying to maintain an awareness of his surroundings. The lane was dark, a single electric light at the far end the only illumination. Someone stood in the shadows, near a jumble of crates that had been left against the wall of the theatre. He was tall, and wearing a shapeless cap. Aubrey couldn't make out his features, but tensed when the man lifted a hand.

'Mr Fitzwilliam?' he called. 'You're intending to see Mr Spinetti, the singer?'

'Without wanting to be rude, what business is it of yours?'

'If you'll just come this way.' He hesitated. 'It's important.'

Aubrey's feet seemed to be assured by the calm confidence of the stranger; he took a step into the lane before he realised what he was doing. He stopped and shook his head. 'I don't think so.'

George appeared at his side. 'What is it?'

Then Aubrey heard Caroline's voice. 'Aubrey? George?'

'In here.'

On the opposite side of the lane from the theatre, a metal door banged open. Two more dark-clad figures emerged. Both of them had the shapeless caps.

The first stranger held up a hand and his two colleagues froze.

It was a suspended moment where nothing was happening. Aubrey knew that the pause wouldn't last, that events would move forward at any instant – for better or for worse.

Caroline came around the corner, saw the tableau – Aubrey, George, confronted by three strangers in a darkened alley – and took matters into her own hands.

Events moved forward again, toward the 'worse' end of the scale.

Before Aubrey could stop her, she slipped past him and kicked at the knee of the first stranger. He jumped backward, but by then Caroline had closed on him. Her open hand whipped upward, catching the stranger flush under the chin.

Aubrey heard his teeth snap together. His head bounced off the brick wall and he crumpled to the cobblestones.

A scream went up from behind them as someone in the theatre crowd decided that reality was much more confronting than make-believe.

George roared and waded in, meeting the advance of the other two strangers. He knocked one over and grappled with the other. Caroline grasped her skirts and leaped over to help.

Aubrey was about to hurl himself into the fray when the sour taste of magic came into his mouth. Spinning around, he saw the first stranger was on hands and knees in the muck, but he'd lifted his head and he'd begun to chant a spell.

Aubrey could feel it taking shape. A simple binding spell, it was a derivative using Greek as its base. He knew he could counter it by snapping out an annulment with a limiter on the duration, effectively ending the spell as soon as it began – but he hesitated, remembering his vow not to do magic.

The hesitation was enough. Someone hit him from behind and his dilemma was suddenly irrelevant.

When Aubrey regained his senses, he was in a brightly lit room that smelled of disinfectant. A bland-faced man was looking down at him.

'Good. I'm MacNamara,' the bland-faced man said. 'Are you fit to get up?'

Aubrey worked his jaw for a moment and glanced sourly at him. 'It depends.'

'On what?'

'On whether you're going to hit me again.'

'I didn't hit you.'

'No?'

'Carstairs did.'

MacNamara gestured to Aubrey's left. Aubrey shifted his attention, discovered exactly what 'woozy' meant along the way, and saw another bland-faced man leaning against the tiled wall. 'Hello,' Carstairs said. 'Sorry about the conk on the old noggin. Couldn't be avoided.'

Aubrey sat up and saw that he was in a hospital bed. He rubbed the back of his head. 'Hate to contradict you, but you could have avoided it by not hitting me on the back of the head.'

'Ah yes, but you were about to do some magic. Had to stop you.'

'No I wasn't. And no you didn't. And what is going on here? Where are my friends?'

'Craddock will tell you,' MacNamara said.

Aubrey rubbed his forehead. The Magisterium. Well, at least he should be safe with them.

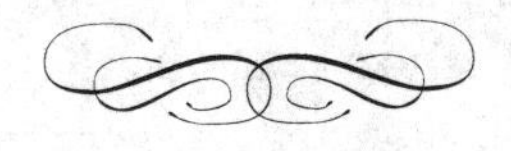

CRADDOCK STUDIED THE NOTEBOOK ON THE DESK IN FRONT of him, then regarded Aubrey across the wooden expanse. 'Well, at least you're safe with us.'

Craddock was a difficult man. Aubrey couldn't imagine having a friendly chat with him. Musings on the weather, one's health or the state of the national cricket team wouldn't come easily to him. 'If you call being assaulted then abducted "safe", then I suppose we are.'

Craddock moved one of his pen stands a fraction of an inch. He picked up a silver fountain pen and balanced it, crossways, on his forefinger. 'Apologies for all that. Bit of a mix-up, really. You were recognised by my operatives and they showed commendable judgement in wanting to get you away. Not so commendable was the way they overreacted. Especially since you're a fellow member of the Magisterium.'

Aubrey rubbed the lump on the back of his head, the tangible evidence of their overreaction. 'What's wrong with the Orient Theatre? And what were your operatives doing in the first place, flitting about in the dark like that?'

'Two things. Firstly, we've had this Spinetti under surveillance for some time. Did I say something funny, Fitzwilliam?'

'No, not funny. Not funny at all.'

'Very well. Secondly, our monitoring section detected another substantial magical flare-up in that vicinity, early this evening. It was very brief, but strong enough for three separate monitors to hit the alarm.'

Aubrey nodded at that particularly interesting piece of news. 'And when I appeared, it sent your people into a spin. Prime Minister's son and all.'

Craddock's expression didn't change. 'It was potentially a tense situation.'

'What aroused your suspicions about this Spinetti? Before tonight's magical surge, I mean?'

'Small things. Enough to make us interested.'

'It would have to be magical, otherwise it wouldn't be a Magisterium matter.'

Craddock flipped the pen and caught it in the same hand. He placed it back in its holder. 'This is novel. I'm usually the one asking the questions.'

Aubrey wondered how much to tell Craddock. Despite some misgivings, he'd come to respect the man, understanding that his integrity was absolute. Beholden to the country, not to any particular political master, his actions were often viewed with suspicion by politicians, but the independence of the Magisterium was guaranteed by the constitution.

And isn't this what I agreed to do? he thought. Working for the Magisterium had seemed exciting. Now, he wasn't entirely sure.

'I have an interest in Spinetti,' he said guardedly.

'I see. I take it that this interest goes beyond his singing? Which, by all accounts, is uncommonly good.'

'I think he's Dr Tremaine.'

Craddock didn't move for some time. He studied Aubrey with his dark, unblinking eyes. 'Well,' he said eventually. 'That is fascinating.'

Aubrey let out a breath he didn't realise he'd been holding. It was hard to surprise Craddock, but he thought that he'd at least managed to take him aback a little. 'I'd begun to doubt myself. No-one else can see it.'

Craddock held up a finger. 'I'm not saying I accept this. I'm simply saying that it might explain some of the anomalies we've noted around him and the area of that theatre.'

'Magical anomalies?'

'To all intents and purposes, he is what he seems. His papers are all in order. He fulfils his obligations. He is adored by the public. But we have operatives on the boat train, especially when foreigners are coming in. When Spinetti arrived, one operative had the distinct impression – for a moment – that his appearance changed.'

Aubrey felt relieved. He mightn't be the only one. 'But the operative wasn't certain?'

'No. Whatever, it was enough to put him on our "To Be Watched" list. Several times since, we've detected magical ripples in his vicinity. Always behind closed doors, nothing overt. And then this substantial flare-up.'

'When I look at him, I see Dr Tremaine.'

Craddock grasped his chin and frowned. 'None of my operatives has reported anything so definite. Suspicions, only.'

'One thing is for certain,' Aubrey said. 'If it is him, he's not here just for his singing.'

'Of course.' Craddock made a quick note. 'Anything interesting to report from the university?'

'No. Especially since I'm not sure what you're after.'

'Have you encountered the foreigner, Lanka Ravi?'

'Lanka Ravi? No-one has. He's been locked away with the bigwigs. Surely you don't suspect him of spying.'

'No, I'm interested in the quality of his magic. If you can, I'd like your assessment of it.'

'I'd like to, but there's no telling when he's going to give a public lecture.'

'Now, how are you getting on with the refugee Holmlanders? Count Brandt and his friends?'

Aubrey wasn't surprised by Craddock's knowledge. 'Harmless? Nefarious? Talkers? Plotters? Who knows?'

'We need to know. Get close to them. Find out their links in Holmland. Report back.'

WHEN CRADDOCK USHERED AUBREY TO A ROOM OVERLOOKING Grainger Square, he realised they were in Darnleigh House, the headquarters of the Magisterium. Waiting for him, with different levels of patience, were Caroline and George.

George looked up from his cup of tea. 'Fine biscuits, Aubrey. We really should come here more often.'

Caroline stood. 'Good. We can leave now. How's your head?'

Aubrey touched the lump and winced. 'Feeling better and better.'

'He has been of some use to us,' Craddock said. 'Thank you for waiting.'

'We didn't have much choice, did we?' Caroline said.

'I hope you weren't inconvenienced too much.'

'We wasted our tickets,' George said. 'And an evening.'

'Of course. May I offer you some tickets to another show, one that's sure to be rather safer?'

'What is this?' George said. 'Is the Magisterium turning into an booking agency now?'

'We have our eye on another performer. One of

ours this time. He's generously given us some tickets.' Craddock produced tickets from the inner pocket of his long coat. 'Perhaps you've heard of him? The Great Manfred?'

'The Great Manfred?' Aubrey would have reeled with surprise, but he was too tired. 'One of yours?'

'We've seen him already,' George complained. 'Haven't you got something with dancing in it?'

'He's very talented,' Craddock said. 'But his major role is counter-espionage. We're making sure he's seen with influential Albionites – newspapermen, politicians, decision-makers of all kinds.'

Aubrey thought he was accustomed to the shifting sands that were the world of intrigue, but he felt positively dizzy at the way things were moving. Craddock had certainly expanded his brief, edging into counter-espionage. He was sure that Commander Tallis, the head of the Special Services, wouldn't be altogether happy about that.

'You're using him as bait,' Caroline said. 'You want the Holmlanders to recruit him.'

'His grandmother was Albionish,' Craddock said. 'He's happy to help.'

Aubrey suddenly saw Craddock's work as a complicated dance – a dance in a smoke-filled room, where the dancers could only glimpse each other, and each of them could hear different music.

While across the Continent, in Holmland, Craddock's equivalents were planning their plans, scheming their schemes and staying awake at night wondering what Craddock was doing.

They left Darnleigh House in a cab. Caroline waited until the Magisterium headquarters had been left far behind before she spoke. 'Did you see who was just ahead of us in the queue for Spinetti's show?'

'Lots of people there,' George said. 'Didn't see anyone important.'

'Important, perhaps not. But interesting? Indeed.'

'Who?' Aubrey asked.

'Count Brandt and his friends. Our refugee Holmlanders.'

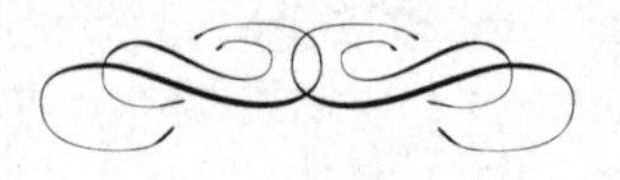

Ten

THE NEXT DAY, BACK AT MAIDSTONE, AUBREY WOKE feeling rested and whole. Political machinations, spying, counter-spying and plots were all manageable when life was non-magical, he decided. He lay in his bed a while, hands behind his head, listening to the early morning sound of the gardeners clipping the cypress hedge.

It was good not to wake feeling as if he were on the edge of falling apart. The struggle to keep body and soul together often meant sleepless nights, which meant exhaustion, which meant matters only grew worse.

Lying there in the dim light, he realised that over the last few months he'd been losing the battle. He'd tried to convince himself otherwise, full of desperate confidence. He'd been sure that finding an answer to his condition was just a matter of working harder at it.

Stopping magic was the simplest solution. After a week of not casting any spells at all, he understood that he should have tried it earlier. He felt well, hearty, complete.

An image came to him unbidden – a fish, refusing to swim, sinking slowly into the depths of the ocean – but he shook it off.

He sprang out of bed, ready to meet the day.

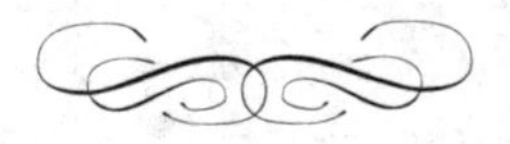

AUBREY FOUND GEORGE IN THE DINING ROOM WITH THE remains of his breakfast on the table in front of him. He was stirring a cup of tea, but his blank gaze was on the window.

'What's wrong, George?' Aubrey asked.

George blinked and then looked at his cup. 'I'll have to get another. This one's cold.'

'Which means you've been stirring a cup of tea so long that it's gone cold. Something must be seriously wrong.'

George frowned. He put down the teaspoon, picked it up again, then thought better of it and placed it on the saucer once more. 'It's Father.'

Aubrey's good humour vanished. 'He's all right, isn't he?'

'Not exactly. A letter arrived here this morning.'

'Sunday?'

'That's part of the problem. It went to college, but I've been gallivanting around with you and Caroline. Luckily, I'd mentioned a thing or two to the head porter about how things were going at home. He recognised the return address and organised a messenger to bring it here. Dashed decent of him.'

'Is it your father's health? He hasn't taken a turn for the worse, has he?'

'No, nothing like that. The ulcer's under control. It's something else.'

'What?'

George pushed the cup of tea aside with an expression of distaste. 'I can't tell you. Not just now. And don't pester me either.'

The horde of questions that had leaped to Aubrey's lips had to be dragged back with some force. 'All right. But you must tell me later.'

'Of course I will. If I can.'

Aubrey didn't like the sound of that. 'Go home. Stubbs will drive you, then wait. If all is well, he'll bring you back to college by this evening.'

'And if it isn't?'

'Stay there. Telephone the Rector. Let me know.'

George swept the tablecloth with his hand, without looking up. 'D'you think it's a good idea?'

Sometimes, Aubrey knew, people wanted someone else to say what they were thinking. 'Of course. Get your things. The motorcar will be at the front door.'

George rose, but stopped halfway, in a semi-crouch. 'And what are you up to today, old man?'

'Oh, this and that.' *A visit to our Holmland friends, for one.* 'I might ask Caroline if she's free.'

George looked doubtful. 'Perhaps I should stay.'

'Don't be ridiculous. You have more important things to attend to.'

George stepped away from the table. 'Thank you, Aubrey. I appreciate this.'

'Family is important, George. We do what we can.'

George noddedly sombrely. 'One other thing. Something I've been meaning to ask you.'

'What is it?'

'Is your condition affecting your magic? Couldn't help but notice, last night, when that Magisterium operative started a spell. I thought that you were about to do something, but nothing happened.'

Aubrey should have known. 'You don't miss much, do you?'

'What's going on?'

'I've given up magic. It seems like the only way to hold myself together.'

'Good Lord.' George digested this for a moment. 'Rather drastic solution, that.'

'A drastic solution for a drastic situation, my condition being the very definition of life and death.'

'Makes sense, then,' George said and Aubrey was surprised at how relieved he was to have his friend's support. 'Perhaps I should stay after all.'

'You're standing. Your legs know you should be off.'

George looked down and blinked. 'I say.'

'The motorcar is ready. Now go!'

A TELEPHONE CALL TO JACK FIGG WAS SOMETHING AUBREY always approached with trepidation. It was one of the more convoluted arrangements Aubrey ever entered into. The number Jack had given him was for a telephone in a sheet music shop near where he was currently living. If the shopkeeper was the only one on the premises – as was usually the case – after taking the call he held a gong out of the window and rattled it noisily. The family next door to the music shop then sent one of their numerous children down the street to Jack's small house. Alerted, he'd scurry back up to the music shop and take the call, assuming the caller hadn't died of old age in the meantime.

Aubrey thought it would have been quicker to send a message by carrier turtle.

When Jack eventually reached the telephone, he was able to tell Aubrey that Count Brandt and his friends were at the hall behind St Olaf's in Crozier, conducting one of their Albionish language schools for their countrymen.

When Aubrey hung up the telephone, he stared it for some time, his chin on his fist. Then he looked out of the window. The study was one of three in Maidstone, and it was Aubrey's favourite not only because it contained a telephone, but because of the view. It looked out over a corner of the garden that was quite overgrown. An old pear tree, still alive but in its latter years, was in the middle of being swallowed up by a wisteria. The purple flowers hung in extravagant profusion, like astonishing mauve grapes. The smell drifted in through the window, which Aubrey had opened an inch or two.

He then wrestled with himself for seconds before he decided that he really must contact Caroline and ask her to accompany him. His reading – and experience – on information-gathering expeditions was that two people were less conspicuous than one. Two could talk to each other, naturally, whereas one tended to look as if he were skulking, no matter how harmless the intent.

It was all perfectly logical.

Aubrey was firm with himself. Just because Caroline

and he had agreed, sensibly, that any deeper friendship was not wise, that didn't mean they couldn't see each other. As long as the understanding was clear that all was above board and sensible, no harm should come of it. Practicality was the key.

He rehearsed a few humorous opening remarks, scratching the best of them on the blotter in front of him.

Caroline's mother answered the telephone and all of Aubrey's preparations fell to pieces.

He hadn't spoken to Mrs Hepworth since the disastrous affair in Lutetia. He'd always liked her and she seemed both amused and intrigued by him, possibly because – some time ago – she had known his father well. Exactly how well was a little unclear, for Sir Darius tended to present a significant silence if that matter ever arose, while Mrs Hepworth simply smiled and kept things to herself.

'Ah, Aubrey, it's good to hear your voice again. Are you well?'

Aubrey closed his eyes with relief. No grudges, it appeared. 'Mrs Hepworth. Yes. Very well.'

'Aubrey, my dear, it's an ongoing battle, isn't it?'

Aubrey had scant belief in psychic powers, but at that moment he was ready to be convinced. 'Well, it has been difficult, but I wouldn't call it a battle, not exactly.'

Mrs Hepworth chuckled. She was one of the few women Aubrey knew who could chuckle stylishly. 'You're thinking of something else, aren't you? I shan't embarrass you by guessing what it is, either.' She chuckled again, but Aubrey thought he could detect affection rather than scorn. 'What I was referring to was the battle to get you to call me Ophelia.'

'Rather than Mrs Hepworth. Sorry.' Aubrey flailed around for a conversational prop and grabbed the first that came to hand. 'How's the painting?'

'Nicely done, Aubrey. Not a totally smooth conversational segue, but not far away from it at all. The painting? As I'm sure you're aware, I have an exhibition at the end of the month, at Greythorn.'

'I know. I'll be there.'

'I'm glad. But the end of the month means I have a great deal of work to do before then.'

'So I shouldn't keep you on the telephone?'

'Now, that was much more deft. You do learn quickly, Aubrey.'

'Well, I try hard. Sometimes it's the same thing.'

'I'll send someone for Caroline. She's in the garden, reading.'

A muffled moment and Mrs Hepworth was back. 'She won't be long. Now, while I have you here, Aubrey, I'm going to be direct with you.'

Aubrey's heart sank. 'Please do.'

'In Lutetia, something you did upset Caroline dreadfully. When she said she wanted to go away with your mother, I supported it. She needed some time to compose herself, but also to think about things.'

'I'm sorry.' It was all that Aubrey could manage.

'I think that's true, otherwise I wouldn't be talking with you. Caroline has told me something of what went on, and you have much to be sorry for.'

'Yes.' Aubrey was enjoying monosyllables. They had great attraction when lost for words.

'But also that all is not lost. I wanted to tell you that.'

'Not lost?'

'No. But here's Caroline.'

For once, Aubrey wanted to talk to her mother more than he wanted to talk to Caroline.

'Aubrey?'

'Yes.' Aubrey made a fist and hit himself on the forehead, once, reasonably firmly. If that response had been any lamer, it would have been taken out the back and shot.

'Good,' Caroline said. 'Now that we've established that you're you, what is it you want?'

'Can I ask a favour of you? Please?' *Better. Polite, reasonable, neutral.*

'What is it?'

'I need to do some more investigating of Count Brandt's people. Would you come with me, please?'

'When?'

'In an hour? I'll have a cab.'

'Well . . .'

'I'll take you to lunch. You name the place.'

'Marcel's. It will remind me of Lutetia.'

'Ah.'

'One hour. I'll be ready.'

She hung up. Aubrey stared at the handpiece, took some time to remember what it was, and then replaced it.

Caroline wanted to be reminded of Lutetia? What did she mean by that?

He groaned. The sooner he was immersed in international intrigue and espionage the better. It was much more straightforward than trying to understand people.

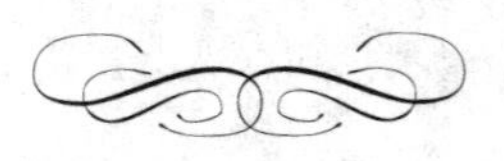

CAROLINE SAT OPPOSITE HIM IN THE CAB. SHE WORE A jacket and skirt over a white linen blouse. Her hat was blue velvet, rather striking. Aubrey found it hard to keep his gaze from her, but he realised – from her startled expression – that the alternative of flicking his eyes around the interior of the cab and out of the windows, never settling for long – made him look quite demented, as well as feel dizzy.

'Are you all right?' she asked.

He gave up and looked at her. She had one small crease, a perfectly vertical one, exactly halfway between her eyebrows. He realised she was frowning.

'Yes. Ripping. Couldn't be better.'

She frowned harder. The crease deepened. Aubrey was lost in wonder.

'Do I have something on my face?' she asked.

'No, no, nothing. Sorry.'

She sighed. 'Aubrey, we can't do anything if you're going to be a goose like this all the time.'

'Quite right.'

'You'll have to learn to manage yourself. More decorum.'

'Of course.'

'I thought it the sort of thing you could do. Most men can't.'

'Ah. An appeal to vanity.' He grinned. 'I'll see what I can do.'

Aubrey sat back. He'd never really considered the issue, how tiresome it must be for Caroline to be stared at. Her occasional brusqueness was perfectly natural when looked at in that light.

'Here's something practical for you to think about,'

she said, 'since a modicum of practicality may be useful.'

Aubrey sat straighter. He adjusted his tie. He clasped one knee, composed his face and nodded. 'How's this? Practical enough?'

She rolled her eyes. 'The Eastside Suffragists. I've mentioned them to you before. We're on a membership drive.'

'Excellent idea. Can't have too many suffragists.'

'Then you're happy to sign up. The fees are reasonable.'

'Me?' With a thought that was quicker than instantaneous, he managed to save himself from utter disaster by going on. '*Just* me, I mean? I'm sure I can convince George to join, and what about Father? That would be a coup for your organisation.'

Caroline looked thoughtful. 'George is already a member, but your father . . .'

'I'm sure he'd do it.' *George is already a member? I must ask him about that.*

'Despite the party? The Opposition?'

'You know he believes in votes for women. It's just that things are slow to move in this area. This might be the sort of thing that could give matters a kick on.'

'It's an excellent idea,' Caroline murmured.

'And here's another. If we can get Father's agreement – and I'm sure we shall – we might be able to seed this in the press via George's work with *Luna*. If he could write an article about it, perhaps interview Father, it would be an achievement for him, and a way of bringing the matter to public attention.'

'Aubrey, your plans sometimes have a touch of genius about them.'

'Well, I try.'

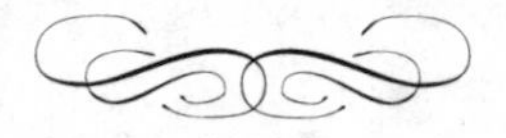

AFTER CROSSING THE RIVER, THE CABBY CIRCLED AROUND a little before finding St Olaf's. It was a squat, blockish church in the Crozier district, right on the edge of Little Pickling. The church was in need of repair, its gutters were sagging, and the belltower had a decided lean. The detached hall at the rear was more modern, but no less shabby. A drone of massed voices came from it.

Inside, three separate groups had divided the hall into fiefdoms. Each one was made up of a dozen or so people sitting on wooden chairs, facing an instructor with a blackboard. The lessons seemed to comprise 'listen and repeat' – traveller's phrases, mostly. One group would stumble over 'Good morning' then the next would raise its collective voice with 'How much is it?' and, to combat this, the final group would be forced to bellow 'Which way is the railway station?' before the first group started again.

Watching this process, Aubrey didn't hear the approach from behind. A hand tapped him on the shoulder. 'Mr Fitzwilliam, Miss Hepworth. What are you here for?'

It was Brandt. Standing next to him was Rokeby-Taylor with a look of honest, and delighted, surprise on his face.

While trying to deal with this unexpected development, Aubrey's brain slipped into his prepared story. 'Count Brandt. Good to see you. I was wondering if you'd like to discuss the details of setting up a clinic in this area.'

'Mr Fitzwilliam,' Brandt said, 'what a fine idea!

But excuse me, I must introduce my good friend, Mr Rokeby-Taylor. He is an important man, knows many powerful people. He has promised much support for our cause.'

'We've met, Kurt,' Rokeby-Taylor said, reaching out and shaking Aubrey's hand. He took Caroline's hand and held it for rather longer than Aubrey thought appropriate. 'Miss Hepworth. You look as if you've recovered from your nautical adventure.'

'I have, Mr Rokeby-Taylor,' Caroline said gravely. 'Thank you.'

Rokeby-Taylor put his hands on his hips. 'A clinic, eh, Aubrey? Should have thought of it myself.'

'No, Clive,' Brandt said, 'you are already doing more than enough. Your generous donations to our cause, your introductions to important people, taking our talented people into your company? How can we thank you?'

'No need, Kurt, no need. We all benefit. I needed good magical talent, your people were unable to get positions here.' He took out a pocket watch and barely glanced at it. 'Goodness. I'm afraid I must be off.' He touched his tie – a striped, navy blue and white number. 'Miss Hepworth, would you be free next Friday evening? I have tickets to a recital at the Regent's Hall. Palliser is playing.'

'I don't think so, Mr Rokeby-Taylor.'

'I see. The day after?'

'I'll have to look in my diary, but I don't think so.'

'Eh? Well, if you do find a gap in your schedule, I'd consider it an honour if you'd telephone me.'

Caroline frowned at the card he handed her, but she tucked it in her bag.

Aubrey was glad no-one had glanced in his direction during all this. He was sure that his face had turned as stony as an Aigyptian statue. It was all he could do to prevent himself from cheering when Caroline declined Rokeby-Taylor's offer.

'Insistent man,' Caroline said when Rokeby-Taylor had left the hall.

'Hmm?' Aubrey said. 'Sorry, I was miles away. Didn't notice a thing.'

Caroline glanced at him sharply, but Aubrey was alert. 'Tell us, Count Brandt, what are you up to here?'

'We are up to as much as we can,' Count Brandt said. 'In exile, we do our best.'

Brandt led Aubrey and Caroline out of the hall. Around the corner was another, smaller hall in a courtyard surrounded by tall buildings. It was full of people – thirty or forty – arranged in old pews. Aubrey recognised Bloch at a lectern, and Madame Albers, but the others were strangers. Bloch was allocating a list of tasks and Aubrey was thankful for his father's insistence on the importance of foreign languages.

Those in the pews were well-dressed, if their clothes were a little out of fashion. Most were taking notes.

'We are exiles,' Brandt said. 'We take care of our own, and such requires organising. We meet, we discuss, we do what we can.'

'Do you discuss going back to Holmland?' Aubrey asked.

Brandt nodded. 'Of course. Delightful though your country is, we are not here by choice. We were in danger if we stayed and in danger if we go back now. Troublesome opponents of the Chancellor have a habit of disappearing.'

'But you must have plans.'

'Plans? He who does not plan lives half a life. We would love for the corrupt regime in our beloved Holmland to come crashing down. If we can help that happen, it is good. How to do it is the question.'

'You must be in communication with those still there,' Caroline said.

'Of course. Carefully.' Brandt shook his head. 'The Chancellor and his government cronies are popular. They build ships, they have parades, birthday parties for the Elektor. There is little support for our cause.'

'There is always an opposition to a government,' Aubrey said. 'What about them?'

'Tame rabbits. Powerless. Equally corrupt.'

Standing at the lectern in front of the small audience, Bloch broke off and waved. 'Brandt,' he called in Holmlandish. 'Leyden here says that his cousin in the navy has been approached by the Circle.' Then he saw Aubrey and scowled.

Brandt shook a finger at Bloch. 'Mr Fitzwilliam is a trusted friend. You can talk in front of him.'

But before Bloch could continue, Madame Albers laughed. 'The Circle. When are they going to do something to match their big talk?'

'Talk?' Brandt said. 'Talk? The Circle is our best hope of return. The offers they've made, the people . . .'

'Many promises, little action,' Madame Albers said. 'We need more than words.'

Bloch glanced at Aubrey for a moment. 'Words are powerful. Look at the Chancellor's new adviser. When he speaks, everyone in the government listens.'

'This Dr Tremaine?' Brandt said, and Aubrey was

suddenly much more interested in what had seemed like an argument over petty rivalries. 'Do you really think he has that much influence?'

'He's a persuasive man,' Aubrey put in and they all stared. He shrugged. 'I've had some dealings with him.'

'Your insights may prove useful,' Brandt said, then he turned back to his compatriots and soon they were deep in discussion about the best ways to return to Holmland.

Aubrey only half-listened. The revelation that Dr Tremaine had expanded his influence from the Holmland espionage wing to the government itself was terrifying. Aubrey didn't want that man close to the highest decision-makers in any country – let alone warlike Holmland.

Aubrey looked up. He had the oddest sensation – as if reality had suddenly creaked at the seams, shifting uneasily before settling again.

'What was that?' he asked Caroline.

'What was what?'

'Nothing. Probably nothing.'

He couldn't shake it off. A curious double feeling took hold of him, one sensation overlaid on another, and he realised he was detecting magic – but he couldn't define it. It was fractured and indistinct.

The meeting broke up. People moved past, nodding to Brandt as they went. All of them glanced curiously at Aubrey and Caroline.

'Ach,' Bloch said. His voice echoed in the nearly empty hall. 'Someone has left a bag.'

'No.' Aubrey grabbed Brandt's shoulder. 'No!' he shouted, but it was too late.

The hall blew apart.

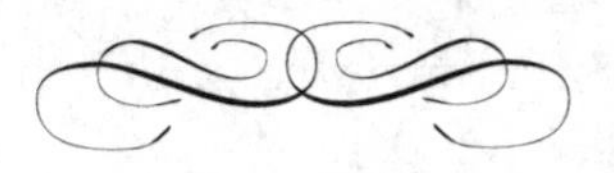

Eleven

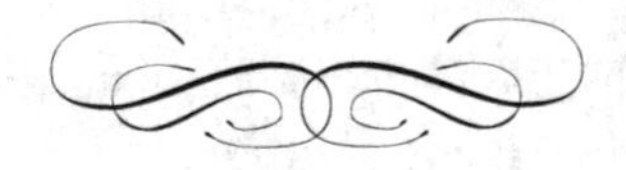

AUBREY WAS ON HIS BACK, HIS HEAD RINGING. HIS cheek hurt. Blurrily, he realised that he was looking at the sky. Boiling upward like a geyser from hell was a whirling mass of black cloud. Lightning shot from it, jagged bolts that hurt the eye, lancing left, right, up and down with manic glee.

Weather magic, Aubrey thought as dozens of individual aches and pains jostled for his attention. *What fool would mess about with weather magic*?

Aubrey had, once, and he'd learned the hard way the First Law of Weather Magic: localised weather changes have effects that can't be predicted. This was why weather magic was discouraged. A simple spell to stop rain falling on a picnic could end up with a massive drought half a continent away. Aubrey had a suspicion that some inherent disorder was at work in most natural processes. When he had some time, he intended to investigate this.

The pocket thunderstorm flattened overhead, as if it had run against an invisible ceiling. It swirled angrily, then gradually dissipated.

He lay there a moment and felt the heart-scurry of panic. His soul. Had it been jolted free again?

Then, a greater fear swamped this one. Where was Caroline?

He climbed to his feet, hurting all over, and faced utter devastation. The hall had been shredded by the thunderstorm. The walls had been flattened, apart from a few splintered uprights. Broken timber was strewn about, as if a giant had been playing pick-up-sticks. The brickwork nearby was studded with shards of wood that had struck hard enough to embed themselves.

Caroline stumbled from behind a pile of debris and Aubrey began breathing again. That instant, when she reappeared, defined what she meant to him. His condition, his hurts, his existence were secondary. His greatest concern was her wellbeing.

His chest ached, but he limped toward her. She sagged to her knees and he nearly cried aloud. She saw him approaching, gathered herself and stood. 'I'm all right.' She frowned. 'My hat's gone.'

Aubrey put a hand on her shoulder and inspected her. He sent a prayer heavenwards when he saw that she was untouched. 'You were lucky.'

His heart began to slow and he took a series of long, slow breaths to steady himself. He took a moment and used his magical senses to inspect his condition.

His body and soul were still united. His recent lack of magical exertion had apparently made his state more robust and he was well pleased.

So intense had been his focus on Caroline and his own condition that it took Aubrey some time to hear the groans. 'Over there.' Caroline pointed.

It was Count Brandt. He'd been thrown ten yards by the sudden thunderstorm and had slammed against a brick wall. He was sitting, splay-legged, amid shards of glass from the empty window above him. Aubrey hurried to his side only to discover that the Holmlander was unconscious.

'He's breathing,' Caroline said. 'Only a few small cuts. There's not much else we can do.'

Carefully, as shouts and cries for help rose from the streets nearby, they picked their way through the remnants of the hall. The floor was intact, if buckled in a few areas. The thunderstorm had obviously appeared and expanded both horizontally and vertically. Aubrey noticed part of his mind cataloguing details, knowing that immediate first impressions from a trained observer could be crucial in any investigation. His magical experience would be useful in documenting what had been, without doubt, a magical attack. Craddock would want to know everything.

'Here, Aubrey!' Caroline was crouched next to the stump of what must have been one of the main uprights of the hall. It was a massive piece of timber, but it had been snapped off as if it were a straw.

Aubrey hurried across the uneven and protesting floor to see that Caroline had found Bloch. She was crouching, cradling his head, but the unnatural angle of his limbs indicated that the Holmlander had been subject to much of the force of the storm.

'The bag,' he said, when he saw Aubrey's face. 'I should not –'

He broke off and his body jerked with a horrible spasm. He started to cough, but hissed with pain and bit it back.

'Rest,' Aubrey said. 'Help will be here soon.'

'I should not have opened it.' Bloch fought for breath after each word.

'It wouldn't have mattered,' Aubrey said, and even as he said it, he realised it was the truth. 'The weather magic was in the bag, but it was compressed.' *That was why I felt more than one layer of magic.* 'It would have expanded some time. Soon.'

Aubrey bit his lip. It was messy magic. Spell compression was useful, sometimes, to let a spell unfold at a bidden time. It could let a non-magician set a spell in place, where a magician was unavailable. But compression was touchy. Templeton's First Law of Compression had been hammered out over fifty years ago, in the laboratories of experimental magic in Greythorn. Professor Victor Templeton had established, after much trial and error, that the force required to keep a spell in compression is proportional to the force of the spell itself. Mighty spells required much power to keep them compressed.

While rebuilding the experimental magic laboratories at Greythorn, Professor Templeton had engraved his Second Law of Compression over the doorway: an inadequately compressed spell, when it works free, will be multiplied in effect by the power of the spell used to compress it. Or, in student shorthand, bad compression leads to horribly bad outcomes.

To which Aubrey was tempted to add Fitzwilliam's Corollary to the Laws of Compression: Compression isn't worth it.

Bloch mumbled, then quivered. 'My arm isn't working,' he said, in a conversational tone. 'My nose itches.'

Caroline scratched it for him.

'I don't suppose it's a good sign,' Bloch said, 'not being able to move my limbs.'

'No,' Aubrey said. He didn't see how he could say anything else.

'I didn't think so.' Bloch glanced at Aubrey. 'It's Fitzwilliam, isn't it?'

'That's right.'

'I thought so.' He paused and grimaced. 'Thought so,' he repeated, softly.

'Don't speak. Save your strength.'

'For what?' Bloch tried a laugh, but the result was horrible – wet and desperate. 'I suppose I should tell you something important, seeing as I'm dying.'

'Sh,' Caroline said. 'Easy now.'

'Don't,' Bloch said. 'I know what's happening.'

'Are you in pain?' Aubrey asked.

'I was. Now I'm not.' He licked his lips. 'There is a plot. To steal Albion's gold. From the bank.'

'The Bank of Albion?'

Bloch nodded. 'Your Albionite friend. The magician.'

Aubrey clutched the man's shoulder. 'It's Tremaine's plot? Tell me more.'

'I will.' He looked puzzled for a moment, and he cocked his head as if listening. Then he glanced at something over Aubrey's head.

And died.

THE POLICE ARRIVED, JUST AFTER THE HOLMLANDERS flooded back. Brandt came to his senses and began issuing orders before realising that nothing could be done. He moved about among his countrymen, attempting to console them.

Craddock and a dozen Magisterium operatives arrived soon after, while the ambulance porters were attending to Bloch's body. Craddock made immediately for Aubrey, while his operatives fanned out and examined the area. He crossed his arms and grimly looked over the ruins of the hall, a scene that still shocked Aubrey with the completeness of its devastation. 'Holmlanders against Holmlanders, here in Albion. Can't have this.'

'What makes you think it's Holmlanders who were responsible?'

'Who else do you think it could be? Disaffected local troublemakers?'

'It's possible.'

'Possible, but not likely. Manfred warned us that the refugee Holmlanders had attracted attention at the highest level back in Fisherberg. He didn't foresee this sort of action, though.' He rubbed his long chin. 'Ruthless or careless?'

'I beg your pardon?'

'Was this action ruthless or simply sloppy work?'

Such practical issues had been far from Aubrey's mind. He'd been too stunned by the ferocity of the attack and – he admitted – too relieved that he and Caroline had survived. They had survived, where Bloch hadn't. In the lottery that was the unfolding of events, it could have happened differently. He could have opened the bag. The spell may not have gone off. Bloch may have taken the bag outside and the effects would have been felt over a wider area.

Aubrey had been lucky. Caroline had been lucky. He was thankful.

With an effort, he turned to Craddock's question. 'I hope they were careless. I'm afraid they were ruthless.'

Craddock nodded. 'This is real.'

'I beg your pardon?'

'Sometimes, we forget that this struggle is real. We see it as a game, a jolly spate of push and shove, of wrangling over who's the best.' He looked tired and Aubrey was startled to find himself feeling sympathy for the man. 'It's murky stuff we're dealing with, Fitzwilliam, down in the depths that no-one sees. Are you up to it?'

'I hope so.'

'Good man. Now, I understand you're interested in forensic magic? Go and see what you can learn from my people. Top notch, all of them. Ah, Miss Hepworth, good to see you're unharmed.'

Craddock went to Caroline. Aubrey winced, and limped a little, as he picked his way over to the nearest of the black-clad Magisterium operatives.

This sort of thing signalled a new world, a world that Aubrey didn't like the look of. It made him even more determined that Holmland wouldn't force a war. With that sort of attitude, it would be a war of a sort that had never been seen before – indiscriminate, callous, but on a scale beyond imagining.

He could hear Dr Tremaine's laughter.

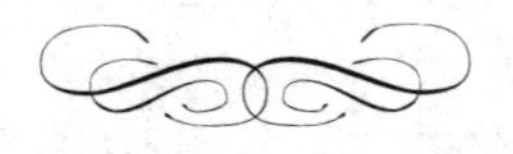

FORENSIC MAGIC WAS A CURIOUS MIXTURE OF THE commonplace and the arcane. Sharp eyes were useful, but more essential was a finely attuned magical sensitivity. Here, Aubrey was able to help. Such a thing was passive, like a mirror catching a sunbeam, and required no magical effort. He could sense magic, taste its flavour and feel its texture, without affecting his condition at all.

After a quick briefing, he became part of the line of Magisterium operatives that picked its way across the site, bent nearly double. He concentrated hard and was only dimly aware of the activity to one side, where the police were blocking off access, hauling wooden barricades across the lanes between the surrounding buildings.

He could feel the magical residue that overlay the disaster area, a wasteful, clumsy sign that tended to suggest the perpetrators were in the careless camp rather than the ruthless. Although he admitted they could be both. Some of the residue had a tantalisingly familiar aspect about it, but he couldn't find enough to be more definitive than that. It could be a Continental approach; it could be a Holmland style of magic. Or it could be someone who'd studied under a Continental master and actually lived around the corner.

A shout came from the opposite side of the courtyard. One of the operatives had a long pole and was fishing about in the denuded branches of an elm tree. Craddock hurried to her side and helped retrieve a singed and battered object that flapped about in the breeze.

'Eyes down,' the operative next to Aubrey – a few yards away – growled, and Aubrey went back to poring over the broken floorboards. He spread his hands, fingers stretched, as if warming them over a fire. He felt the buzzing magical leftover, and he did his best to break it into its constituent parts. What was the exact nature of the spell? Where did it come from? And, more importantly, could he detect any fragment that hinted at the final element of a spell, the identifying signature?

He grappled with what he was sensing, but although he could identify parts, he couldn't grasp the larger picture. He needed more information, and there was only one way to find it.

Eyes down.

Some hours later darkness fell, putting a halt to any further investigation of the site. Around the corner, in the Incident Room set up in the vestry office of St Olaf's, he listened to each of the operatives report their findings to Craddock. The operatives were packed in, shoulder to shoulder. Craddock stood at a desk, his hands behind his back. He had the manner of a man who'd prepared himself for the worst, only to have his expectations exceeded.

Aubrey sat against the wall and felt as if he'd been hammered all over by gnomes with rolling pins. He knew he'd have bruises in the morning. Caroline sat next to him and listened carefully. He wondered where she'd been while he was intent on his magical business. He started to ask her, but she hushed him with a look.

The most interesting contribution came from the tree raider, the operative who had fished the object from the tree. It was placed on a table for all to examine. Aubrey peered over shoulders to see that it was the remains of a leather bag.

'No doubt that this contained the spell?' Craddock asked.

'None,' the pole-wielding operative said. 'Feel the residue. I'm surprised the bag lasted as long as it did.'

Craddock looked up. 'Fitzwilliam. You were there. Tell us what you saw.'

The operatives drew back and allowed Aubrey space. He took a deep breath, regretted it when a pulled muscle tugged on his ribs, then reported on the events leading up to the explosion. He went on to describe the thundercloud's passage and disappearance. He began to tell of Bloch's strange final words, but he held back. He told himself that he wanted to clear up any possible doubt that it was Dr Tremaine that Bloch had meant. It was an excellent reason, he decided. 'Weather magic,' he concluded.

'Obviously,' Craddock said.

Aubrey shuffled a little. 'The bag could have been put there by anyone at the meeting.'

'Or it might have been placed there before the meeting by persons unknown.'

The operatives – and Craddock – turned to see Caroline standing. 'True,' Craddock said. 'But not very helpful.'

'It's only helpful if it reminds us that our potential suspects are not limited to those at the meeting,' Caroline pointed out.

'And that the suspects need not be magicians,' Aubrey put in.

'Go on,' Craddock said.

'Well,' Aubrey said, 'one of the uses of compression spells is to allow non-magicians to use magic. They can transport a spell, site it, then let it go off, provided the original magician has limited the time variable accurately enough.' Aubrey blinked. *Is that what happened on the* Electra*?*

'And that's a question,' Caroline said. 'Did the spell go off when intended? Or was it too late? Or too early?'

'Did you two work this performance out beforehand?' Craddock said, with chilly amusement.

Aubrey looked at Caroline. She looked at him. 'No,' they said simultaneously.

'Pity.' Craddock moved on. 'It is as you say. Many questions. Few answers.' He raised an eyebrow. 'Unless you two have answers as well as questions?'

'No, nothing helpful,' Aubrey said. 'But you could ask Rokeby-Taylor if he saw anything suspicious. He was here right before the explosion.' Aubrey paused. Rokeby-Taylor was in the *Electra*, too, when it was magically attacked. Unlucky, or . . .

Aubrey's train of thought was completely disrupted when Craddock went on: 'Rokeby-Taylor? Good idea. He's on Tallis's payroll so he's used to keeping an eye open.'

Aubrey actually swayed a little at the unexpectedness of the revelation. Rokeby-Taylor working for Special Services? With his connections he could be a useful source of information, however unlikely an operative he seemed. And it could provide another reason for his presence at St Olaf's, other than generosity.

Or mayhem.

Craddock looked at the frowning faces of his operatives. 'Does anyone else have anything? No? Right, back to Darnleigh House with the lot of you. Fitzwilliam, Miss Hepworth, would you mind waiting behind a moment?'

Obediently, the operatives filed out.

'What is it, Commander?' Aubrey asked, but he was stunned into silence by the figure who slipped into the room.

'Ah, Manfred,' Craddock said. Aubrey had thought that Craddock had looked tired, but any sign of exhaustion vanished at the entrance of the Holmland performer. 'Let me introduce Miss Hepworth and Mr Fitzwilliam. You've been asking to meet them and here they are.'

The Great Manfred bowed. 'I am honoured to meet both of you. Especially the son of the Prime Minister.'

He wore a dark grey topcoat over a dark suit. His black gloves and bowler hat looked expensive. Aubrey decided that the sleight-of-hand business must pay well.

Or perhaps it was the spying business.

'It's been Manfred's investigating that suggested all is not well between Holmlander groups in this country,' Craddock said.

'Indeed,' Manfred said. He seemed remarkably unaffected by the attack. Aubrey wondered what he was accustomed to. 'It would appear as if the obvious culprits come from a rival group here. Count Brandt has made few friends in the established Holmlander community.'

Aubrey frowned. 'So you don't think it's the work of the Holmland espionage agencies?'

'Unlikely. My information does not support this conclusion. I have made the recommendation that your government may have to begin interning Holmlanders who are in sensitive positions.'

'What?' Caroline said. 'How can such an action be taken in good conscience? We're not at war.'

'Not yet,' Manfred said.

'But it's inevitable,' Aubrey said, 'isn't it?'

Manfred shook a finger at Aubrey. 'Mr Fitzwilliam, you should come to our country, you know. Top members of the Circle are eager to have you visit, so you could see for yourself how strong the pro-Albion sentiment is. There is a chance we can stop this war before it starts.'

'The Circle?'

'Bloch mentioned them,' Caroline said. 'Arguing with Brandt.'

'Not all Holmlanders support the Chancellor and his government,' Manfred said. 'The Circle is a secret group of those against him. Powerful people. Influential people. Come, meet them, you will see for yourself that there is a chance to topple the Chancellor and stop this madness.'

It was appealing. Aubrey had never been to Holmland and he was all in favour of forestalling a war.

'I don't think so,' Craddock said before Aubrey could respond. 'The Prime Minister's son on a clandestine mission to talk to chief opponents of the Chancellor's government? The relations between our two countries is much too delicate for that.'

'I beg you to reconsider, Craddock,' Manfred said. 'It could be important.'

'Perhaps. We will monitor the situation.'

Manfred bowed. 'I hope we can facilitate this. It may be vital.' He adjusted his gloves. 'One more thing, Craddock. Count Brandt needs twenty thousand pounds. He has a chance to sow serious dissent in Fisherberg and we can't miss it.'

Aubrey had trouble believing what he heard. Twenty thousand pounds?

'It shouldn't be a problem,' Craddock said and Aubrey's astonishment was redoubled. *Twenty thousand pounds, just like that?* 'See me at Darnleigh House tomorrow.'

Manfred left. Aubrey felt as if he were a shop assistant and he'd been handed another sale item to fit into an already crowded window display. He stood, hesitated, glanced at Caroline, then hesitated again. She nodded, very slightly, and he knew they were partners in intrigue.

'Yes?' Craddock said. 'Is there something else?'

'No, no. Just trying to make sense of everything.'

Craddock laughed a little. It was a quiet, almost noiseless, laugh, mostly in the intake of breath. Aubrey couldn't imagine the man putting his heart into a laugh. 'If you can make sense of everything, let me know. It's a grand aim.'

Aubrey paused, then decided that giving Craddock something might deflect the man's natural suspicions. 'Bloch mentioned that Dr Tremaine is advising the Chancellor now.'

'Bloch mentioned this, did he?' Craddock nodded. 'Of course, it's something we've known for a while, but it's useful to hear it from another source. Well done.'

He nodded to Caroline, then left, and Aubrey felt guilty at not telling him everything, but also irritated that Craddock hadn't shared his information about Dr Tremaine with him.

'Can I walk you home?' he said to Caroline.

'Why didn't you tell him what Bloch said about Dr Tremaine's plot?'

'I was just wondering that myself.' Aubrey shrugged. 'I thought we could investigate a bit more, first. Clear things up.'

'Good. That's what I thought too.'

'We're holding a live grenade here,' Aubrey said. 'This information could be vital.'

'I know. Let's not drop it.'

ONCE THEY WERE AWAY FROM THE VICINITY OF THE attack, Aubrey saw that the streets were themselves again. In the north, toward the river, was the great brewery of Rawlinson and Sons. A soupy, yeasty smell hung over the whole neighbourhood. Various industrial yards were strung out, silent in the darkness. A derelict pumping station stood forlornly outlined against the night sky.

Aubrey thought of catching the underground, but the stations were few and far between south of the river. Instead he and Caroline walked, side by side, silently for a time, making their way towards Earlchester Bridge.

'You want to catch Dr Tremaine by yourself, don't you?' Caroline said. They were passing an old cable car terminus. Aubrey wondered if they would ever rebuild it.

'I'm not the only one, I'm sure. But I'd like to be the successful one.'

'I don't suppose I could interest you in something else? Something perhaps more immediate?'

'Ah. You've been withholding information from Craddock, too?'

'I made myself useful while you were busy. I talked to people.'

'Information gathering. Commander Tallis would be pleased.' He looked sharply at her. 'You didn't tell Craddock what you found because you're going to tell Tallis, is that it?'

'I haven't told anyone yet. I'm about to tell you. Then we'll see what we'll do.'

'Excellent.'

'I wasn't just gossiping. We had injured among the Holmlanders who hadn't left the area. I helped your Dr Wells, from the Broad Street Clinic, tend to them, and assisted those who seemed to know what they were doing. A number of the Holmlanders were doctors, you know, and one was a surgeon.'

Aubrey nodded. 'I thought they seemed well-educated.'

'I did notice one young woman who wasn't doing anything. She was on the edges of the crowd, observing, it seemed.'

'Holmlander?'

'Oh yes. A Holmlander suffragist – apparently a very difficult thing to be. After some prompting, she was quite scornful of Brandt's people.'

'Brandt's people aren't her people?'

'What she told me supports Manfred's story. Brandt's group is only one of several Holmland ex-patriate communities in Trinovant. Not all of them are friendly toward each other.'

'Why should they be?'

'It's not just unfriendliness. My suffragist friend was downright suspicious of Brandt's group. Too aristocratic, she said. Couldn't understand what they were doing here.'

'Things move quickly in politics. People fall out of favour. Alliances shift.'

'But my informant was adamant that Count Brandt is great friends with the Elektor's younger brother. They hunted together, and my young friend worked in the kitchens and as a serving maid. She said they were thick as thieves.'

'So why did Brandt leave the country?' Aubrey wondered. Then he remembered something. 'And last night . . . he was on his way to see Spinetti, you said.'

'What does that mean?'

'It could mean the Holmlanders simply enjoy his singing. Or it could mean something much more sinister, if Spinetti is Dr Tremaine.'

'But how does this explain the attack today?'

Aubrey shrugged. 'It doesn't. But once I apprehend Dr Tremaine, then his web will be revealed.'

'I see. As easy as that?'

Aubrey stopped. They'd reached the bridge. Traffic clattered across it, while a steam barge chuffed its way underneath, smoke easing its way from under the vaults. 'Apprehending Dr Tremaine easy? I don't think so.'

'Then why are you so determined to do it? And do it alone?'

Because the greatest magician of our time might have the answer to my condition.

'Does it have something to do with your condition?' Caroline said suddenly.

Aubrey was glad no-one appeared and poked him with a feather, for he would have toppled like a sawn-off tree. 'What?' he said weakly.

She looked at him solemnly, as if she were enquiring about a cold. She held her bag in both hands. 'Your condition. Your soul. Your self-inflicted half-life. What *is* your current state?'

'You know?' He gathered himself and immediately

headed off a protest. 'Of course you know. You're not stupid.'

'Thank you.' She frowned and seemed to choose her words. 'It's mostly been observation, you know. I saw your interest in my father's notebook, then how ill you looked in Lutetia . . . After that, I asked a few questions of people at Stonelea, read some notes of my father's. And I put two and two together.'

'But why didn't you say anything? It's been difficult, hiding it from you.'

'I thought as much. But you seemed so intent on keeping to yourself. And George.'

'He told you?'

'No. But I assumed he'd know. And you've just confirmed it.'

'Ah. Yes.' Aubrey leaned on the parapet of the bridge. Lights were streaking the water, reaching from one bank to the other. Some met in the middle, and muddled together in a whirl where the wash of boats combined. 'Who else knows?'

'No-one that I know of. Your father might suspect. And your mother. But neither has said anything to me.'

And here I was, thinking I was so clever. 'My condition is stable,' he said, answering her question. 'Thank you for asking.'

'It wasn't a polite enquiry. I'm concerned.' She held up a hand as he brightened. 'Concerned, that's all. I wouldn't like to see anything happen to you. And don't read anything into that.'

'I shan't.' *I shall.*

'I thought it might help, if you don't have to go to the effort of hiding it from me.'

'So I can be myself? Weak and feeble Aubrey?'

'Are you weak and feeble?'

'Just now? No. Things are well enough.'

'But you're not improving.'

'Nor deteriorating. It's satisfactory.'

'You'd never be content with satisfactory. Exceptional is your minimum acceptable standard.'

'I aim high.'

'So do I.'

'We're alike like that,' he said, more as a tactic than with any real hope.

'Yes,' she said, but her expression wasn't hopeful. It was sombre as she looked over the river. 'I blame our fathers.'

Caroline was one of the few people who had the ability to consistently flabbergast Aubrey. 'And what do our fathers have to do with this?' he said when he finally managed to put words together.

'Quite a lot, really. Look at mine. A brilliant, world-wide authority on magic. A master in his field. Consulted by governments here and abroad.' She sighed. 'It's quite a lot to live up to.'

Words eluded Aubrey again. He grasped at them, but they slipped away like eels. 'I thought I was the only one.'

She glanced at him and smiled a little. 'I guessed as much. Driven to try to emulate a great man? Always being asked about following in his footsteps? Trying to succeed, your own way, despite all this?'

'That sounds familiar.'

'And expectations.' She scowled over the bridge. 'Don't talk to me about expectations.'

'Your parents' expectations are too high?'

'What? No. They haven't had any. Or they didn't express them. They always said they didn't want to crush me with their dreams. They wanted me to find my own future.'

'So you have to try to guess what their expectations are, for fear of disappointing them.'

'That's right.' She looked squarely at him. 'Oh. It's like that for you, too?'

'For as long as I can remember.'

'Hmm. But what you don't have to contend with is a mother who is also famous and brilliant.'

'I do have a mother who is world-renowned and exceptionally accomplished. Lady Rose Fitzwilliam? You've heard of her?'

'Well, yes, but being a male you don't have to live up to her.'

'So you have to live up to your father's name as well as your mother's?'

'Raised in a prominent suffragist household like ours? Of course.'

'So you have it harder than I do. You have two parents to live up to.' It was a novel thought. Aubrey had always felt that he had a unique situation in as far as living up to parental expectations went.

'People call me driven,' Caroline said. She rested her arms on the parapet and bent to put her chin on them. 'Or ambitious. They don't realise that the only way to live up to these unstated hopes is to excel. To triumph. Even then, I'm not sure.'

'So we are alike.' As Aubrey said it, he realised that he'd placed a little too much hope on his words. He turned around so he was facing the traffic. 'So where does that leave us?'

'On a bridge. In Trinovant. Trying to do the best we can.'

'That's not what I mean.'

She looked at him and he nearly swooned at the sweetness of her smile. 'I know, Aubrey. But let's let it rest there for now, please.'

'Of course.' He straightened a jacket that didn't need straightening at all. 'Will your mother be worrying about you?'

'It's not even eight o'clock.'

'Excellent. Would you have time for the dinner I promised? Marcel's is just on the other side of the bridge.'

'I thought you'd forgotten.'

'A promise is a promise.'

Caroline was merry, entertaining and wickedly witty as Marcel himself served them. She charmed him, the other waiters, and – of course – Aubrey, but he thought that underneath her sparkle, a wistfulness lay. They ate excellent soup, fine fish, and a dessert that was both delicate and sweet. Beyond that, Aubrey couldn't remember any details about what was served to them.

When they finally reached the Hepworths' city flat – a quiet, gently curving street in Mortonbridge – they stood at the bottom of the stairs. The streetlights were lit, and the windows of the houses on both sides showed that families were in residence.

Caroline held her bag in front of her like a shield. She didn't look at him. 'Aubrey.'

He'd been waiting for this. 'I know. You think it best if we don't see each other for a while.'

'I beg your pardon?'

'It's too much, you're not ready, something like that.'

She did look at him this time. 'Is leaping to conclusions a speciality of yours?'

Aubrey went over the conversation in his mind and decided that a brief retracking was in order. 'You were about to say something?'

'Thank you. You went haring off in completely the opposite direction, you know.'

'Opposite? Do we have a future together?'

'Yes. No. Not exactly.' She paused. 'You do make things awkward, don't you?'

I was thinking the same thing of you. 'Apparently. Sometimes on purpose, too.'

'There is much to be said for not seeing you. I realised that after your poor show in Lutetia.'

Here it comes. 'I'm not going to pretend that never happened. But I have sworn it will never happen again.'

'A noble aim. But I do worry that you tend to get caught up in things. Big things. And when important events are in train, I fear that you lose sight of the people around you. They become less important.'

Aubrey wanted to squirm, but resisted the impulse. 'I did. Not any more.'

'As you say. Forgive me if I harbour reservations about that resolution.'

His face fell. 'I shall miss you, you know.'

'There you go again, getting ahead of yourself. What I'm trying to say is that *despite* all that, I still want to see you.'

'You do? Why? I mean, that would be wonderful. If you're happy, that is. And if you're not, then I'm sure something can be done.'

'You're babbling again, Aubrey.'

'Sorry. Go on.'

Caroline was silent for a moment. A cab trotted past. The driver tipped his hat to them. 'It's exciting, you know.'

'Exciting?'

'This world you've introduced me to. The plots. The spies. The subterfuge. The adventures. It's thrilling.'

'Oh yes. Makes the blood race.'

'When Commander Tallis offered me a position, I thought he was joking. But after the Lutetian affair, I was elated.'

'Me too.'

'We stopped the world going to war, Aubrey. We skirted death, we foiled plots, we rode magical towers, we nearly had our souls stolen.'

'And we danced at the embassy ball.'

'Yes. That too.' Caroline looked up at the evening sky. 'You see, for years I'd had my head down with one goal in mind: I wanted to be a scientist. You've shown me that there is more, and it's tempting.'

'I've always been torn,' he said. 'Magic. The army. Politics.'

'Exactly. My efforts for women's suffrage have suffered of late. I need to do more. Seeing how you've worked for your father – and how he has worked – has shown me the sort of thing that needs to be done.'

'You aim to be the first female member of parliament.'

'If I can.'

'If you can manage it with all the other goals that are calling you.' He pursed his lips. 'I have one word of advice for you: wax.'

'Wax?'

'Do you remember the classical story of Odysseus and the sirens? He had his crew tie him to the mast as they sailed past, so he could hear the sirens' tempting song and not plunge over the side to join them and be eaten.'

'And the wax, Aubrey?'

'That's the point. All his men, working at the oars, had their ears stuffed with wax so they couldn't hear the siren song. That's what you need.' *And that's what I need, too.* 'Special wax so that you won't hear the siren songs you don't want to. Wax will help you avoid the temptations that the world has to offer. Wax will allow you to ignore distractions. Metaphorically, of course.'

'Then I will offer you a metaphor in return: juggling.'

'I know this one. A juggler is perfectly fine as long as all the balls are kept in the air, kept moving, kept in balance.'

'I was thinking more along the lines of those mixed jugglers: balls, knives, plates, indian clubs, kittens.'

Aubrey was intrigued. 'You've seen a kitten juggler?'

'Once. A long time ago, a friend of my father's. They didn't look happy, but they weren't harmed.'

'Amazing.' He nodded. 'Yes, it's like juggling futures, isn't it?'

'Juggling futures. A neat way to put it, Aubrey.'

'And the immediate future?'

'We have to do something about Dr Tremaine. If it is him.'

'It is.'

'And he may have plans to rob the Bank of Albion.' Caroline shook her head impatiently. 'I must go back to the university tomorrow. I have studies to attend to. Another item to add to the juggle.'

'Of course. As do I.' Aubrey stopped and hummed a little. Bloch's hinting at an attempt to rob the bank was a bombshell. But how trustworthy was it? 'I think I'll drop in and see Jack Figg before I go.'

'Tonight?'

'Jack is always happy to see me. Besides, I have a notion that could be helpful in our investigating Dr Tremaine's plans, something that might help us gather more information.'

Caroline nodded, then mounted the stairs where she stopped and turned. 'You'll catch the morning train?'

'Bright and early. I'll see you at Greythorn?'

'We'll have to meet regularly. To share information and suchlike.'

'Of course. Entirely proper.'

Caroline paused with her hand on the brass door knob. 'Aubrey, I realise that I'm being difficult.'

'Not at all.' Puzzling, maybe. Difficult had too many negative connotations for Aubrey's liking.

'I don't want you to get the wrong idea. It's just that I'm having trouble knowing what the right idea is.'

'That's a predicament I know well.'

'I want everything, you see. The future is there in front of me. A thousand futures – more. I want all of them. I suppose that sounds greedy.'

'It sounds exciting.'

And it sounds like me.

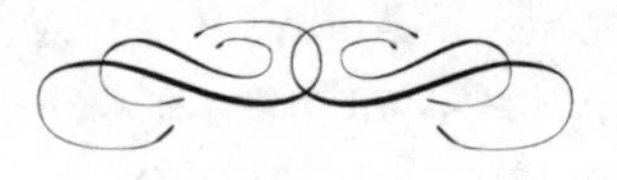

Twelve

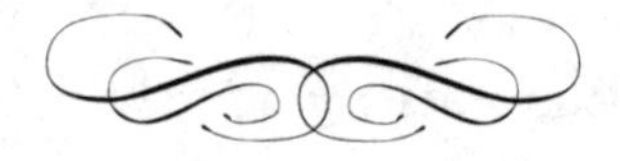

JACK'S HOVEL WAS ONE OF THE CLEANEST HOVELS Aubrey had ever seen. Two cats were waiting outside – one on a dustbin, the other sitting on the step like a miniature sphinx.

'Hello, puss,' he said, more out of politeness than friendliness. He'd never warmed to cats. The one on the dustbin eyed him as if it knew exactly that and would take the first opportunity to trip him up when it presented itself.

The door opened. 'Oh, it's you, Aubrey. Come in.'

'You looked surprised, Jack. Who were you expecting?'

'No-one, no-one. Sit anywhere.'

Aubrey looked around the tiny room that opened directly onto the street. Apart from the desk, it was full of boxes, some piled three high. 'On one of these boxes?'

'That's all there is, I'm afraid. Tea?'

'Thank you. More pamphlets in here, Jack?'

'Of course. The struggle for justice and equality can't get enough pamphlets.'

Aubrey worked his hand under a lid. 'Ah. "Votes for Women". I didn't know you were a suffragist, Jack.'

Jack stood there with a brown teapot in his hand and a vacant expression on his face. 'What? Of course I am. Only an idiot would be against votes for women. It's a struggle, and I'm on the side of justice here. Speaking of such, what's your father doing about it?'

'What he can. The party is undecided. Lost something?'

'The kettle. It was here a minute ago.'

'It's on top of that pile of boxes. It has a kitten in it, I think.'

Jack found the kettle, tipped two kittens out of it, and disappeared through one of the doors that opened onto the room. Some clattering, clinking and shuffling later, he reappeared. 'That won't take long to heat up. Now, what's brought you here?'

'I need your help, Jack.'

'Again.'

'Again. It's the Holmlanders.'

'Our foreign friends.' Jack sat on the desk and sucked his teeth for a moment. 'I had a feeling you were going to ask about them.'

'Why? Are you suspicious?'

'I deal with many people, as you know. Many foreigners, too.'

'You're a prince, Jack.'

'I'll have none of that aristocratic nonsense here.' Jack grinned. 'I have a different view of patriotism from most, I'll grant you. I see us all belonging to the community of humanity, first and foremost. Crowns and kings and borders come a distant second.'

'I'll grant you that many ills have been perpetrated in the name of patriotism.'

'That they have. And it's worse than ever, in my books. Just read the papers, or listen to your politicians. It sounds as if some of them can't wait to go to war. As if they'd be the ones going.'

'All the more reason to do what we can to prevent it. Tell me what's troubling you about the Holmlanders.'

'For one, they seem very well-off for poverty-stricken refugees.'

'They're aristocrats. They must have smuggled out some funds.'

'True, but it's the pattern I'm intrigued by. They seem to be flush with cash for a while, then it disappears and they have nothing to show for it.'

'Perhaps they're selling off the family jewellery and sending the proceeds back to family in Holmland.' *Or using it to buy influence*, Aubrey thought, *or even to fund the Circle's activities.*

'Could be, could be. I've seen that done before, too, but it's always with gloom and tears. Not Count Brandt and his crowd. It's money, not family heirlooms, that's keeping them afloat.'

'Hmm.' Aubrey rested his chin on his hand. 'On another matter altogether, how are Maggie and her Crew, Jack? Still hard at work?'

'Best messengers and errand runners in the district.'

'Of course. I was going to say that it keeps the urchins off the streets, but that's not quite the case, is it? They're scampering up and down the streets all day long.'

'Gainful employment. Mostly.' Jack took off his glasses and polished them on his vest. 'I hate to think what they'd be doing if she didn't have work for them.'

'School being out of the question.'

'Here? Not enough schools for a start. Among the younglings, not one in ten can read and write.'

Aubrey made a mental note. He could see a project on the horizon. 'I may have some work for Maggie's Crew.'

The whistle of the kettle brought Jack to his feet. 'Good. They like it when you have a job. You tend to pay.'

The tea was surprisingly good. Aubrey cocked an eyebrow at Jack.

'One of my friends at the docks supplies me.'

'From cargo that's gone missing?'

'Could be. Who's to say? Call it the workers' share.' Jack put his cup down on top of another box. 'Drink up. Then we'll go and find Maggie.'

'At this time of night?'

'She and her Crew have an unconventional working schedule. Around the clock, if needs be.'

Aubrey gulped the tea and stood, taking care that the floor was cat free. 'Take me to them.'

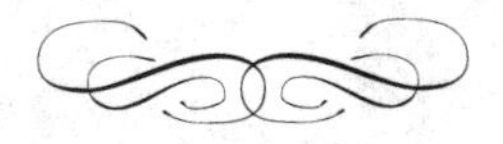

Little Pickling was a district of contrasts. Mostly a warren of rooming houses and rundown tenements where once-grand houses had been subdivided and subdivided again, it also hosted many factories and warehouses and a large gasworks. Jack wound his way through this sparsely lit industrial part of Little Pickling until they reached a freestanding building that had once been impressive.

'The Society for the Advancement of Knowledge,' Aubrey read aloud from the carving over the rather grand entrance. 'A noble aim, I would have thought.'

'Noble, but doomed. The society may have wanted to advance knowledge, but the founders had no idea about money. It went broke.'

'Sad.'

'Of course, they weren't the original owners of this place. It was built for Beauchamp's engineering project. It went broke, too.'

Aubrey was about to raise the possibility of financial bad luck being integrated into a building when a low whistle came from overhead. Aubrey looked up in time to glimpse a silhouette that dropped behind a parapet.

'We've been noticed,' Jack said.

'That's bad?'

'That's good. Much better for us to be expected than unexpected.'

Just before Jack reached the boarded-over doors, he turned left. 'This way.'

The stairs seemed to go down forever, much further down than the level of the basement of the building. At irregular distances, candles in jam jars had been left, just enough to make the darkness difficult instead of impossible.

Jack held up a hand to caution Aubrey. 'Almost there.'

'Almost where?' Aubrey said. He looked around at the platform that stretched to left and right from the end of the stairway. 'This tunnel isn't part of the railways, is it?'

'Not as you know it.' Jack ran his hand along the tiled wall and stepped out onto the platform. 'This is all that's left of the hydraulic railway.'

Aubrey stopped dead. *The hydraulic railway.*

Great engineers were great engineers for many reasons. Great magicians, likewise. Sir Cosmo Principality Beauchamp was both. The first member of a famous engineering family to show any magical aptitude, he went on to fuse magic and engineering in ways that had never been conceived of before.

Beauchamp fascinated Aubrey, especially his tragic end. As a young man, he had immediate success in designing bridges. He managed to blend high quality steel and spells drawing on the Laws of Attraction to span gaps many thought impossible. He moved on to shipbuilding, aqueducts and other structures, all stunning in design.

Then, forty years ago, Beauchamp had fallen in love with railways.

His obsession began easily enough, engineering the Moulton–Snapesby line with its cuttings and river crossings. Soon he was engaged to construct stations, locomotives, rolling stock of all kinds, one of the many men who were bringing steam rail to the countryside of Albion.

Beauchamp's great vision was elsewhere, however. He wanted to free the choked streets of the capital, to transport people from one side of the city to the other in speed and comfort. It was the beginning of the age of the underground railway.

But being a visionary, Beauchamp scorned the normal approach of tunnels and steam engines. He had a grand plan, one that removed the steam engines from the depths and put them on the surface, for easy maintenance and repair. Instead, he dreamed of a hydraulic railway. Tunnels, not to keep water out, but to keep water in. Watertight carriages, huge steam-driven pumps to move the water – and the carriages – in smooth, quiet, cushioned grace. No wheels, no engines, no smoke, simply comfortably upholstered capsules to seat dozens of passengers.

It all fell apart, of course. The seals on the tunnels weren't tight enough to allow efficient pumping. The huge engines on the surface were plagued with problems. The tunnels leaked; the capsules ground to a halt. Beauchamp died, penniless, of lung rot brought about by supervising his workers too closely when tunnelling.

Only a short, experimental stretch of the hydraulic railway was ever finished and Aubrey was now standing in it.

'Aubrey.' Jack nudged him. 'Are you all right?'

Aubrey blinked. 'I'm fine, Jack. Just impressed.' Dozens of candles gleamed. The air still smelled damp, years after the last hydraulic capsule had come to rest.

The platform was in the outer of the double tunnel – Beauchamp's brilliant idea. It was essentially a long walkway, a concourse, with doors that opened onto the inner tunnel, the water-filled one where the capsules ran. Aubrey counted twelve black openings in the long, convex tiled wall, and imagined passengers filing through, stepping into the capsules that were ready to surge to the next station.

It was a grand idea and a grand failure. Nevertheless,

Aubrey admired Beauchamp for the audaciousness of his vision.

The platform had never looked like this when Beauchamp was in control, Aubrey decided. An assortment of battered furniture, most likely rescued from rubbish heaps, had found its way down to the depths, to give the place the appearance of a long, narrow parlour, albeit one decorated with a complete lack of consistency or taste.

Candles and the occasional lantern were propped up on tables; lamp stands, bookcases, kitchen dressers, ironing boards and other spliced-together pieces of furniture made the place look like a particularly jumbled jumble sale. Aubrey thought he saw a tall construction that was part pulpit, part dog kennel.

He frowned and rubbed the back of his neck. The tingle of magic brushed him; it was distant, low-level, but intriguing. He wondered if Beauchamp had used magic in his construction and he immediately had an urge to explore, but Jack had moved on.

Jack marched along the concourse, past figures reclining on hessian bags, swathes of tattered fabric that still had curtain rings attached, piles of clothing too ragged to be worn. The faces that stared up at them were curious, guarded, grubby and young.

None of them older than ten, I'll warrant, Aubrey thought as he followed Jack.

'No parents,' Jack muttered as they approached a large dining table. A paraffin lamp stood at one end, while three children sat, solemnly, like a panel of high court judges.

'None of them?'

'No. They're lucky to have each other. I help when I can. Now,' he said. 'Hello, Maggie. This is Aubrey Fitzwilliam.'

Aubrey couldn't judge how old Maggie was. Fourteen? Fifteen? He settled for young, even though she was clearly older than anyone else in the disused station. She studied him carefully and he assumed it was her customary approach, something she would have learned on the streets. She had long black hair, in a single plait. She wore a green dress and yellow cardigan. Both were threadbare, but they were clean, as was her face. She stood and offered Aubrey a hand, which was also clean. 'Mr Fitzwilliam. Thanks for the work you've sent our way in the past.'

The two boys either side of Maggie were tall, strong looking, and didn't say a word. She glanced at the one on her right and in an instant he was fetching chairs for Aubrey and Jack.

'How's things, Maggie?' Jack asked.

'Well enough, thank you, Jack. We haven't lost anyone lately.'

'Lost anyone?' Aubrey said. *Old before her time* was the phrase that echoed in Aubrey's mind, but in Maggie's case it had little of the sadness it usually carried. Her gaze was direct, her speech was measured and careful.

'No-one looks out for us, you understand, Mr Fitzwilliam. Living this way, we have a habit of disappearing, one way or another. The Crew look after each other, where we can.'

'Safety in numbers.'

'You might say that. This is our home. We have food, a bit of money. It's better than what we'd have otherwise.' She looked troubled. 'Apart from the stinks.'

'Stinks?' Jack said.

'From the tunnel. Doesn't happen all the time, but rotten smells come out of it. Didn't used to.'

Aubrey looked at the gaps in the tunnel walls. They were holes into space.

'Business is thriving, I hope,' Jack said.

'You should know, Jack,' she said primly. 'You send most of it to us.'

She glanced at Aubrey. 'You were expecting someone older, weren't you?'

'Perhaps. I didn't know what to expect, really.'

'I am the oldest, you know.' She gestured at the two or three dozen who were watching the discussion with varied levels of interest.

'And she has the best head among them,' Jack said. 'She keeps a ledger, even.'

'I learned some figures, some reading,' she said. 'Before Ma and Pa died.'

'It was TB,' Jack said softly. 'Your clinic helped, Aubrey, but it couldn't save them. Maggie has no other relatives.'

'There was just me,' she said, 'so I decided to do what I could.'

'She started the Crew,' Jack said. 'Just a few, like her, in the beginning.'

'Now we have more than we can take on,' Maggie said. 'That's no good.'

'She's tough with them, too. They have to do lessons a few days a week. She won't have any stealing.'

'I won't abide thieving,' she said. 'It's the road to ruin.'

'I'm impressed,' Aubrey said. 'And I'd like to do more business with you.'

'Very good. What do you need? Errand runners? Delivery boys? Dog walkers?'

'Watchers.'

Aubrey outlined his plan. Maggie listened carefully, asking questions, adding suggestions along the way. Jack sat back, arms crossed, pleased at how his protégé was managing.

'Done,' Maggie said finally. The boy on her left produced a large, leather-bound book. She opened it and whipped out a pencil. The boy on her right moved a candle closer. 'Around the clock watching of one Mr Spinetti, the singer, for one month,' she said slowly as she wrote.

Aubrey had initially thought two weeks would be sufficient, but had found himself persuaded to take on a month. 'That's it. With daily reports.'

'Daily reports,' Maggie repeated, writing this down. 'We'll get letters to you, all right?'

'Excellent.'

'Half now, half when we're done.'

'I beg your pardon?'

'You pay half our fee now, straightaway. At the end of the month, we get the rest.'

Aubrey reached inside his jacket for his wallet, without much reluctance. 'If I'm satisfied with the quality of your work.'

'You will be.'

Maggie handed the cash over to the boy on her left. He counted it, laboriously, and nodded. Then he reached down and deposited the notes in a metal box.

'In the special place, Irwin,' Maggie said.

The boy nodded again. Then he looked at Aubrey and Jack.

'Don't worry about them,' Maggie said. 'Go, go.'

Irwin disappeared into the shadows at the far end of the platform, evidently to Maggie's satisfaction. 'Safe as houses,' she declared.

Aubrey cocked his head. The low-level, background magic he'd felt ever since he'd entered the tunnel had suddenly surged, peaking in a powerful upwelling that made his eyes widen. He tried to locate it, but the magic disappeared before he could tell which direction it came from.

Then he felt the concrete beneath his feet start to vibrate.

'What's that?' Jack asked.

'Where?' Maggie asked.

'It's coming from the tunnel,' Aubrey said.

He stood. A rumbling noise was definitely coming from the inner tunnel. Along the platform, children were rising, some half-asleep, others more curious, eyes shining in the candlelight.

The noise grew louder. Soon, it was an angry, bellowing sound and Aubrey could feel it as much as hear it. The floor shook and dust trickled down from overhead. He was on his feet, but uncertain whether to run – and in what direction.

'Aubrey?' Jack asked.

Aubrey hushed him with a gesture. He closed his eyes, frowned, then opened them again. 'It's not magic. Not any more.'

'Then what is . . .?'

With a hissing roar, water burst out of the inner tunnel, a solid stream smashing through the first doorway. Jetting with such force that it looked like a solid bar of metal, the water slammed into the wall opposite. Instantly, the air was full of spray. With the moisture, all the candles went out, leaving only the few lanterns to shed any light.

The thunder of the water shook the whole platform. Over the shrieks and cries of the children, another jet burst through the second portal, then the third, and the next, and the next right along the length of the platform.

Each jet slammed into the wall opposite and exploded, venting its fury in all directions. Water surged upward, roaring along the curve of the tunnel, and to either side. The concourse became a world of spray and panic, underscored by the growl of an ocean let loose.

Aubrey barely had time to grab a brass pipe running along the wall when he was engulfed. His breath was taken away by the cold, but by the time he could cry out, it had rolled over him and was gone. He shook the water from his eyes then another wave struck and tried to tear his grip loose. For an awful instant, his fingers felt as if they were slipping. Aubrey had visions of being swept away, smashed against the tiles by the hurtling water, unable to draw breath. He gritted his teeth and hung on.

After these two surges, the flood slackened. Aubrey let go, panting, his clothes sodden and heavy. The water was waist-deep. Desperately, he sought for Jack and Maggie but couldn't find them. He was surrounded by children who were floundering, panic-stricken, wailing and cursing. The water regathered its strength and roared through the doorways.

Abruptly, the flood began to ease. Each doorway became a mere torrent, then a cascade, and – to his vast relief – Aubrey was able to slog through the water.

By the time he reached the first of the children, the doorways were dribbling like a tap on the top floor of a tenement building.

Jack appeared through the misty gloom. He looked as if he'd been dunked in the village pond. His glasses were fogged. 'What can we do?' he said stoutly enough, with only the barest quaver in his voice.

'Ignore the ones who are crying.'

'What?'

'It's the ones who are unable to cry who may be hurt worst.' Aubrey forced his way through floating bundles of cloth and furniture. He scanned the bedraggled Crew. 'If they have enough energy to cry, we can safely tend to them later.'

Not far away, a small form floated. Desperately, Aubrey staggered through water that was only knee-deep, but his heart fell when he made out that the child was face down.

He scooped the young girl up in both hands. Her eyes were closed, but she rewarded his efforts with a huge, gasping cough, and another. 'Take her, Jack.' He thrust the girl on his blinking friend.

Maggie and some of the older children joined the search. Aubrey found more in distress. One was unconscious, a lad of five or six, drifting on his back. He had a gash on his forehead, but he was breathing. 'Can you get him to a doctor?' he said to Maggie, who'd joined him in his task. 'Easy there,' he said to the small boy, who groaned and opened his eyes.

Right at the end of the platform, he found a boy tangled in a tattered woollen blanket. He wasn't breathing.

Aubrey remembered his cadet training. He made sure the boy's mouth was clear, then pumped his chest with his hands, squeezing the water from him.

The lad hawked, choked, then drew in a deep, shuddering breath. He opened his eyes and sat up. 'I'm all wet,' he said with wonder.

Aubrey's body responded. His knees gave way and he sat, with a splash, in a puddle, as around him the children dragged themselves about, crying, chattering, looking for somewhere dry.

The water had almost drained away, leaving a scene of devastation. Furniture was overturned and sodden. Heaps of bedclothes had fetched up against the walls, like seaweed after a storm. A few candles were being relit with tapers from the surviving lanterns.

Maggie sloshed over. 'I think we've got a broken bone or two. We're taking them to Dr Wells.'

Aubrey stood. He started brushing himself off, but quickly gave up. 'Isn't that a long way to go?'

'He'll treat them for nothing,' Jack said, 'and he doesn't complain about being woken up.'

I must make sure Dr Wells is handsomely paid, Aubrey thought.

'Does this sort of thing happen often, Maggie?' Jack asked.

'Never seen it before. I thought we were safe here.'

Aubrey looked toward the doorways. 'Are you in a hurry to go, Jack?'

'Why?'

'I'd like to do a little exploring.'

Aubrey leaned through the portal and held out his lantern. The inner tunnel was completely round, made of iron segments twice the height of a person and – as Maggie had noted – it smelled.

Just inside the first doorway, he could make out the huge iron ring that would slow down a capsule as it came into the station and hold it at the right level for embarking and disembarking. The leather padding on the inside of the ring was hard and cracked, and still dripping from the flood that had thundered through.

He turned to his left and saw four more great rings, each with slip-sockets to allow release and capture of the capsule.

He shook his head in admiration at Beauchamp's daring. It was a folly, but a glorious, spectacular folly.

'D'you think this is a good idea?' Jack said from behind him.

'Possibly not. We'll know soon enough.'

One-handed – the other holding the lantern – Aubrey climbed through the portal and down the curved ladder.

Even though the sloping sides of the tunnel were still wet, he was able to stand without slipping into the knee-deep water at the bottom. His lantern glinted on it and reflected off the wet metal sides, scoured clean by the flood that had disappeared as fast as it had come.

Behind him, a curse and a splash. He turned in time to see Jack stagger to his feet, dripping. 'I didn't think I was wet enough,' he said, and he wiped his face with a hand. 'But this should do it.'

Aubrey studied the weak current in the bottom of the tunnel, then turned and edged in the direction the water was coming from. He'd only gone a hundred yards or so – with Jack gamely following – when he came to the bricked-up end of the tunnel.

'Aubrey.' Jack tugged on his arm and pointed.

A ragged hole had been punched through the metal of the tunnel on the left, a few feet from the brickwork. A yard or so across, Aubrey couldn't imagine the sort of force required to make such a rent. Water still trickled from it. He bent, but couldn't see far, and had to jerk back his head when a wave heaved out, splashing into the tunnel. Jack danced aside with a cry of dismay, the sort that a wet man gives when he realises he's just become wetter.

Aubrey could hear the sound of rushing water coming through the gap, and a strange, whirring clatter, but he couldn't see a thing.

'Any ideas?' Jack asked.

'The river's down that way. It could be an aquifer, a drain, something diverted down in this direction.' Aubrey straightened. 'The water was clean.'

'Relatively. I take it you mean that it wasn't sewage. Thank goodness.'

'Quite. No, this was river water. What time is it?'

Jack looked startled, then consulted his pocket watch. 'Just after one.'

'High tide.'

Aubrey hummed a little. If the tidal surge up the river had become diverted into a nearby tunnel, which couldn't cope and burst, diverting water this way . . .

'Are there any other tunnels around here?'

Jack laughed. 'The city is full of 'em, Aubrey, I thought you knew that. Not just the underground, but access tunnels for repairs to building basements, sewer mains, even private pneumatic tunnels and miniature railways that some companies have put in, electrically driven, to scoot packages all around.'

It was a subterranean world Aubrey had never really contemplated. Pipes, wires, tunnels, it was a veritable jungle underneath the staid old city. 'I think Maggie had better look for a new headquarters,' he said. 'I don't think this one will be habitable for some time.'

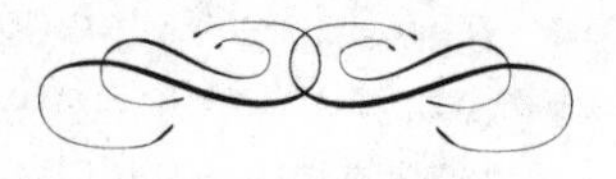

Thirteen

Bleary-eyed, Aubrey staggered onto the Greythorn train just before it left. He threw his hat and his travelling bag onto the luggage rack, hung his jacket on the hook by the door and blessed the designers of the first-class carriages for their forethought in providing seats that were plush, comfortable and conducive to sleep. An extra bonus, one that he couldn't attribute to the designers, was that he was alone in his compartment, with no-one he had to be polite to.

He ached from his battering in the underground flood and the pocket thunderstorm, but it was healthy bruising rather than the pernicious pain that came when his body and soul were drifting apart. He felt perversely satisfied after the subterranean adventure, glad he'd been able to help Maggie's Crew, and pleased that – with his surveillance in place – he was making a positive move in this strange struggle with Dr Tremaine. It was almost as if it were being conducted by correspondence – a move, then a lag, then a response.

But all the time, Aubrey had the feeling of forces being marshalled, battalions being manoeuvred and battlefields being chosen. A confrontation was looming, but when?

He settled himself in. *A minute*, he thought. *I'll be asleep in a minute.*

The train moved out of the station and Aubrey closed his eyes. He could feel the easeful embrace of sleep starting to enfold him.

The train dropped off the edge of the world.

Totally unprepared, Aubrey flew out of his seat. His stomach shot up, slammed off the roof of his mouth and smacked back down again. Desperately, he flailed for a handhold, and then – of all things – he banged his funny bone. He hissed as sparks of pain ran up and down his arm, turning it into a limp, fuzzy, useless object. Handholds forgotten, he landed back on the seat with enough force to wind him.

When his arm returned to normal, he noticed that the compartment was almost completely black. With the shouts and cries for help, Aubrey had an awful moment when he thought he was dreaming, taken back to the flood in the hydraulic railway station. Then a guard – tall, sandy-haired, missing his cap, but with a good, steady bullseye lantern – threw open the door. 'You all right, young sir?'

'I'm fine. Just a little shaken. Can I help?'

'Just make your way to the back of the carriage, sir, if you please.'

'What's happened?'

'Not sure, sir. Looks as if the train's fallen into a hole.'

Suddenly, the compartment dropped a further foot. Amid the renewed crashing and groaning, both Aubrey and the guard grabbed at the walls to steady themselves. The guard grinned, nervously. 'Better step lively, sir.'

The guard moved along the passage, offering his help to the other compartments in a solicitous, calm manner that made Aubrey proud to be a Albionite. In crisis or upheaval, the ordinary man in the street (*or woman*, he added mentally, hearing Caroline's voice in his head) could be relied on to button down and soldier on. It was part of the Albionite makeup, like knowing how to wait in a queue, enjoying the company of dogs and understanding the rules of cricket.

Another conductor was waiting at the end of the carriage. He held a lantern to help passengers off the train. When Aubrey alighted, he saw that they were in a tunnel, but the track directly under the locomotive had subsided. This meant that the first three carriages of the train – and the locomotive – were at a forty-five degree angle, more or less. The locomotive was canted to the right, but all its wheels were still on the track.

The conductor pointed Aubrey back toward the station, which was only a few hundred yards away. He looked at the line of passengers making their way in that direction, and he decided that a fortunate set of circumstances had come together to prevent a disaster. The train was still picking up speed after leaving the station and the subsidence occurred under a straight section of track. If either of this had been different . . .

He shuddered.

Navvies were already hurrying along the tracks, against the flow of passengers, carrying tools, ropes and lengths of heavy timber. Every second man had a powerful lantern. Aubrey stood for a moment, then turned away from the station and joined the first wave of heavy-booted labourers as they made their way to the distressed locomotive.

Last night's incident in the old hydraulic railway tunnel was on his mind. A second subterranean anomaly might be totally unrelated, but Aubrey couldn't let his curiosity go unsatisfied.

He searched in his pockets until he found an old railway timetable. With that folded over, and a pencil in his hand, it provided enough of George's protective colouration to allow him to mingle with the navvies unchallenged.

No need for an invisibility spell, he thought smugly as he pretended to scrutinise one of the driving wheels of the locomotive. *No magic needed at all.*

The engineer was uninjured, to judge from the wrathful indignation he was venting on the impressed navvies. The thoroughly soot-coated individual sitting on the ground had to be the stoker, Aubrey guessed. He was holding a startlingly white handkerchief to his forehead but otherwise seemed to be in fine fettle, joking with those around him.

Aubrey's thoughts turned to wondering how the authorities were going to get the train out of the mess it had wound up in. Magic, muscle or machinery? Or a combination of all of these?

The leader of the navvies was a middle-aged man, bewhiskered and wearing a bowler hat that had seen better days. He swung a pick lazily in his left hand as he listened to the engineer sound forth on the poor quality of the new tunnelling works. When the engineer finally petered out, the navvy boss leaned his pick against the locomotive's bumper and led the applause.

Just the sort of man who knows what's going on, Aubrey thought. The navvies had broken up their admiring circle and were trudging to the front of the locomotive. Aubrey fell in beside the boss. 'Can I help?'

The bewhiskered man glanced sideways. Aubrey saw him take in his clothes, his soft hands, his youth. 'Thank you, young sir. Best if you don't get in the way.'

'Last thing I want to do. I was in the train, though, when it happened. I thought I could tell you what went on.'

'No need for that, no disrespect intended. It's pretty clear, it is.'

'Is it? What happened?'

The look the navvy boss gave him wasn't contempt. Not quite. 'Fell in a bloody big hole, begging your pardon.'

'Of course, of course.' Aubrey realised he was doing a fine job of confirming every low opinion the navvy boss had ever held about the well-off. 'This sort of thing happen often, does it?'

Contempt shifted to a strange sort of pity. 'Not really, no.' He shot a look at the sleepers and ballast under the tracks. 'Though I'm not surprised on one of Rokeby-bloody-Taylor's jobs, begging your pardon.'

Mild interest suddenly became a raging curiosity. 'Rokeby-Taylor? What do you mean?'

'It's his company as what's put in this stretch of track, and the tunnel, from here to Brown Box Hill. Just like the Southern Line tunnel under the river. Made himself a lot of money, I'm sure, but not by overspending on planning or materials, if my meaning is plain enough, begging your pardon.'

'Quite plain enough.' Aubrey stared at the locomotive. The engine was still steaming, but Aubrey could see the boiler was cracked. The locomotive would require a great deal of work before it would run the tracks again.

Rokeby-Taylor. The cost-cutter. The pocket-liner. The gambler. A man whose affairs were catching up with him, if Aubrey's father could be believed. But a man still well embedded in Albion society.

The thought leaped into his head, unbidden and unanticipated. *What a perfect target for Holmland blackmail.*

A loan from an agreeable foreigner at first, then a larger one, and before he'd know it, he'd be enmeshed. Then how would it go? 'Well, Mr Rokeby-Taylor, if you can't pay back your money, how would you like to clear your debt by doing us a little favour? Nothing difficult. Just some papers we'd like to see.'

At first.

'Platform's that way, young sir,' the navvy boss said. 'And thanks for your help.'

'I . . . well . . .' He shrugged. 'Sorry. I was getting in the way, wasn't I?'

The navvy boss pushed back the brim of his hat and scratched his brow. He looked thoughtful for a moment. 'That's not what I meant, Mr Fitzwilliam. Was talking about your Broad Street Clinic, the one your family set up. Saw you there when it opened. Dr Wells saved my daughter, he did, young Dorothy, when she had the gripe.'

Aubrey thrust out his hand. 'She's well now, I hope.'

The navvy boss's hand was huge, but his grip was gentle. 'Thriving and singing like a bear.'

'Bird.'

'No, a bear. Joy of our life, but not much of a singer, is our Dorothy.' He turned Aubrey's hand over and inspected it. 'Not done much shovelling lately, I see.'

'No, not lately.'

'Then leave this to us.' He put his fingers to his lips and whistled, one short, hard blast. 'Come now, boys, let's see what we can do to save bloody-Rokeby-bloody-Taylor's train line.'

A derisive cheer greeted this and the gang of navvies surged past, with wheelbarrows, picks, shovels, planks, crowbars, ropes and lanterns. Aubrey wanted to stay, but he minded the boss's words. These men had a job to do.

BACK AT THE STATION, AUBREY AND THE OTHER PASSENGERS were directed to another platform. The roundabout remedy took them via underground to Knoxton station, north of the disaster zone, where a new Greythorn train was waiting for them. Their luggage, they were assured, would follow them. Aubrey was sceptical, but didn't say anything. The authorities were doing their best.

This time, he did manage to sleep.

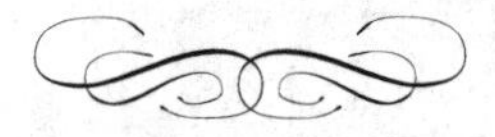

WHEN AUBREY FINALLY GOT TO HIS ROOMS, AN HOUR OR so after an uninspiring railway lunch, George was waiting for him.

He let his newspaper sag. 'You look in one piece, at least. Thank goodness.'

'Hello, George. It's good to see you, too.' Aubrey stared. His travelling bag was on the floor next to his bed. 'When did that get here?'

'Railways chap delivered it an hour ago.'

Aubrey made a mental note not to be so sceptical about Albionite railways. He yawned. 'How are things at the farm?'

'They've been better,' George said shortly. He started to add to this and then appeared to change his mind. 'Caroline rang and left a message. She said that your train had been involved in some sort of accident or other.'

'She was worried?'

'Hard to say. She wanted more information, is how I'd put it.'

'Oh.' Aubrey threw himself on his bed. He lay with his arms behind his head. 'I feel like a chef, George, with a pudding of many parts. It hasn't quite come together yet, but I think with some brisk beating and a good, hot bake in the oven, it might reveal itself.'

'That'd be a metaphor, I take it,' George said. He stood, stretched, then spun around one of the wooden chairs and sat with his chin resting on his hands.

'Indeed. I thought I was looking for Dr Tremaine, but it turns out that things are much more complicated than that.'

'Hmm. That's a change.'

'I know, I know. But remember the Scholar Tan: *A forest is not always a forest. It is a thousand different plants of a hundred different types. But sometimes, it's just a forest.*'

'You know I can't remember the Scholar Tan, never having read him. In fact, I sometimes wonder if you don't make up half of the things you say he said.'

'I don't tell you half of what he said because I don't think you'd believe me.'

Aubrey sat up. 'George, I'm sorry. I've done my usual thing here. I've bustled in, full of my concerns and thoughts, and simply assumed that they're the most important in the world.'

'Don't worry, old man. I'm used to it.'

'But you were saying that things weren't good at home and I let it go straight through to the keeper. Tell me what's happened.'

'Caroline *is* having an effect on you, isn't she? Good show.'

'Caroline. My mother. My father. You. You're all having an effect on me for the better.'

'Now there's a change. No more complete confidence that you know everything?'

'It's a thing of the past. Mostly. Now, tell me about home.'

George's face fell. He stood and started to pace the length of the room. 'It's actually worse than I thought. They've been keeping things from me.'

'Parents have a habit of doing that,' Aubrey said, thinking about his mother's incidents in the Arctic.

'They certainly did in this case. Remember the landslip we had last year, where we lost those outbuildings down the side of the hill?'

'Of course.'

'We had to take out a loan to rebuild. Which we did, without much problem. But the harvest this year was poor, and cash has been hard to come by.' George sighed. 'The short story is that the bank wants money that we don't have.'

Aubrey swung his legs over the edge of the bed. 'You know my father would help.'

Aubrey's father and George's father had been in the same unit – Sir Darius as commanding officer, William Doyle as sergeant-major. Their closeness had resulted in their sons growing up together.

'I know that. You know that. Father knows that. But there is no way in the world that William Doyle would accept money from anyone, no matter how bad the situation is. Stiff-necked, proud buffer that he is, he has to find a way out of this mess himself.'

'George, this is horrible.'

'Oh, it is that. Makes me want to weep.'

'I wouldn't blame you.' Then, without realising it, Aubrey started to hum.

George looked at him sharply. 'Don't.'

'Don't? Don't what?'

'You're scheming. You're trying to devise a clever way to do something about the farm.'

Aubrey winced, but George was right.

This was a circumstance he could do something about. Without anyone knowing it, a quiet word with his father – or his mother – and the Doyles' financial situation would immediately be rectified. Aubrey knew that his family was rich. Not just comfortable, but wealthy. The amount of money needed to pay off the Doyles' debts wouldn't make a dent in the family fortune.

He'd already started thinking about the best way to go about it, to find a way to pay off the debt without

Mr Doyle finding out who was responsible. Maybe getting the money directly into his hands so he could pay the bank. Burying a treasure trove where he'd be bound to find it? A long-lost relative dying in Antipodea? Or just work with the bank, who'd then let Mr Doyle know that the debt had disappeared.

'You've started again, haven't you?' George said gruffly.

'Me?'

'I know you, Aubrey. You can't help yourself. When you see a problem, you want to do something about it.'

'Well, yes.'

'It's more than that, though. It becomes a challenge, something personal. You can't leave things alone.'

'Ah. You're saying that I'm an interfering busybody.'

'That's a harsh description.'

'But accurate?'

'When you're at your worst, yes. But the trouble is, it's also you at your best. It doesn't seem as though we can have one without the other.'

'You don't know how comforting I find that.' Aubrey blew air in and out of his cheeks for a moment. 'I do want to help, you know.'

'I know. But you can't. It would break Father if you did.' George looked at him carefully. 'Look, Aubrey, I want you to promise me something.'

'What is it?'

'I want you to give me your word of honour that you won't interfere here.'

'All right.'

George stopped his pacing. 'No, Aubrey, that was too fast. I want you to *think* about this. I didn't ask you as a negotiating gambit, something for you to counter and then find a way around it. It's your honour that I'm relying on here. Your integrity. Your worth as a decent and trustworthy person. The person that I respect and admire.'

'Oh.' Aubrey, once again, was humbled. He *had* been treating George's request as a feint. He *had* been thinking of ways around it.

He hadn't taken his best friend seriously.

'George,' he said. He sought for the words. 'I want you to know that I'm not doing this because I feel trapped into it, or that I feel shamed into it. I'm doing it because I think I understand and I *want* to do it.' He took a deep breath. 'George, I give you my word of honour that I won't interfere in your family's financial problems. And that I won't try to find a sneaky way around it, either.'

George held out his hand. 'Old man, I take you at your word.'

Aubrey shook and was grateful – for the ten thousandth time – that he had such a friend as George.

George shook himself, like a dog climbing out of a river, and sat again. 'Now, what's all this about a train accident?'

Aubrey told George about the mysterious subsidence and the interesting conversation with the navvy. Then, of course, he found he had to jump backwards and explain the whole business with Jack Figg, Maggie and her Crew. Then he had to backtrack and tell George all about the thunderstorm attack on Count Brandt's Holmlanders, which seemed a very long time ago.

'Busy weekend,' George said, when Aubrey finished. 'A lot to chew over there.'

'That'd be one of your metaphors, then?' Aubrey said.

George threw a book at him, without much malice or force. Then he straightened, eyes bright. 'I tell you what, this is dashed exciting stuff, when you look at it.'

'What is? The explosion? The Holmlanders? The hydraulic railway?'

'Well, all of it really. But I was most interested in the Rokeby-Taylor goings-on. I mean, everyone knows about Rokeby-Taylor, but all this about his shoddy business dealings is fascinating.'

'You're not thinking of your journalism again, are you?'

'It's the sort of hard-hitting stuff that makes reputations. Imagine the headlines! "Rich Dandy Betrays the Country by Not Doing the Right Thing".'

'I think they have people to do the headlines, fortunately,' Aubrey said. 'But let's not get too carried away.'

'You know, I might skip *Luna* entirely. I'm sure I could approach the proper newspapers directly with this. Then those Lunatics would have to sit up and take notice.'

'George. Stop. Wait. Listen for a moment, please?'

George blinked. 'Aubrey?'

'It may not be the best idea to bruit these suspicions about right now. There's more investigating to be done, and even then I'm not sure about how useful it would be to publish such details.'

George jabbed a finger at him. 'You're talking about silencing the voice of the people. Censorship. I'm shocked, I tell you. Shocked.'

'George, it's not the voice of the people I'm talking about. I'm talking about your possibly writing a piece about events and people without foundation. There are such things as laws of libel.'

'Ah, libel. Yes.'

'And as well, there is the tricky area of things that are kept silent in the national interest.'

'Lovely phrase, that. It can mean whatever you want it to mean. Especially if you're the one making the decisions.'

'No doubt it has been used for ill in the past. But surely you can imagine a situation where it could be important to the lives of innocent people to keep some things out of the public gaze?'

'Now, that's a slippery argument. No-one is going to argue against the lives of innocent people. But once a precedent has been set, then it's always easier to find other cases where secrecy is useful.'

'You're right.' Aubrey scowled. 'Hmm. What about if I leave it to you? You need more information before you can put together anything meaningful. I need more information before I can see if there *is* anything useful or meaningful. Then you decide what you'll do with it. As long as you talk with me before you send anything anywhere.'

'Dash it all, old man, of course I'd talk to you. And your father, too. I'm not a simpleton. These are delicate times, for all of us.'

'That they are. And Caroline? She's back in college?'

'Arrived before you did. Obviously caught an earlier train.'

'She didn't have a midnight excursion to the hydraulic railway to contend with. Not that I saw, anyway.'

'Mustn't underestimate Caroline Hepworth.'

'Not under any circumstances.' Aubrey stood and brushed off his jacket. 'Now, if I hurry, I can do my pre-reading for my Parameters and Parallels lecture.' He groaned. 'Don't you hate it when professors try to come up with a snappy title for their subjects?'

'Smacks of desperation. They may as well call it "Dry as Dust: an Introduction".'

THE NEXT DAY, AUBREY WAS LIKE AN ARROW. DESPITE HIS misgivings, his Parameters and Parallels lecture was stimulating, full of knotty stuff. Professor Maxwell covered the blackboard with dense equations, using strange Eastern characters, intermingled with more modern operator symbols. Then he wove a freeform lattice of connectors and explanations until the whole array was a tangled basketwork of fiendish complexity. The professor – a rotund, balding fellow – stood back and smiled at his handiwork before asking, without any guile at all, whether the group had any questions.

After that it was Introduction to Ancient Languages. Just as stimulating, but in a completely different way. Aubrey found he needed two notebooks – the first to jot down the course of the lecture, another to scribble down his thoughts about a universal language of magic, thoughts that were continually sparked by Professor Mansfield's points. At the end of the lecture, with some ambivalence, Aubrey realised the second notebook was much, much fuller than the first.

As Aubrey wandered out of Professor Mansfield's lecture he felt as if his head was bursting. Language was the key to magic, it was a well-established principle.

The more he learned about early languages, the closer he came to the basic building blocks of enchantment.

It made his head buzz.

A blow came from behind and nearly knocked him off his feet.

'Sorry, old fellow,' the gowned undergraduate who had collided with him said, but he didn't wait to see if Aubrey had been hurt. He galloped off with a number of others, all heading along the cloisters in the same direction.

Aubrey shook his head to clear it and realised that dozens of others – students and dons – were all on the move. Portly, gangly, old, young, it was as if the entire campus had become lemmings and were stampeding towards a particularly juicy cliff.

Then Aubrey realised where they were going. His feet came to the same conclusion a few seconds early so that he was already moving when he confirmed that the Sheffield Lecture Theatre – one of the largest on campus – lay ahead.

He was quickly part of a throng. 'What is it?' he asked a frantic-looking don who was waddling as fast as his bulk would allow.

'Haven't you heard? Ravi is going to give his first lecture!'

Aubrey soon left the don behind, which was fortunate, because he just slipped into the lecture theatre before the doors were closed.

The seats were all taken. Aubrey contented himself with standing at the back.

Dwarfed by the massive lectern, Lanka Ravi was arranging his notes.

Lanka Ravi was a small man, extremely neat in

everything apart from his hair, which was black and shiny. It had been pushed back behind his ears but threatened to escape at any minute. If it did, Aubrey feared for those in the front row of seats.

The excited chatter in the theatre ceased immediately Lanka Ravi looked up from his notes. Then he launched into his presentation.

For an hour, the small man detailed several new spells, applications of the Law of Action at a Distance. These spells covered the blackboard and were clever, if not startlingly innovative. His voice was as his appearance: neat, precise. He had a distinct Tamil accent.

Aubrey was starting to wonder what all the fuss was about when Lanka Ravi cleaned the board and returned to the lectern. He shrugged, gave a small smile and held up a finger.

'We all know and appreciate Verulam's Law of Transformations,' he said and Aubrey was immediately alert. 'This law is a fundamental part of our understanding of spell-casting. 'Indulge me, if you will, while I write this law on the blackboard.'

In a clear hand, Ravi wrote: 'The bigger the transformation, the more complex the spell.'

No-one stirred in the lecture theatre. It was an anticipatory silence. The audience was learned enough to understand that such a simple opening was only a preliminary to more complex findings.

'In Baron Verulam's time this was a revolution, such a bold and clear statement of something that had hitherto been half-understood and imperfectly applied. Since then, it has been proven again and again by rigorous experimentation.'

Lanka Ravi looked up from his notes. He smiled, hesitantly. 'Baron Verulam's principle applies very specifically to the magic of transformations, of turning one thing into another. He, of course, proposed a second law, the Law of Transference. Much as for transformations, this law says that the further a magician proposes to move an object by magical means, the more complex the spell. This, too, has been shown to be the case, through repeated experiments.'

Ravi paused and winced. He took a handkerchief from his pocket, coughed into it, and frowned before going on. 'Of course, Baron Verulam's revolutionary work on Transformations and Transference has pointed the way to more general understanding of how magic works. In the centuries since his groundbreaking work the community of magic has established the Principle of Complexity – the more powerful the spell, the more complex the spell construction – and the Principle of Cost – the more complex the spell construction, the more effort is required from the spell-caster.' He looked up and gave his small nervous smile again. 'But, of course, I am telling you things that you already know.'

For a long moment, Ravi shuffled his papers. Remarkably, there was no impatient murmuring, no clearing of throats, no restless shifting of position. The audience had a shared understanding that this was an occasion of great importance; the anticipation, however, was mixed with curiosity. What was he going to say next?

He looked up. He blinked, slowly, then began. 'Magic and humanity,' he announced, and an almost silent wave of satisfaction rolled through the audience. This was what they were waiting for. 'The connection between the two has been much speculated upon. I now believe I can encapsulate the relationship in quantifiable terms.' He abandoned his notes. He took two steps to the blackboard and seized the chalk. 'Let *x* represent the measure of individual human consciousness . . .'

Aubrey knew that magicians tended to either be theorists or pragmatists. The theorists had always wondered at the source of magical power. The pragmatists didn't care – if magic worked, it worked.

But now, as Ravi's flying chalk and mesmerising voice pressed on, he could see the two camps coming closer together than ever. Ravi had derived quantifiable, measurable ways to determine the strength of magical fields – and thus the potential power of a spell. This had always been hit-and-miss in the past, with much effort put into the inclusion of careful limiting factors in spells. Ravi's work could point the way to a dramatic increase in the magnitude of spell effect. If it led the way to calculated manipulation of the force of spells, it could change the face of magic forever.

And if the content of Ravi's revelations wasn't exhilarating enough, the way he presented his findings threatened to have the same effect on Aubrey as a sledgehammer would on a gong.

Ravi was using a symbolic language to fill the blackboard, describing the way that human consciousness interacted with the universe to create a potential magical field. But it was as if the standard symbols used for describing abstruse magical elements weren't good enough any more. Ravi had made up many of his own – and was using old symbols in completely different ways.

Aubrey was frozen – the only part of him that could move were his eyes as they flashed across the unfolding wonders of Ravi's insights. He was absorbing almost without conscious thought, as if the revelations were simply passing through his skin. At the same time, though, his brain was racing in a hundred different directions, making connections, leaping ahead, thinking of alternatives, seizing on implications.

He was spellbound without a hint of magic in the air.

Some time later – it could have been ten minutes, it could have been ten years – Lanka Ravi stood back with a nubbin of chalk in his dusty fingers, gazed at the blackboard and said, 'I think I'll stop now.'

It was as if a bomb had gone off. Everyone was on their feet. Half the lecture theatre was cheering and applauding, the other half shouting angrily. Professor Bromhead appeared and shepherded Lanka Ravi out of the lecture theatre while Aubrey sat, transfixed.

Lanka Ravi's revelations had the immediate crystal clarity of truth. Aubrey was certain Ravi was right. His simple articulation of principles was perfect. It was as if Ravi had provided a lens, making things focused that had previously been blurred.

Aubrey went to stand and flinched. He stretched, barely avoiding the flailing arms of an over-excited don. While he remembered, he scribbled a note to Craddock, assuring the head of the Magisterium that Lanka Ravi was a first-rate theoretician – perhaps unique.

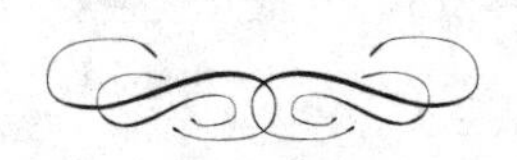

FOR THE REST OF THE WEEK, AUBREY FELT AS IF HIS BRAIN was being stretched in all directions. He revelled in it. This is what he wanted. More than that, it was what he needed. He gave his studies all his attention, for that was what they demanded.

Notes came from Maggie's Crew, written in a large, bold hand and signed – simply – 'Maggie'. Day after day the surveillance was constant and unrevealing. Spinetti sang, ate at the best restaurants, went to clubs, was entertained in high society and in all ways did what was expected of a feted visiting baritone. Which was exactly what Aubrey expected. Tremaine was very, very good. He wasn't about to make amateurish slips – but his arrogance was sure to lead him to do something that would leave him exposed.

He saw Caroline once, briefly; it was like opening a door into summer. She pumped him for details of goings-on in Trinovant. He gave her a précis of his meeting with Maggie and her Crew, the flood, and the plummeting train before she rushed to her commitments in the Science faculty.

She left him breathless.

On the Thursday evening, after a sound dinner, he was poring over Allday's *Fundamentals of Resonance* when he was diverted into checking some mathematics to do with rates of change. In his battered school calculus text, he stopped at a marginal note he'd written last year.

Immediately, it took him back. Stonelea School, before his disastrous experiment. A more uncomplicated life, certainly. But somehow less rich, less challenging.

Then he read his scrawled marginalia and remembered more.

It was half in jest, half serious, an effort toward defining a law of human experience, rather than of magic. 'Have you ever found yourself seeing a grey horse, suddenly, unexpectedly, and then seeing grey horse after grey horse all that day?'

Patterns. There must be something in the human ability to see patterns. Finding them when they're only hinted at. Seeing them when they're *not* there.

Was Dr Tremaine there at all, or was Aubrey seeing something because he wanted to see it?

He gnawed on this bone for some time, then he sat back in his chair and crossed his arms. 'Well,' he said aloud, 'what if Dr Tremaine is working on this principle too?'

He looked around to remind himself that he was alone, George having gone to an editorial meeting with the *Luna* crowd.

Could Dr Tremaine be interfering with people's innate pattern-sensing ability? Had he concocted a spell that would stop people from noticing those details that added up to Mordecai Tremaine-ness?

Why am I resistant? he thought – silently this time. And then he nearly fell off his chair when the answer hit him like a deftly applied mallet behind the ear.

They'd been connected. In the moment of magical struggle over the kidnapped and ensorcelled Sir Darius, Aubrey and Dr Tremaine had been linked. Aubrey had thought it a momentary thing, a by-product of their magical grappling that had passed.

But what if it lingered?

Connections. Aubrey put his head in his hands. It was all to do with connections. His body and soul. Himself and Dr Tremaine. Even the more ordinary magic that bound Aubrey to his parents, to George, and – though she might deny it – to Caroline.

No-one was a totally free agent, untouched by others, but now Aubrey understood that he had a magical connection with Dr Tremaine. Exactly how deep and what it meant, though, he couldn't tell.

Not yet.

IN THE MIDDLE OF THE NIGHT AUBREY'S EYES SNAPPED open. A furtive sound had woken him.

He waited, but nothing further happened. He tugged on the cord of his reading lamp. On the other side of the room, George moaned and rolled over. 'Not more study,' he mumbled. 'Can't it wait until morning?'

Aubrey ignored him. He sat up and then saw the envelope that had been slipped under the door. Even in the dim light, he recognised Maggie's handwriting.

The message was terse, quite unlike the detailed, itemised account of the hour-by-hour movements of Spinetti.

Come as soon as you can, it said, but it didn't say where to find her.

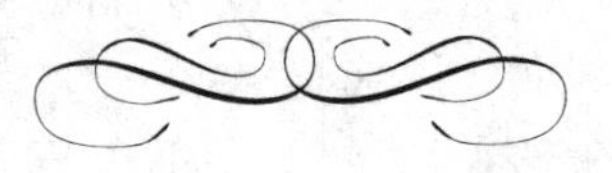

Fourteen

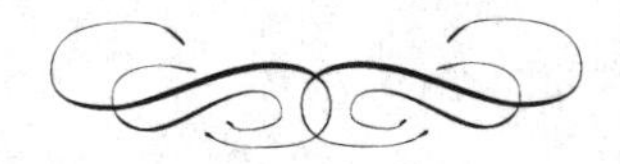

LATE FRIDAY AFTERNOON, AUBREY, GEORGE AND Caroline eventually tracked down Jack Figg in Densmore, working at the Society for Moral Uplift. Jack hadn't heard where Maggie had been staying after the flood in her underground headquarters, but promised he'd find out and let them know as soon as he did.

After leaving the Society for Moral Uplift, they walked for some time, looking for a cab. When a motorcar came toward them, Aubrey was blinded by the headlights. He didn't realise it had slowed until a voice cut through the engine noise. 'Get in. And put the pistol away.'

Aubrey squinted. 'Commander Tallis? What pistol?'

'It's gone,' Caroline said. 'I'm sorry, sir, I didn't realise it was you.'

Pistol? Where was she hiding a pistol? 'Look, Tallis, I'm getting a little tired of being abducted by law enforcement agencies.'

'Quite right,' George said. 'What ever happened to the good old days, when abductions were done by thugs and cutthroats? Doing them out of a job, you are.'

'Get in,' Commander Tallis repeated and his tone of voice indicated that playful banter would be a capital offence if he had anything to do with it.

COMMANDER TALLIS TOOK THEM STRAIGHT TO LATTIMER Hall, the headquarters of the Special Services.

Aubrey and George were kept in a waiting room while Tallis spoke to Caroline alone. Aubrey fumed, but he assumed it was because of Caroline's irregular status with the Special Services. She hadn't been asked to do much, to his knowledge, but he had no doubt that Tallis had his eye on Caroline as a full-fledged Special Services operative.

After some time, Aubrey decided he may as well keep his watch in his hand. It would save him taking it out of his pocket every five minutes to check.

Idly, he polished the Brayshire Ruby. Then he turned the watch from side to side and saw how the heart of fire deep inside the jewel shifted, winking at him.

He flipped open the back plate of the watch and sat for a time, appreciating the work of Anderson and Sutch. The watch's workings were a thing of beauty. The mainspring that drove the whole, complex mechanism set the balance wheel oscillating back and forward diligently, both parts perfectly fitting together. With no more than a daily winding, the watch would keep ticking for years, finely crafted, finely tuned machinery.

He peered closer and saw the jewelled bearings – two or three dozen tiny sapphires and rubies that kept the wheels turning in their ceaseless round.

Aubrey was lost in admiration. In his hand he held the pinnacle of a craft, something so unobtrusively complete that few people even thought about it – however much they relied upon its accuracy.

Caroline appeared after exactly half an hour. 'He was interested in my studies,' she said after Aubrey had asked what Tallis wanted. 'And he wants to speak to you,' she added absently.

Aubrey made a face. Commander Tallis had never liked him. He was sure he was in for a grilling.

Tallis's office was much longer than it was wide. It had no windows, no wall decoration and the desk was bare except for a large black telephone. Tallis sat behind it and glowered at him.

'Sit,' he said. He drummed his fingers on the desktop. 'Now, what's Craddock up to?'

'Sir?'

'Has he told you about the attempt on the Bank of Albion?'

'No, sir.' Had Dr Tremaine moved on the Bank of Albion already? Surely Aubrey would have heard if the most wanted man in the land had been captured.

'He hasn't?' Tallis nodded bleakly. 'I'm not surprised. If it wasn't for the Special Services, the blackguards might have succeeded. We caught them red-handed, trying to dig a tunnel from a building across the road.'

'Why would Commander Craddock be involved?' Aubrey asked cautiously. Much was going on here and he strained to catch every nuance.

'Apparently some magical methods were involved in the attempt. Magisterium operatives investigated, after we'd rounded up the culprits, but we haven't heard anything about what they've found.'

Tallis drummed his fingers on the desk.

'Commander Craddock hasn't mentioned it at all,' Aubrey said.

'Don't you find that interesting? Especially since his operatives found some evidence of involvement from Dr Tremaine?'

'Oh.' *Bloch was right!*

'Yes, and we both know that you have some interest in the movements of this particular individual.' He eyed Aubrey. 'You're sure he hasn't contacted you about Tremaine?'

'Not in relation to any bank robbery, no.'

Tallis snorted. 'It wasn't a bank robbery. It wasn't even a very good attempt at a bank robbery. Dr Tremaine can't be such a mastermind if he hires help like these idiots. They practically asked to be arrested.'

This didn't sound like Dr Tremaine at all. 'They brought themselves to your attention?'

'To police attention. After a few weeks, they'd managed to tunnel close to the foundations of the bank. But a hole opened in Woolcroft Street, thanks to their efforts. Left them exposed, rather.'

'And the bank is safe?'

'As ever. The police called us in, just in case there were any international implications, the Counting of the Coins being so close.' Tallis sat back in his chair and laced his hands on his chest. 'We've checked all around where they dug, and they hadn't even started to penetrate the foundations. We've backfilled their tunnel, made everything more secure than ever. No need of any of this magic stuff, either.'

Aubrey was busy trying to work out what Dr Tremaine's part in this failed robbery could have been – such a fiasco didn't sound like his plotting – but Tallis's remark was pointed enough that he couldn't ignore it.

'Is there something wrong with magic, Commander?'

'It's a lot of mumbo-jumbo if you ask me. It's just a way for some agencies to demand – and get – extra resources.'

Aubrey was dismayed to see such professional jealousy, but also irritated by the aspersions Tallis was casting. 'I'm sorry you see magic that way, sir, but it's changed. It's a rational discipline now.'

'Rational? What's rational about magic? Trumped-up, self-important poseurs making things happen that have no right to happen. Dangerous stuff.'

'Of course it's dangerous stuff. But electricity is dangerous stuff, too, and I'll warrant that you have it wired into your own home, your own bedroom.'

'I don't,' Commander Tallis said stiffly. 'I have gas.'

'And gas is perfectly safe, is it? You've never heard of gas explosions, gas suffocations?'

'Magic is altogether different.'

'Magic is something that needs a careful, intelligent, rational approach. It's vital for our future that we understand it and harness it properly.'

'And this is what Craddock thinks, is it?'

'I can't presume to know what Commander Craddock thinks,' Aubrey said. 'I just know that this rational approach is how all magical research is conducted throughout the world, wherever modern, enlightened thinking takes place.'

Tallis snorted. 'That's what you say. And what has Craddock told you about his research, then?'

Aubrey felt as if he'd been standing on stilts and suddenly had them sawn off underneath him. 'Research? The Magisterium is conducting research?'

'So he hasn't told you about that? Little wonder. I don't suppose the PM knows either, or the Parliament.' Tallis smiled a little and shook his head, as if amused at the things people will get up to.

'The Magisterium doesn't do research,' Aubrey repeated. 'It's not part of its charter. It has no research budget.'

'I see. Craddock wouldn't have any unconventional ways of diverting funds, would he?'

Aubrey blinked. He remembered how easily Craddock had found twenty thousand pounds for Count Brandt.

Tallis gazed up at the ceiling. 'In any case, his operatives put their hands on valuable items every day of the week. Seizures of contraband magical artefacts, the sort of thing that would fetch a lovely price in an auction in the Levant.'

'Not something that the Special Services would stoop to,' Aubrey said, in an attempt to wrest back control of the conversation.

'You leave that sort of thing to those that know best. Just to show you what a fair-minded fellow I am, I'll just point out that Darnleigh House is a big place. Much bigger than it looks from the street, am I right?'

Aubrey remembered. 'It goes down a long way. Below street level.'

'Four levels. Officially, that is. Plenty of room for research labs down there, even if you don't count the other two levels.'

'Other two?'

'You weren't aware of them? Doesn't surprise me. Not many are. Just Craddock and a few of his inner circle. Special access. Guarded twenty-four hours a day. It's where Craddock's most top secret stuff happens, by all accounts.'

'And how would you know all this?'

'Now, that's something I can't tell you. It's a secret of my own. Suffice to say, I'm in the intelligence game. And looking out for my own back means knowing what people like Craddock are up to.'

'You're not asking me to spy on the Magisterium.'

'Of course not. I just want you to be aware, to have the whole picture. If matters change, you'll be able to make considered decisions.' He narrowed his eyes. 'Just be careful of that Rokeby-Taylor.'

'I've already had my suspicions about him.'

'Good. He's a Magisterium informant, very important to them. Which means you can't trust him.'

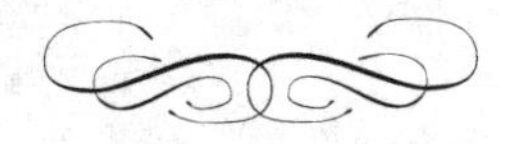

WITH A SERIES OF GLANCES AND GESTURES, CAROLINE insisted Aubrey keep his silence during the entire motor-car trip to Maidstone.

It was only when the Special Services driver left the gates and they were standing alone at the elegant front entrance of the house that Caroline looked around and – finally satisfied – relented.

'Do you recall Commander Craddock's telling Manfred he'd give all that money to Count Brandt?'

'A fortune, it seemed to me,' Aubrey said.

'Yes.' She pursed her lips and frowned. 'It's just that Commander Tallis told me he was organising a similar amount for Count Brandt and his friends.'

'A double fortune,' George said, impressed.

'That's not all,' Aubrey said. 'Since we're talking about double games, both Tallis and Craddock think that Rokeby-Taylor is working for the other.'

'Good Lord,' George said. 'This whole situation is getting stickier and stickier.'

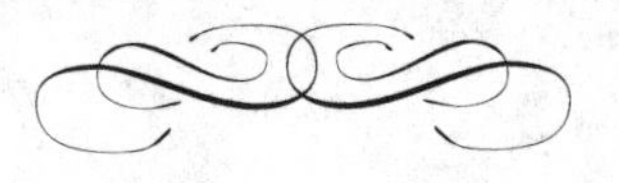

Fifteen

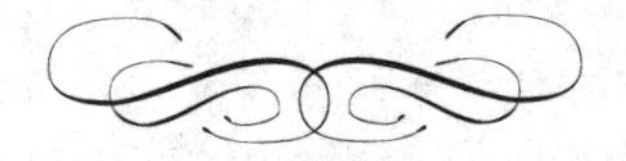

AT DINNER THE NEXT DAY, IN ACCORDANCE WITH A Fitzwilliam tradition that went back to when Lady Rose first joined the family, it was her turn to sit at the head of the table. Sir Darius sat at the other end. George and Aubrey were on one side, Caroline on the other, with Lady Maria next to her.

Naturally, Aubrey was pleased that his mother had asked Caroline. As far as he was concerned, she made any occasion more delightful. The dinner also gave him a chance to put aside his thinking about the dizzyingly complex situation they'd found themselves in with Craddock, Tallis, Manfred and Brandt.

Lady Rose didn't take long before her opening salvo. Soup had barely arrived before she pointed her butter knife at Aubrey – but addressed Caroline. 'I think you're far too forgiving, Caroline, consenting to associate with Aubrey again.'

'Thank you, Lady Rose. I do wonder about myself, sometimes.'

'It's all right, Mother,' Aubrey said. 'We've worked things out.'

'I'm glad to hear it,' Sir Darius said. 'And it appears as if the arrangements are amicable, at least. Now, dear, I think we should move on. How are things at the museum?'

Lady Rose attacked her roll. 'Darius, that's the sort of question you only ask when you want to divert matters, and I'm going to make you suffer by telling you.'

So through the soup and almost until the end of the salad course, Lady Rose entertained the table with her scurrilous opinions of the board of the museum and most of the directors. 'Tin-pot dictators, all of them,' she finished. 'They wouldn't know a specimen if it jumped up and bit them. And with the lack of funds spent in conserving some of our pieces, I wouldn't be surprised if that actually happened.'

'It's never a place for a lady,' Lady Maria said severely, 'and especially not a Fitzwilliam lady.'

'Thank you, Lady Maria,' Lady Rose said. 'I agree. It needs much more money spent on it before it would be fit. Darling,' she said down the length of the table, 'how is that bill going, the one with an increased budget for the Albion Museum?'

'I wouldn't know, dear. Arm's length, that sort of thing. I put it Marlow's way. The museum falls under his purview.'

Lady Maria was vexed at how she'd been outflanked. She looked as if she'd been on the verge of winning a point, but the long rally had somehow turned around.

Of course, the signs of her irritation were minute, and only someone as long accustomed to her as Aubrey could see exasperation in the way she dabbed twice at each corner of her mouth with her napkin. A slight narrowing of her eyes, however, indicated she had something up her sleeve.

'And the Rashid Stone, Darius,' she said. 'I see posters around the city, saying that the stone is on display for the last time before it leaves Albion for good. Surely you're not really letting the Holmlanders claim it.'

Sir Darius grimaced. Lady Rose bridled. Aubrey was prepared to grant Lady Maria a point for a very fine serve.

'It's appalling,' Lady Rose said, finally managing to put together words. 'The museum has had the Rashid Stone for a hundred and fifty years. And now the Holmlanders want it back?'

Aubrey had seen the Rashid Stone, years ago. Covered with indecipherable inscriptions, it was an object of great antiquity, and great mystery.

'It belongs to them,' Sir Darius said. 'At least, under international law. It was taken from Aigyptos, which is a Holmland colony.'

'Colony,' Caroline said. 'Isn't that a polite word for a place that has been taken over and exploited by bullies?'

'Colonialisation is a difficult issue. Albion has colonies. I hope we've treated our colonies better than some other countries have.'

'The Holmlanders looted the Rashid Stone from Aigyptos,' Lady Rose said. 'One of our warships happened to intercept the Holmlander carrying it. Ever since, the museum has taken care of the stone. Custodians, rather than owners.'

'Waiting to give the stone back to Aigyptos?' Caroline said archly.

'The political situation is awkward,' Sir Darius said. 'Holmland rules Aigyptos. If we give the stone back to the Aigyptian governor, Holmland would simply claim it.'

'Why do they want it so badly?' Aubrey said. 'And why now?'

'The Elektor's birthday. Its return is meant to be part of the celebrations, along with unveiling a host of battleships, things like that.'

Lady Rose had one last broadside. 'We could give the Rashid Stone to the Sultan of Memphis. He's the rightful ruler of Aigyptos. And a fine antiquarian.'

'Holmland doesn't recognise the Sultan. He's a rebel leader according to them. If we deal with him, it would be a decidedly unfriendly act. We're doing our best not to provide Fisherberg with any excuse for hostility.'

This was a decided dampener. Sir Darius realised it and rallied. 'University, George. It's treating you well?'

'It's busy times, Sir Darius. Very busy.'

'Not too busy to write to that charming Sophie Delroy, I hope? You and she seemed to be getting on so well at the embassy ball in Lutetia.'

Aubrey knew George hadn't written to Sophie for some time, so he swooped in. 'George has been involved in the university paper, the *Luna*.'

George shot Aubrey a thankful look, then launched into a description of his journalistic endeavours. The discussion that this prompted went on until dessert, with much cutting and thrusting over public opinion, newspaper ethics and state secrets. The term 'muck-raking' was used freely, as was 'freedom of the press'. A scoreless draw, the arguing was enjoyed by all.

As it wound down, Aubrey took the chance to drop in something that had been on his mind. 'I met someone who knows you, Mother. She said to say hello. Professor Mansfield.'

'Anne Mansfield?' Lady Rose said, smiling. 'I haven't seen her in ages. Brilliant woman. You remember her, don't you, Darius?'

Sir Darius patted his mouth with a napkin. 'Of course. Remarkable person. Wonderful dancer.'

Lady Rose lifted an eyebrow, but went on. 'I've never known a better linguist. She's working with Ancient Languages now, isn't she?'

This led Aubrey into the story of his adding Ancient Languages to his studies, to the interest and approval of both his parents, for which he was relieved.

Politics, however, was the topic for dessert, which Aubrey was glad to see was a lemon tart. Somehow it wouldn't be right to have anything too sweet with politics as an accompaniment.

It was Caroline who asked the leading question this time. 'Tell us, Sir Darius, what exactly is the situation with Holmland at the moment?'

Sir Darius smiled. 'Do you want the answer I give to journalists, the answer I give in Parliament, or the answer I give in Cabinet?'

'Pish, Darius,' Lady Rose said. 'Tell them the truth, instead. They're well on the way to being grown up.'

Sir Darius turned to his wife. 'Did you say "pish", my dear?'

She waved a hand and did something rare for her. She

blushed. 'I didn't notice.' She sipped from a glass of water. 'It must be the Mannerford I'm reading.'

'Re-reading,' Sir Darius corrected. 'Things are difficult at work, then?'

Caroline was frowning, baffled. Aubrey leaned across the table with a stage whisper. 'My mother has a fondness for the novels of Mrs Mannerford. She has them all.'

'Harmless fun,' Lady Rose said. 'Vastly entertaining.'

'I don't suppose Mrs Mannerford has a huge Holmland readership, though,' George said.

'Well done, George,' Sir Darius said, 'a deft nudge for all of us back toward the topic. Although I do love a diversion.' He sat back in his chair and steepled his fingers. 'Holmland is extraordinarily active, in a way that does not bode well. It is building its fleet, adding to its infantry, giving every appearance of a country that is going to war. All of this is open and clear. Beneath the surface, it's engaged in much diplomatic manoeuvring, making demands of its neighbours over disputed borders and the like. Then there is espionage.'

'Sordid stuff,' Lady Maria said. 'Your father would have none of it.'

'Sorry, Mother, but that's not quite accurate. Father did use spies, when he had to. He simply didn't tell you about it.'

Lady Maria touched the brooch at her throat. 'I don't believe you. Your father was a statesman, a diplomat, a man of principle.'

'And I understand that you're dedicated to preserving that image. But he was also a general involved in more than a few nasty affairs, and a politician who survived five governments. He appreciated the need for espionage in the defence of the realm.'

This was news to Aubrey. Lady Maria was ferocious in perpetuating her particular view of her late husband, Aubrey's grandfather. She'd commissioned the standard biography of him, and she was currently organising another 'to flesh out the man'.

While Aubrey had never thought of the Steel Duke as a saint, he'd only heard a few whispers of anything other than pure integrity. What his grandmother didn't understand was that this made the old man more fascinating rather than less.

'And now, Aubrey,' Lady Rose said, steering the conversation from her position at the head of the table, 'your father wants to know how your work with the Magisterium is coming along.'

Sir Darius touched his forehead. 'I've just taken a hit and I didn't see it coming.'

Lady Rose smiled sweetly. 'I do my best to keep you on your toes.'

'Er,' Aubrey said, 'did you want to know? Or not?'

'We're both interested, naturally.' Sir Darius shot a glance at his wife. She leaned slightly to her right and let it pass over her shoulder, still smiling. 'Craddock did inform me of his plan, of course.'

'Of course.' Aubrey wondered if this were strictly true, or if it was the other way around. Did his father approach Craddock, put pressure on him to give his son an opportunity? If so, it rankled. Aubrey was determined to make his own way in the world, for that would be the only way for him to know his own worth – by doing it himself.

He gave a sketchy account of Craddock's requests, enough to have both Sir Darius and Lady Rose nodding their heads. Lady Maria looked disapproving, but as that was her normal 'at rest' expression, he wasn't too bothered by it.

'I know it's pointless reminding you to be careful,' Lady Rose said, 'but do try to limit your life-threatening scrapes to one or two a week.'

'I'll do what I can, Mother.'

'And Sir Darius,' Caroline said, neatly making use of the conversational pause, 'when are you coming to speak to the Eastside Suffragists?'

'The Eastside Suffragists? Tell me more.'

'Ah.' Caroline glared at Aubrey. 'You haven't been told?'

'It's on my list,' Aubrey said and immediately felt he'd started digging another hole for himself, but – helplessly – he kept on excavating. 'I've been having some trouble with the membership form.'

'Filling it in?'

'Finding it, then filling it in would be more precise. I think I lost it.'

'You never asked me for it.'

'I didn't? I was sure I did. Didn't I, George?'

George blinked. 'Sorry, I missed that. What were you asking?'

'Never mind.' Aubrey took a deep breath. 'When can I get some membership forms from you, Caroline? Please?'

Lady Rose and Caroline looked at each other. 'I'm afraid, my dear,' Lady Rose said, 'this could be a long-term project.'

Coffee and chocolates revealed little new, which gave Aubrey some time to think as he was able to hold his end up by dropping in an observation every so often, nothing too taxing.

He was concerned for George, who appeared more and more distracted as the dinner went on, rallying gamely whenever he could to take part in the conversations that rolled around the table.

George's level of distraction worried Aubrey. His friend usually enjoyed the dinners at Maidstone, especially when Lady Rose was present.

And then there was Rokeby-Taylor's dangerous double game. Or was it a triple game? Money flowing in all directions around Count Brandt. Whose side was he actually on? And where were Maggie and her Crew?

And of course there was Dr Tremaine. The elusive Dr Tremaine. Where was he?

Too many questions, not enough information. Aubrey needed something more than speculation and supposition.

He needed information – but where would he find it?

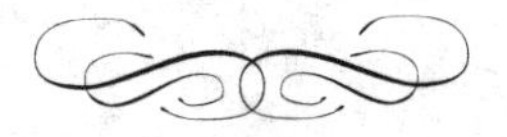

STUBBS WAS IDLING THE OAKLEIGH-NASH AT THE FRONT door. Aubrey and Caroline stood under the porticoed entrance. 'What's keeping George?' Aubrey said. 'He said he wanted to see you off.'

'He seemed thoughtful tonight,' Caroline said. She looked out at the night sky.

'Some trouble at home. Nothing serious, but it's on his mind.'

'Whose mind?' George said, bustling out of the door. He was smiling broadly. 'Sorry to interrupt, but I must tell you that Sir Darius has agreed to an interview about the suffrage issue. I just have to tee it up with his press secretary. Cedric Westerfold will be green with jealousy.'

'Cedric Westerfold?' Caroline asked Aubrey.

'George's journalistic nemesis. It's a long story.' He clasped his hands behind his back, sought for a witty remark and found that – for some reason – Caroline's bare shoulders were preventing him from thinking of one.

'It's been a pleasure,' he managed to say.

She arranged her shawl around her. 'I've enjoyed myself.'

She stepped into the motorcar. Stubbs closed the door behind her.

Aubrey stood there, hands behind his back, and hummed.

Caroline slid back the window. 'What are you thinking about?'

Aubrey blinked. 'Pardon?'

'You're humming. That means you're planning something.'

'It's nothing, really. I'm just thinking of a fact-finding outing, to help sort out things.'

'Now?'

Aubrey looked at George, who shrugged. 'Time is at a premium, so now seems most apt.'

'You're not going without me,' Caroline said.

'Sir?' Stubbs said from the driver's seat.

'Are you sure?' Aubrey asked Caroline.

'Perfectly.'

'Thank you, Stubbs. It looks as if Miss Hepworth won't be requiring the motorcar right now.'

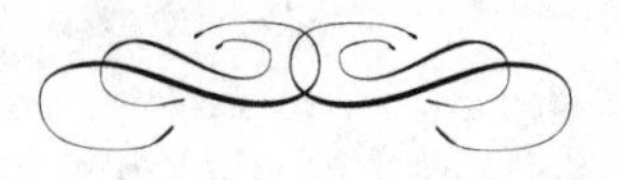

Sixteen

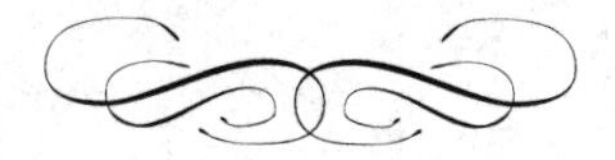

'I SEE WHY YOU ASKED ME TO BRING THIS ALONG, OLD man.'

George hefted the pry bar. He slapped it in his palm while he studied the heavy boards over the entrance to the hydraulic railway.

Before they'd left for Little Pickling, Aubrey had time for some preparations. Not needing any magical apparatus, it was simple enough to find appropriate tools in a garden shed.

'You seem to have a knack for this sort of thing,' Aubrey said. He held up the oil lantern the better to see their task.

'For breaking and entering?'

'You know what I mean. I'm willing to learn, though. Let me have a go.'

George held the pry bar to his chest. 'Do I look like a fool? This is a dangerous implement. No knowing what it could do in the hands of an amateur.'

Aubrey grinned. 'Go to it, then. Be my guest.'

The nails groaned as George wrenched the boards off the entrance. Aubrey always felt that clandestine noise carried more weight than ordinary noise, so he was glad they were in a deserted part of town.

'Wait,' Caroline said once they'd climbed in through the splintered timber. 'Turn away.'

'What? Why?' Aubrey said.

'This dress may not be ideal for underground exploration.'

'Ah. Oh.'

It was a matter of seconds, but Aubrey and George contemplated the dusty concrete walls for what seemed like an eternity while, behind them, a complicated rustling went on.

'Very well,' Caroline said. 'You can turn around now.'

Aubrey had prepared himself, but he still swallowed hard. He held the lantern so he could see her more clearly and he hoped that she wouldn't notice his hand trembling. 'You wore your fighting suit on a visit to Maidstone for dinner?'

'Preparation is a very useful thing.'

Caroline's fighting suit was a loose black silk outfit, a version of those worn by the oriental teachers her father had organised. The jacket was tied at the waist and the trousers ended mid-calf. She was fitting black slippers to her feet. Her dress and evening shoes were bundled in a corner.

'Useful,' Aubrey repeated. 'You do look that.'

'It's practical, Aubrey, you should realise that by now. And what about you? How have you prepared for our excursion?'

'I've changed my footwear. Good hiking boots, these.'

'George?'

George held up the pry bar. 'A tool with many uses. Mostly destructive, I'll grant you.'

Aubrey rallied. 'I'll have to rely on my wits.'

'Wise. Always play to your strengths.' Caroline nodded. 'I hope we can come back here. I always liked that dress.'

Aubrey led, feeling remarkably vulnerable. For years, he'd had the fallback of spells at his fingertips. Quick thinking and magical power had extricated him from tricky situations again and again. Now here he was, deprived of the magical option by his own decision. He felt hobbled, lame, half a person.

He shrugged and the yellow pool of light bobbled ahead of them. Deep down, he ached to use magic. Just a little.

The tiled walls echoed with their footsteps, in a way that promised emptiness ahead. It was damp and dank, much different from the last time Aubrey had been down this way. The prickly-festering smell of mildew was omnipresent, thick and unappetising.

Aubrey hated it; he was reminded of rot and decay and death, the appallingly physical side of his struggle to keep his body and soul together.

'Impressive,' Caroline said and her words echoed in the empty space.

The concourse was too large a space for the lantern to illuminate fully. It became a place of shadows and rippling light. Mounds of broken furniture became hulking monsters ready to pounce. Heaped-up mattresses were rotting balefully. Water hadn't swept the place clean, it had merely turned it into a garden of decay.

'Cheery place,' George muttered. 'Can't see why this Crew made it their home.'

'Beggars can't be choosers,' Caroline said, 'but this is depressing.'

'It was better than this,' Aubrey said, 'before the flood.'

'It was cosy? Homely?' Caroline said.

'Not exactly. But it was better.'

The doorways into the inner tunnel stared at them. If anything, the blackness there was more intense than the shadows that swirled around them. *Hungrier*, Aubrey thought, but decided this was not an entirely helpful – or morale-building – description.

'And you think Dr Tremaine is somewhere around here,' George said.

'I didn't say that. It's the last place Maggie and her Crew were seen. I thought we could do a little poking around.'

'But Dr Tremaine is on your mind.'

'He could be. In a healthy, non-obsessed sort of way.'

'It's a fine place to hide,' Caroline said. She went over and leaned through the nearest gap. 'You could scurry around for years down here.'

'Like a rat,' George said.

Aubrey hummed a little. 'Which way is the Bank of Albion from here?'

Caroline frowned, then turned a little before pointing. 'That way.'

'Far?'

'No, not really. Less than a mile, in a straight line.'

'That's what I thought.' Aubrey sauntered along the concourse for a moment, hands behind his back. Then he stopped. 'I wonder if we can get there from here.'

'The Bank of Albion?' George asked. 'Why don't we just pop upstairs and hail a cab?'

'The bank isn't open at night, George. Besides, it's not what's on top that I'm interested in.'

'Aubrey,' Caroline said, a pensive expression on her face. 'When is the Counting of the Coins?'

She was remarkable. Aubrey felt a wave of desire and admiration, but it was overlaid with the sweet, painful ache of knowing that he could do nothing about it. 'You've seen it, haven't you?'

'Seen what?' George asked.

'The connection. It's come together.'

'I'd appreciate it if you'd be a little less obscure,' George said. 'Slowly now.'

'The Counting of the Coins is on Monday,' Caroline said. 'A good part of the coinage from all over the kingdom is in the vaults of the Bank of Albion, waiting for the King.'

'He won't actually count the coins,' Aubrey said. 'He just picks up a few and shuffles them from hand to hand. After that, it's considered that he's counted them all. The King's touch has blessed the lifeblood of the realm and that blessing will spread from coin to coin to coin.'

'A ritual important to a nation of shopkeepers,' Caroline said.

'That's right,' George said. 'I remember old Mr Tompkins at the Post Office near home. Whenever a gold sovereign went over his counter, he'd hold it up and say "Been blessed by the King himself, that has."'

'A tenth of all the commercial gold in the land has been shipped to the vault, too, ready for this,' Caroline said. 'Bullion from the regional banks. After the King has done his duty, it all goes back, just like the coins.'

'So now would be a perfect time to steal the whole lot?' George said.

'Perfect,' Aubrey said.

'Wait, wait,' George said. 'They *tried* to break into the bank. Last week. Unsuccessfully.'

'Exactly. And security has been doubled and redoubled. The tunnel was filled in, the underground approaches to the bank have been fortified, reinforced, made impregnable.' Aubrey rubbed his hands together. 'What a perfect time to break in. No-one would suspect it.'

Caroline nodded. 'It fits Tremaine's double-dealing mind. Organise a few dispensable types, promise them riches, let them do some of the dirty work, then watch as they make a botch of the whole thing. Watch, and learn.'

'It's just like him,' Aubrey agreed. 'It was a blind, a feint, and it's now lulled everyone into a false sense of security.'

George looked unconvinced. 'Or a true sense of security? The bank is alert now.'

'Knowing Dr Tremaine, a plan is no good without a plan hidden inside it, like one of those Cossack dolls.'

Aubrey went to the gap and began to climb down into the hydraulic tunnel. 'Let's see if we can go underground to the bank, shall we?'

The source of the flood hadn't been repaired. The gaping hole still yawned onto the unknown, but no water cascaded from it.

As Aubrey leaned in through the rent in the iron wall and held up the lantern, the skin on his hand began to prickle. It was a rapidly intensifying sensation that worked its way down to the bone.

Magic.

He closed his eyes and braced himself for a moment. Then he let his innate magical sense feel the residue of the powerful spells that had been in this area.

Stability. Preservation. Solidity. The magic had something to do with these factors. But what caused his heart to pound was the flourish at the end. It was a cryptic, oblique signature but it had a resonance that was unmistakeable to Aubrey.

It was the work of Dr Mordecai Tremaine.

'Are you stuck there, old man?' George said from over his shoulder. 'D'you need a boost?'

'We're on the right track. Dr Tremaine has been spell-casting here.'

'Good,' Caroline said and Aubrey heard the determination in her voice. If he was obsessed with Dr Tremaine, then how would Caroline's preoccupation be described?

Aubrey paused a moment. He could still hear sounds of rushing water in the distance. As well, the heavy, throbbing thud of machinery came to him, a regular, pulsing beat. It was disturbing, setting his teeth on edge.

He handed the lantern to George, then he scrambled through. Caroline came next, easing herself past the sharp iron edges. George used his pry bar to help himself over.

It was a shaft, more than a tunnel, and it showed signs of recently being bored: round, a good ten feet in diameter, and the earth on all sides appeared compressed. Along the bottom of the shaft, the flood had left a tide of debris: broken bricks, roofing tiles, glass, timber. Aubrey crouched and inspected the rubbish more closely to find a number of long steel cables snaking through the detritus. They were spotted with rust, but otherwise looked surprisingly new.

Puzzled, Aubrey stood and ran his fingers along the wall, then wiped his hands together. The earth was damp and crumbling.

What keeps it up? he wondered. The tunnel had no timber bracing, no metal sleeves to hold the earth at bay. He looked back at the hole into the hydraulic tunnel. Something had excavated this shaft, boring along, then it had run into and pierced the metal sleeve of the hydraulic tunnel. It had then withdrawn, somehow leaving the shaft stable and unshifting.

Aubrey skipped across a shifting shoal of broken roof tile, running his hand along the wall.

He stopped, hissing, and pulled his hand back, nearly slipping on the loose footing.

'Steady.' George put a hand on his back. 'What is it?'

Aubrey wrung his hand and stared at the wall. He passed the lantern to George. 'Shine the lantern up here, please.'

Carefully, Aubrey touched the offending section of the shaft with just his fingertips. It felt different: harder, more like ceramic than earth – even compacted earth.

'Feel this,' he said to Caroline.

She ran her hand along the wall and narrowed her eyes. 'Peculiar. It stops about here. Ordinary earth after that.'

'It's about a yard wide?' Aubrey asked. Caroline nodded.

George hung the pry bar from his belt. He rapped the wall with a knuckle. It made a hard, sharp sound. He reached up as high as he could go, then used the pry bar to extend his reach. Each tap rang back at them.

Finding a narrow piece of timber to balance on, Aubrey crossed to the other side of the shaft. With some reluctance, he touched the wall. Even though he was ready for it, the intense magic made him grit his teeth. 'It's over here, too,' he announced.

He looked up. 'I'll warrant that it goes right overhead, too.'

Caroline and George joined him. Caroline crossed the timber easily, George with a frown and a near-disastrous misstep. 'It's magical,' Aubrey told them. 'Dr Tremaine is boring along underground and stopping the tunnels from collapsing through magic.'

'You knew he'd been here, didn't you?' George said. 'It wasn't just a lucky stab in the dark.'

'I didn't know I knew, if that makes any sense. After the hydraulic station was flooded, a number of things made me think. I'd felt a magical intrusion in the area, just before the flood. But I needed to come down here to see if I was right.'

They pushed on. Four or five yards ahead, Aubrey tapped on the wall with a stick he'd picked up. 'Here it is again. These stabilising rings are like the metal sleeves that were used in building the underground railway. Uncommon sort of magic.' *And brilliant. The man's a genius.*

'Boring along underground?' George said. 'What for? Some sort of strange hobby? "Excuse me, dear, I'm just off for a bit of a bore."'

'Here's a question,' Aubrey said. 'What part of the Bank of Albion lies under the ground?'

'The vaults,' Caroline said.

'Exactly.'

'But the Bank of Albion is over there,' George said. 'What's Dr Tremaine doing boring a tunnel over here?'

Aubrey held up a finger. 'Yes. Two good questions. Answers to follow. As soon as we find them.'

'To the bank, then, if we can,' Caroline said, and with that, they were off.

As they went, Aubrey's heart decided to lift its tempo, apparently feeling that the dark, the shadows and the uncertain destination were good enough reasons. His palms began to sweat, in sympathy. Noises alternated, echoing then muffled. Their footfalls and voices made sounds that took on a life of their own, whispering along curves of the shaft.

From all around came tiny groans, clicks, rustlings that seemed to fall silent when they neared, only to start again when they passed.

Side tunnels appeared, opening up at irregular intervals, right and left. Most sloped downward and these showed signs of flood damage. Others curved upward, toward the surface.

All of them had bundles of cable, or chains, or pipes running along the bottom. Sometimes they were buried, sometimes they ran exposed along the bottom of the tunnel. Aubrey grew used to picking across intersections where wires or ropes criss-crossed before disappearing off into the darkness.

Aubrey's sense of the underground world beneath the city grew as they crossed shafts that admitted light from grates high overhead – gas street lights, he assumed. Pipes crossed their paths, emerging from tunnel walls and disappearing again on the other side. These pipes were mostly cast iron, but some were large-bore earthenware pipes and others, on closer inspection, were tarred bundles of wires. They stepped over or crawled under these with extreme caution.

Throbbing. As they pressed on, Aubrey thought he could hear throbbing. No, more than hear it – he felt it through the soles of his boots. It was as if mighty engines were at work around them. But the sound didn't disappear as they moved; it was with them constantly, as much a background noise as one's own breathing.

After half an hour of stumbling and slipping, George stopped and cursed with unaccustomed vehemence. When the lantern light moved and shifted, Aubrey turned to see his friend crouching. 'Resting, George?'

George didn't answer immediately. He used his pry bar to shift some loose earth. 'Vandal,' he growled.

'Who?' Caroline peered at where George was working.

'Dr Tremaine or whoever it was that drove this shaft through here. He's smashed through . . . Here.'

George handed Aubrey a shard of rock. Aubrey turned it over and saw the incised letters. 'What is it?'

'It's marble.' George grunted, then put the pry bar aside and used his arms to scoop earth away, ignoring the disastrous effect this was having on his jacket. 'Latin inscription. Tremaine has shorn off the corner of a Roman ruin.'

A few minutes' work and George had enlarged the hole in the wall enough for Aubrey to see the remains of a pillar.

George leaned back and wiped his brow. 'Roman. From when Albion was part of the empire. Nearly two thousand years.'

'And what's it doing down here?' Aubrey asked.

'Cities are built on the remains of what went before. I hadn't realised how literal this was, until now.' George leaned into the hole with the lantern. 'Mosaics.' He leaned back. 'It's collapsed, in places, but looks pretty solid.'

'You want to explore,' Aubrey said.

'This is exciting stuff,' George said. 'We're the first to see this place for thousands of years. We can't ignore it.'

'It does sound exciting,' Caroline said.

Aubrey had reservations, but shrugged. 'Two out of three. Who am I to argue?'

Climbing down into the ruin was easier than Aubrey expected. Shattered sections of pillars acted as stairs. Some were wobbly, but plenty of handholds made the climbing simple.

Once down, Aubrey could make out what had happened. The ceiling was curved – not a dome, a barrel vault. It had come crashing down, unevenly, but mostly in one solid piece, strong enough to resist being crushed as rubble piled around it and on top. It was a bubble, a gap in the earth that preserved the world of two thousand years ago.

Inside, it was a ruin – mounds of broken stone, vast drapes of spiders' webs, collapsed pillars and broken floor tiles. The lantern threw shadows around that swooped as George swept his arm, surveying the space.

'This would be a high-class building, originally, George?' Caroline asked.

'It'd need a fair bit of study to work out exactly what it was,' George said. 'Private home? Municipal building? You're right, though, definitely not a worker's cottage.'

Carefully, they picked their way through rubble and cobwebs. Ahead, maybe twenty yards away, was a wall of solid, compacted stone and earth. 'No way forward,' Aubrey said.

'Hello. What's this?' George squatted on one knee, right where the edge of the vault met the floor, and inspected a slab of stone – low and about six feet long, running parallel to the line of the vaulted ceiling.

'A bench?' Aubrey guessed.

'Don't think so. Can you lend a hand?'

Caroline took the lantern. Aubrey joined George.

'Now,' George said, 'let's see if we can shift this thing.'

'Shift it? Something that's been sitting here for two thousand years?'

'If I'm right, it was meant to be shifted.' George pushed, and hissed with effort.

Aubrey put his shoulder to the stone and added his weight. 'No good.'

'Let's try the other end,' George said, wiping his hands together.

Aubrey lost some skin from his knuckles, but the stone did indeed slide aside. Panting, he looked down into a narrow flight of stairs.

'Now we're onto something,' George said, beaming.

'How did you know, George?' Caroline eyed the gap into darkness.

'Something I read. Some of these old Roman places had secret shrines underneath.'

A small bell rang in the back of Aubrey's mind,

something he'd come across in one of Professor Mansfield's recommended books. 'So these weren't the ostentatious, showy sort of public shrines?'

'These were private, or only known to a small group. Not official, you see. These people were worshipping something that would get them into trouble if it was widely known.'

'They used them for magic, too,' Aubrey said. 'Outlawed magic.'

'I hadn't heard that,' George said, 'but it would make sense. Fortune-telling, divination, magic like that went hand-in-hand with some of this sort of worship.'

The possibility of discovering traces of ancient magic removed any doubts Aubrey had about this side expedition. 'Well, I can see that you're eager to inspect this shrine, George. I suppose we can spare the time.'

'You're awfully keen, all of a sudden,' Caroline said.

'Just being accommodating.'

'That's why I'm suspicious. What about being careful?'

'Ah. Yes. George?'

'Looks sound enough. If it hasn't fallen down in two thousand years, I don't think it's about to collapse on us now.'

'You mentioned magic, Aubrey,' Caroline said. 'Any danger there?'

'Let me see.'

Aubrey stood for a moment and extended his magical awareness.

It was like listening hard for faint sounds. The world seemed to go away as he focused. Without realising it he turned slightly from side to side, as a sunflower turns to follow the warmth of the sun.

'Aubrey?' Caroline said.

He opened his eyes. 'There's magic down there. Weak, a trace of a residue, I'd say.' He rubbed his hands together, as if they had dirt on them. The magic was of a flavour that he'd never encountered before. Rough, coarse, even, but it held a ghost of power. In its day, it was probably impressive. Now, all he was feeling were echoes across the centuries.

'Is it dangerous?' Caroline asked.

'No. Probably not. Almost certainly not.'

'Hardly reassuring, that.' George lifted his pry bar. 'I hope this thing doesn't come in useful.'

Aubrey bit his tongue. If magic were involved, a pry bar probably wouldn't be much help.

'I'll go first. Caroline, can you take the lantern and come next? George at the rear.'

The third step was where Aubrey started to feel uneasy.

It was a gradual thing. He shivered on step three, but he told himself he was imagining it. Step four added to his sense of disquiet, but he decided he needed more proof.

He took the next step down – five – and at that moment Caroline, behind him, said, 'Oh.'

Aubrey stopped. 'You felt it too?'

'Felt what?' George asked.

'Yes,' Caroline said. 'It was like stepping into an ice bath.'

'So I wasn't imagining it.' The chill he'd encountered at first was now swirling around his calves, biting right through the fabric of his trousers. The cold was ominous enough, but it was the swirling that made him even more alert. Something was moving down there.

'Wait a moment.'

Slowly, he stepped onto the sixth stair. The cold rose to his knees. 'Brace yourselves,' he said. 'It's freezing down here.'

By the time he reached the bottom, he was totally immersed in frosty air. His breath steamed and he shivered. Any exposed skin was nibbled by icy teeth.

Aubrey touched his cheek, then scratched it. Everything about the place made him alert – the shadows, the slightly dank smell, the sound of water trickling nearby – but his caution had nothing concrete to fasten on. The unfocused nature of the potential danger made things worse, and he clenched his hands into sweaty fists.

The room was small – two or three yards long, half that wide. The blocks of the walls, ceiling and floor were roughly dressed. At the far end stood a stone table – a slab resting on a solid base.

Caroline joined him. She'd wrapped her arms around herself and she held the lantern close for its warmth. 'Why is it so cold?'

George tapped a wall with his pry bar. His voice was harsh, strained. 'So this is our hidden shrine. Any clues, Aubrey?'

'Don't move for a moment. I must think.'

Hostility. Aubrey could feel it oozing from the walls. It was similar to the concentrated emotion spells perfected by Caroline's father, but cruder. He wondered, briefly, if Professor Hepworth had gone back to Roman roots for inspiration for his particular branch of inquiry.

The stone table shook.

Aubrey shuffled back a few steps. He felt Caroline's hand on his shoulder, then George's reassuring bulk on his left. His heart threatened to crack a rib with its pounding.

'We're intruders,' he said through a throat that was suddenly hoarse. He opened and closed his fists, realising they were aching from being clenched so hard.

'Intruders?' Caroline breathed. He glanced to see that she was holding out her hands in front of her, as if feeling the texture of the air.

'This is a holy place,' he said. 'A *secret* holy place. Guardian magic, I'd expect.'

'What can you do about it?' George said.

'We can try to convince the place that we're harmless, before it decides to use more active deterrents than just fear and cold.'

'How do we do that?' George asked.

'Ah. I'm afraid that's as far as I've got with my planning.'

'Keen though I am to see its full extent,' Caroline said, 'I'm not sure if you've got time for a comprehensive plan.'

'P'raps we should just leave?' George said.

The shadows behind the stone table moved. 'Too late, I'm afraid.'

'Rarely good words, those,' George said.

Then, as suddenly as if a switch had been thrown, the chamber was no longer freezing. A drift of dust trickled from above. Aubrey glanced at the ceiling, held the lantern up and his eyes widened as the solid stone blocks *rippled*.

'How far are we from the stairs?' he asked.

A grinding noise, as if a tombstone were being dragged along rock, came from behind him.

'What stairs?' George said. 'They've just disappeared.'

'The room is reshaping itself?'

'A wall moved, swallowing the stairs. It's a bit crooked in that corner, but you'd never know they were there.'

'Careful,' Caroline said. 'The floor.'

Aubrey had felt it, too. The stone had flexed, as if a great beast had pushed up from underneath. He winced. There was such a thing as having too good an imagination.

A sudden, sharp blow from under their feet sent them staggering. 'George!' Aubrey shouted. 'Look out!'

The wall near his friend bulged menacingly, but it was so slow and ponderous in its movement that George had no trouble avoiding it. 'It'll have to do better than that.' He straightened his jacket.

Caroline had ended up in the corner where the stairs had once been. 'Careful,' Aubrey said.

She looked irritated by his unnecessary advice, then on either side of her, the stone walls lurched inwards and tried to trap her in the corner.

Again, the ponderousness of the movement gave Caroline time to skip away and back off, grimacing. 'Slow. But it's getting faster.'

They came together in the middle of the room, back to back to back, as far from the walls as possible. 'Keep the lantern up, Caroline,' George said. 'And I'd suggest we find a way out of here very, very quickly.'

It seemed like a time for unnecessary advice – Aubrey's brain had been whirring at full speed for some time. The problem was that he was facing a magical threat and he couldn't meet it with magic. Not if he valued his soul.

Dread and terror. Aubrey could taste them, and he knew they were being generated by the room. They came from inside. A pulse fluttered at the side of his neck like a trapped butterfly. He swallowed and it was as if a grapefruit had lodged there.

The stones of the room quivered, sequentially, a ghostly finger running along piano keys.

It's not used to moving, Aubrey thought. He had the unnerving certainty that it was learning quickly.

It began with the floor. It suddenly lifted underneath George, tilting and sending him staggering until he met the nearest wall. Caroline, too, was thrown off her feet. She tumbled and landed easily, bouncing on her toes, ready for whatever came next.

The stones underneath Aubrey heaved. He fell and, spreadeagled, found himself on top of a column that burst from the floor and threatened to mash him against the ceiling. He flung himself to one side, tumbling to the floor. The column and the ceiling met with a crash.

Aubrey crouched, panting. George picked himself up and stumbled toward him. Caroline eased closer. 'Now what?'

'Nothing good.' Aubrey tried to look in all directions at once. When would the shrine realise that it could drop the entire ceiling and get rid of them that way?

They were intruders. He had to convince the place that they belonged there.

The rear wall of lurched. It shuddered, stopped, then began to grind toward them.

Helplessly, they backed away. Aubrey's stomach was an empty, yawning hole the size of all creation.

'Time to pull something out of the bag, Aubrey,' George muttered.

Aubrey had a solution at his fingertips. He was sure that a variation of his identity spell, the one he'd used in Lutetia, would work. Not just identity, but texture and flavour of identity could be captured by the spell. He was sure he could cloak them in enough 'Romanness' to placate the shrine's awareness.

But he couldn't use magic.

George shouted and pushed Aubrey aside. A mass of stone fell, sending up a cloud of dust. Aubrey cannoned into Caroline. She twisted, keeping her balance, but Aubrey lurched to one side and slammed his head against the wall. Black streaks clawed at his vision.

Through his grogginess, movement caught his attention. Behind George, on the other side of the room, a huge mouth had formed and was snapping at him. Made of the stone blocks of the wall, its lips flapped and snarled obscenely. George cried out and recoiled, but the floor beneath his feet bucked, throwing him straight at the hungry teeth.

A few yards away, Caroline was on her back, scrambling away from a hole that had opened in front of her. The floor tilted, doing its best to slide her into the gap.

Aubrey flung off the last vestiges of terror. His friends were in danger. Nothing else mattered. He had to save them, even if it cost him.

The spell leaped to his lips, as if it had been waiting for the chance. He began to chant.

The spell was dense; each individual term was short, but the linking and sequencing needed to establish identity was demanding. Sweat sprang to his forehead as he spat out each Chaldean syllable, biting off each one as clearly as he could. The spell writhed on his tongue, having a life of its own. It looked for any chance to baffle him, to go wrong, or to tease him into slurring or mispronouncing.

He refused to be beaten. Each element came to him as he needed it, whole and clear. He shunted them to his mouth and marched them off, not allowing any mistakes.

Finally, he slammed out the final syllable, his signature and conclusion.

All strength vanished from his legs. He grunted and, boneless, he slumped to the floor.

He watched, blurrily, unable to move, hoping he'd done enough and trying to remember another spell, just in case he hadn't, but his mind was leaden. Nothing came to him.

All movement in the shrine – apart from Caroline and George's desperate efforts to avoid their traps – ceased. They scrambled to the centre of the room, breathing hard, eyes darting.

The mouth in the wall shrank, shifted, then disappeared. The stone made itself whole again. The gap in the floor closed up, the stone blocks rumbled back into place. In the far corner, stairs projected from the wall, floor and ceiling.

'Aubrey!' George called and hurried to his side. 'What have you done?'

Aubrey shook his head, then he bit down as a sharp spasm seized him.

His body and soul were coming apart.

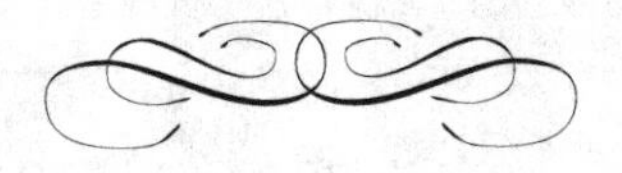

Seventeen

AUBREY DOUBLED UP, HIS KNEES ALMOST TOUCHING his chin. He hissed, trying to let out the agony. Dissolution had never been this acutely painful before.

He felt George's hand on his shoulder. 'Steady, old man.'

'Trouble, George,' he managed to gasp. His vision wavered and blurred before settling. He felt as if he were being jabbed all over with icy needles.

'I gathered as much. Here, can you make it to the wall?'

Caroline brought the lantern close. 'What's going on?'

Aubrey gave a weak laugh. 'This is what I didn't want you to see.'

'Your condition?' She glanced at George. 'I know, you know.'

'Magic.' *Pause, gather breath – not too deep.* 'I convinced the shrine that we belonged here.' He shuddered as another wave of pain rolled through him, his soul wrenching at the confines of his body with enough force to make him nauseated. He used his magical awareness and wasn't surprised to see that the golden cord was shining brighter than ever.

The mystical golden cord. Every soul was bound by two aspects of the golden cord. One disappeared into the portal that leads to the true death. The other linked the soul to the body. When the time was right, the golden cord that linked body and soul melted, and the surviving cord guided the soul to the true death.

It was the natural order of things. The order that Aubrey had messed up with his experiment.

His time was not due, but the true death called him constantly, tugging his soul towards the final journey. Now, its summons was greater than ever.

George eased him down so his back was to the wall, near the stone table.

Caroline crouched and held the lantern so it wouldn't shine in his eyes. A wisp of hair had escaped the knot she'd tied at the back of her head. She pushed it away irritably, but with such grace and economy of movement that Aubrey nearly wept.

'You idiot,' she said. 'What have you done?'

'That's all right,' he croaked. 'Any time.'

'What?'

'Sorry. I thought you were thanking me for saving you.'

She thought about this for a moment. 'No. I was upbraiding you.'

'Ah. That's what it was.' Aubrey closed his eyes for a moment. The darkness behind his eyelids swelled and surged in time with his pulse.

'Is there anything you can do?' she asked.

'I hope so.' He concentrated on his breathing. It seemed to help.

'Is it like this all the time?'

'Like this?' *Small breath in, tiny breath out.* 'No. Not all the time. My hold has been loosened.'

'What caused it then?'

'Magic. Strains me. Weakens my grip.' He probed at his teeth with his tongue, checking to see if any were loose.

'I see. You tried not using magic, didn't you?'

'You noticed?'

'It was as if you'd stopped talking.'

'Ah. That noticeable.' Aubrey took a breath, a deep one that didn't hurt, and he saw that as a good sign. He counted another ten painless breaths, and then – hesitantly – felt he may have things under control. Apart from the iron spike being pounded into his head. And the tremors in his hands. And a hundred other small symptoms that he was going to address by hoping they'd go away.

'Indeed.' She studied him. 'You can't stop doing magic, Aubrey. It's too important to you.'

'That's what I discovered.'

'So we'll just have to manage you. Somehow.'

She rose to her feet in one lithe movement. Aubrey followed her by tilting his head back and staring, unmindful of how this made him look.

Did she say 'we'?

Before he could query her, George spoke up. 'Aubrey. I think you should have a look at this.'

Caroline offered him a hand, but Aubrey didn't think his dignity could stand it so he dragged himself up via the wall.

His soul was uneasy, but at least it wasn't battering at its confines any more. His head was tight and he thought he was slightly feverish. He resigned himself to being on the roundabout of feeling out of sorts once again.

Aubrey limped to where George was crouched in the corner of the room. 'What is it?'

'A stone tablet, broken into fragments,' George said. 'The writing has been defaced on all of them, so it's unintelligible. Except for this bit.'

He held up a piece of stone, roughly five-sided, about the size of his hand. It was covered with minute script, in three distinct bands.

'It's Roman?' Caroline asked.

'As the expert here on Roman history, I can confidently say that the writing at the top is Latin. Most of it. Of a sort, anyway,' George said. 'But there are two other sorts of writing. This spiky one in the middle, and that mess at the bottom. Or are they pictures?'

Aubrey squinted. The writing was almost microscopic, and the light wasn't the best, but he could make out some sections. 'The middle one, the spiky one, is cuneiform. Late cuneiform, the writing of the Sumerians. I think the Latin section is a translation of the cuneiform, or the other way around.' He stared. 'They're both talking about magic.'

'Magic, eh? That'd fit. I'd say that this tablet was broken as part of a ritual,' George said. 'See the black soot on the other bits? Someone poured oil over them and lit it.'

'Whatever for?' Caroline asked. Her eyes gleamed with interest.

'Who knows? Maybe sending a message to the gods, or someone in the afterlife. Or a ritual attempt at destroying them. Educated guesswork, this is.'

Aubrey leaned closer. 'If the top two scripts are translations of each other, it would stand to reason that the bottom one is as well.'

'Interesting.' Caroline leaned on Aubrey and peered at the stone. He nearly buckled at the knees but managed to hold himself up. 'I've seen something like it before,' she said.

'Really?' George said. 'Where?'

'In the museum. The Rashid Stone.'

For a moment, excitement drove away Aubrey's terrible weariness. 'You're right. The messy script. That's the Rashid Stone script!'

'Good Lord,' George said, and his voice was hushed, almost reverential. 'You understand that this means we could crack the mystery of the Rashid Stone? After two hundred years of trying, we stumble across a touchstone.'

'It's more than that,' Aubrey said. 'This could be an early treatise on magic. Maybe the earliest we have.'

Aubrey's heart pounded, but with exhilaration this time, not fear. The few bits and pieces he could make out suggested that stone was dealing with fundamental aspects of magic – where it came from, how it was influenced by people, how to shape it to one's will, and some terms that seemed to be about city magic, which was a puzzle to him, a small one in the larger puzzle of the stone itself.

If the unknown language was early, primeval, could it be closer to a source language, something which could serve as a universal language of magic? He blew on the stone, trying to clear the dust, and more characters emerged.

Death. Protection. Soul. Three cuneiform characters became clear and he nearly dropped the stone. He checked the Latin inscription above and it seemed to echo the Sumerian. The corresponding characters in the unknown script were distinctive, but puzzling.

'I need to study this. I need to talk to Professor Mansfield.' Aubrey rubbed his thumb on a soot-stained section. Was that the Latin word for 'connection'? He tried to remember, but his Latin was more than rusty; it was badly corroded and in need of major restoration.

'Not now, I think,' Caroline said. 'We have a mission ahead.'

Aubrey was torn, but he reminded himself that Maggie and her Crew were still missing – and Dr Tremaine was still out there. This could wait. 'Of course.'

'I'll keep it safe,' George said and he wrapped it in his handkerchief before slipping it into his pocket. 'There. Safe as the Bank of Albion. Or safer, really.'

They hurried from the tomb and quickly worked their way through the marble vault. After a scramble out of the Roman ruins, where Aubrey delightfully had to assist Caroline, they were back in the main tunnel. Once there, Aubrey leaned against the wall for a moment while George and Caroline argued about the way ahead. With glum certainty, he realised that his magical expenditure had already come at a cost. He ached, and shivering threatened to seize hold of him.

As he tried to steady himself, he realised that, for the present, this was his lot. He couldn't stop using magic.

It was like deciding not to use one of his arms – awkward, difficult and potentially dangerous.

Live with it, he thought, *and live long enough to find a way to sort things out.*

He controlled his shivering through an act of will and straightened to join his friends.

The main tunnel trended upwards for a few minutes, then it opened out into a larger tunnel: a wide, open drive. It was long, and wide as a boulevard, with some bracing timbers as well as the magically stabilised earth. Along one side of the excavated area Aubrey could make out the foundations of buildings, the first reminder he'd had of the world overhead for some time.

Sitting in the middle of the underground boulevard, twenty or thirty yards ahead, was an elaborate machine.

George and Caroline stared. 'I think we've found our tunneller,' Aubrey murmured.

The machine was the size of an omnibus, completely enclosed in smooth steel apart from a window at the front. A large auger projected from the front, twice the height of a man, and it was surrounded by immense electric lights in wire cages. Large metal plates ran around all four wheels and Aubrey was startled to see that these plates were connected, like links in a chain. He squatted, taking the lantern from Caroline as she peered at the welding, and inspected the undercarriage of the contraption, growing increasingly excited at what he was finding.

By the lantern light, he saw that the cabin had a single seat. No room for passengers; this was a solo craft. Levers, knobs, switches were arranged within reaching distance. All were mysterious, unlabelled except for one brass handle – 'Ignition'. Automatically, Aubrey tugged on it but was not surprised when he found it locked – magically locked, to judge from the tingling in his fingertips.

A set of three large brass rings – each as tall as George – jutted from the rear of the machine, one behind the other. Hundreds of silver rods ran around the perimeter of each ring and linked them together so that they were a handspan apart. When Aubrey touched the rings, he felt the magical residue and immediately knew what they were for.

'They belch out the stabilising sheaths.' He stood and wiped his hands on his filthy trousers. 'The auger digs, the machine pushes aside the earth, and the rings shoot out stabilising magic that locks the earth into place.' He shook his head with admiration. 'It's a masterpiece.'

'A Dr Tremaine construction?' Caroline said without a trace of admiration.

'I'd say so. Dr Tremaine is a man for elegant machines.'

'So where *is* he?' Caroline demanded. 'If this is his machine, shouldn't he be nearby?'

The thought gave Aubrey a momentary alarm. Then he placed his palm against the cowling of the tunneller. 'It's cold. Hasn't been used for some time. Dr Tremaine could be anywhere.'

Aubrey walked along the length of the tunneller, then around to the far side. He lifted the lantern and faced the mighty foundations of a building.

Thrusting down from the overburden were large stone blocks, reinforced with steel bars driven through each and bolted, linking them together. They rested on solid bedrock. Aubrey looked up. The weight resting on these foundations meant that they were immoveable, part of the rock itself, as if they'd grown there. 'He's excavated right along the foundations of our Bank of Albion. I'd say the Vault Room is through here.'

George broke off from studying the tunneller's gearing and joined Aubrey's inspection of the foundations. 'How thick are they?'

Aubrey cast his mind back to his day in the vault with his father. 'Ten, twenty feet? There's no getting through that lot.'

'Then how is Dr Tremaine imagining he'll waltz in?' Caroline said.

Aubrey looked along the length of the foundations. 'Does the tunnel continue past the bank?'

'It does. And that doesn't answer my question.'

'No, but it's a step toward answering it.'

Aubrey was sure he was close, that answers were dancing just a few inches beyond his fingertips. He was tired, aching, filthy and suffering from the disunity of his body and soul – but he was buoyed by an urgency that came from his desire to succeed whatever the circumstances.

He walked along the length of the foundations. It wasn't long before he was on the edge of Caroline's lantern light and entering the realm of shadows. He tripped on a sheaf of tarred wires that emerged from the earth and vanished into the darkness ahead, but he barely noticed them.

Another tunnel, at right angles to the main shaft, had been bored along the side of the bank's foundations.

The tunnel mouth became clearer, shadows fleeing. 'Someone wants to see as much of the bank as he can,' Caroline said. She held the lantern up, and Aubrey could see the calculation in her eyes. 'Was he trying to find a weak spot?'

'In the bank?' George said, joining them. 'No-one's managed to break into the Bank of Albion. Ever.'

'Dr Tremaine is a man for firsts,' Aubrey said. He scuffed at the earth of this side tunnel. It wasn't as compacted as the main tunnel. Was it more recent?

His scuffing uncovered something that clinked when he nudged it with his foot. With astonishment, he realised that it was a chain.

He gouged at the earth with his heel and discovered that the chain seemed to run underneath the tunnel floor, extending into the distance.

'What is it?' George asked.

'An enigma.'

'One of those spiny anteater things from Antipodea? How did it get here?'

Aubrey lifted his head only to see George grinning at him.

'Now,' George said, 'for a second, you actually thought I'd confused enigma and echidna, didn't you?'

'Touché, George. Now that you've kept me on my toes, I'll ask you – what's that behind you?'

'I feel like I'm in a pantomime,' George said. He turned, but slowly, ready to disengage himself from any upcoming joke.

Twenty or thirty yards away at the edge of the lantern's light, was a shadowy bulge, an irregularity in the straight, sheer stone of the foundations.

'Something worth investigating, in my book,' Aubrey said. He led the way, cautiously.

The lantern light revealed that the side tunnel ended

in solid rock. An arm of the rock projected, punching through the corner of the foundations, which were built right up to it, butting up against it with a combination of masonry skill, iron work and reinforced concrete.

'North,' he said. 'Which way is north?'

Caroline frowned, but pointed back in the direction they'd come. 'That way.'

'Yes. Of course.'

'This rock is part of the bank,' George said. 'It's been built around it.'

Aubrey tried to remember the layout of the Vault Room. What was where?

Then he had it. 'It's the Old Man of Albion. The rest of him, anyway.'

George stared. Even Caroline looked impressed. 'This goes right through into the bank?'

'Oh yes. Part of the history and soul of the place.' Aubrey slapped it. Then he lifted his hand and stared at it. 'Of course, I could be wrong.'

'Now, Aubrey,' Caroline said, 'being inscrutable doesn't help us at all here. What's going on? Plain, simple explanations, please.'

Aubrey rubbed his temples. Plain simple explanations for fiendishly complicated phenomena? 'I'll try.' He rubbed his hands together. 'It's a fake.'

George gaped, but Aubrey could see Caroline speeding through the implications. 'Dr Tremaine?'

'It's his back door,' he said. 'After the first robbery attempt, the foundations were reinforced from the inside – thick steel plate and whatnot. Except for the Old Man.'

George reached out and tapped the rock with his pry bar. 'Sounds real enough to me.'

'Magic, George. For all intents and purposes, this is as solid as mountains. But Dr Tremaine has removed the original Old Man of Albion and replaced it with a lookalike.'

'Lookalike?' George said. 'Sound-alike and feel-alike too.'

'He's no petty magician.'

'The possibility of your making a mistake here is a remote one?' Caroline said.

Aubrey debated this for a moment. Then he shook his head. 'I don't think so. But remind me if this goes spectacularly wrong, will you?'

'Naturally,' she said, but she smiled.

Aubrey had an instant to regret how he'd mishandled everything to do with Caroline, but an instant is as long as a lifetime when it comes to self-chastisement. Aubrey managed to kick himself a good number of times in between one tick of his watch and the next.

If only things had gone differently, he thought and then rephrased it. *If only I'd done things differently*. Sharper, less pleasant, but more accurate.

He sighed, caught it, and turned it into an exhalation that he hoped signified urgency, determination and fortitude.

'Asthma, Aubrey?' Caroline asked.

'Asthma? Me? No.' He thumped his chest and winced. 'Like a bell, I am.'

'Excellent. Now, what are you proposing?'

'If Dr Tremaine left this as a back door, he must have some way to get in.'

'A key?' George suggested.

'Metaphorically speaking, that's right. This key, however, will be some sort of spell.'

'Shouldn't be too hard,' George said. 'You were able to sneak into that Banford Park place, where Dr Tremaine had your father hidden. You tricked his security spells there.'

'Yes. And I don't think Dr Tremaine is a big enough fool not to have realised what went on there. He would have changed any spells he's using for such a thing.'

Caroline nodded. 'It'd be like leaving locks unchanged after burglars had broken in and made off with your keys, as well as the silverware. To extend George's metaphor.'

'Extend away,' George said. 'I'll set them up, you two can run with them.'

Aubrey examined the stone. It had every appearance of solidity. He could even see scrape marks where dirt had been cleared away. If it was an illusion, it was a perfect one.

He put his hands against it. No doubt about it, he could detect faint traces of magic – and it had the hallmarks of a Tremaine spell. Aubrey guessed that most magicians would be unable to feel the residue, and none but him would be able to determine the spell-caster's origin. It was turning out to be another aspect of the peculiar magical bond he'd established with the renegade.

Which was well and good, but it didn't give him a clue as to how to get into the vault.

He began humming as he inspected the rock where it joined the foundations. Not a crack showed. Aubrey doubted that he could fit a piece of paper between the dressed stone and the substance of the Old Man – or the fake Old Man.

Perhaps he could work on some sort of osmotic principle, changing his body so that it could ooze through the rock. He shook his head. No, a stupid idea. It would take too long, and what use would that be anyway? How could anyone get out again with loot?

Still, he was pleased. His brain was working, throwing up possibilities.

'I'm going to have another look at that tunnelling machine,' George said.

'Do you think that's wise?' Caroline said.

'Aubrey's thinking. He could be some time.'

'Are you sure?'

'I've seen this before. Best thing to do is to leave him undisturbed. If we stand around, we're just a distraction. You more so, naturally.'

Caroline shook her head. 'Very well. Let's see what we can find out about that tunneller, shall we?'

Aubrey was left alone, but he hardly noticed. He conjured up a small glow light, barely the size of a pea, without really thinking about it – without noticing that this simplest of spells sapped his energy, added to the strain of holding onto his soul.

He stood in front of the mass of stone and plucked at his chin. A key. This special back door needed a key.

What sort of magic had Dr Tremaine used? Without knowing exactly what branch of magic, Aubrey assumed the spell would be unusual, outlandish even, and would pay very little heed to established conventions. It might be crude and powerful, or elegant and subtle.

Which is like saying it could be anything at all.

He flexed his fingers, then rubbed his hands together. He leaned close to the rock of which the Old Man of Albion was but an extension. When he put his ear on it he relished the coolness. Slowly, he spread his hands and placed his fingertips on the surface of the rock, either side of his head.

He closed his eyes. As much as it was against his nature, he allowed himself to become entirely passive. He waited, receptive, allowing the magic to come to him, ready to sense the faintest touch, the merest hint of its nature.

Time passed, but Aubrey was only aware of it in an abstract sense. He opened his eyes. His fingers tingled when he took them from the rock. Frowning, he rubbed them together.

The rock was a sham, it was clear. A cleverly constructed magical facsimile, it had all the appearance and solidity of the real thing, but with the right magical key a substantial part would vanish, leaving a comfortable access into the vaults of the Bank of Albion.

All this he had been able to sense quite quickly; the revelation was that the key was a spoken one.

It was a crucial discovery, but it still left the doorway locked.

The standard technique in these matters would be to construct a spell that would generate and articulate words, one at a time, until the correct one was stumbled upon. This also showed the limitations of brute force, as the process could take a lifetime or two.

What Aubrey needed was a crib, a hint as to the type of key word that had been used. But where to start?

Aubrey whirled, heart racing, and stared back along the tunnel. His silence had been suddenly interrupted by a short, sharp explosion. It was followed by a growl, a deep mechanical rattling which stuttered and cut off.

Then all was quiet except for George's cursing.

Aubrey was already racing towards the disturbance when he registered that George's swearing wasn't shocked or fearful. It was the heartfelt tone of voice he reserved for recalcitrant machinery.

Rounding the corner, he slowed, both astonished and amused at the sight before him.

George had his head and shoulders buried in the innards of the tunnelling machine so far it looked as if the contraption was eating him. Caroline was in the cabin, scowling at the instrument panel.

Without removing his head, George flapped a hand. 'Try again!'

'Get out of the way first!' Caroline called.

George straightened. He'd removed his jacket and he had a large grease smear on one cheek. He smiled at his friend. 'Aubrey, we've got this thing working –'

The rest of his words were cut off by a deafening blast from the belly of the tunneller. Smoke erupted from a dozen different vibrating places. The whole thing shook like a volcano that had decided enough was enough and it *really* needed to clear its throat.

George stood back, beaming. 'Splendid, what?'

Aubrey was about to offer his congratulations when the tunneller coughed, missed more than a few strokes, and ground to a halt. George eyed it menacingly. 'Ghastly machine.' He glanced at Aubrey. 'I thought those printing presses were uncooperative. This thing makes them look as placid as a draught horse.'

Caroline leaped down from the cabin. 'I think the fuel line might be choked, with all the rock dust that must have been flying around. Would you like me to check, George?'

Aubrey finally found his words. 'How did you get it started?'

Caroline frowned. 'What?'

'It was locked. I checked it when we first found it. The ignition control was locked by the same sort of spell I'm grappling with up there.'

'Oh that.' Caroline waved a hand with a gesture that was so elegant it would make a ballet master cry. 'It was a magical key lock, verbal.'

Aubrey goggled.

'I thought everyone knew that,' George said smugly.

'Yes,' Caroline said. 'I would have thought you'd see that, with all your magical experience.'

'Key. The key word.'

'Yes, that's the nub of the problem, isn't it?' she said. 'Once I had it, the lock fell away and I could engage the ignition. Now, if only George can clear this fuel line . . .'

'But how did you find out the key word? Luck?'

'I don't trust to luck, Aubrey, you know that. It lets one down at the most awkward times.' She smiled, wickedly, and Aubrey saw how she'd been playing with him.

'I apologise,' he said quickly.

'What for?'

'For whatever I've done to make you keep me in suspense like this.'

'Oh, you've done nothing in particular. This time. Just keeping you on your toes.'

'Consider my toes totally extended at all times. Now, can you tell me how you came up with the key word?'

'It was written on a piece of paper pinned to the instrument panel.'

Aubrey blinked. 'I may be forced to revise my estimate of our foe's omnipotence.'

George shrugged. 'So he's forgetful. He can still be dangerous, you know.'

'And what was the key word, out of interest?' Aubrey said.

'It wasn't a word. It was a phrase.'

'Good idea. Even harder to guess.'

'Except if it's written down right in front of one,' George said.

'Of course. And what was this phrase?'

'The Lady of the Lake.'

Aubrey narrowed his eyes and stared at the rocky roof overhead. 'The Lady of the Lake,' he repeated. 'It must mean something to him.'

'Of course it does,' George said. 'It's the name of that show. He sings songs from it. I read about it in the newspaper: "A charming, romantic fantasy."'

'An opera?'

'Light opera,' Caroline said.

'I thought it was an operetta,' George said, interested.

'Regardless,' Aubrey said, 'Tremaine sings songs from it?'

'In his stage show. As Spinetti.'

Aubrey stood motionless as thoughts bounced around in his head. It could be the crib he was looking for. Music was apparently on Tremaine's mind – the reviews showed that he wasn't taking his role as a singer lightly. With his penchant for plots, counter-plots, false plots and plots that look like plots but are – underneath – schemes masquerading as plots, small things like key words could be hard to remember. What better way to remember them than to use something that was already on his mind?

'Let's leave the tunneller for now,' Aubrey suggested. 'I need your help to get into the Vault Room.'

'Happy to.' George actually gave the tunneller a kick. It was a light one, but the machine boomed hollowly, as if remorseful.

'How, Aubrey?' Caroline asked. 'Magic is your area of expertise, not ours.'

'True, but between us we might have a good coverage of musical theatre.'

Caroline's expression was a marvel of economy. In one tiny raising of her eyebrows, a hint of a twitch of the right corner of her lip and a slight, sceptical movement of her cheek, she managed to communicate that she had some doubts about Aubrey's sanity, but she was willing to go along with his suggestion because querying it now would result in a convoluted and long-winded attempt at explanation.

George merely slipped his jacket on. 'Right you are. This way?'

Half an hour later, they were all slumped around the false Old Man of Albion, defeated.

'We've tried the names of operas.' Caroline rubbed her forehead. 'Gallian, and from every part of Italia.'

George was sitting with his back to the rock. He had his eyes closed. 'We've tried light operas, operettas, comic operas, folk operas and every variation we could think of.'

'We've tried the names of singers, composers, lyricists, arrangers and costumiers,' Caroline said. 'Nothing's worked.'

Aubrey was bone weary. He leaned, arms crossed on his chest, against the foundations. 'I know,' he said. He groaned. 'But we're close. I can feel it.'

'I'm glad you can,' George said. 'Because all I feel is tired and sweaty.'

Aubrey straightened. His eyes widened. 'Oh, for an extendable and flexible leg.'

Caroline pointed at him. 'Clarity, please.'

Aubrey touched the rock. The magic still hummed under his fingertips. 'I need an extendable and flexible leg to kick myself with.'

'What have we missed?' she asked.

'Holmland. Tremaine has been in Holmland for some time now. He must have been listening to Holmland music, Holmland operas.'

'Holmland has operas?' George said.

'Of a sort. Long, long musical dramas about destiny, the gods and heroism.' He turned to the rock. '*Siegfried's Sister*.'

The rock disappeared.

While George scrambled to his feet, Aubrey couldn't keep a satisfied smile from his face. 'Schroeder's masterpiece,' he explained. 'A man searches for his long-lost sister, overcoming monsters, temptation and the irritating fact that the same stirring theme is played each time he strides onto the stage. It's become a point of national pride in Holmland to stage it on every conceivable occasion.'

Aubrey paused. Sister? Had Tremaine seen some personal parallels in *Siegfried's Sister*? Aubrey filed this one away for later consideration.

Caroline bent and peered into the gap that had

appeared in the wall of the foundations. 'It's overrated. Long, loud and laughable.'

'You've seen *Siegfried's Sister*?' Aubrey asked.

'My mother and father took me. While we were in Fisherberg.'

Caroline had been in Holmland? Aubrey hadn't known that. He put it with all the other reasons to be impressed by Caroline Hepworth.

Aubrey was first through after Caroline. Every sense was alert, and he carried an over-stoked traction engine in his chest where his heart had once been.

Hissing came from the gaslights in wall sconces. They cast a gentle radiance on the waist-high stacks of metal bricks, making them gleam with a lustre that could be only one thing.

'Gold,' he breathed, staggered by the sheer amount of it before him. Hundreds of bars of bullion beckoned to him, each with the unmistakeable stamp of the Bank of Albion.

'Good Lord,' George said as he entered. His head moved slowly from side to side, surveying the field of gold.

'Why isn't it in the actual vaults?' Caroline asked. She moved slowly in the Vault Room, with the reluctance of someone not wanting to disturb a pleasant dream.

The massive doors to the inner vaults were closed. 'I don't know,' Aubrey said. 'All ready for the King to bless?'

George squatted in front of the nearest pile. 'They're on trolleys. They're either going out of the vault or just going in. And I'll warrant that these chests are full of sovereigns.'

Aubrey felt strangely reluctant to approach the gold. Instead, he stood and surveyed the scene, trying to ease the tension from his shoulders.

His gaze fell on an ominous black box in the far corner of the vault. It was slim, featureless, about shoulder height, and it was so discreet that Aubrey had – at first – ignored it as a fixture of the room.

Then he realised that an identical unit stood in the other corner.

He took a step further into the vault and saw that the corners nearest him also sported the black boxes.

While George and Caroline marvelled at the gold, picking up bars and exclaiming at their weight, Aubrey inspected the nearest of the black boxes. Then he had a thought. He took out his handkerchief and shook it. He plucked a simple spell from his memory, one of the first he'd ever learned, just after he'd turned ten. He spoke it softly, but clearly, and let go of the handkerchief.

The spell cost him a bright bolt of pain right behind his forehead, but it worked. The handkerchief fell a little, then caught itself in mid-air. It twisted itself into a vaguely human shape – four limbs, a trunk, a head – and bobbed in the space between his two hands. It danced there for a moment, until he cancelled the spell.

Aubrey glanced at the inert black boxes and stowed his handkerchief in his pocket. *All is not as it seems, it seems.* He shrugged. With Dr Tremaine involved, why would he expect any different?

'No time for party tricks, old man,' George called. 'Come and look at the riches of Albion.'

Aubrey strolled over, humming something remotely Holmlandish. 'We have a mystery here.'

Caroline raised an eyebrow. 'Of course. Why should the vault of the Bank of Albion be any different to everywhere else we've visited?'

Aubrey pointed to the black boxes in the corners of the vault. 'Those units are magic suppressors.'

'Like the Great Manfred had for his stage act?' George said. 'Good show. Should stop any magical mischief around here.'

Caroline said nothing. She merely pointed to the gaping hole in the wall. George scratched his chin. 'Or not, as the case may be.'

They both looked at Aubrey.

'I tried some small magic, something that should have been impossible within the anti-magic field, but it worked.'

'The magic suppressors aren't active?' George said.

'What's this mean?' Caroline said.

'I think it important to find out,' Aubrey said. 'George, do you still have that pry bar?'

Some muscle work later, Aubrey was convinced. The magic suppressor had been tampered with.

Inside the slim black box were three separate compartments. Each was sealed, but proved to be no match for George's handy implement. The top compartment was full of components that looked like the interior of a radio – valves and wires, wrapped tightly in rubberised cloth. The middle compartment was a solid block of a hard, black ceramic. The bottom compartment was the largest, and contained four metal bars that stretched from the top of the compartment to the bottom. When Aubrey touched one of the bars, it vibrated. An instant later, the other three bars began to vibrate in sympathy.

'But you say it's not working?' Caroline said.

'No. All the components look whole and complete, but something is missing.'

'Or tampered with,' George suggested.

'Rokeby-Taylor's company makes these,' Aubrey said. 'Why does that prompt suspicion?'

'The units are sealed,' Caroline said. 'If an outsider had tampered with these things, the evidence would be obvious.'

'But if the tampering were done at the factory? They would seem to be one thing, and actually be another.' Such a state of affairs was not unusual where Dr Tremaine was concerned. Aubrey's gaze fell on the astounding collection of gold. Frowning, he approached the nearest chest and opened it. Hundreds of sovereigns glinted back at him.

He guessed that the Vault Room held enough gold to finance a moderately-sized nation. 'Dr Tremaine wants to steal the gold.'

'Well, he won't succeed,' George declared. 'Not now that we've found the back door he organised.'

'No.' Aubrey wasn't convinced. 'A Holmlandish battleship is sailing for Fisherberg later this week.'

'Elektor's birthday,' George said. 'The *Imperator* must be there for that.'

'With a few tons of gold in its hold?' Caroline wondered.

'And the Rashid Stone, don't forget,' Aubrey said.

'So Dr Tremaine planned to get all this gold out of here, through the tunnels and down to the docks?

Incredible.' George shook his head. 'What an outcry that would make.'

'Outcry?' Aubrey said. 'It certainly would. Scandal, uproar, outrage. Messy, but not crippling.'

'Not crippling?' Caroline said. 'All this gold vanishing?'

'Probably not. The empire could cope. It might even unite the country, especially since it could be seen as a direct insult to the King, his not being able to complete one of our traditions.' Aubrey picked up one of the sovereigns. He'd been expecting the weight of it, but it still took him by surprise. It was unexpectedly warm, too, quite unlike holding a similar silver or copper coin.

He hefted the coin and then replaced it in the chest.

'I wonder,' he said, then he paused.

'That's quite dramatic enough a pause,' Caroline said, tapping her foot. 'Finish your sentence.'

He swept a hand over the stacks of gold. 'I wonder if this is gold at all.'

Silence.

'If it's not gold,' George said eventually, 'it's a very convincing substitute.'

'Exactly. Surely you've heard of fairy gold?'

'Fairy gold?' Caroline said. 'It's a fairy story.'

'It's an example of life imitating art,' Aubrey said, slipping into his instructional mode. 'The Holmlanders, especially, have been fascinated by magic stories for children, handed down over the generations. Some of their researchers have been studying these stories to see if there are any truths to be found. A few years ago, Professor Esselbach in Vessenheim managed to establish a spell that – for all intents and purposes – mimicked that of fairy gold.'

'What?' George said. 'Something that looks like gold, but vanishes in the bearer's pocket?'

'Esselbach drew on the Law of Similarity and the Law of Permanence. His gold looked like gold, felt like gold, but after a pre-determined period of time, it evaporated and left nothing behind.'

'Nice party trick,' George said.

'With some practical applications I can think of,' Caroline said.

'Imagine what would happen to the economy of Albion,' Aubrey said, 'if fairy gold was distributed throughout the land. Especially after the King had laid his hands on it.'

George's eyes widened. 'I wouldn't like to be the shopkeeper who opened his till to find his sovereigns gone.'

'It's more than that,' Caroline said slowly. 'Once suspicions are roused about the genuineness of the currency, it could cause financial instability. A run on the banks, at the very least, I'd say.'

'Lovely mischief-making for an enemy power,' Aubrey said. 'It would slow down our economy dreadfully. Much more than a simple theft of bullion.'

George slapped his pry bar in his palm. 'And it'd put a brake on our armament program. Especially our shipbuilding.'

'And if Dr Tremaine could somehow get the real gold into the hold of the *Imperator*, it would be a double win for Holmland.' Aubrey chewed his lip. With Dr Tremaine's penchant for plots within plots, he wouldn't be surprised if some of the gold went missing on its way to the docks. Dr Tremaine had never been known for frugal living.

'And is it fairy gold?' George asked. 'How can you tell?'

'That's the point,' Aubrey said. 'You can't.' He scooped up some sovereigns and poured them from hand to hand. 'Without magic.'

Caroline crossed her arms. 'Go to it, then.'

Aubrey dropped all the sovereigns but one. He held it close, examining its inscription, the portrait of the King, the slightly grainy sheen of gold. He flipped it and it spun, catching the gaslight. Deftly, he caught it in his palm and covered it with his other hand.

He closed his eyes and extended his magical awareness.

There, he thought. A faint, tell-tale quality that spoke of a magical rather than a natural origin. It was like a hint of a scent, a tickling greenish smell with the distinctive, veiled signature of the enemy.

He opened his eyes. 'It's not real. And it was conjured up by Dr Tremaine.'

Caroline glanced at the gold with some disappointment. 'Oh.'

'What is it?'

'What would be worse than fairy gold crippling our economy?'

'Worse?' George said. 'Dashed hard to think of anything worse, old girl.'

Caroline shot George a look. 'Old girl?'

'Sorry,' he said. 'Don't know what got into me. *Caroline*, I meant to say.'

'Thank you. Where was I?'

'Worse than a crippled economy,' Aubrey said.

'Thank you, Aubrey.'

'I hang on your every word.'

She shot him a look as well, but continued. 'The bank always waits for the King's ceremony before undertaking certain customary transactions. It's tradition.'

'It does? How do you know this?'

'Norman Hood. The chief governor was a friend of my father's. He made sure Sir Norman gave me a number of lessons in the functions of the bank.'

'So you're talking about annual transactions? Annual transactions that would require moving around a lot of gold?' Aubrey's heart sank as he anticipated Caroline's next words.

'Settling international debt, in particular. Traditionally, Albion has waited until after the King's blessing before shipping gold off to any nation we owe money to.'

Suddenly, Aubrey realised, a potentially enormous problem had just become even larger.

'I see why you're upset,' George said. 'It'd be a nice way to offend any potential allies, wouldn't it? Offering stacks of gold to settle a debt only to find out some time later that it melted away.'

Aubrey knew that every nation on the globe was scrambling to cement friendships in this precarious world. With every indication that a war was imminent, allies were vital. If Albion was seen as untrustworthy or – even worse – duplicitous, it could find itself alone in a hostile international landscape.

He raked back his hair with both hands. 'Well, it looks as if we've managed to prevent this, at any rate. Should we go upstairs and raise the alarm?'

Caroline gave him a look of approval and he vowed to do his best to earn more of them.

He was about to offer her his arm when George

cleared his throat. 'Sorry to be a wet blanket, but I've just been thinking about these magic suppressor thingies.'

'Thingies?' Deep inside, a misgiving or two woke, as if they'd heard their name being called.

'Well, they must have been working when they were first installed. You saw the units in the main banking chamber in action, didn't you?'

'They worked perfectly.' Aubrey winced. His misgivings were now rampaging around inside his stomach. 'And the governors would have insisted on testing these units, especially after the failed break-in.' He bounced over to the nearest suppressor, frowning, and ran his fingers over it, peering at its flat black surface. 'So if anyone was going to do anything magical in here – such as replacing the Old Man of Albion and creating a mountain of fairy gold – these suppressors must be able to be shut off at a distance. Radio, perhaps?'

A voice came from the corner of the vault nearest the Old Man of Albion. 'Interesting idea, but no. I used magic. A neat little application of the Law of Opposites, actually.'

It was as if the space between Aubrey's Adam's apple and navel had been replaced by a block of ice. Slowly, he turned, while George let out an oath.

Dr Tremaine stepped forward, brushing dust from his shoulders.

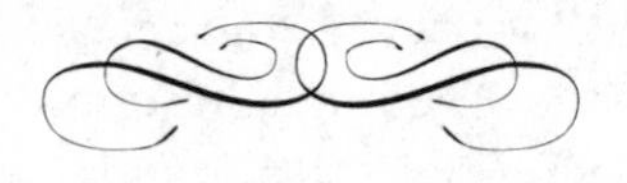

Eighteen

'TREMAINE,' AUBREY GROWLED. HE'D GROWN TOO accustomed to the renegade's mercurial behaviour to be surprised at his appearance, but his casual demeanour made Aubrey extremely wary.

Dr Tremaine shook his head, as if Aubrey was a slow student. 'I was afraid you'd missed the implications of my little plan entirely. Luckily, you have Miss Hepworth to help you.'

He bowed in Caroline's direction. She gazed at him steadily with such venom that Aubrey was surprised the ex-Sorcerer Royal didn't drop dead on the spot.

'And your remarkably unimaginative friend even managed to play a part.'

'Who?' George said. 'Me? I'm offended by that, Tremaine.'

Tremaine bowed again. 'I aim not to disappoint.' He glanced at a watch on his wrist. 'Now, Fitzwilliam, I must say that your timing is abominable, as usual. Interrupting my important work like this? Most regrettable.'

The ex-Sorcerer Royal behaved as if he belonged in the vault of the Bank of Albion. Tall, broad-shouldered, with long black hair, he leaned against the wall and yawned. He wore a midnight blue frock coat, cutaway, and he held a cane. 'And just in case you were wondering why you couldn't see me as I stood here, listening to your ponderous deductions, I played around with Dimensionality, just like the batteries in the *Electra.*'

'That *was* you, then.'

'Sinking it was a daft idea, I tried telling the Holmlanders that. A waste of fine engineering. Nevertheless, heads of intelligence services will insist on having ideas of their own, won't they?' He held up his cane. 'Recognise this, Fitzwilliam? It should have a pearl on top, and I've a mind to reclaim it.'

'That can wait,' Aubrey said. His palms prickled with sweat.

'That's your problem, Fitzwilliam. You get your priorities mixed up. You put the public ahead of the personal.'

'I do? I mean, isn't that the way it should be?'

Dr Tremaine laughed. 'You couldn't be more wrong, my boy. The personal always comes first. Always, always, always. It's the only way to achieve anything.'

'Well, you're not achieving your goals with this little scheme, are you? We've messed it up for you, well and truly.'

Dr Tremaine clapped his hands together. 'That, of course, depends.'

'Depends? On what?'

'On your getting out of here alive.'

It was the combination that took Dr Tremaine by surprise. George roared and charged from his left, swinging the pry bar. At the same instant, while his attention was taken by the whistling length of steel, Caroline slipped up from behind.

But even then, Aubrey had bad feelings about this multiple attack. Tremaine was as far away from the traditional notion of a namby-pamby magician as one could get. He'd boxed several noted prize-fighters to standstill, both gloved and bare-knuckle. He was also a fine wrestler.

And he's the most powerful magician in the world.

Tremaine moved towards George's wild charge. He side-stepped just enough for the pry bar to hiss past his nose. This put George off balance and Dr Tremaine reached out, grabbed his arm and wrenched. George cartwheeled away and crashed into the wall.

With balletic ease, the ex-Sorcerer Royal pivoted in time to meet Caroline's challenge. He grinned like a crocodile. 'Ah, Miss Hepworth! I see you've been instructed by Master Wu. Very fine indeed!'

Caroline didn't answer. She turned side on and advanced.

Aubrey normally would have been fascinated to watch Caroline move so gracefully, but his thoughts were elsewhere.

He desperately needed to activate the magic suppressors.

Dr Tremaine was playing with George and Caroline. He didn't need to meet any physical challenges – he'd have a hundred spells he could use to disable them. But if Aubrey could make the magic suppressors work again, the odds could be evened – especially if Tremaine was unaware of this change of events.

Dr Tremaine said he'd used the Law of Opposites. Could it be as simple as thinking of the magic suppressors as having two possible states – active and inactive? With the correct spell, a magician could change the state of an object, flip-flopping from active to inactive, from hot to cold, from light to dark. The effect was simple, the spell fiendishly complex. Completely reversing a state, in its most fundamental aspects? Lanka Ravi's work suggested why this was difficult. Most magicians wouldn't even try.

But it was just the sort of thing Dr Tremaine would attempt – and succeed at. It was uncommon, difficult, and needed sheer brilliance to achieve.

And, Aubrey thought, *it's a red herring.*

Where Mordecai Tremaine was concerned, Aubrey had learned that jumping to conclusions was a deadly pastime. When an answer fitted perfectly, it had to be wrong. He had to find the solution behind the solution.

A spell couldn't work in the field of magic suppression cast by the devices, not even a clever spell using the Law of Opposites. Tremaine was lying, Aubrey should have known that.

But what did that leave?

Aubrey sprinted for the nearest suppressor. He tore it open and scanned the contents feverishly.

Nothing.

He straightened to see the improbable sight of Dr Tremaine flying through the air, his coat flapping like a vast pair of wings. He lost his grip on his cane and it clattered onto the nearest stack of fairy gold. He landed like a sack of wheat thrown from a first-storey window, grunted, but rolled to his feet immediately. 'A fine throw, young lady,' he cried. He slapped at his coat, dusting himself off. 'But even Master Wu has his limitations, as you're about to find out.'

Aubrey's impulse was to help Caroline. But while she looked pale and strained Aubrey knew what a formidable fighter she was – he'd only get in the way. He raced for the next magic suppressor, knowing that all Tremaine had to do was disable one and the suppressors would be unable to generate a field.

Aubrey cursed. Its workings were exactly the same.

Except . . .

With a knuckle, he banged on the block of black ceramic in the middle of the box. It made a hollow noise, as if it were a mere eggshell. Gritting his teeth, he made a fist. He punched the ceramic and it shattered.

Inside was the workings of a clock.

Aubrey actually turned away and then looked back, unwilling to believe his eyes. The second time, he realised that while the gears and springs may have been clockwork, it had never driven a pair of hands to tell the time. It was a machine set to disable the magic suppressor.

A small pair of spring-loaded, very sharp blades had been arranged either side of a wire which ran between the top compartment and the bottom. The clockwork mechanism was attached to these blades. When it unwound, it released the tension on the blades and they snapped shut, severing the wire. A crucial wire, Aubrey had no doubt.

It was simple, it was ingenious, it was nearly foolproof.

But all it needed was for the wire to be reconnected for the suppressor to work again.

Feverishly, Aubrey tore away the clockwork mechanism and flung it to the ground. He dragged his new watch out of his pocket and yanked. The chain tore away the button and it dangled, loose. The Brayshire Ruby winked at him.

He spared an instant to regret his actions, then he went ahead. He tugged, the chain parted. He slipped the watch into his pocket and caught the chain before it fell.

With quick, precise movements, he bent the remains of the wires and linked them with the gold chain.

Heart pounding, he swivelled in time to see Dr Tremaine block a lightning-fast blow from Caroline. He was grinning, fiercely. 'Good!' he shouted. 'But this is better!'

He twisted, moving both forearms against each other, catching Caroline's fist in mid-strike. She was flung aside as if she was a doll. The wall was too close. Before she had time to cry out, she crashed into it.

Dr Tremaine turned, panting, and faced Aubrey. 'Ah, the child wonder! You're still here?'

'Where else would I be?' George was slumped on the floor near Tremaine. Aubrey was relieved to see that he was still breathing, even though his eyes were closed.

Where was that pry bar?

'And that's the pity of it.' Dr Tremaine's dark eyes glittered. 'You should leave well enough alone, Fitzwilliam. Stay out of things that don't concern you. Adopt a quiet, contemplative life. It's the only way to ensure your integrity, shall we say?'

Aubrey blinked. While Dr Tremaine had been talking, he'd made his way halfway across the vault, weaving in and out of the stacks of gold. Aubrey hadn't even noticed.

'If you're talking about my condition, I've made some significant improvements there. It's no longer an issue.'

'I'm sure you've done what you can. But death magic is a perilous area to work in for the uninitiated. And leaving yourself unprotected, as you did, is a difficult mistake to remedy. Adopting the life of a recluse is best for you, you know that. No strain, no excitement. You should be able to live out a relatively normal span, if a boring one.'

Aubrey was strangely heartened by Dr Tremaine's advice. It showed that despite his powers, he didn't know everything. *If he thinks I'd be happy mouldering away, living as a hermit, he's insane.* 'Excellent advice,' he said to Dr Tremaine, who had sidled his way to within a few yards. 'After I make sure you're safely imprisoned, I'll think about it.'

Dr Tremaine shook his head. 'You disappoint me, like everyone else.' He sighed and let his hands drop to his sides. 'Despite that, I will try to make this as painless as possible. Which is an interesting point in itself, as no-one has ever come back to report on the pain levels of this particular method of demise.'

Aubrey backed against a stack of gold. Dr Tremaine barked a spell – a long, convoluted series of expressions that Aubrey recognised as Akkadian. It ended with a flourish – not a cryptic one, but a defiantly Tremaine-esque finial that stamped the ego of the originator on the spell.

Nothing happened.

Aubrey took great delight in the expression on the magician's face. Disbelief, astonishment and fury warred for possession, with the result that the great ex-Sorcerer Royal stood looking as if he'd been struck between the eyes with a cricket ball. He actually rocked on his feet, then his eyes narrowed and he snarled. 'The magic suppressors.'

Aubrey shrugged and scrabbled behind his back. 'Good machinery. It was a shame to see them sitting idle.'

'So I am left to my own resources.' Dr Tremaine flexed his shoulders and strode towards Aubrey. 'I don't imagine this is going to be much of a problem. More painful for you, I'm afraid, but you've brought it upon yourself.'

Heart pounding, Aubrey lifted the gold bar he'd separated from the stack behind him. Crying out with the effort, he heaved it at the charging figure of Dr Tremaine.

With a sickening crack, it took him flush on the chest. Dr Tremaine grunted and fell sideways. He sprawled across the nearest stack of gold where he clung, one-handed. 'That, Fitzwilliam,' he gasped, 'was uncalled for.'

'Uncalled for?' Aubrey picked up another gold bar. 'You were going to kill me!'

'For the greater good.' Dr Tremaine groaned. 'For the greater good.' He closed his eyes and rested his head on the bullion.

'For the greater good? Whose greater good?'

Dr Tremaine opened eyes that were full of contempt. 'Mine, of course, you idiot.'

He struggled upright, using the stack of bullion for support. His right arm was held tightly against his side, but now he had a revolver in his left.

Aubrey couldn't help it. Part of his brain noted that it was a Symons service revolver, the Mark V model, not the more common Mark IV, and that it had been well used. It was large: a .450 calibre. It was more than enough to punch a hole right through him from this distance.

'I always have backup.' Tremaine's voice was hoarse and he had blood at the corner of his mouth. He winced as he breathed. Aubrey hoped he'd cracked a rib. 'Noisy, messy, but it should do the trick.'

Tremaine coughed and grimaced. As a distraction, Aubrey decided it was as good as it was going to get. He flung himself sideways behind the nearest stack of bullion. The revolver roared. The air was instantly full of cordite smoke and the enclosed space of the vault echoed with disapproval.

Aubrey crawled as fast as he could through the aisles made by the stacks of bullion, his back itching as he imagined Dr Tremaine rounding the corner. He went left, then right, then the revolver fired again, but it was followed by bellowing and a string of quick, heartfelt curses.

Aubrey risked a quick head bob. Dr Tremaine was standing in the middle of the stacks of gold. He was trying to complete the difficult task of clamping one arm to his side while using it to cradle his other wrist. The revolver was nowhere to be seen, but the handy pry bar was. Spinning on top of the bullion, it was the object of Dr Tremaine's wrath.

'Call it an unimaginative throw, Tremaine,' George cried. 'I think it worked well enough.' Then he hefted a bar of gold and heaved it at the wounded magician.

Dr Tremaine ducked and let out an almost animal growl. He glanced at George, then at Aubrey, then at the gold. He glowered, bared his teeth, then, with an enormous effort, he used his damaged hand to extract a glass globe from the inner pocket of his coat. It was the size of an orange, but something green inside it swirled ominously.

'Look out!' Aubrey shouted, but Dr Tremaine dismissed him with a snarl. He hurled the globe to the floor and immediately the vault was full of dense, white smoke.

'Stop him!' Aubrey called. 'The door!' He choked, then coughed, and groped for clearer air. The smoke was thick, and stung his eyes. He knew he wouldn't be able to see if an elephant happened to choose that moment to stroll though the Vault Room. He took a step, but collided painfully with a chest of sovereigns.

'Which door?' George shouted.

'The Old Man of Albion!'

At that moment, revolver fire cracked – once, twice, three times. Aubrey dived for where he hoped the floor was and flung his hands over his head. Exactly what good that would do, he wasn't sure, but he was grateful when the floor was where it promised to be.

A dark-clad figure loomed in front of him. Ears ringing, Aubrey lifted his head, but all he could see were black trousers and a revolver dangling at knee height in front of him. He was relieved to see that the legs in those trousers were infinitely more attractive than Dr Tremaine's.

'Get up, Aubrey,' Caroline said. 'I think I hit him.'

'You hit him?'

'Oh yes. He managed to lock the Old Man of Albion behind him, but I got in three shots before it materialised fully. And I don't miss. Not at that range.'

'I don't doubt it,' Aubrey said fervently.

IT TOOK SOME TIME – AND SEVERAL TELEPHONE CALLS – before they could establish their credentials to the satisfaction of the nightwatchman who'd been aroused by the commotion. Despite Aubrey's best efforts at persuasion, he kept them waiting behind the locked, barred gates of the Vault Room. Even after Caroline slid the revolver to him, the nightwatchman continued to eye them with the sort of caution that rabid dogs usually inspired.

It was only when Sir Darius appeared – looking immaculate, even though it was nearly four o'clock in the morning – with Sir Norman Hood that the nightwatchman used his keys in the lock. His every movement promised that some time soon he'd be saying to someone: 'You'll never guess what happened at work tonight . . .'

'Miss Hepworth,' Sir Darius said immediately, 'you're unhurt?'

'I'm quite well, Sir Darius. Thank you.' She nodded at Sir Norman.

Bells sounded from the street. 'That will be the police,' Sir Darius said. 'I alerted them. Be prepared for several squads, plus people from Special Services and the Magisterium.'

'Of course, Prime Minister,' Sir Norman said. 'The only thing that could be done, in the circumstances.'

'Please let those in charge know that I'll have these young people at Maidstone, ready for interview once they've had some sleep.'

Sir Norman huffed and puffed like a steam locomotive and shepherded them through the hordes of uniformed officers that were pounding over the marble floor of the main banking chamber. The whole bank was lit, and Aubrey wondered what nocturnal passers-by would be thinking. All-night bank-note counting? A bank tellers' knees-up?

The Oakleigh-Nash was waiting outside the bank, Stubbs ready at the rear door. Aubrey was reassured to see that underneath the driver's greatcoat was the tell-tale shape of a pistol.

'Miss Hepworth,' Sir Darius said. 'I hope you'll accept an invitation to a room for the night at Maidstone. I'll contact your mother the first thing in the morning, but I don't feel that rousing her this early would be polite or helpful.'

'Thank you, Sir Darius. I appreciate it.'

He bowed, slightly. 'I'm glad. I'm sure the authorities might have insisted on taking you, otherwise.' He assisted her into the car, then glanced at Aubrey. 'You have a story to report, Aubrey?'

'It's Dr Tremaine, sir. He's definitely back.'

'You're sure?'

'It was him, Sir Darius,' George said. 'No mistaking it.'

'You've saved the nation again, I suppose?' his father said.

Aubrey gestured at his friends. '*We've* saved the nation again.'

Aubrey stood with one hand on the polished roof of the Oakleigh-Nash. The sky was brighter, the buildings about more distinct. 'A new day,' he said, and it felt good. Even though his exertions had left him exhausted, bruised and drained, it still felt good. The night's escapade was thrilling, hair-raising and utterly, utterly addictive.

He wanted more of it. The trouble was, he wanted more of everything.

And right now, he thought, *some sleep is what I want most.*

He yawned.

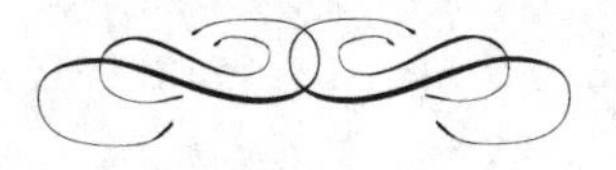

Nineteen

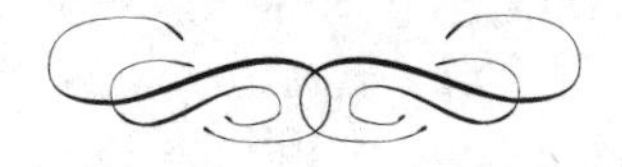

SATISFACTION AT HAVING FOILED DR TREMAINE'S PLOT gave Aubrey some solace as he suffered from the effects of his exertions in the Vault Room of the Bank of Albion. He was exhausted, but had found it hard to sleep. He had a thundering headache and he was dismayed to find that he'd had a nosebleed in the night. His pillow looked as if someone had cut his throat and he had to expend some energy to calm Tilly, who brought his morning cup of tea, when she saw the gore.

Despite the summons to an urgent meeting in the library, Aubrey took his time, limping through his ablutions and doing his best to gather himself before fronting to what he imagined would be an inquisition. He chose a bold, green-striped tie, hoping it would take some attention away from his slightly trembling hands.

His satisfaction dwindled as he washed his pale, drawn face and saw in the mirror his deeply bloodshot eyes – evidence of the consequences of his decision to return to magic. He shrugged. He would have to endure it.

The head of the Urban Police was John Pierce, an experienced officer in his sixties, large-framed, grey-haired, alarmingly whiskered. He was renowned as the scourge of villains throughout the city, and a man with forty hard years on the force.

Yet he sat behind the table, looking both wary and intimidated by the two men either side of him – Tallis of the Special Services and Craddock of the Magisterium.

While he was a phlegmatic man, he could not have been unaware of the tension between Tallis and Craddock. Without a harsh word being spoken, without an unprofessional look, the two were waging an invisible war. Pierce kept glancing from side to side as if he were suffering from incidental blows to the head.

Wearily, with limbs that felt as if they'd doubled in weight, Aubrey admired the seating arrangements that had been hastily set up in a vacant room on the second floor of Maidstone. The table behind which the heads of the concerned authorities sat was big enough for the three men, directly in front of and a good five yards away from the straight-backed chairs where Aubrey, George and Caroline sat.

Sir Darius was in an easy chair, situated against the wall, near the door, halfway between the questioners and the questionees. Whenever he contributed, the questioners had to look to their right, and the questionees to their left. It broke the confrontation beautifully.

'So you're saying that the gold is now in the hold of the *Imperator*?' Tallis said to Aubrey.

'Most likely. What's left in the vault of the bank is mostly fairy gold.' Aubrey held his hands together in front of him to disguise their trembling.

Craddock tapped the table with his forefinger. 'I have a squad of operatives testing it. I'm sure it's as you say.'

'So we have an incident on our hands,' Sir Darius said. 'It seems as if I'll need to summon Cabinet.'

'We can't just go marching onto their battleship and demand to examine below decks,' Aubrey said. He straightened, feeling slightly stronger as a plan unfolded in front of him. 'Some tricky negotiation ahead, I'd say.'

Sir Darius nodded. 'Quite.'

'And you think you shot Dr Tremaine?' Tallis said to Caroline. 'How could you be sure? You said the vault was full of smoke.'

'I don't think I'd miss the man who killed my father.'

Tallis blinked, then suddenly found the papers on the table in front of him very interesting. 'Of course.'

'Besides,' George said. 'He had a broken wrist and a few cracked ribs to contend with. He wasn't at his most nimble.'

'It's remarkable then,' Tallis said, 'that we've found no trace of him.'

'You've sent operatives after him?' Aubrey wasn't optimistic.

'Of course,' Craddock said. 'We would have liked to examine the tunneller you spoke of, too. It sounded like a fascinating piece of machinery.'

'Would have?' Aubrey echoed. He knew congratulations had been premature.

'We couldn't find it,' Tallis said. 'At least, it wasn't where you said it was.'

If Tremaine had activated the tunneller, then there was no doubt he'd escaped.

'It might interest you to know,' Tallis went on, 'that a certain singer, an Arturo Spinetti, didn't appear for his show last night. According to the theatre manager, he's been abducted. The theatre district is in uproar. Although how anyone can tell the difference, I have no idea.'

'It's a flimsy excuse,' Craddock said, 'and this circumstance does tend to support your story that Spinetti could be Tremaine.'

'He is. Was.' Aubrey had mixed feelings. He felt vindicated, but also a touch guilty. If he'd raised more of a hue and cry, could Tremaine have been stopped earlier?

In the pause, Pierce saw an opportunity to play some part in proceedings. 'You'll all have to come down to headquarters and make a statement, you understand.'

Tallis frowned. Craddock looked at the police officer as if he was a performing dog. 'I'm sure there's no need for that,' he said. 'The Prime Minister will make sure that these young people write everything down. It will get to you as soon as we've gone over it.'

Pierce frowned. His bushy eyebrows were two caterpillars muscling up to each other.

'Only if that is acceptable to you, Pierce,' Sir Darius said carefully. 'Otherwise, I'll bring them to your headquarters immediately.'

Pierce visibly chewed on this. He glanced at Tallis and Craddock. 'We have our processes.'

'Agreed,' Sir Darius said.

'But it's been a shock, no doubt. The statements can wait.'

Sir Darius stood. 'Very well then. But if you change your mind, we'll be at Barker Street promptly.'

Caroline stood, as did Aubrey and George. Aubrey rubbed his forehead, but a thought occurred to him. 'Commander Craddock, have you read the memo I sent you about Ravi's recent breakthroughs?'

'Go on.'

'It's just that I was thinking about the Law of Displacement. Perhaps.'

'Aubrey?' Sir Darius said. 'You're not speaking very clearly.'

'Sorry, sir. I'm still rather tired.' He cleared his throat. It was thick and cloggy. 'The fairy gold and the real gold. That's what I'm thinking of. With some careful spell construction, it should be possible to switch the two.'

'Ingenious,' Craddock said. Tallis sat back and wrinkled his brow.

'Circumstances won't get any better,' Aubrey went on. 'The fairy gold and the real gold share weight, dimensions, almost everything, really. The variables are kept to a minimum.' He warmed to his subject. 'Of course, distance is a factor, but we know where the *Imperator* is docked. I'm sure the fairy gold could be moved to a warehouse nearby to make the transference easier. I'm happy to help your people, if you like.'

'No need,' Craddock said. 'I have a squad of operatives ready to work on matters such as these.'

'You have? Oh.'

'Mr Ravi has been working with this special squad for some time. I'm sure they'll be able to swing onto this task.' He allowed himself a thin smile. 'The Holmlanders won't even know what happened. Not until the fairy gold disappears.'

Lanka Ravi was assisting the Magisterium now? That was news. Things must have moved apace after Aubrey's report.

And how did this fit with Tallis's revelation of the Magisterium doing original research?

'I'm sure you were going to tell me about this in due course,' Sir Darius said to Craddock, but his tone said otherwise.

'Naturally, sir. When matters were a little closer to resolution.'

'It changes the situation,' Sir Darius said. 'But it's even more reason for me to call Cabinet together. This is going to affect Defence, the Foreign Secretary, the Chancellor of the Exchequer, the Home Secretary.'

'Once the bullion reaches Holmland, it's bound to be put into circulation, eventually. Imagine the Holmland armament manufacturers when their gold evaporates,' Aubrey said. 'It's going to put a dent in their war effort if we can pull it off.'

'Which isn't a bad thing,' George said. 'Maybe your Holmlander friends might be able to make use of this, Aubrey. They could expose Dr Tremaine and his cronies as thieves or incompetents, ruining the Holmland economy. Brandt and his cohort could sail back into Fisherberg as saviours?'

Craddock shook his head. 'I don't think so. Manfred has reported that Brandt and his people are moving their plans forward in a different direction, with encouragement from their well-placed friends in Holmland.' He studied Aubrey. 'He still wants you to reconsider the offer to accompany him to Fisherberg. I told him that this was not feasible.'

'Sorry, Aubrey,' Sir Darius said. 'Not a wise idea, I'm afraid.'

Aubrey rubbed the back of his aching neck. He had no sense of this multiple-headed affair coming to a conclusion. It was like trying to cross a room scattered with ball-bearings that kept skating off in unexpected directions.

Or was he being *steered* in directions?

He nodded to his father. 'If it's all right, sir, I'd like to get some more rest.'

Sir Darius looked to the interrogation table. 'Gentlemen?'

At that moment, the door was flung open. Lady Rose stood there, hands on hips. 'What on earth is going on?'

WHILE SIR DARIUS SAW OUT THE THREE LAW ENFORCEMENT officials, Lady Rose ordered Aubrey, Caroline and George to her drawing room. Amid the tribal masks, bark paintings and dried-flower arrangements, she listened as Aubrey recounted the night's events all over again. He didn't even pause when his father slipped in and joined Lady Rose on the shot silk sofa.

'And so we saved Albion from financial ruin,' he finished. 'Have I missed anything?'

'Of course,' Caroline said. 'But I'm trying to decide how much of it was deliberate and how much is simple forgetfulness.'

'What about this Maggie and her Crew, Aubrey?' George said. 'They're still missing.'

'Ah. I did forget that. I'm sorry. I shouldn't have. I'll have to let Jack Figg know we haven't found them.'

'Jack Figg?' Lady Rose said. 'I hope he's over his cold.'

Aubrey, Caroline and George stared at Lady Rose. 'You've seen Jack lately?' Aubrey asked.

'I asked him to the museum a few days ago, and we went to lunch. I wanted to discuss a new project with him.'

'Another clinic?'

'One attached to his home for unemployed miners. He's doing fine work.'

Aubrey shook his head. His mother – both his parents – were sources of ongoing wonder to him. 'You do understand that he's actively working to bring down the government, don't you?'

'Good luck to him.' Lady Rose leaned over and shifted a vase of feathers so they wouldn't obscure an outstandingly ugly statue. 'Healthy dissent is the sign of a robust democracy. Isn't it, dear?'

'I don't agree with everything Figg stands for,' Sir Darius said, 'but I'm glad to have him as an active voice. It stops us getting fat and lazy, taking things for granted. He shines a light on areas that need it.'

'So what are you three up to now?' Lady Rose said.

'Rest,' Aubrey said. 'I'm exhausted.'

'You do look pale,' Lady Rose said. 'Are you sure you're not coming down with something?'

Aubrey didn't know quite what to say. 'I'm well enough.'

'I should be getting home to see Mother,' Caroline said. 'She likes to be kept informed about our excursions.'

'Excursions?' George said. 'That's a nice way of putting it. Slogging through underground tunnels, battling a renegade magical genius . . . "Excursion" makes it sound comfy, like a nature ramble.'

'Exactly,' Caroline said. 'Perhaps we could meet and catch the train back to Greythorn tomorrow evening, Aubrey, George?'

'Delighted,' Aubrey said. Caroline made her farewells to Lady Rose and Sir Darius, and was shown out. Aubrey watched her go with the wistfulness he always felt when she left.

'If you're just going to lie about,' George said, 'I'll dash up and see how the parents are getting on. I can catch a train from Fasham Square, just before lunch.'

'Hmm,' Sir Darius said. 'You can ride a motorcycle, can't you, George?'

Aubrey thought George's grin was half-hearted. 'Motorcycle? What country lad can't?'

'I have a Kenyon Special in the stables. It's in good shape, but hasn't been ridden for ages. Needs the cobwebs blown out of it.'

'What? No, I couldn't, Sir Darius.'

'You'd be doing me a favour, George. '

'Well, if I can help . . .'

'Excellent.' Sir Darius rang the servant's bell. A quick conversation with Harris, the butler, and all was arranged. 'Fifteen minutes, George. Stubbs will have the machine waiting at the front door.'

When George had gone, Aubrey draped both arms over the back of the chair and groaned.

'You're not really going to sleep all day, are you?' his mother said.

'It sounds appealing, but I don't think so.'

'I'm at the museum this afternoon. Darius?'

'A hastily arranged Cabinet meeting for me, I'm afraid. I may not be home until very late.'

'Don't worry about me,' Aubrey said. 'But if you're not busy, I thought I might drop in and see you at the museum, Mother.'

'Me? Whatever for? Are you volunteering to document the backlog of specimens I have to sort out?'

'I wanted to see the Rashid Stone. Perhaps talk to someone about it.'

Sir Darius cocked his head. 'Now, I know you well enough, Aubrey, to realise you rarely do anything on pure whimsy. You must have some sort of motive here.'

'It doesn't matter what his motive is,' Lady Rose said. 'He can't do it.'

'Er . . . Am I confined to quarters?'

'Tempting notion, but that's not it,' Lady Rose said. 'The Rashid Stone has been packed away, ready for its trip back to Holmland on the *Imperator*.'

'I didn't know that negotiations had been finalised.'

'It's all about the Elektor's birthday,' Sir Darius said. 'A number of things have become urgent, apparently. Urgent enough for Count Brandt to speak to the King.'

'Who intervened on behalf of his cousin, the Elektor,' Lady Rose said, unhappily. 'The museum governors didn't think it wise to refuse a direct approach from the King.'

'Wait, Count *Brandt* spoke to the King about returning the Rashid Stone? That doesn't make sense. He hates the Holmland government.'

'It makes political sense,' Sir Darius said. 'By doing this, Count Brandt shows that he supports the Elektor, who is still phenomenally popular in Holmland, just as our King is here. Brandt also shows that he can do something the Chancellor couldn't, so his reputation goes up. It's a clever move, but it suggests that Brandt isn't planning to stay in Albion long.'

'He wants to return to Holmland and become Chancellor himself.'

'Which would seem to be better for us than the current Chancellor,' Lady Rose said.

Sir Darius nodded. 'In any event, the *Imperator* is sailing on Monday. It'll give the current Chancellor a chance to crow, I suppose, and tell the whole world that Albion wants to appease Holmland.'

'You can't do anything about it? Simply refuse?'

'I'd like to. The Holmlanders looted the stone from Aigyptos. They don't have any intention of returning it to its rightful owners.'

'They rule Aigyptos with an iron fist. It's the oil, you see, and it's a shame,' Lady Rose said. 'The Sultan is a thoughtful man. He had a keen interest in finches, the last time I spoke to him.'

'The Sultan of Memphis,' Aubrey said. 'Didn't he attend Greythorn?'

'Thirty years ago,' Sir Darius said. 'They still talk about his batting. He's a good man.'

'You've met him.'

'Back then, certainly.'

'More recently?'

Sir Darius grinned. 'Now, Aubrey, it wouldn't be seemly for the Prime Minister of Albion to meet a rebel leader.'

'That's not a "no", is it?'

'No.'

Lady Rose gazed at the ceiling. 'If you boys are just going to fence with each other, I'm leaving.' She gazed at the inspired disorder of the drawing room. 'I had one of those posters around here somewhere. The Rashid Stone posters. I wonder if Caroline would like it.'

Aubrey spied a rolled up tube of paper on a table nearby, wedged in between a collection of rock crystals. 'Is this it?'

He unrolled it and, for an instant, the whole world went away. The central aspect of the poster – a large photographic reproduction of the Rashid Stone itself – was all that he could see.

It was an excellent reproduction. So much so that he could make out the first three characters in the baffling script before it was overwritten with details of the exhibition. And, if his quick translation of the stone they found in the underground Roman shrine was correct, they read: Death. Soul. Protection.

He was insensible to the world around him for some minutes while he frantically thought through the implications of this. He must have made intelligible responses, for he had a dim notion that the conversation went on around him without any strange looks.

Aubrey stood and re-engaged with the world around him. 'I really must get some rest.'

Sir Darius rose. 'And I must get to the Houses of Parliament.'

He dashed to the sofa, kissed his wife on the cheek and dashed out again.

Lady Rose looked at the doorway. 'I knew it would be like this when I married him.' She stood. 'That's why I promised I wouldn't sit around at home, waiting. I'm off to the museum.'

And Aubrey was left alone.

WITH THE HELP OF A MAGNIFYING GLASS AND A STRONG electric desk lamp, he spent some hours peering at the mysterious fragment from the underground shrine. He made little headway, finally admitting he needed expert help.

He'd made some tentative notes, enough to excite him about the link between the fragment and the Rashid Stone. He was sure the possibility existed that one, or both, of them might hold some clue to curing his condition.

He was unwilling to hope too much, but the chance was there that the knowledge of the ancients might come to his aid. Protection of the soul was a fundamental aspect of working with death magic – something he had come to understand all too late. And death magic was a major concern for early magicians, so perhaps they had ways forgotten to modern magicians, methods to reunite his body and soul permanently.

He rubbed his eyes, sat back, snapped off the desk lamp. The weariness he'd been holding at bay descended on him like a thick, black fog. He stumbled to his fish tank and hid the tablet under the sand, right outside the octopus's cave.

Sleep beckoned. Left alone, the house quiet apart from the muffled noises of the servants going about their business, it should have been the perfect time for napping.

So, naturally, Aubrey lay on his bed, unable to sleep. Somewhere along the way, he'd apparently decided to substitute worrying for sleeping.

He was worried about George, and his family. Aubrey knew that George's father was a modern farmer in most ways, adopting the latest techniques in scientific farming. He'd not been averse to investigating magical techniques, either; his apple orchard sported several bird scarers that used a clever derivation of the Law of Opposites.

But in one way in particular, William Doyle was an old-fashioned man: he was loath to accept help, especially financial help. Aubrey could imagine a financial situation getting steadily worse and worse, while Mr Doyle tried one thing then another, and then one day waking up to discover the farm was owned by someone else.

Aubrey could think of several ways to fix the debt. It would be fun, organising a complex nesting of identities, a trail of Person A paying Person B who owed money to Person C and somehow having the Doyle farm ending up safe and secure. He itched to do it.

But he wouldn't. He'd promised.

Even if the Doyles lose the farm? a voice whispered.

George was no financial wizard, Aubrey appreciated that. But perhaps his unequalled ability as a good listener and sounding board would be of some help to his father. Aubrey hoped so.

And Caroline. Aubrey worried about her and about the goals she was setting for herself. Even though the world was changing, it wasn't changing quickly enough for a girl (*young woman?*) of Caroline's abundant talents and ambition.

At the back of his mind, he'd always taken perverse

pleasure in the hard row he'd set himself to hoe. To excel in multiple areas – magic, the military, academia and politics – was foolish, overreaching, impossible. But it suited him. Some people enjoyed a challenge. Aubrey was bored to death without one – and more than one, preferably.

He had a difficult road ahead. But he had to admit, Caroline's aims seemed just as lofty – those she'd disclosed – but her sex was going to make them even more difficult to achieve. Aubrey worried that the realities of an unequal world would break her spirit. It was something he didn't want to see.

His father? Well, he was a fairly minor concern. Sir Darius was the subject of political plotting, backstabbing and general malfeasance, but he knew how to take care of himself. He'd managed for years – although the added strain of dealing with the shifting international situation was something that Aubrey wouldn't wish on anyone. If Albion went to war, Sir Darius would be responsible for the lives of hundreds of thousands, perhaps millions.

His mother was fearsomely capable as well, but he did worry about her worrying about his father's worrying. His mother put great store on appearing unaffected by weighty matters of state, and by her husband's commitments. She had a rich life, she was prepared to tell anyone, one that was not dependent on her husband. This credo shocked many, to which Lady Rose declared she gave not a fig.

But lately, Aubrey had seen the hint of anxiety in her face. This tended to coincide with newspapers announcing further Holmland aggression on the Continent, or more fractiousness in the Goltans.

Both his parents were busy people and Aubrey was glad of this. Without their various distractions, he worried that they would notice his condition. He'd managed to keep it from them, but with his decision to use his magical powers, despite the dangers, they may notice his physical condition go up and down more than previously. He didn't welcome their intelligent regard turning in that direction.

Aubrey found worrying seductive. It was tempting to brood, sorting out 'Should have' and 'Why didn't I', teasing apart the strands of regret, fear and hopelessness. It was all-consuming.

Eventually, he shook his head and sat up. Worry was all well and good, but it wasn't achieving much – and going around and around over the same ground was so *boring*. If he wanted his worries to lessen, he should do something about them.

He glanced at the window, then stared. Evening had stolen in. The gaslamps in the street were already lit. A hansom cab trotted by; its lanterns were bright in the gathering shadows.

Somewhere, sometime, he'd slept, right through lunch. He'd worried before falling asleep, then dreamed worrisome dreams, then woken to more worrying, all without noticing the transitions.

'Well, that's enough of that, then,' he said aloud. He poured cold water into his basin and dipped a facecloth in. A vigorous face rub later, followed by an energetic application of his hair brushes, and he was almost a new person. That is, if he ignored the pinched look about his cheeks, and the redness around his eyelids, and the disturbing amount of hair his brushing had dislodged.

He stretched, squared his shoulders and decided it was hard to be gloomy when he had a plan in front of him.

After what he'd discovered from the mysterious inscription, he simply had to see the Rashid Stone before it was shipped to Holmland. Copies of its inscriptions were no good – he wanted to put his hands on the actual stone itself.

Which meant he was going to break into the Albion Museum.

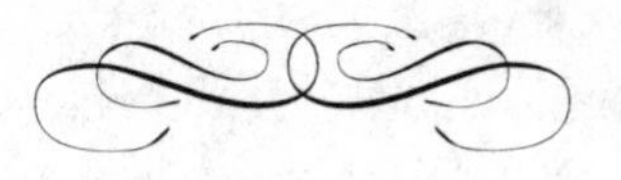

Twenty

The Albion Museum had occupied a number of different buildings throughout its history. The current edifice faced Fanthorpe Square and had been built in the reign of King Stephen, the current king's grandfather. It had miles of galleries, four substantial wings, and was a devil to heat in the winter.

Aubrey had always had an affection for its ugly hotch-potch of architectural styles. King Stephen's favourite architect had been Lionel Willoughby, who proudly proclaimed he'd never had an original idea in his life. His genius, he confided to everyone within earshot – and for those who missed it, he wrote a five-volume autobiography – lay in bringing together great styles from around the world. When he was successful it was a harmonious – if startling – whole. On an off day it resulted in buildings that made people cry out in horror if they came upon them unexpectedly.

The Albion Museum was one of Willoughby's triumphs. Vaguely classical, with more pediments and pillars than were strictly necessary, it looked serious, impressive and weighty, perfect for the pre-eminent museum in the country.

With an effort that left him doubled over and panting, Aubrey managed to scramble over the tall iron fence and lose himself in a clump of may bushes near the museum's eastern wing. The windows on this side were dark, but he knew that nightwatchmen patrolled the corridors. The museum held many invaluable treasures from antiquity, so the guarding wasn't perfunctory.

He'd come equipped. Not with George's trusty pry bar, though the prospect had tempted him, but with magical props.

He patted his pockets to make sure he hadn't lost anything while scaling the fence. Chalk, always useful. Beeswax. A bunch of assorted keys he'd collected over the years. Matches. A small bottle of bicycle oil with a sunflower seed in it. A silk scarf.

Now, to find a window. He had a cunning spell ready, one that could use a prepared key on a lock at a distance . . .

He heard footsteps and froze, not even daring to breathe. The footsteps were careful, deliberate, authoritative.

They stopped right in front of his hiding place.

'You'd best come out of there.'

Aubrey stood and stared. 'Mother?'

Lady Rose wore a white gaberdine coat over her dress. She had no hat – her hair was pulled back in a bun. 'I thought you'd appear sooner or later, Aubrey.'

'I . . . but . . . it . . .'

'Don't stand there gawping like a goldfish. This way. I'll let you in.'

He pushed through the bushes, not even noticing when a branch thwacked him across the face.

Lady Rose took him around a corner. A door stood open. 'Here. I'll answer your questions once we're inside. There's no telling who's lurking about these days.'

Numbly, Aubrey shook his head and followed her inside. Lady Rose locked and tested the door, then studied him. 'Generally you're a mystery to me, Aubrey, as I imagine all children are to their parents. But sometimes you're as clear as a pane of glass.'

'I try to be honest with you.'

'I know that, and I know that there are ways to remain completely honest while keeping people in the dark. Don't protest, you'll only tie yourself in knots over that one.'

Aubrey gave up and simply nodded.

'Very good. This morning, your interest in the Rashid Stone was obvious. When you didn't pursue your father on stopping its shipment, I knew that you had plans.'

'Plans are a good thing.'

'Really, Aubrey, the sooner you go into politics the better. That was a perfect politician's statement: it appeared to have something to do with what I said, but it actually said nothing at all.'

Aubrey decided a full frontal assault was the only course left. 'I was thinking I'd steal the Rashid Stone.'

'Excellent. I was hoping you were going to say that.'

Aubrey couldn't have been more astonished if his mother had suddenly turned into Dr Tremaine. 'I beg your pardon?'

'A temporary appropriation, rather than stealing, I'd call it,' Lady Rose said. 'Much better than letting the Holmlanders take it away.' She frowned at him. 'I'm assuming you want to return it to its rightful owners?'

'Er . . . I was just going to have a look at it before it was shipped out.' He saw his mother's expression. 'Of course, I'm happy to revise my plans. You think we should stop the Holmlanders from having it?'

Lady Rose made a face. 'I feel sorry for Holmlanders. Some fine people there, excellent scientists, but their government seems to have more than the usual number of blockheads in it. I know that politics attracts a certain sort of person, but really – ' She broke off and looked seriously at Aubrey. 'That's really why I want you to go into politics, you know. Your father is a good man, but he's outnumbered by scoundrels and buffoons. It might even up the odds if you and Caroline get in.'

Aubrey jumped. 'What? What did you say?'

But Lady Rose had already disappeared through a doorway.

When Aubrey found her, she was in a darkened corridor. The only light came from a window that looked out on the gaslit street. She put a finger to her lips. 'There are bound to be people in offices and workshops.'

She led him along the corridor. On the left the wall was half glass, venetian blinds obscuring what lay behind. Lady Rose opened the sixth door on the right.

Aubrey hadn't been in his mother's workshop for months. It was unrecognisable. When he was there last, it was tropical birds. Dozens of brightly coloured specimens in glass cases, waiting to be classified. Now the whole place was full of boxes, stacked up to ceiling height in some places. It smelled of fish. 'Sea birds of the north,' Lady Rose said when she saw Aubrey's wrinkled nose. She lifted the top from the nearest box.

'Albatross?' Aubrey hazarded.

'Of course it's an albatross. Look at that beak.'

Aubrey peered closer. 'I'll take your word for it.'

'It is,' she said gently. 'But is it a waved albatross or a young short-tailed albatross? The captain of our ship had it mounted on a perch, quite proud of it he was, but insisted I take it when he saw our other specimens.' Lady Rose replaced the lid. 'Now, let's find this Rashid Stone.'

Aubrey felt like an unprepared challenger in the ring with a heavyweight champion. He was still reeling from the shock of his mother's appearance and support for his spot of burglary, when he walked into this most recent uppercut. 'You want to come?'

'I'm here. I know the layout of this place. I'm not incapable of clandestine activity.'

'No,' Aubrey said weakly. 'I mean, I imagine not. If you put your mind to it.'

'Hmm. Ask your father to tell you about the time I freed him and his squad from the Articari partisans, while still keeping my collection of jungle beetles safe.'

'I will.' *At some moment when it might be useful to surprise him*, Aubrey thought. Information was ammunition.

Lady Rose took a bullseye lantern from a shelf. Aubrey had a match ready.

'Shall we go?' The light caught his mother's eyes and Aubrey realised that she was serious about accompanying him. And she was excited.

Lady Rose had never embarrassed Aubrey, which he'd discovered was a rarity. It seemed as if the roles of most boys' mothers was to embarrass them often, in public, and with a total lack of understanding as to what was going on. Lady Rose had never been like that. Aubrey had always been proud of her calm, her self-assurance, her ready wit and élan.

But this was different.

'Do you *have* to come?' he said.

'Yes. Now, straighten your collar. You look quite disreputable.'

'Well, I am dressed in clothes that are meant to make it easy to break into a major national institution. Disreputable would seem to be part of the job description.'

'I see what you mean.' With a quick movement, she took off her white coat. The dress underneath was a dark emerald green. 'This should be less noticeable.'

Aubrey knew there was no sense arguing about it. Once his mother had made up her mind, she was as unstoppable as the tide. 'Which way?' he said, as if his mother came with him on nefarious activities every day of the week.

'It's crated up in one of the workshops. Best if we cut through Aigyptian antiquities.'

Echoing footsteps announced the presence of the nightwatchmen well in advance, and they took their duties seriously enough for Aubrey and Lady Rose to scamper aside a number of times. However, the many large stone statues, stelae and sarcophagi provided useful hiding places.

An unmarked door next to a jackal-headed god opened onto a workshop. At first, Aubrey thought he'd taken a dramatically wrong turn and ended up in a cabinet-maker's shed. By the dim light that struggled through grimy windows, he could make out racks of timber and tools. The floor was covered with sawdust and shavings, and the smell of cut wood was clean and sweet. For a moment, Aubrey was reminded of William Doyle's workshop at George's farm, where the young Aubrey and George had admired Mr Doyle's careful woodwork, turning rough timber into delicate objects – spoons, bookends, buttons.

Suddenly, Lady Rose drew him into the shadows near the entrance. She blew out the lantern, then she brought her mouth close to his ear. 'The rear doors. They're open.'

Aubrey dropped to the floor. Carefully, he eased his head out from behind the coat rack that stood near the entrance.

Four or five figures – it was hard to tell in the indirect light – were clustered around a crate in the doorway, arguing in low but agitated voices that seemed to require much finger-pointing. The crate stood about five feet high and looked very weighty. Despite the burliness of these intruders, it seemed as if the crate had defeated them.

Aubrey pulled his head back. Someone else wanted the Rashid Stone.

Why can't anything be simple? he thought. *All I wanted to do was break into the foremost museum in the land and have a good look at one of their treasures. Is that too much to ask?*

He wished that he'd come prepared for hand-to-hand combat rather than simple burglary.

Matches. He had matches. He could work with that. In fact, it might turn out beautifully. Scare off these unwelcome guests, take the stone, then call the police and give them the description of these villains, who'd take the blame for the theft. It was a fine line, but Aubrey decided that they deserved a good interrogation, at the least. Even if they hadn't stolen the Rashid Stone, they *intended* to steal it. Later, once the stone had been reunited with the Sultan, Aubrey could let the authorities know the truth of the matter. Leaving his name out, of course. Perhaps some sort of moniker would be in order. The Liberator? The Guardian of Looted Antiquities?

A crash came from the direction of the crate. The cursing that followed was intense, and all the more interesting for its restraint. It was conducted totally in whispers, even though one of the cursers sounded as if he was in considerable pain. Aubrey added 'well-disciplined' to the description he was ready to give to the police.

He took out the box of matches. The applications of the Law of Intensification were well understood. Certain processes could be intensified if the spell were very precisely phrased. The precision was important, otherwise the intensification could run rampant and get totally out of hand. Aubrey had seen a practical demonstration go badly wrong when a tuning fork's sound had been shoddily intensified. The whole class had to flee the room, hands clapped over ears, and all the windows of the room had shattered before one of the senior masters came and cancelled Mr Lapworth's spell.

Mr Lapworth hadn't remained long at Stonelea School, even though he was the headmaster's wife's nephew. The last Aubrey had heard, he was in Antipodea and making a good fist of banking.

Aubrey had always used Mycenaean for his intensification spells. It was a difficult, rigid language, but its very rigidity gave him confidence where intensification was concerned. He knew that an explosion was merely very rapid burning, *intensified* burning, as it were, and he didn't want an explosion in the confines of a museum workshop.

He undertook an elaborate mime with his mother, finishing with an injunction to cover her eyes. She nodded and he gave thanks for all the hours the family had spent playing Charades.

He held the box of matches in the palm of his hand. Just as he was about to start the spell, another thump came from the clumsy villains, and another stream of hushed cursing.

It was perfect timing, covering Aubrey's whispered Mycenaean. He pronounced each agglutinative syllable carefully, concluded with a modest signature flourish, then he threw the matchbox over his head and clapped his hands over his eyes.

Even though Aubrey had confined his intensification to light, he felt a wave of heat roll over him at the same time as hard, white radiance crept through the cracks in his fingers.

This time, the oaths weren't muffled.

Aubrey removed his hands from his eyes and stood. 'It's safe.'

His mother took her hands away and blinked. 'I haven't seen your spellwork for ages, Aubrey. You have improved.'

Aubrey was about to answer, modestly, when he realised something wasn't right. If all had gone smoothly, the villains should have been dazzled, then run off, afraid that their doings had been discovered. The dazzling had happened, as planned, but he couldn't recall hearing the sounds of villains decamping the scene, in a northerly direction or any other.

He peered around the corner of the coat stand to see the burglars advancing on their position, making their way through crates, boxes and piles of horsehair packing. In the quick glance, he saw that they were blinking, wiping streaming eyes, and furiously unhappy.

He withdrew his head and cursed his luck. Not only had he stumbled on antiquity-loving burglars in the middle of a job, but they were hard-bitten villains, not easily scared, and looking as if they were more interested in settling scores than getting on with good, honest thievery.

Or they don't want witnesses, he thought and his stomach turned to stone. The game had suddenly become much more serious.

He pushed his mother toward the door. She didn't stop to argue, for which he was grateful.

Outside, Aubrey skidded on the parquetry floor. 'Which way?'

'Which way to where?' Calm, a little puzzled, Lady Rose made sure she closed the door behind them. Softly.

'To somewhere away from here. They're after us.'

'Ah. This way, then. Through the Oriental Hall.'

They'd only made it halfway to the arched entrance to the Oriental Hall when a shout went up, then a shot. Aubrey ducked, instinctively, and flung an arm around his mother.

She shook it off. 'You can run better without such niceties,' she snapped and ducked past the pillar at the entrance.

A few lights were on in the Oriental Hall, enough for Aubrey to make out that it was a long, uninterrupted stretch of display cabinets in two long columns, all as tall as he was, with an aisle in the middle and space between the cabinets and the walls on either side.

Aubrey summed it up in an instant. Fortunately. If they wove in and out of the cabinets, no-one could stand and shoot at them from the entrance with any likelihood of success.

Of course, someone could simply run down the middle of the hall and tackle them.

Therefore, make pursuit more difficult, he thought. Time was important. The nightwatchmen must have heard the gunshot. They'd be converging at any instant.

'Light the lantern,' his mother ordered.

'What?'

'Now,' she said calmly. She held it up in front of his face. 'Light the lantern.'

A simple ignition spell jumped into his mind and the lantern was alight.

'Now,' she said, 'let's see if this helps.'

She swept the beam of the lantern down the hall, through the glass cases. Immediately, it bounced and bent, and the room was full of dozens of shards of light, flashing across walls and ceiling. Some cases were full of brightness, but lost it when the beam moved on. Other cases sent the light in unexpected directions as it reflected off curved surfaces, gold and silver.

'*Sow confusion where you may*,' Lady Rose said. 'Or so the Scholar Tan says, apparently.'

The evening had turned into a session of complete gob-smackery for Aubrey, so his mother's quoting the Scholar Tan was only mildly flabbergasting.

He grinned. She smiled. Then they were off.

They darted down the middle aisle, then flitted left at a cabinet holding a beautiful, globular water jug, Lady Rose keeping the lantern beam moving in jerky, erratic sweeps. They paused for a moment, then they ran along the wall, before slipping right across to the other wall and racing for the far-off exit.

Aubrey took out the bottle of bicycle oil just as a voice called out from the entrance to the hall. 'Stop right there!'

Aubrey had momentary visions of aeronautical pigs, then he uncorked the bottle and splashed it on the ground as they ran, the sunflower seed rattling inside the bottle. They crossed to the other side of the hall, sprinting past cabinets of ewers and silver plate which reflected the lantern light beautifully.

Aubrey dribbled oil as they ran.

Starting to pant, he chanted a spell, doing his best to make it as clear as possible. The sunflower seed had been in the bottle of oil for months now, preparing for a use such as this. The Law of Proximity. In the time that the oil and the seed had been close to each other, they had absorbed some of the characteristics of each other – helped by some judicious spells, of course. Now, the seed had a special oiliness about it, while the oil had taken on some of the qualities of the seed. With a little magical nudging, the oil had the desire to grow, just like a seed.

Aubrey pushed out the last of the spell, a dimension-limiting element, giving a rough idea of width and breadth. He added his signature and immediately staggered. It hadn't been a difficult spell but on top of his exertions in the ruined shrine, it was taking a toll.

His mother grabbed his arm. 'Aubrey! Are you all right?'

The spell had drained him. The effort had struck him like a punch to the stomach. 'Fine. Run.'

Behind him, he heard a thud, a crash, renewed cursing, then a shot, but he was too tired to get worked up about it. More thumps, curses, crashes, cursing. It sounded as if a herd of bulls had taken it into their heads to do a spot of china shopping.

'They're floundering on the floor, can't stand up at all,' Lady Rose reported. Whistles sounded from nearby. 'Ah. Watchmen. The oil will disappear soon, I hope.'

'Ten minutes. Was all I could manage.'

'It is enough.'

They dashed out of the Oriental Hall. Lady Rose shone the lantern both ways, then hurried Aubrey toward a nearby doorway. 'The Arctic Display. It's being redone. We won't be disturbed.'

Aubrey would have thought that the entire museum in the middle of the night was a place not to be disturbed, but events had convinced him otherwise. He leaned against a lumpy, canvas-draped shape. The canvas slipped and Aubrey was unsurprised to be staring at a polar bear. He shrugged. 'Can you get us back to the workshop?' he asked his mother. His pulse was loud in his temples. He rubbed them, but it didn't help.

'I can. But I don't think that's wise. We shouldn't be found here.'

'We won't be found here. If you can get us there unseen.'

'Aubrey, you're not making sense.'

'If we can get there, I think we can still spirit the Rashid Stone away.'

Lady Rose put both her hands together, as if she were trying to hold a piece of paper between them, then put them to her lips and studied him over the top. 'Exciting though this has been, I really should get you away from here. Enough is enough.'

'Mother, this could be a last chance to restore the stone to the Sultan. If we don't do something now, Holmland will have it forever.' He put a hand to his forehead. 'Or whoever those thieves are working for.'

And that's something I have to think about. When I have time.

Lady Rose dropped her hands. She looked at Aubrey with exasperation. 'You're determined to do this, aren't you? Despite the danger, you still want to do the right thing?'

He straightened himself and stifled a groan. 'It's our best chance. I think we have to.'

'You're just like your father.'

With that, Lady Rose set off, not looking back, marching deeper into the shadowy maze of canvas and scaffolding that was the Arctic Display under reconstruction.

A door near a fire hose opened onto a short corridor, lit by a single electric light globe in a wire cage. 'I don't think anyone knows this building in its entirety,' Lady Rose said over her shoulder.

The corridor ended in a metal door. Aubrey added his weight – ignoring the burning pain it sparked in his shoulder – and the door screeched open. 'But you've done some exploring,' he said.

His mother nodded. 'This is tricky. Hold my hand.'

Linked, they shuffled along a narrow, concrete corridor that smelled of damp. Aubrey trailed his spare hand along the wall and it came away wet.

'Careful,' Lady Rose said. 'Stairs. We're going down.'

The stairs were metal. Aubrey felt for each one and clung to the handrail with strength that surprised him. A watery light beckoned at the bottom of their descent.

'Cellar?' Aubrey looked around. The place was full of trees. 'Forest?'

Lady Rose swept the lantern beam and it ran across dozens of tree trunks. Some were slender, some were broad and gnarled. Branches and leaves completed the unexpected picture. 'These are props. We use them for dioramas. You know: "The Animals of the African Plains" and suchlike.'

Aubrey had seen some strange things underground lately, but he'd never expected to see an underground forest.

'Careful,' Lady Rose said as Aubrey turned away from the trees.

Directly in front of him was a gap in the concrete floor. It was a few feet across, and when his mother pointed the lantern down he stared.

Tracks. Tiny train tracks a foot or two across. He followed them and saw that they disappeared into the wall.

'It's a parcel railway,' Lady Rose said. She pointed the lantern up the tunnel, but the darkness ate the beam before it made any real impression. 'Between the Art

Gallery, the Houses of Parliament and St Michael's Hospital, for some reason. It's fallen out of use, but it once had a regular, circular route.'

Aubrey felt as if he was learning about a hidden side of an old friend. 'The underground life of this city astonishes me.' He toed the rusty rails with his boot, then frowned. Had the rail just shuddered?

He drew back his foot to try again, but his mother tugged on his jacket. 'We should hurry.'

Reluctantly, Aubrey allowed himself to be led away from the mysterious parcel tunnel.

Lady Rose took them through unlit corridors and dusty, cobwebbed staircases. In some places, they had to squeeze past forgotten crates, stacked high against the walls. Other passages were empty and echoed to their footsteps. It was as if they were in another world.

The workshop was quiet. From other parts of the museum, however, Aubrey could hear the noises of pursuit – whistles, shouts, ominous crashes. Further away again, sirens and bells spiralled through the night, suggesting that urgency was a useful attribute.

One side of the crate had been removed. With his mother holding the lantern steady, Aubrey crouched and peered inside.

Cloth had been torn aside. Nestled inside it was the irregular black shape of the Rashid Stone.

'Can you leave the lantern, please, Mother? And listen at the door? Let me know if we're likely to have visitors.'

'Very well.' She composed herself. 'I was working late, became extremely worried by all the commotion, tried to find out what was going on and ended up here.'

'Excellent. Who could doubt you?'

After she left, Aubrey spared himself a moment of awe. This fragment was a time voyager. It had travelled four thousand years – and several thousand miles – with its mysteries intact. It had messages which had lasted longer than kings and queens, longer than empires.

But underneath it all, the Rashid Stone was still a very large, very heavy lump of granite. *And I want to walk out of here with it.*

This, at least, was something he *had* prepared for. His makeshift spell in Lutetia, which had levitated a whole building, was one he'd spent some time refining since that adventure. He felt confident about applying it to the Rashid Stone to reduce its weight. He didn't want it bobbing along like a balloon, though, as a slab of granite drifting through the air was likely to attract attention.

He wanted to slip it in his pocket.

Weight-negating, then, was under control. But he needed to compress the size of the stone to something more manageable.

And this is where his pondering over the dimensionality spell he'd seen in action on the submersible came in handy. By combining aspects of his levitation spell (the Law of Reversal) and the dimensionality spell he could produce something which would shrink the stone to an unnoticeable size, but not leave it in a state where its weight would be unmanageable.

Of course, such a novel combination of spells, crossing distinctly different principles, was something that needed careful experimentation, in controlled laboratory conditions, so that variables could be noted and countered, the results could be tabulated and mused over, a paper could be written on 'Some Aspects and Applications of

Combining Spells Derived from the Law of Inversion and the Principle of Dimensionality', preferably with the name of a respected professor attached, the one who dropped into the lab looking for his tea cup.

With no time for that, Aubrey took a deep breath and started.

The thrill he felt at embarking on a new magical direction almost overcame his exhaustion. He'd done much of the preparatory work on the way to the museum, and he pulled out the scrap of paper he'd used while in the cab. It was hard to read, even when he angled it to catch the lantern light. He'd hammered out the variables for duration (open-ended – he didn't want to be held up on the way back to Maidstone and have a suddenly massive chunk of stone tear a hole in his pocket) and direction (heavier rather than lighter) but he hadn't been able to do much more before seeing the slab. He squinted and worked up some dimensional and positional parameters, translating them into Demotic as he went. He'd felt that using the ancient Aigyptian language might be fitting in this circumstance; he'd had some experience using it for spells that dealt with physical variables.

He stood, knees popping alarmingly, fixed his gaze on the stone in the crate, and began.

It was a long spell, of necessity. It had many elements to control, and all had to roll out in the correct order. It helped that the language was pleasing to work with; Aubrey had always enjoyed it. When he used Demotic, it felt as though he was constantly talking about flowers.

He finished with his signature element and closed his eyes. The wave of exhaustion that struck him wasn't unexpected, but even so he had difficulty not slumping to the floor. His legs trembled, his chest felt tight. His stomach was hollow as if he hadn't eaten for days, but the thought of food made him nauseated. He swayed, steadied, and opened his eyes to see that at least one aspect of the spell had worked. The Rashid Stone had disappeared.

He bent, not trusting himself to crouch, but it was nearly a mistake. His vision swam, little black suns swelling and bursting in front of his eyes. He gasped and caught himself on the edge of the crate, rubber-legged. After a moment, he groped inside with his other hand.

He found something in the bottom of the crate, something important that wasn't there. By not thinking about the contradiction, he was able to push his lump of beeswax over it.

Carefully, he straightened, still swaying a little, with the non-dimensional, light-as-air Rashid Stone pressed into the beeswax. He slipped it into his pocket.

'We should go,' he croaked just as his mother appeared.

She was by his side in an instant. 'You sound terrible.'

'A cold. Coming on.'

'I hope not. Fitzwilliam men are terrible invalids.'

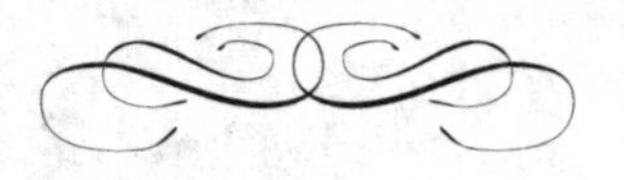

Twenty-one

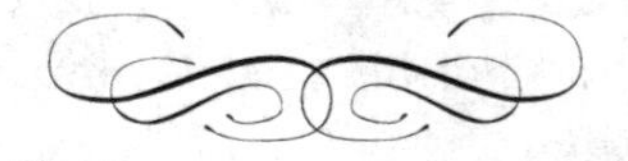

THE NEXT MORNING, A TENTATIVE KNOCK CAME AT the door. It opened and Tilly stepped in. 'If you please, sir, Sir Darius would like to see you in his study. He's just got in and is asking for you.'

Aubrey straightened and rubbed his eyes, grateful that this Monday was a public holiday and he hadn't had to rush back to the university. He glanced at the sheets of paper on his desk, filled with his transcriptions from the Rashid Stone and from the mysterious Roman fragment. The fragment was proving to be what he hoped: a key to unlock the mystery script.

'Ten minutes, Tilly. I'll be there.'

He was exhausted by the effort of restoring enough size to the Stone to allow him to transcribe the inscriptions and then shrinking it again for concealment, but the pleasure of discovery had kept him working, for now – and helped him ignore the tell-tale tenderness of his gums, another symptom of bodily dissolution.

Already his studies with Professor Mansfield were proving valuable. The Rashid Stone was definitely a treatise on magic; he'd managed to puzzle out some references to light magic, healing magic – and death magic.

Aubrey needed more time, but he thought he had some hints toward a solution for his condition. Hints, clues, suggestions – but he needed more time to be sure what he was finding.

He jotted down a few last notes from the central section of the Rashid Stone. It dealt with urbomancy, which apparently was concerned with collections of humanity and accumulated consciousness. Some of the references were disturbing, hinting at animating entire settlements, but most of it remained unclear. He'd searched through a number of reference texts before he found even the slightest mention of it, but it was singularly unhelpful, simply noting it was a 'minor, and forgotten, art'.

The trouble with having a well-developed sense of curiosity was that it made researching difficult. Sidetracks and byways opened up all over the place, beckoning alluringly.

Aubrey's curiosity couldn't let such a tantalising description pass. It was so curt, so dismissive that he wondered what was going on. Even with the little information he had, the field sounded intriguing and, unless he was mistaken, could shed some insights into the nature of magic itself. Numbers of people coming together was the beginning of true magic. Surely urbomancy was a part of this?

He sat back and linked his hands on his chest, thinking.

His research into his condition had brought him to many arcane and recondite texts. He'd become attuned to scholarly arguments over fine points of magic, or interpretations of fine points of magic.

He'd also stumbled on areas that were best left alone – according to learned opinion. Death magic's perils, for instance, were well known and highlighted in many, many texts.

Another way, however, to steer the foolhardy away from dangerous areas of magic was to pretend it didn't exist – or was only of minor, boring importance. This was never the result of anything formal – Aubrey snorted at the idea of a Council of Wizards controlling magical research – but a consensus was nevertheless reached among like-minded scholars.

Was urbomancy one of these areas? If so, why?

Frowning, he tapped his pencil on his teeth. The Rashid Stone was proving to be a treasure, but a frustrating one.

AUBREY ADMIRED HIS FATHER'S CONSTITUTION. WITH NO sleep, after a night of political push and shove, Sir Darius looked as if he was ready to swim the channel.

When the maid had closed the door behind her, Sir Darius leaned back in his chair and eyed Aubrey. 'Rokeby-Taylor. Count Brandt. Dr Tremaine.'

It was a hot chance, but Aubrey took it with both hands. 'You're asking if there's a connection.'

'I could be suggesting that there is a connection but I don't know what it is.'

'This is what Cabinet was discussing?'

'We were discussing the Holmland situation in more general terms, but those names kept coming up. Then I had some time with Craddock and with Tallis where they came up again.'

'And I imagine that those conversations were separate.'

'I did my best to make sure that each didn't know about my chat with the other. No guarantees there.'

'Of course not.'

'I need your insight here, Aubrey. You're bound up in all of these goings-on and you might be able to shed some light. The others are all protecting their little areas. Too much posturing for my liking.'

'I'm happy to help, sir.'

'I don't doubt that.' For a moment, Sir Darius smoothed his moustache thoughtfully. 'But before we go any further, I need to know if you have any knowledge of a ruction at the museum early this morning.'

Aubrey should have known his father would have heard. 'I may have.'

'I see. You were out last night, I take it?'

'Yes.'

'Without Caroline and George?'

'I had Mother with me.'

Sir Darius's gaze instantly became intense. 'Tell me about it.'

Aubrey was in agony as he sorted through the implications of this simple request. 'I don't think I can.'

'I beg your pardon?'

'If you know about it, you might have to do something. Or tell someone if they ask you about it. But if you don't know, you can't. And they won't know if you don't know.'

'That, surprisingly, makes sense, but I'm not sure I agree.' Sir Darius scowled.

Aubrey remained silent.

'I see.' The pause that followed this statement weighed more than a hundred Rashid Stones. 'You were with your mother, you say.'

'Yes.'

'And she and you are safe and – perhaps just as importantly – unidentified?'

'Yes and yes.'

Another massive pause pressed down on Aubrey as his father scrutinised him. 'At an appropriate time, you will tell me, both of you, what happened.'

Aubrey sighed with relief. 'Naturally. In full detail.'

'And I'm sure I don't have to tell you that it would be most awkward if any missing treasure that belonged to another nation was ever found in the Prime Minister's own residence, do I?'

Aubrey thought of the fish tank in his room where he'd buried the dimensionless, weightless Rashid Stone: right next to the Roman fragment, outside the octopus's lair. 'It would be improper.'

'Let us move on, then,' Sir Darius said. 'Now that we understand each other. At least, you understand me – I hope. I'm not sure if I'll ever claim to understand you.'

'Sir,' Aubrey said. It was a meaningless response, but it filled in the gap in the conversation nicely.

'I know you keep an eye on the bills moving through Parliament. Has anything pricked your interest lately?'

'The battleship bill. You're voting on it later this week.'

'And why are you interested?'

'Rokeby-Taylor. Five new battleships and his shipyards are in a good position to win the contract, once Defence has been allocated the budget. He's been taking on new magical experts, Holmlanders this time . . .' Aubrey's voice trailed off.

'Go on.'

Aubrey threw up his hands. 'Rokeby-Taylor is everywhere I turn these days! His companies are cutting corners, a menace to the public. He's well connected, well thought of, has his fingers in dozens of pies. Dozens of fingers.'

'Just the sort of person who would be an excellent enemy agent.'

'I'd thought of that. But just because he's a bounder, it doesn't make him a traitor. Does it?'

'I'm not sure. You saw that he wanted to borrow money from me. I've found out that his financial position is even more dire than he'd let on. This sort of leverage is gold for enemy intelligence operatives.'

'But the battleship contract! Rokeby-Taylor would make a fortune and it would put a dent in Holmland's naval ambitions at the same time. He'd be a hero, not a traitor. Unless . . .'

'Yes?' Sir Darius raised an eyebrow.

'He takes Holmland's money *and* the Navy's money, builds the ships but does something to them? Sabotages them?'

'Who'd be in a better position?'

'You know him best. Would he stoop to something like this?'

'He dearly loves his money. Or the life it buys him, anyway. Could he be tempted? Yes. Would he betray his country? I don't know. Would he risk his own life to do so? Almost certainly not. Remember how dismayed he was when the *Electra* sank.'

'Dr Tremaine,' Aubrey said, almost without thinking about it. 'Once you bring him into this equation, everything changes.'

'Ah, the elusive Dr Tremaine.'

'If he has a hold on Rokeby-Taylor, it changes everything.'

'But what sort of hold? More than blackmailing him over money?'

'Something magical.'

Aubrey tried to recall his meetings with Rokeby-Taylor. There was something about the man that had prodded his curiosity, even then. But Tremaine's hold couldn't be something as trifling as a poison administered and an antidote withheld. It would have to be something that worked on Rokeby-Taylor's weakness, something that could be exploited.

His greed.

'Supposition,' Sir Darius said. 'We have no proof, only suspicions. Clive's turning up at every inconvenient point, his uncharacteristic philanthropy –'

'Count Brandt's Holmlanders. Are they of interest, too?'

'Yes, but not in the same way. From all reports, they're genuinely opposed to the present Holmland government. Brandt would like us to consider them an opposition in exile, but their organisation is too haphazard to deserve that.'

'And Rokeby-Taylor's supporting them financially.' For a moment, Aubrey wondered at Rokeby-Taylor's source of funds. If his companies were doing as badly as it seemed, then where was the money coming from?

'Or supporting *someone* financially,' Sir Darius said. 'It seems as if Brandt is channelling much of the money he receives to the Circle, this mysterious opposition group in Holmland. I'm very nervous about this.'

So was Aubrey, but it was well down the list of things to worry about. 'What about Craddock and Tallis? What's going on there?'

'Rivalry. There's no more powerful motivator when people reach a certain level, unless it's naked ambition. Of course, the two often go hand in hand.'

'They're not traitors?'

'Craddock and Tallis? Traitors?' Sir Darius's laugh was sour. 'I'll warrant that both of them suggested that about the other. Tallis, reasonably bluntly. Craddock, so subtly that you hardly noticed at the time.'

'They're valuable men.'

'In their way. But they must put aside petty jealousies like that. It's time-consuming and very, very dull.'

Aubrey bit his lip. 'I've heard that the Magisterium might be conducting research.'

'Who better to research magical espionage issues?'

'But isn't it against their charter?'

'Not any more. We changed that months ago. Didn't make any sense to stifle their investigations like that.' The front doorbell rang and he stood. 'Thank you, Aubrey. This time was useful.'

'Wait,' Aubrey said. 'I'm sorry if I sound suspicious, sir, but did Commander Craddock suggest you talk to me?'

'Craddock? No. I do have my own thoughts occasionally, you know.' Sir Darius studied his hands for a moment. 'Your conduct lately has been impressive. I can talk freely with few people, and few of them have your acuity and incisiveness.' He looked at his wrist watch. 'I must go. I have a meeting with the Minister for Defence.'

With Dr Tremaine still unaccounted for, Aubrey was very uneasy. The rogue magician had shown in the past that he was willing to strike at the Prime Minister and events seemed to be coming to a head. 'Be careful.'

'Don't worry. Stubbs will be driving me.'

'He'll be . . . well kitted out?'

'It's the wisest course of action for now. You can reassure your mother of that.' He cleared his throat a little awkwardly. 'I've asked Tallis to make sure his men are extra alert in guarding this place for the next few weeks. They're also keeping an eye on Ophelia Hepworth's flat. I thought you might like to know that.'

Aubrey had much to think over after his father left, but he had no time. George bustled in. He was red-faced, dressed in the same clothes as when Aubrey had seen him last. He had his cap scrunched up in one hand. 'On your feet, old man. Jack Figg's here.'

'George, when did you get here? How are things at home?'

'Just now, and no good news at home, I'm afraid. Come on, I think Jack has something important to tell us.'

'Jack can wait. In fact, the whole country can wait. What aren't you telling me about your father?'

George sank into a chair. His attention was entirely on the cap he now held in both hands. He wrung it back and forth, back and forth. 'It looks as if the farm is gone,' he said softly.

'What?'

'The bank marched in on Friday and demanded immediate payment. Father couldn't, of course. He was left with no choice but to sign it over.'

'But that land has been in your family for generations!'

'Funny, that didn't seem to make much difference to the bank manager.'

'But what happens now?'

'The land, the house, the stock will be auctioned off in a few weeks. If there's any money left over after paying the bank, we'll end up with it. I think Father would choke before he took it.'

'Your mother will take care of any money,' Aubrey said absently. 'But how did this happen?'

'Bit by bit, really. Like a boat slowly sinking – when we noticed, it was too late to do anything about it.' George gave his cap a particularly vicious wrench. 'Father says they'll have to come to the city. He'll look for some sort of job.'

Aubrey felt a stab in the heart. 'And you?'

The hat wrenching stopped, but George didn't look up. 'I'll have to leave college, of course. Get a job, too.'

'No,' Aubrey said. 'I'm sure we can do something.'

'Father won't allow it. Pride, remember?'

An enormous hollow opened in Aubrey's chest. He felt as if his entire being could cave in and disappear at any moment. 'George, this is horrible.'

'It's a nightmare.'

'What happens now?'

'I don't know. But I know what *won't* happen now. Aubrey Fitzwilliam won't ride to the rescue.'

'Even though I could.'

'That's right. This has crushed Father. Accepting help would destroy him.'

George stood. Then he shook himself, like a dog emerging from a river. 'Let's go and see what Jack wants. If we're lucky, we can head off and do a spot of saving the country. It's just the sort of thing I need.'

Jack Figg was waiting in the drawing room. He'd just finished blowing his nose and when the handkerchief disappeared into his pocket it was plain he was in a state of shock. His hands shook until he clasped them together. His face was pale. 'I have word of Maggie and her Crew,' he said in a trembling voice.

'Did you call the police?' Aubrey asked.

Jack gathered himself. 'Police? What do you think I am? Cooperating with the bully boys of the establishment? Not on your life.'

Aubrey sighed. Jack Figg had a whole hive of bees in his bonnet, police being one of them. At times like this it didn't make things any easier.

'As much as I'd like to discuss the proper role of law enforcement in a civilised society, I gather that time is an issue here.'

'Where is she?' George asked.

'She's at the clinic.'

MAGGIE LAY ON THE HOSPITAL BED, PALE AND SHAKING, eyes closed, moaning with pain. Her hospital gown was soaked with sweat.

'I've never seen anything like it in my life,' Dr Wells said. He pushed his glasses back on his nose and looked for something to do with his hands. He finally stuck them in the pockets of his white coat and frowned at his patient.

'What's caused it?' Aubrey asked.

'Nothing natural.' Dr Wells mopped at the young girl's brow with a flannel, but it caught on the wire protruding from her temple. With extreme delicacy, he detached it. 'It must be magic. The wires are all through her body.'

Aubrey's whole being wanted to crawl away from what he was seeing. He heard a whimper and he hoped it wasn't his.

Maggie had been transformed. Hundreds of bright copper wires stuck out of her skin in horrid profusion. Many were at her joints – elbows, knees, shoulders – but just as many were in random clumps, bursting out of her neck, her feet, her hands. Wires snaked around from underneath her, and it made her look as if she were lying on a bed of metal straw.

The skin around the wires was red and angry-looking, but it wasn't bleeding. It appeared to have closed up around the wires, giving the appearance of the metal belonging there, a natural – if hideous – growth.

The loose ends of the wires were twisted, some were knotted, and all showed signs of having been broken or snapped off.

'This is ghastly.' George's face was pale. 'Can you do anything, Aubrey?'

'I can't. But I know who might. She must go to St Michael's Hospital. They have some of the new X-ray photography machines and some fine medical magicians on staff.'

George swallowed. 'But how did this happen? Who did it to her?'

Jack Figg hadn't said anything since they'd entered the small, brightly lit ward. He wiped a hand over his face, knocking his glasses askew, but he didn't seem to notice. 'She staggered into the Society for Moral Uplift, delirious. She collapsed and we brought her here.'

'Did she say anything? Anything useful? Where has she been? Where are her Crew?' Aubrey asked.

'She mumbled about the underground, tunnels, the hydraulic railway. And the dark. She's afraid of the dark.'

In a dreadful, jerky movement that set them reeling backward, Maggie sat up. Her eyes flew open. Someone gasped.

Her eyes were glazed and feverish, heavily bloodshot. She stared straight ahead, seeing something that wasn't there, while wires sprang back and forth. They caught on bedclothes and wafted in the air like seaweed on a drowned corpse.

'The dark,' she grated, in a voice that was thick and pained. 'Don't go down where the dark is.'

Aubrey was the first to recover. 'Why not, Maggie? What's down there?'

'The dark is down there. It's down there everywhere. It's alive.'

'What is?'

'Darkness. Power. Darkness.'

Her teeth clicked together and she spasmed, hurled backward by the force of the seizure. Wires clashed and tangled and Aubrey was astonished they didn't tear out. Ignoring any sharp ends, Dr Wells took the young girl's shoulders and held her to the bed. 'Leave,' he snapped over his shoulder. Aubrey and the others hustled for the door with no pretence of hesitating, only to find Caroline Hepworth hurrying into the clinic.

Aubrey was brought up short. 'Caroline! How did you know we were here?'

'Harris told me.'

'We've found Maggie,' Jack said abruptly. 'But don't go in there.'

Aubrey flinched. Jack hadn't had as much to do with Caroline as he had. Telling her what not to do usually wasn't productive.

When Caroline emerged, all the colour had fled from her face. Her blue eyes blazed with fury. 'Who's responsible for this?'

'We don't know,' Aubrey said. 'But I know what I'm going to do about it. I'm going to find the rest of Maggie's Crew.'

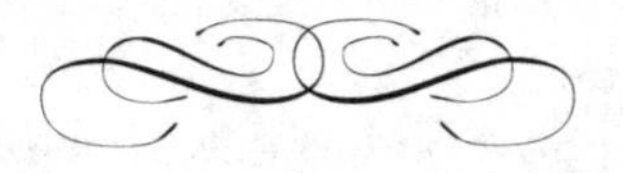

Twenty-two

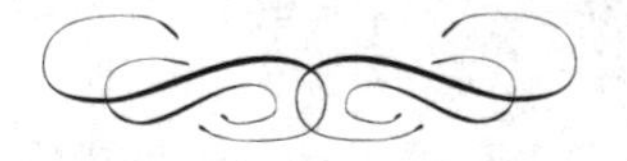

It was a dilemma. Aubrey had weightier matters at hand, more important concerns than a handful of street urchins. The world was lurching toward war, spies and agents were at work, the economy of the nation was under threat.

But he didn't hesitate at all. He liked Maggie's pluck, her independence, the way she'd been making a go of things. Her torment angered him in its callousness.

And this callousness, added to her tortured warning about the darkness, made Aubrey chillingly certain that he could see Dr Tremaine at work.

Ready to rush out of the clinic to find the rest of her Crew, to right the wrong done to her, he pulled himself up short and struck himself on the forehead.

He had no destination.

Planning. He burned to spring into action, to do something to help the poor girl and her friends, but he forced himself to stop, to think.

The reception desk of the clinic was vacant, the nurse having gone home for her midday meal. Aubrey searched the cupboards, the shelves behind the counter, the desk drawers until he found a map of the city, a new one that had been used to note the addresses and neighbourhoods of patients, the sort of thing that a doctor would need when summoned on a house-call. He unrolled it and George and Jack weighed down the corners with a penholder, a blotter, a small jar of boiled sweets and a steel ruler.

'Here's the hydraulic station,' Aubrey said. Caroline reached over and circled it with a pencil. 'And the Bank of Albion is there.' Another circle. 'And here's where Maggie was found, near the Society for Moral Uplift. Count Brandt's headquarters.' Circle.

Aubrey stood back. The patterns of the map swam and moved, starting to fall into place.

'The Southern Line railway tunnel,' Caroline said before he could. She pointed. 'It connects the Bank of Albion with the hydraulic station, near enough.'

George shook his head. 'It stops short of both of them.'

'The part of the tunnel that we know about stops short of both of them,' Aubrey said.

'But what would make you think that there is anything suspicious about it?' Jack asked.

'It's a Rokeby-Taylor construction,' Aubrey said. 'That makes me suspicious.'

Aubrey studied the map. It had the underground lines marked, as well as the above-ground lines of the City Rail Corporation. They extended to the edge of the map and criss-crossed each other, linking in an irregular way that made Aubrey think of a fishing net constructed by a worker who had his mind on other things at the time.

For a moment, despite the urgency, he lost himself in the intricacies of the map. Roads intersecting and connecting, looping about on themselves, splitting and reuniting. The map also indicated the major electricity supply lines for the city, so people would know which company was providing for their neighbourhood. Aubrey knew that no matter how recent the map was, this aspect must be out of date because of the rate at which these companies were spreading their wires though Trinovant.

He tried to picture the subterranean layers of the city, the world he'd lately been shown. Water pipes, gas pipes, sewerage pipes ran in all their which-ways, underpinning the world of the surface. Wires for telephones ran under streets, pneumatic tubes connected offices – and mysterious chains and cables ran along Dr Tremaine's tunnels, even though the tunnels were recently made. Why? With Dr Tremaine nothing was insignificant. Could they be some sort of new weapon?

'What's here?' he asked, pointing to a spot just to the south of Rokeby-Taylor's railway tunnel under the river. It was situated halfway between the tunnel end and the hydraulic station, a gap of half a mile or so. And it was very near where Maggie had been found.

'The Southern Electricity Generating Station,' Caroline said promptly. 'It's another of Rokeby-Taylor's.'

'It is?' Aubrey said. 'How on earth do you know that?'

'Mother was approached to paint a mural inside it. She refused.'

'Good thing,' Jack said. 'I've seen it. It's a monstrosity.'

'She was given a commission document that specified certain aspects of the mural. The dominant figure of The Rise of Commerce was to be modelled on Rokeby-Taylor himself. Mother couldn't stomach such strictures, nor such appalling big-headedness.'

'This is worth investigating,' Aubrey said, chewing his lip.

'Shadwell Phelps took the commission,' Caroline went on. 'He could never do people. Has trouble with hands. And faces. Bodies cause him some difficulty, too. He's quite competent on ankles, though.'

Aubrey stared at the location of the electricity generating station. The Southern Line passed nearby, obviously, and it wasn't far from the river either.

'Jack, you know this area. Wasn't there a canal here?'

'The old Bedford Canal. It was roofed over, years ago. I doubt if it's there now.'

Aubrey was prepared to believe otherwise.

'I think I see what you're on about,' George said. He pointed. 'Unless I'm completely wrong, the main sewerage drain on the south side of the river goes right past this electricity station. The pumping station is on the river's edge, directly north of the place.'

Caroline drew a star on the location of the electricity station. 'It's right on top of a junction of these underground lines.'

'A nexus,' Aubrey said. 'A place that all roads lead to.'

'I understand that they're having guided tours,' Caroline said.

'You know this because your mother was invited?' Aubrey said.

'She declined. She has no interest in bad art, nor electricity generating stations, and the combination made her feel positively ill.'

'I have a strong stomach,' Aubrey said.

'I can take notes without looking suspicious,' George said. 'And who knows? It might turn into a genuine article.'

Jack Figg wanted to go with them, but Aubrey convinced him to stay with Maggie while she went to St Michael's. Jack agreed, reluctantly, and Aubrey was glad. He had an inkling that Jack might slow them down. Despite his enthusiasm, Jack wasn't the sort who'd be first choice for a commando unit.

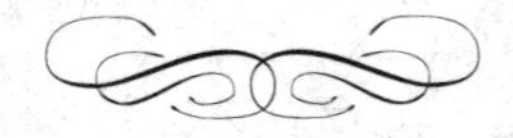

THE SOUTHERN ELECTRICITY GENERATING STATION WAS A hulking brick building that took up an entire block – a block that had been cleared of slums. As they approached it along Tartar Street, Aubrey had the unsettling feeling that the building was crouching below the level of the ground, waiting for them.

It may have taken up an entire city block, but it was set back enough from the street to allow a circus in front of it.

A large red-faced man ground away at a barrel organ, entertaining a crowd of youngsters, most of whom were more interested in the candy floss that was being handed out free of charge. A sweating clown in a spangled jacket had his own audience as he put his troupe of trained dogs though their paces. Other entertainers did their best to make the visitors see an electricity generating station as a place to have fun.

They alighted, and Aubrey paid the cabby. 'Mr Rokeby-Taylor,' Aubrey said as they strolled through the crowds. 'Mr Bread and Circuses.'

'This sort of display must be expensive,' Caroline said. A juggler wandered by, showering a mixture of balls and plates, and smiled at her. 'I wonder where he's getting his money from.'

'A fine, useful question to which I'd very much like the answer,' Aubrey murmured. 'For someone in financial difficulty, he's remarkably free-spending.'

George snorted. 'You know what they say. If you owe the bank a thousand pounds, you're in trouble. If you owe the bank a million pounds, the bank is in trouble.'

Aubrey didn't blame George for his sour outlook on banks, but he wasn't accustomed to seeing his friend so cynical. George's troubles were affecting his usually happy-go-lucky ways, Aubrey was sure, and it pained him to see his friend so. If only he could do something about it.

No, he thought, *I gave him my word*.

But the vow hurt.

Aubrey turned his attention to the task at hand. He patted his pockets and felt the chalk, the handful of brass tacks, and the string that he'd stowed – just in case. The assorted needles stuck in cardboard were a precaution against unknown circumstances. The small bag of glass marbles, on the other hand, was simply insurance, the sort of thing that could be useful in facing powerful forces. With the application of some clever magic.

Immediately Aubrey saw the mural in the gigantic entrance hall, he knew why Ophelia Hepworth had refused the commission. It was vast, taking up a whole wall the size of a tennis court. But it wasn't the size that would have made Mrs Hepworth unhappy, it was being dictated as to the contents and the style.

He couldn't imagine an artist inventing this appalling display. They stood, transfixed, while people moved around them, averting their eyes.

It was the style that Aubrey had become used to on the sides of fruit boxes and packets of soap powder. It was a sort of Commercial–Industrial–Propagandist approach, but with none of the subtlety or humour that that school of art was renowned for.

Aubrey guessed it was a paean, a tribute to the power of Hard Work or such. Hordes of blocky figures were tilling soil, harvesting crops and digging mines. Quite a bit of mine-digging really, and plenty of hauling mountains of what must be coal, towards something that vaguely represented the Southern Electricity Generating Station, in the same way that the face on a coin resembled the reigning monarch.

Smiling beneficently down on this scene of activity was a giant figure in a white robe, surrounded by clouds and golden birds who – Aubrey assumed – were singing songs of praise.

'That's Rokeby-Taylor, isn't it?' George asked.

'Yes. Give or take several dollops of idealising, but who's that behind him?' Caroline asked. 'Right on the edge of the picture. Side profile, looking towards him.'

Aubrey moved closer. Lurking on the edge, almost disappearing into the corner, was a figure.

'Tremaine,' Aubrey said softly and a number of pieces began to lock together. While it may not have stood up in a court of law, it was the first substantial evidence they'd had linking Rokeby-Taylor and their nemesis. 'It's Dr Tremaine.'

Then Aubrey had a moment of self-doubt. Was he imagining Dr Tremaine again? Was it obsession? And if it was him, would the others see him this time? He hoped that having encountered him in the flesh had interrupted the confusion spell that Dr Tremaine had been using in his guise as Spinetti. 'At least, I think it is.'

'What do you mean?' Caroline said fiercely. 'Of course it's him.'

'I wonder who insisted on including him?' George said. 'Rokeby-Taylor?'

'That's something worth considering,' Aubrey said, relieved that they could see Tremaine too. 'Or is someone else in control? He loves a puppet, does Tremaine. Rokeby-Taylor would be perfect.'

'This place is Rokeby-Taylor's triumph,' George said, 'but I don't see him around here.'

'With the battleship bill at a crucial stage, I imagine he's doing what he can to persuade members to pass it.'

They joined a guided tour, where a bowler-hatted gent who must have been chosen for his loud voice conducted a group through heavy steel doors into the main part of the electricity generating station. The whining of the turbines was like the shrieking of a thousand chained-up demons.

The guide managed to make every third or fourth word intelligible, but he supplemented this with extravagant gestures at intake pipes, furnace hoppers and the squat, massive turbines themselves. It was an eloquent, if puzzling, dumbshow.

On one level, Aubrey could appreciate the work that

had gone into the place. He was impressed by the technology, bringing light to homes that had, for years, had to battle with difficult, dangerous gaslights – or oil lamps, which caused more than their own share of fires.

He could sense, too, the magical refinements that had gone into the place. Bearings and turbine blades had been magically protected, while some of the thermal efficiency of the furnaces was monitored magically.

Overhead, the pillars of the smokestacks thrust up through a roof that was a stark curve. Skylights were set amid the reinforcing struts of the roof, allowing sunlight to illuminate the immense space. Aubrey shaded his eyes and squinted upward. His eyes opened wide. He clutched the railing with enough strength to turn his knuckles white.

In the heights, running between the beams, was a meshwork of metal wires, spread in all directions. Bright, shiny copper wires that looked just like those that had infested Maggie.

With a glance and a gesture, Aubrey made sure that Caroline and George lurked at the back of the crowd. When the guide conducted the group along a walkway toward the coal intake area, they passed a staircase that headed downward. Aubrey, Caroline and George dawdled, inspecting walls and dials with the avidity of Wall and Dial Inspectors, then they darted down the stairs after the tour group had left them behind.

The cellar was huge – a deafening, wet, pillared hell where the bulk of the furnaces had residence. Immediately, Aubrey saw that this was the place where the dirty work went on, while upstairs was the showcase. It was chokingly hot, with rattling conveyor belts feeding the never-ending hunger of the fires. Above, in the generation chambers, was the polite face of the coal-devouring monsters. Down here, it was the sweaty, grinding reality.

The place smelled of coal, dirty water and the ozone created by electrical activity. Large electric lights in the ceiling lit the space, but despite their size they seemed to struggle with the soupy atmosphere in the cellar.

They were immediately drenched in the foggy heat. Aubrey found distances hard to judge. Hasty stacks of timber, bricks and metal were flung willy-nilly around the place and he could imagine the panic as opening day had drawn nearer. The cellar was out of sight of the public. Anything that wasn't bright and shiny had been thrown down here, so that even though the facility was only months old, the cellar had the look of an abandoned industrial wilderness.

'Which way?' Caroline asked. She'd changed into her fighting suit and stowed her dress in a small bag she wore at her waist. This time Aubrey managed to pretend it was a matter-of-fact transformation.

'Down,' he said with certainty. 'Our answer lies underground.'

Aubrey's head ached from the noise and the humidity made him feel nauseated but he welcomed these as mere physical sensations, relatively simple to bear. More worrying was the blurring of his vision, something he couldn't blame on perspiration running into his eyes; he was sure it was a symptom of his body and soul disuniting.

It would need attention. When he had time. Right now, he had enough to worry about with the increasing certainty that they were reaching the domain of

Dr Tremaine. Maggie's tortured warning about the depths was becoming more ominous as they edged through the dark and oppressive realm.

Aubrey's lips were dry with apprehension as he peered through the shadows. He could feel his heart racing, rapping his ribs from the inside. The notion of turning around and heading home suddenly had great appeal. A bath, a good meal, a rest and come back some time when better fortified.

No. He thought of poor Maggie. *I want to find him now.*

They trudged along, trying doors and hatches as they came to them. They climbed around piles of building debris, some of which looked as if it had been merely dropped from above. They worked by the feeble light of the dirty electric globes and a lurid red light that came from the slitted grilles and air intakes of the furnaces.

'Another door,' George grunted as they slogged through a pool of ankle-deep water. It was warm, and Aubrey could see the eyes of rats swimming in the near distance. He peered through the gloom. *At least, I hope they're rats.*

The door was heavy steel, bolted and barred. Aubrey hammered on it, but the door was so solid it didn't make a sound. Thinking hard, he rubbed his fist.

Caroline wiped her brow with the back of her hand. 'We've been right around the perimeter. We've found closets, storage rooms, switchboards, nothing useful.'

'This is the only door that's been secured,' George pointed out. He leaned right next to it. His face was red.

'Then I think we may have found our way into the underworld,' Aubrey said.

'What makes you say that?' Caroline asked. She took an unruly strand of hair that was plastered against her temple and, with both hands, fixed it behind her head.

'When I thumped the door, I felt a magic residue. A familiar one.'

Caroline narrowed her eyes. 'Concentrated on the area near the lock, I assume?'

'Dr Tremaine?' George said. He raised his fists, as if he thought Tremaine was going to burst through the door at any minute.

'Correct, both of you. It's the same security spell he used on the Old Man of Albion, and the tunneller.'

'So I missed him,' Caroline said flatly. She clenched her fists.

'Maybe not,' Aubrey said. 'Tremaine is . . . I don't know . . . not like normal people?'

George rubbed his chin. 'Are you saying like one of those werewolves in the stories? Do we need a silver bullet to finish him off?'

'No, nothing like that. It's just that things that would stop an ordinary person won't stop him.'

'I see,' Caroline said and Aubrey knew that she was taking careful note of this information. It wouldn't make her give up her quest for revenge – it would just make her more careful to do it properly next time.

'He's down there,' Aubrey said, 'so it's time for some ifs.' He counted them on his fingers. 'If it's Tremaine, and if he managed to escape from the Bank of Albion and find somewhere to recover, and if he's still down there, then he'd suspect that his security spell was compromised. He'd change his password.'

'So we're stuck?' George said.

'Maybe not. I might have an idea about a replacement password.'

He spread his left hand on the metal, just above where the bolt slid home. He felt the tingle of magic and had no doubt that it was Dr Tremaine's. 'This has been set recently. Within the last twenty-four hours.'

He ignored Caroline's sharp, hissing intake of breath.

'Sister,' he said, clearly and carefully.

The lock didn't budge.

'Sylvia.'

Nothing.

He chewed his lip, then had an inspiration. 'Pearl,' he said, and the lock's tumblers ticked, clicked, shifted. The bolt slid back and, with grim satisfaction, Aubrey realised that he may have found his enemy's weak spot.

He wrenched the door open and was greeted with a welcome gust of cool air. 'Journey with me,' he said grandly, 'to the centre of the earth.'

Without a word, Caroline stepped through. George followed, mumbling, 'I hope we don't have to go that far.'

Aubrey took a moment to prop the door open with a few bricks, then darted after his friends.

The stairwell was poorly lit. Mechanical noises echoed along its brick walls – clanking, vibrating sounds that made Aubrey think of clockwork toys run amok – but toys the size of buildings. By the time they reached the bottom of the stairs, his knees and calves were aching, but the pounding of his heart didn't come from exertion. His whole body was gripped by tension as they approached their destination, and – not for the first time – he wondered what foolishness had prompted him to plunge into the unknown like this.

Next time, he thought, *I'm going to have a crack squad of magical operatives, sappers and marksmen with me. As a bare minimum*.

He hoped there would be a next time.

In the lead, Caroline held up a hand and they stopped. The light that fell on her face made her look heartbreakingly beautiful and determined. She beckoned them forward and slipped out of the doorway.

Aubrey followed, then the outrageousness of the scene struck him. All his breath ran out in a single, awed exhalation.

The chamber was vast, the ceiling soaring cathedral-like overhead. The walls to the right and left were thirty or forty yards away but he couldn't make out the far wall, for the chamber was almost choked with a dizzyingly tangled meshwork of chains, cables and conduits. Pipes and wires of a thousand different sizes and colours emerged from the walls, floor and ceiling and dived into the central snarl, a tangled interweaving that defied the eye to unravel it. Plumes of steam gushed from its depths, and it vibrated, rattled, throbbed, hummed and pulsed with enough energy to seem alive.

Aubrey stared, numb, assaulted by the complexity of the array. He guessed that the entire structure must have plenty of open space, but the overall effect was of overwhelming solidity, of the coalescence of uncountable elements into a massive, compound whole. It reminded him both of a lattice and something organic, something that had grown, branched and grown again.

And he could feel waves of magic rolling through the fantastic construction, waves that came from a single source.

'Where's the light coming from?' Caroline whispered.

Aubrey whispered back, not sure why he kept his voice low, but it seemed most appropriate in this unsettling place. 'In the middle. Where the magic is coming from.' He moved his head from side to side. Light flickered across his face, scattered by the jungle of pipes and wires.

'Must be big. And it's moving,' George said. 'Look around.'

On the walls and ceiling, shadows moved, sliding along, overlapping each other, slipping at speed, then being swallowed by others. 'The light is rotating,' Caroline said.

Aubrey crossed to the edge of the structure. He peered past a series of parallel cast-iron pipes, each only as thick as his thumb, but it was like looking into a thicket; he could see only three or four feet. He put his hand on a brass pipe, a modest one a handspan in diameter, and narrowed his eyes as he felt a tingle of magic moving through it. The pipe emerged from the wall near the stairwell and plunged directly into the structure at about chest height; but as soon as it entered, it bent at ninety degrees and shot upward.

Aubrey edged his head in underneath an earthenware pipe and a sticky bundle of wires as thick as his thigh. He tried to follow his brass pipe to see how high it went. He thought it bent again at right angles and ran parallel to the front edge of the cube for about ten yards. There it met a three-way junction and he lost it.

Aubrey's grip tightened. A few yards away, wrapped around a large cast-iron pipe, was a loose mat of copper wire, the same wire that had infested Maggie.

He shuddered, but forced himself to inspect the malignant wire more closely. The mat was thick, like weed, and it oozed magic. It dangled from the cast-iron pipe and linked it to a bright steel beam that was standing vertically amid a riot of other wires, pipes and struts, interlinked in a structure that hinted at organisation. He was tempted to try to find the underlying pattern, but it defeated him.

'Rails,' George said. Aubrey withdrew his head, catching his ear a stinging blow on a square wooden duct. He hardly noticed.

'What?'

'About twenty yards in that direction. A narrow gauge railway comes out of a tunnel and heads into that mess.'

'And we have a canal over here,' Caroline said, appearing from the shifting shadows. Motes of light flashed across her face. 'A tiny one, only a few feet across.'

'It could be a drain,' George said.

'With miniature wooden barges?'

'Miniature barges?' Aubrey said. 'What on earth?'

'I assume they're barges. They might be just boxes. They're definitely manufactured, and just like the rails, they disappear into the middle of that thing.'

Aubrey looked up, then down, then all around. 'From all directions, they go in there.'

'It depends on how you look at it, old man,' George said. 'They could be leaving the middle of that thing and going outwards.'

'Or some might be pumping inward, and some flowing outward,' Caroline said.

Aubrey's head started to ache with the possibilities. 'But

pumping what? And flowing what? Water? Electricity? Steam? What's going in? And what's going out?'

'Boats?' George said. 'Maybe it's a strange new communication system that uses miniature naval craft to convey information.'

'That is probably one of the more bizarre suggestions I've heard for a long time,' Aubrey said, 'and I'm frightened because I'm considering it seriously.'

'Naturally,' George said, looking pleased with himself. 'But whatever else it is, it's a mystery.'

'It's only a mystery until we find out,' Caroline said.

'And how are we going to do that?' Aubrey said. 'It's a maze in there. A ferret couldn't squeeze its way through.'

'If we can't go through and it's pointless to go around,' Caroline said, 'then we must go over. A better vantage point, a position of strength. We may be able to see into the centre from up there.'

Aubrey raised his head, then leaned back. It was difficult to tell in the shifting light, but it looked as if the structure ended a good ten feet before the ceiling.

Caroline grinned. 'Let's see how you two are at climbing.'

The going was reasonably simple, at first, and Aubrey certainly found it easier than climbing most trees. Solid, rigid pipes were always close at hand, and if he put his weight on something that flexed ominously, an alternative was always nearby. Many pipes were conveniently sized for gripping, but even the large bore mains were simple enough to clamber over. Chains and cables infested the meshwork, too, and provided useful handholds.

But to Aubrey's increasing unease, he found that many of the interweaving strands carried traces of magic.

He avoided wires, singly or in bundles. He had a healthy respect for electricity, as he did for most things that could kill him. Whenever he saw the bright copper mesh, he kept well away from it.

They climbed straight up the outside of the structure. Caroline went first, offering advice to both Aubrey and George as they followed. She appeared to have no difficulty with heights, and often hung from one hand as she looked back to check their progress.

George climbed doggedly, muttering under his breath each time he came to an obstacle that had to be skirted or squirmed around.

Aubrey climbed a few yards away. A construction that looked suspiciously like a miniature aqueduct appeared just above him, emerging from the wall opposite and disappearing into the depths of the labyrinth. Aubrey hoisted himself up and found that it was, indeed, open on the top and carried water. He added it to the list of unbelievable things he'd recently seen.

Once on top of the structure, the going was easier. Instead of lifting their own weight, all they had to do was scramble on all fours. They had to work around any pipes, wires or cables that thrust down from the ceiling (or up from the mass below?) and they had to be sure anything underfoot would bear their weight, but the challenges were few.

Aubrey found himself staring downward as he went, admiring the intricacy that resulted from the myriad interconnections. At times he thought he could detect movement, but he decided it could simply be water, or one of the miniature barges Caroline had seen.

Caroline paused and glanced back quizzically. Heart

pounding, Aubrey nodded, then crawled until he could see that she had reached a gap in the structure. He sought the walls of the chamber and realised they'd reached the centre of the immense meshwork. He found a good foothold on what felt like a solid concrete beam and gazed at the light that filled the gap.

He had to shade his eyes. The light was fierce, a flickering, dancing radiance that licked upward like a bonfire on Empire Night. Aubrey felt its power even at this distance and it daunted him. It wasn't heat that battered his skin, it was raw magical power, redolent with potential – and a hint that was unmistakeably Dr Tremaine.

Gritting his teeth, he crawled closer until he could see more.

A column of cold flame, white and blue, writhing and spinning, filled the gap in the lattice. Mostly, it was half the height of the array, but it occasionally burst upward, as if in joy, sending an arm of flame lancing toward the heights.

'I can see someone down there,' George said.

Aubrey started and nearly lost his grip. He hadn't heard George approaching.

'How many?'

'Just one, I think.'

Caroline made a sound deep in her throat. 'It's Dr Tremaine.'

She lifted her head and scanned the area. It was obvious to Aubrey that she was looking for a way down. She wasn't about to shirk a confrontation with the man who killed her father.

Aubrey tried to think of a good enough argument to change her mind, counselling caution over impulse.

He blinked and almost smiled when he realised that this was just the sort of advice he'd ignored over the years, from some of the best.

Caroline glanced back the way they'd come and her face fell. 'Oh.'

Aubrey followed her gaze and immediately saw the danger. He did his best to appear steely calm, turning a groan of dismay into what he hoped was a determined grunt, while his whole being insisted that elsewhere (anywhere!) was a better place to be.

A swarm of glittering motes was speeding toward them. Insects was what immediately came to mind – bees or wasps – and Aubrey became aware of a humming that was quite different from the background noise from the structure. It was an angry sound, full of intent. The swarm bent in their direction and the humming became furious as it dived.

Aubrey started scrambling on all fours, grasping whatever came to hand. Finding action a good antidote to terror, he set off in a different direction to Caroline, trying to draw the swarm away. He hoped George would do the same and perhaps one of them could escape.

He'd only managed a few frenzied yards when one of the insects struck him behind the ear with stunning force. He fell forward, barely catching himself, then he was struck again, just under the shoulder blades, and he grunted with pain.

It felt as if he were being pelted with stones.

A pistol sounded, once, twice, three times in quick succession. He hoped it was Caroline and he hoped she'd done some good.

One of the insects struck the pipe he was clutching and it rang like a bell. He stared and saw that it was, indeed, a winged insect – but it was made of bright, coppery metal. The insect was chillingly unformed. No features, no details apart from the segmented body, legs and wings. It staggered a little, as if dazed, then it dropped off the pipe and vanished into the depths of the structure.

Dragging a fine copper wire behind it.

Horrified, Aubrey jerked his head back as another insect hummed past his eyes. It curved around and he was dismayed to see that it, too, was trailing a fine copper wire.

Another crashed into a steel cable near Aubrey's hand. He stared at it, but couldn't make out where the insect ended and the wire began. The insect was an extension of the wire or the wire was an extension of the insect.

And it doesn't matter! he thought frantically. He tried to assemble the beginnings of a spell – any spell – but the copper insects had found him. They bombarded him, scores of them, stinging his back and legs with bruising force.

The gap in the structure beckoned. Perhaps if he reached it . . .

The hail of insects kept on, wave after angry wave, battering at him with brutal, senseless ferocity. Aubrey put his head down and crawled.

Then a wire snaked around his ankle.

He pulled loose, but another snagged at his wrist. Desperately, he jerked his head around to find that the insects were crawling over his legs, scuttling along pipes, looping their trailing wires around his body and limbs.

Aubrey thrashed, trying to free himself from the insistence of the wire, not caring if his struggles took him to the edge of the lattice. Revulsion seized him as he realised that this is what must have happened to Maggie and his skin shrank from the evil attention of the creatures.

This gave him renewed energy. He threw himself from side to side, ignoring the bright pain that came when he struck elbows and knees on pipes and chains. He cracked his head with enough force to make his teeth snap together. Stars jumped in front of his eyes, but he couldn't throw off loop after loop of copper wire that kept coming. He tucked in his chin, fearing he'd be strangled.

While he struggled he heard a steady stream of oaths and shouts from George, who seemed to be trying to keep the insects off by power of voice. Aubrey was appalled to hear his friend's shouts growing angrier and angrier, until they became wordless, strangled growling.

At the same time, he heard more pistol shots from nearby. When he rolled to avoid a squad of manic insects descending on his throat, he saw Caroline springing across the framework like a gymnast. One-handed, she swung on an upright and blasted three quick shots that seemed to have some effect on the swarm of insects gathering around her. Even in his difficulties, Aubrey had time to be astonished at her marksmanship, but he groaned to see the pistol plucked from her hand and a blanket of copper wire swirling around her.

Then he had troubles enough of his own. The insects descended like the Furies. He tried to raise a hand to protect his face but found that his left arm was pinned by his side. His right arm had been trapped diagonally across his body. His legs were wrapped together. Unable to move an inch, he snapped his jaws, trying to bite at the insects as they scuttled across his face.

Finally, he was immobilised. He couldn't even attempt a spell – the wires criss-crossed his face, making clear speech impossible.

With the sort of calm deliberation that comes after horror has become too much, he wondered when they would start to penetrate his skin.

A painful clanking sound echoed through the pipes Aubrey was lying on, as if a giant gear had just slipped a cog. It rattled his teeth. Then it was a series of chuffing, pounding thumps, one after the other, like giant footsteps.

Steam washed over Aubrey and he gagged at the hot, oily smell.

A voice cut through the cloud. 'Ah, Fitzwilliam and friends. Just in time.'

Aubrey threw off the heavy hand of dread and decided that bravado was all he had left. He strained until he had some slack in the wires over his jaw. 'Give up, Tremaine,' he slurred. 'It's all over.'

Dr Tremaine loomed into view, stepping off a platform that hadn't been there a moment ago. He was dressed in a green jacket that was so dark it was almost black and he carried a familiar cane. He crouched and studied Aubrey's copper-wrapped face.

'Fitzwilliam, you overrate your comedic talents.' Tremaine plucked at one of the copper wires. It snapped against Aubrey's cheek, but he'd steeled himself. He didn't want to give Tremaine the pleasure of seeing him flinch. 'Now, let's descend to the anastomosis.'

Aubrey couldn't help himself. 'Anastomosis?' he asked mushily.

For once, Dr Tremaine showed irritation. 'Juncture. Nexus. Chiasma. Confluence.' He snorted. 'Never mind. You'll see. It might be the last thing you'll see, but you'll see.'

He clicked his fingers. A copper insect appeared. It hurried backward and forward, tightening copper wire over Aubrey's face until he was well and truly speechless.

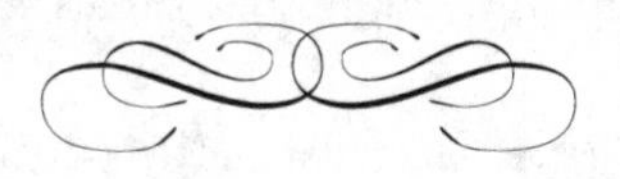

Twenty-three

AT THE BOTTOM OF THE GAP IN THE MIDDLE OF THE invigorated framework was a circular walkway. It ran around the edge of a pit, some twenty feet or so across.

It was the pit that held Aubrey's appalled attention. From it grew the leaping, mounting pillar of magical fire – cold fire, raw magic on the verge of being shaped into something terrible. This was the focus, the origin of the waves of magic that were rolling through the lattice-work. Erratically, it sloughed off magical power that Aubrey felt as if it were handfuls of hail.

From his vantage point, Aubrey could see the pipes, wires, chains and beams funnelling into the flame. They weren't consumed; they were channelling the awesome power of the flame outward, radiating through the latticework. They tightened, clanking or trembling as the magic pulsed.

And then? Aubrey thought and dread seized his innards in an icy grip.

Stalking along the walkway, attention on the magical flame, ignoring his captives, was Dr Tremaine.

Aubrey, Caroline and George were each enmeshed in copper webs, pinned against upright pipes. Aubrey could move his head only fractions of an inch, but it was enough to see his friends. In the flickering light, he could make out the strain in their faces as they struggled with their bonds. To make his situation worse, the conduits running behind Aubrey's shoulderblades throbbed and pulsed with malignant regularity, jarring his teeth and shaking his vision.

Aubrey had been in better positions. In fact, he decided that every other part of his life was rather better than where he found himself right now.

Dr Tremaine's angry pacing took him along the walkway directly in front of Aubrey and his friends, only a few yards away. He looked deep in thought, but reserved, as if this was an ordinary magical laboratory and he a comfortable don. He occasionally paused and contemplated the magnificence of the pillar of cold flame, rubbing his chin and frowning before uttering sharp, coarse spells. After each, the pillar of flame would change – growing, twisting, writhing in an agony of growth – and Aubrey would feel magic sleeting from it in indiscriminate bursts of power. The latticework around them groaned and shook like the rigging of a ship in a storm.

He managed to make a noise – a hurtful grunt – and Dr Tremaine glanced at him. 'Don't worry. Your time will come very, very soon.'

With implacable efficiency, the ex-Sorcerer Royal went about his business.

And his business chilled Aubrey to the core. With a proficiency that would have impressed Professor Mansfield, Dr Tremaine roamed across dozens of ancient languages, some of which Aubrey knew, some he had knowledge of, and others that were totally alien to him, to create a dense, interwoven series of spells.

Each individual spell was fiendish in its length and complexity, but Tremaine seemed to be unaffected by the Principle of Cost – he didn't flag at all.

In addition, he regularly broke a cardinal rule of spell construction – he used a number of different languages within the same spell.

Under other circumstances, Aubrey would have been fascinated to watch a master at work. This eclectic, individual approach was a virtuoso display. He would have questioned, taken notes, and felt privileged to observe such craft.

Instead, he was trapped with a rapidly increasing feeling of alarm as each of Dr Tremaine's refinements made the pillar of flame grow, clawing upward with greedy fingers that boiled with power.

Dr Tremaine was attempting some sort of animating magic. It was like that which they'd encountered in the Roman shrine, but only in the same way that a kitten resembles a tiger. This was immeasurably more powerful, more complex, more wide-ranging. Apparently he'd had some success already, judging from the copper wire insects and Maggie's appalling condition.

The tower of cold fire was at the heart of Dr Tremaine's conjuring. He stoked it with spells and it grew with baleful splendour. Its power – the power of animation – was channelled outward through the pipes, wires and cables that speared into it.

And where does it go then? Aubrey thought, but he was already beginning to form conclusions – and none of them were joyous.

With a cry of exasperation, the sorcerer cut short his current spell. He whirled. 'You fool! Don't you know you're endangering the whole project by interrupting me!'

Aubrey started, even though he couldn't imagine how he'd interrupted. Flicking his gaze to either side, he could make out that Caroline and George were both still bound – but then he saw that someone was joining them.

A figure squirmed through a small gap between a twisted bundle of rusty chains and a red-painted steam pipe, head and shoulders emerging with much grunting. He was grimy and dishevelled, smeared with grease. His clothes, once fine and expensive, were a mess, and Aubrey saw with bleak satisfaction that he was wearing a red tie with a green suit and the combination clashed horribly.

The intruder's mouth fell open at the sight of the trapped Aubrey, Caroline and George. 'What are they doing here?'

'What does it look like, Rokeby-Taylor? Quantity surveying? Landscape painting?'

'You're not going to embed them?'

'Of course I'm going to embed them. Human consciousness is vital to animating my magnificent creation.' Dr Tremaine heaved a huge, theatrical sigh, then cocked an eyebrow at his captives. 'I really must get a better quality of henchman. But there's not a lot to choose from, these days, when it comes to toadies and traitors.'

Rokeby-Taylor heaved himself out of the latticework, but fell heavily. Picking himself up with awkward solemnity, he tried to straighten his clothes and brush off the mess but only made it worse. He shook his head and wiped his hands on his jacket. 'The tunneller has broken down again,' he said to Dr Tremaine, 'but I've finished the last connector.'

'And placed the vivifying wires?'

'I think so. If the infernal machine worked properly.'

'It's good to see you've done something right,' Dr Tremaine said absently. He flexed his shoulders and considered the cold flame. 'Especially seeing as the last thing you managed without cocking it up was concealing that thunderstorm spell at Count Brandt's little meeting.'

It was Caroline who succeeded in squeezing out a wordless cry of outrage. Aubrey simply felt despair. He'd been right in his first suspicions – Rokeby-Taylor had played a part in that atrocity. Why hadn't he listened to himself?

'I'll have you know,' Rokeby-Taylor said to Aubrey, Caroline and George, trying to regain some dignity, 'that I don't approve of this embedding.'

In his confining mesh, Aubrey sagged until the wire threatened to cut into his skin. He'd had his suspicions, but deep down he'd tried to convince himself it wasn't so. To see Rokeby-Taylor, the epitome of the Albion gentleman, in league with the foremost enemy of the land was a blow.

Dr Tremaine sneered at Rokeby-Taylor. 'You don't approve? I'll show them what you approved of without an instant's hesitation.'

He spat out a short spell. A section of the structure began to extrude itself from the meshwork, pushing out into the central vantage point. Pipes, wires, rails thrust forward, clanking and shunting, telescoping, growing while steam hissed around it. Sparks ran along its length, crackling with glee.

It was a cube, three or four yards on a side, connected by an arm that was composed of beams and pipes intertwined with the bright copper wire Aubrey had come to loathe.

It chuffed and ground its way toward the beckoning Dr Tremaine.

At that moment, in this nightmare world of intersections and junctions, Aubrey himself made a connection. He saw the city as a map, but a map of many levels, extending deep beneath the surface. Dr Tremaine had learned to animate the network that connected the underworld. Pipes, wires, rails, cables, canals all criss-crossing, interlinking and interweaving throughout the substrata of the city and Dr Tremaine was uniting them under his will. The animating power of the cold fire was permeating all Trinovant.

He began to tremble as his imagination supplied details. Dr Tremaine's reach wouldn't be confined to the realms beneath the city. Wires, pipes and drains penetrated every building in the modern city, joining them in an elaborate grid, a web with a malevolent genius at its centre.

Aubrey's heart raced – pointlessly, for he was unable to

either fight or flee. He was worried that it would take matters into its own hands, burst from his chest and try to escape.

The cube continued to ratchet forward. The clanking made Aubrey wince; it sounded poorly constructed, metal grating on metal, but it continued its jerky movement with no sign of weakness. Finally, with the sound of clashing gears, it dropped to eye height.

'See?' Dr Tremaine poked at the cube with his cane. 'Mr Rokeby-Taylor was quite happy for poor urchins to be embedded. His righteousness didn't extend that far.' He stroked his chin. 'It's a pity the girl got away. I have no idea how she managed to tear herself free.'

Sickened, Aubrey gazed into the heart of the cube.

Maggie's Crew. A dozen small bodies were implanted in a dense mesh of copper wire. It was as if they were sprouting bizarre copper hair from all over, making it hard to see where the wire ended and their body began.

Even in the extremity of his own situation, Aubrey mourned for them. They didn't deserve what had happened to them. Life's victims, for a brief moment – with Maggie's help – it had looked as if they had hope, but they had ended up as dead as the other lost children on the streets of Albion.

A moan came from his left and he saw that Caroline had closed her eyes, trying to keep the horror away. George, on the other hand, was straining against the copper wire, a snarl coming from his tortured throat.

Then the nearest embedded urchin opened his eyes. Aubrey would have screamed if he had been able.

'Oh yes,' Dr Tremaine said, chuckling at Aubrey's distress. 'They're still alive. Alive and vital. It's the vitality that is useful, after all, feeding into the process. Human consciousness and great magic go hand in hand. Magic, the universe, humanity, all intertwined, all available for manipulation.' He pointed with his cane. 'And we have all sorts of other life wired as part of this beautiful creation too, to add to the piquancy of the creation. I was particularly interested in life that we found down here. Indigenous to the area, you might say.'

'Put them away, Tremaine,' Rokeby-Taylor said. His face was drawn and haggard; his eyes darted uncertainly. He swallowed before continuing. 'Just put them away, there's a good fellow.'

Dr Tremaine gave Rokeby-Taylor a look that very clearly said that he wasn't anyone's good fellow, but he growled out another spell. With a chuff of steam, the cube and its supports shunted away until it was an undistinguishable part of the structure again.

'We have life aplenty embedded in the array,' Dr Tremaine went on, as if Rokeby-Taylor hadn't interrupted. 'Rats – thousands of them – pigeons, bats, a surprising number of foxes, a few badgers. And humans. Nothing like a bit of human to add vigour to a spell, I always say.'

The ex-Sorcerer Royal crossed his arms. He contemplated the majesty of the cold fire. Its light flickered on his profile.

'But not them, Tremaine,' Rokeby-Taylor said. 'Not the Prime Minister's son. Not the girl.'

Aubrey immediately felt offended – and concerned – on George's behalf. And it felt grubby, having his life pleaded for by Rokeby-Taylor. He wanted to go and have a good wash.

The cold light lingered on Tremaine's face. 'Are you still sure you want to do this, Rokeby-Taylor? Do you really want to destroy the greatest city in the world?'

Rokeby-Taylor fumbled with his tie. 'It was your idea.'

'Naturally it was my idea. No-one else in the world would have been capable of conceiving such a thing. Animating Trinovant? Only Mordecai Tremaine would dare. Urbomancy is not something that small minds can contemplate.'

Urbomancy. Of course. Aubrey closed his eyes. Dr Tremaine was not a man for small plans. Trinovant in this era was different from the urban civilisations of the past. Not even the Romans, fine engineers though they were, had the extensive underground skeleton that electricity, gas, water, sewerage and transportation provided. Tremaine was using it to animate all Trinovant.

The horror came to him with swift, punishing clarity. Railway tracks rising like giant serpents, intertwining and crushing buildings. Electrical wires lashing panicked pedestrians. Pipes wrenching themselves from the ground and flattening entire neighbourhoods, before jetting gas, steam and water to wreak havoc. The earth itself rising, held together by the web of power, shedding itself of shops, homes and palaces the same way a dog shakes off fleas.

He felt sick.

'It's beyond me,' Rokeby-Taylor said, but then he looked sharply at Dr Tremaine. 'Not that I have a small mind, Tremaine.'

'Of course not.' Dr Tremaine pressed both hands together. He strolled over and brought his face close to Aubrey's. 'Now, my interfering friend. Soon you will belong to the city in a way of which you couldn't even dream.'

Aubrey decided that Dr Tremaine had a very low opinion of his dreaming abilities.

He was experiencing a peculiar mixture of emotions. He was scared, but that seemed natural enough in the circumstances. However, it wasn't the crippling fear of panic; it was the heart-thumping fear of consequences, the hollow pit of the stomach that came from thinking what could happen if they couldn't get out of this.

But understanding where his fear came from had helped him control it. It was almost as if he'd managed to pack it into a box and park it in a corner. This cleared his thinking so he could train it on trying to devise a way out of their predicament. The trouble was, nothing came to mind – except an understanding of what Dr Tremaine was planning.

For the lack of anything better, Aubrey began to struggle. Dr Tremaine threw his head back and laughed. 'At last! Someone who doesn't disappoint me!'

Rokeby-Taylor looked most put out. 'What on earth do you mean, Tremaine?'

'Young Fitzwilliam. He's worked out what I'm up to, with very few hints at all.'

'How do you know?'

'Look at him. He was quiet, thinking, and now he's all a-flutter. He's no idiot, Rokeby-Taylor, not like you.'

'Steady on, Tremaine. No need to be offensive.'

'No need, but it's a pleasure anyway.' Dr Tremaine shook his head. 'For all the money I've given you, Rokeby-Taylor, I haven't asked you for much. But you've messed up just about everything I've tasked you with.'

'A run of bad luck, Tremaine, that was all.'

'I could have used the Rashid Stone to help with these spells but you managed to mess up procuring that in a way that I thought impossible. Even if your minions failed to steal it, I was going to have access to it on board the *Imperator*, but now it's disappeared.'

Aubrey should have known that Dr Tremaine would have had some interest in the Rashid Stone. He was glad he'd managed to put a stick in those spokes.

'That's hardly my fault,' Rokeby-Taylor said. He didn't whine. Not quite.

'And then there was the *Electra*. You managed to get yourself aboard, but because you insisted on using your cheap magicians you nearly killed Sir Darius instead of wrecking the boat in the deep water test it was due to undertake on the very next day.' He glanced at Aubrey. 'I suppose I should thank you for preventing that. Now isn't the time for your father to be removed. That will come later.'

Any trace of fear disappeared from Aubrey. It was replaced with cold, hard anger. Tremaine's casual assumption that he could play with the lives of those Aubrey loved was a reminder of what the man was – a menace that must be defeated.

Rokeby-Taylor made an attempt at dignity that fell short by a league or two. 'Listen here, Tremaine, I was nearly killed myself in that escapade. I risked my life for you.'

'And what about the tunneller?' Dr Tremaine went on remorselessly. He glanced sideways as a trail of sparks fizzed along a chain and disappeared into the latticework. 'You had a few easy connectors to dig and you managed to flood the old hydraulic tunnel. Then you made your own railway line collapse. I couldn't believe it.'

'Could have happened to anyone. Who knew that tunnel was still down there?'

'I did. You should have.' Dr Tremaine looked at Aubrey for a moment, then he uttered a short, spiky spell. Copper insects scuttled over Aubrey's face. His skin crawled, but in seconds his jaw and mouth were free. He worked it from side to side, testing it warily.

'What do you want?' he asked Tremaine.

'I want to know what conclusion you've reached.'

'Why?'

'I'd like to be surprised. I so rarely am.'

'You're going to turn the city into a monster.'

'Not the best choice of words, but I see what you're thinking.'

'You're animating the city, using the tunnels, the wires, the pipes as connectors, like veins, arteries and nerves.'

'Yes, yes, like ligaments, sinews and tendons. And have you ever noticed how a metaphor can actually reduce the object of comparison? No? Very well, what will happen next?'

'The city must have reached a critical level of connectivity to facilitate this.'

'Yes, well, partly that's due to Rokeby-Taylor here. His electricity generating plants have been important in achieving this – as you put it – critical level of connectivity.' Tremaine paused. 'I like that phrase.'

'So Rokeby-Taylor's responsible for this.'

'Don't be foolish. He does what I tell him.'

'Is that right, Rokeby-Taylor? Why?'

Rokeby-Taylor glanced at Dr Tremaine, who grinned. 'Go ahead. You can answer.'

Taylor wouldn't meet Aubrey's eye. 'Dr Tremaine has offered me eternal life.'

Aubrey's eyes widened at the absurdity of the offer. Eternal life wasn't something to be handed around like a box of chocolates. Dr Tremaine's plans for eternal life for himself involved long and meticulous planning, committing a whole continent to war. 'Eternal life? I thought you wanted money.'

'I do. Bucket loads of it. But what good is money if you only have one lifetime to spend it?' He frowned, as if it should have been obvious.

Aubrey sighed. Rokeby-Taylor's betrayal was for such a petty motive. He wanted the good life, but he wanted it to go on forever. Nothing elevated there, no appeal to a philosophical ideal, just base and sordid greed.

'You see,' Dr Tremaine said, 'Rokeby-Taylor here has sold himself to me, in exchange for his heart's desire. A simple transaction, with benefits to us both.'

'And disadvantages for Albion.'

'There you go again, taking a lofty view of what is essentially a personal matter.'

'Personal matter? You'll turn Trinovant into a monster and then . . .' Aubrey thought hard. Apart from ruining the financial centre of the Empire, what else would he do? 'Send it rampaging across the countryside to destroy what? Our munitions factories? Shipyards? Railways?'

Dr Tremaine waved this away. 'I'm sure I'll find some use for a city-sized creature. Once I *have* a city-sized monster.'

A flat, deadly voice came from Aubrey's left. 'You killed my father. And you tried to kill Lady Rose.'

'Eh? Ah, Miss Hepworth. I thought I'd cancelled that insect's work after it freed young Fitzwilliam. Never mind.'

'You killed my father,' Caroline repeated, 'and you tried to kill Lady Rose.'

'Now you're getting tedious,' Dr Tremaine said. 'I told you about your father, and how unavoidable that was. Lady Rose, though, that's another matter. I've found that those Holmlander espionage agencies need something to keep them busy, something to keep their noses out of my business. A simple assassination or two is just the sort of thing.'

'They failed,' Caroline said.

'Yes. Most of humanity is less competent than I am, but I can't do everything. Now, I need to concentrate.'

This gave Aubrey some hope. Dr Tremaine could still be stopped; he hadn't finished his work.

The magician snapped out a short spell and Aubrey felt the hated copper insects crawling over his face. Within seconds, they'd bound his mouth again. At the same time, he saw insects shuttling across Caroline's face. Despite her furious struggling, she, too, was silenced.

He strained against the wires, desperately hoping the insects had left some slack this time. The wire bit cruelly into his cheeks and lips, but he didn't give up until blood trickled from a cut on his upper lip.

In his desperation, he realised that this was a small victory. He worked his neck, one of the few tiny movements available to him. The cut opened. Blood smeared on his skin. Ignoring the pain, he continued, working away, straining a fraction of an inch this way, a fraction of an inch back.

Until he felt the wires slip, lubricated by his own blood.

Hope flared in him and he looked toward Dr Tremaine. The sorcerer was locked into his cycle of spells. His voice – vast and majestic – rolled around the chamber and the pillar of flame responded, roaring upward, swollen with power. Sparks crackled along chains and cables, turning the latticework into a shadowy fairyland. Pipes shook. Metal quivered with the force of the magic it channelled.

And the latticework was alive with sound – low whistling, a multitude of creakings and shiftings, a humming just on the edge of perception.

Aubrey shifted, flinched, then thrust a little with his chin. The bloody wires separated, freeing his mouth just enough for him to articulate a spell. A very short, very simple spell.

So I'll have to start small.

It appealed to his sense of irony. Against prodigious magic, he was forced to use a humble spell. But if it worked, it would be a step toward foiling the destruction of Trinovant. If he could find a spell to free his mouth properly, he could then cast a more substantial spell – one that could stop Dr Tremaine.

He recalled his flirtation with the violin at university. Two days of dogged practice had left his fingertips sore and tender, so his instructor had used a spell to harden them. After this, he was able to press on the strings with no problem at all, as if his fingertips were little blocks of wood. The effects didn't last long, just for a practice session, but that was all that was required. Naturally, Aubrey had been intrigued by the spell. At the time, he had sworn off magic – but he had played around with some of the elements, in a strictly theoretical manner.

This time, though, he needed something harder than wood – and it wasn't his fingertips he was hardening. It was his tongue.

He constructed a spell sequence, adjusting the hardness factor. He wanted the tip of his tongue to be as hard as steel. As hard as diamond!

In the clanking, hissing world of the pipeworks, Aubrey didn't think he could be heard, but he kept his voice low in any case, barely above a whisper. Five short terms then a clipped final signature and he was done.

Unsure if the spell had worked, he tapped his tongue against his teeth and was reassured by the solid 'clink' it made.

He went to work. The copper wire was no match for his diamond-hard tongue. He sawed the edge against them and, one by one, they parted. First on the left side, then the right, and soon his whole mouth was free. He cancelled the spell, stretched his mouth, and he was ready.

Now he could do some serious magic, but he was frozen by the sight that confronted him.

Even with a small audience, Dr Tremaine did not neglect the dramatic. As his spells grew, rising in volume and complexity, he thrust up a hand, summoning and harnessing the power of the cold flame. It quivered in response, and all the connectors vibrated with the power it was pumping out to the edges of the city.

Rokeby-Taylor had backed away until he was pressed against a huge, vertical pipe. His expression was one of avidity and excitement, a man seeing his heart's desire, but unwilling to believe it was so close. His hands trembled even though he held them together.

Aubrey had time for one spell. Even though he could work his mouth properly, he doubted that Dr Tremaine or Rokeby-Taylor would allow him the luxury of a long, uninterrupted casting, so something short and useful would have to do.

His mind was awhirl with the possibilities, but what could he do to combat Dr Tremaine's power, face to face?

Then he realised he didn't have to meet him head-on. Dr Tremaine had embarked on a careful series of interlaced spells. His admonition to Rokeby-Taylor not to interrupt him wasn't just an artist's petulance, it was vital. If one component of the spell matrix was incomplete, the whole program could fall apart.

All Aubrey had to do was break up his spell-casting, but interrupting someone with such a focus, such an iron will, was not going to be easy, however much magic Aubrey had at his disposal.

So he turned the problem around. Not magic, anti-magic.

The Rashid Stone, the mysterious Roman fragment, his work on Ancient Languages, had all helped to refine his understanding of the basic nature of magic – and how language shaped it. Added to this, Rokeby-Taylor's magic suppressors showed that magic could be damped, neutralised. All he had to do was work out a way of achieving it here.

His mind seized on the rods inside the magic suppressors. They vibrated. If they generated magic that was equal to and opposite any magic performed in the area, everything would be effectively cancelled out – much as the sound-deadening magic that Aubrey had some experience of, back at Stonelea School.

Aubrey grasped at this fundamental application of the Law of Opposites. The difficulty was setting up the spell so it had duration – and that it also adapted to cancel out any magic within its range.

Feverishly, he plotted out the elements, the variables and the constants. Striving for potency, he reached back and used Sumerian, hoping that the primeval language would have the simplicity needed for such a weighty spell.

It was intricate. Aubrey had doubts about its effectiveness, and the variable for dimensionality seemed to be intimately linked with the intensity constant. It meant he couldn't cast it very far away – it was an extremely proximate, localised spell. He realised it explained the restricted field generated by the suppressors, and how carefully they had to be situated.

He could affect Dr Tremaine, but not the fountain of animating flame.

It was enough – he hoped. If he could interrupt Dr Tremaine, it should stop his careful spell-casting.

When he had it mapped in his mind, he ran through it twice, then began.

Immediately, he faced a struggle.

What he was doing was fundamentally inconsistent. He was casting a magical spell to negate magic. Each syllable resisted him. He had to force his mouth to make the correct shapes and spit them off his tongue. His split lip flared with sharp, lancing pain at each movement. Sweat sprang from his forehead and his jaw ached with the effort of speaking each element. They were heavy, dragging his lips downward so that he had to compensate in his delivery. He felt as if he were being strangled.

His throat started to close as the final term loomed. He dropped his chin as much as he could, hoping that gravity would help the term fall from his mouth.

It did; finally all he had left was his signature. It, too, was weighty, as if infected by the other parts of the spell, but he forced it out. He was done.

Dr Tremaine continued chanting.

Aubrey slumped against his metal bonds, oblivious of their cutting into him. He had no triumph to keep away the avalanche of fatigue that swept over him. No strength was left in his limbs. His head felt too heavy for his neck. He was defeated.

Then Dr Tremaine stopped chanting and whirled, eyes blazing. 'Magic suppression! Magic suppression! Do you know what you've done, Fitzwilliam?' He raged over the increasing noise of the flame. 'You've ruined everything!'

He stormed to Aubrey and thrust his face close. He snarled, baring his teeth like a great beast. 'Wretched boy! You dare to interpose yourself in my plans?'

In a blur of motion, he slapped Aubrey across the face, once then again, backhanded. Aubrey's ears rang with the force of the blow.

Dr Tremaine glared at him, jaw clenched so tightly that the tendons stood out on his neck. He panted, sucking air in through his teeth. 'You've destroyed the spell.'

With difficulty, Aubrey lifted his head and smiled. 'If that means I've stopped you destroying Trinovant, that's good enough.'

Tremaine stared at him for a moment then threw back his head and laughed. 'That you may have, boy. But at the cost of your own life.' He studied Aubrey. 'In that case, you won't be needing this.'

With a fingernail, Dr Tremaine sheared through wire as if it were butter. He plucked Aubrey's watch from his pocket and held it up. The light from the cold fire made the Brayshire Ruby glitter like a red star.

Aubrey threw himself against his bonds, anger making him oblivious to the pain. He hissed, then locked eyes with his tormentor and their connection was re-established.

An instant lasted for an eternity, an instant where Aubrey knew Dr Tremaine. He knew his roaring confidence, his unbounded dreams, his utter selfishness. He also knew his sorrow and frustration at never being able to find his sister. A vision came to Aubrey of Sylvia, but it was ghostly, vague, a portrait seen by cloudy moonlight.

Above all, Dr Tremaine's self dominated the experience – raw, wild, untouched by anyone apart from his sister. He was more a primeval force than a human being – a storm, an earthquake, a volcano. Aubrey shuddered and shied away from such unalloyed power.

At the same time, Aubrey was aware that Dr Tremaine had touched him. He lay exposed – his ambitions were naked, his confidence and insecurities on display, his skill and talents up for measure.

Then it ended, a heartbeat where they were blended and aware of another human being as few are.

Aubrey was dazed. Numbly, he stared at Tremaine, who looked back thoughtfully, tapping his chin. 'My, my, my,' he said, and the sheer banality of this utterance brought Aubrey back to his senses.

He managed to make his mouth work again. He wanted to demand the heirloom back, but he refused to give Tremaine the pleasure. 'You're a petty thief as well as a failed traitor, Tremaine.'

Dr Tremaine shrugged. 'You have something precious of mine, Fitzwilliam. It's only fair that I have something of yours.' A bass rumble from the column of cold fire made the magician glance over his shoulder. 'I always say that a true genius knows when to abandon a plan and when to try to resurrect one. Now is the time to abandon this one, I fear.'

Aubrey couldn't help himself. 'You didn't say that.'

Dr Tremaine frowned. 'What?'

'That's one of Scholar Tan's axioms. You stole it and just pretended you made it up.'

Aubrey had fought hand-to-hand with Dr Tremaine. He'd engaged in a magical struggle with Dr Tremaine. But judging from the almost embarrassed scowl, this time he'd managed to slip right under his guard and pierce his pride. Hastily he chalked it up as a point to himself and steeled himself for Dr Tremaine's reaction.

The rogue magician ignored it. Pretending he hadn't heard Aubrey, he went to make his exit.

Aubrey had an instant of satisfaction, then he did what he could. 'Stop him, Rokeby-Taylor!' he cried. 'Before he gets away!'

'Yes, stop me, Rokeby-Taylor,' Dr Tremaine said, having gathered his composure. He chuckled. 'Do something useful instead of standing there. Use the revolver in your pocket.'

Obediently, Rokeby-Taylor took out the revolver. He blinked at it, owlishly. 'I say, Tremaine, it's not for you. It's for protection.'

'Stop him, you idiot!' Aubrey shouted.

'How can I confer eternal life on you, Clive, if you shoot me?' Dr Tremaine said. He appeared to be enjoying this immensely, but Aubrey noted how he kept one eye on the shifting column of flame. 'Now listen. You stay here, guard these troublemakers, and I'll come back and get you in a few minutes.'

Rokeby-Taylor stared at Dr Tremaine, then he glanced at his revolver. He weighed it in his hand, then, slowly, he reached out and snapped off the safety catch. 'I've been called many things in my time,' he said, and he looked like someone who believed he was dreaming, 'and I put up with them because I knew what I wanted.'

'And you'll get it, Clive, you will,' Dr Tremaine said. 'Keep your back to the flame and all will be well.'

'I was a fool,' Rokeby-Taylor said, in the voice of someone discovering something for the first time. 'And it's all come to this.'

'You'll be able to laugh at all those who scorned you,' Dr Tremaine said. 'When they die, you will be alive. What better revenge can anyone have?'

Rokeby-Taylor considered this. 'I could show them that they were wrong.'

'Yes,' Aubrey said. 'Do that. Show us we were wrong. Show us you're not a traitor. Stop Tremaine and you'll be a hero.'

'A hero, a fool, and a disgrace.' He pocketed the revolver. 'No. On the whole, I'd rather have eternal life.'

Aubrey closed his eyes as hope ran away. Rokeby-Taylor had a chance at redemption, but had passed on it.

Dr Tremaine clapped his hands together. 'Excellent. Now, remember that you're in charge until I get back.'

He strode to the latticework of conduits. Aubrey thought he was going to crash right into it, but just as he neared, the pipes, wires and chains drew back, making a Tremaine-sized hole that closed behind him.

The flame he left behind continued to grow in bulk and height. It now licked the ceiling with hungry vigour. It began to branch, side jets flaring with their own greedy life. Aubrey knew that, now the flame was released from Tremaine's control, it would build on itself, a runaway column of raw power. The chamber would be consumed, swallowed in the boiling chaos of uncontrolled magic.

The flame bowed, shifting enough so he just make out Caroline and George. Both were struggling, but Aubrey knew how pointless it was. Still, he was proud that neither of them was giving up without a fight.

Rokeby-Taylor paced along the walkway, his back to the flames. He was a long way from the well-dressed man about town that Aubrey had met in his townhouse. He was unshaven, filthy and he mumbled as he marched. His shoulders were hunched and he kept his head down as if uncertain about this whole walking business. 'I'm not a bad man,' Rokeby-Taylor said suddenly, popping his head up. 'Just greedy.'

'I'm afraid I don't really care at the moment,' Aubrey said. 'I have to stop this flame from exploding. Look at the way it's building.'

'I can't. Tremaine said not to look at it.'

'And you believed him? He's been lying to you all along, you know. He has no intention of giving you eternal life. It's a trick.'

'No it's not. I'm crucial to his plans, he told me.'

Yes, thought Aubrey, *but not in the way you think.* 'Look, the flame's getting bigger. Move away, at least.'

'What?'

At the last moment, Rokeby-Taylor did glance over his shoulder at the flame, Aubrey's urgency overcoming his obedience. He was in time to see the column split and send a branch snaking in his direction. Rokeby-Taylor straightened, and for a moment it was as if the years had melted from him. His eyes sparkled as he threw himself to one side, rolling and coming to his feet with a grin. He looked toward Aubrey and touched his nose with a gesture that suggested that this was all a jolly lark.

Then the tentacle of flame snapped back and wrapped itself around him.

Rokeby-Taylor's eyes flew open wide and his hands clawed at the flame. His mouth gaped, but no scream came out. The process was too quick for that. He was frozen in place, trapped in the middle of terror. In an instant, he became transparent, like smoked glass. Then he was an outline, a sketch of a human being, an empty husk. A burst of light and he was gone, as if he had never been.

Aubrey cried out, but it was far, far too late. All the breath went from him as if he'd been punched hard in the stomach. He had no time to spare for pity, but he couldn't help but be moved by the fate of a fellow human, no matter how misled, how corrupt, how avaricious.

The column of flame was broader, taller, more solid. The blue-white was shot through with deeper, shimmering folds of gold. It began to roar like a mighty wind; it battered at him with sheer, unfocused magical power.

He had to stop it.

His mind worked in double time, dividing each second into a hundred parts. He riffled through possibilities and solutions, testing and discarding, pressing for a solution.

He couldn't imagine dousing it like an ordinary fire. Could he smother it, choke it? How had Dr Tremaine summoned it? How had he controlled it? What was its fuel?

Fuel. He seized on this. A fire needed fuel, but this cold flame had reached a stage where it was growing beyond any supply of fuel. It was sending out infinitely more power than could possibly be supplied to it.

It was feeding on itself. The Law of Intensification played a part here, he was sure, but it had sent things spiralling out of control. Intentionally or otherwise, it didn't matter. The flame had achieved a stage where the magic it was generating was spawning further magic, which further fed the beast. It would grow on itself, getting bigger and more powerful, faster and faster.

Unless he could interrupt it. He had to control it, to absorb some of the magic it was breeding. If he could, this would stop the process, for good.

It was a hastily constructed theory, but it was the only one he had.

He had to adapt the magic suppressing spell. He couldn't cancel the magic of the column of flame – it was too fierce, too powerful for that. Instead he wanted a spell to *absorb* it.

The image was perfect and he seized on it. He pictured administering charcoal to a patient to absorb poison, sponging up the deadly stuff and making it harmless.

The metaphor helped, but he realised he had no time to work out a careful spell. He had to launch into it straightaway – and trust to his ability to extemporise.

He recalled his anti-magic spell and began, adjusting each element, starting with intensity, duration, direction and dimensionality, before moving on to the individual variables and constants that shaped such an involved spell. He hurried through it, adapting on the run. It was easier this time as he wasn't negating magic, he was simply mopping it up.

He gasped when he finished, slapped by a wracking pain, but was astonished when he saw his spell create a jet black rod, two yards or more in length, a few inches in diameter. It appeared out of the air and toppled into the heart of the flame – his absorption metaphor made real.

For an instant, the flame buckled, then it roared back as fierce as ever.

Aubrey repeated the spell, gritting his teeth against the combination of pain and fatigue that assaulted him. Another rod appeared and joined the first.

This time, Aubrey had no doubt. The flame flinched. It folded in on itself, wavered, but then jetted upward again in defiance.

Aubrey cast the spell again. And again. And again. His throat grew hoarse, his vision blurred.

He lost count of the rods that popped into existence and fell into the flame. The fire collapsed, grew again, collapsed, wavered, grew and collapsed until Aubrey was lost in a haze of light, sound and magic.

And pain.

It was the quiet that made Aubrey stop. He found it hard to breathe. He couldn't move his head and he struggled to lift his gaze.

The flame was gone.

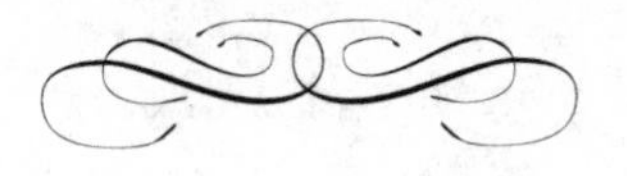

Twenty-four

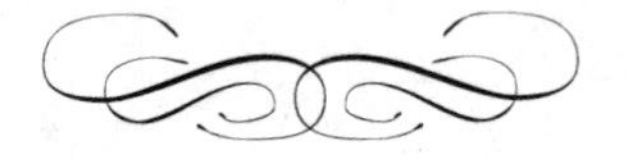

Craddock's operatives found the exhausted and battered Aubrey, Caroline and George stumbling through the tunnels after freeing themselves. Through a haze of pain and fatigue, Aubrey listened to their explanations as they half-dragged him through the tunnels.

Dr Tremaine's urbomancy had set off multiple alarms in the Magisterium's magic monitoring department. The intensity of the magic was enough for Craddock to send a Flying Squad to find the source of such a gargantuan disturbance. Too late to have been of any assistance in quelling the magical fire, but well timed to render some useful first aid.

Dimly, Aubrey was glad Craddock insisted on physical fitness in his operatives. Shivering, he leaned heavily on the two agents who assisted him and he let his head loll. It was simply too much effort to hold it up. Besides, he'd seen more than enough tunnel to last him a lifetime.

A WEEK LATER, AUBREY WAS AT ST ALBAN'S, MUCH recovered and studying hard, when the door opened. A large cardboard box entered. Carrying the box, sweating and panting, was George.

Instantly, Aubrey was on his feet. He winced at a dull pain in his back, but was inordinately pleased, too. A week ago, after the efforts of quelling the magical flame, he was in a horrible condition – weak, aching, shivering uncontrollably, wincing at bright light. Leaping out of chairs would have been right out of the question. 'What's the news?'

George didn't answer. Gently, he placed the box on his desk. Whistling a tune, he cut the string with penknife and opened the package.

'George?'

George raised an eyebrow, but simply continued his whistling. He reached into the box and pulled out a small, muslin-wrapped bundle, which he tossed to Aubrey.

Aubrey unwrapped it. 'Ham?' He sniffed it and the savoury aroma made his mouth water, his appetite a sure sign that his condition had improved.

Another bundle sailed toward him. Hastily, he put the ham on his desk in time to catch a cold roast chicken wrapped in a linen tea towel. Looking up, he found a jar coming at him. He let out a yelp, but managed to catch it in the crook of one arm. He had time to see that the jar was full of pickled onions before he had to put down both it and the chicken. More foodstuffs were arcing toward him.

George kept whistling and kept up a barrage – sausage, gherkins, relish, mustard, loaves of freshly baked bread, two large bottles of ginger beer, apples, pears.

With frantic speed, Aubrey caught each of the flying foods and added them to the growing pile on his desk. When George flung two enamel plates his way, Aubrey plucked them out of the air and waved them over his head. 'Enough! Enough!'

George grinned. 'I thought you'd never surrender.' He peeked into the box and took out a bread knife. 'Good timing, as I only had these left.' He held up two stoneware mugs, which he proceeded to fill with ginger beer. 'A toast, before we feast.'

Aubrey took his mug and tasted the ginger beer. He looked sharply at George. 'This is yours, isn't it?'

'From Mother's special stock.'

'And the ham. That's yours too.'

'When only the best will do.'

Aubrey surveyed the fare spread out on his desk. His textbooks were buried under edibles. 'The news is good, I take it.'

'We're not going to lose the farm.'

Aubrey held out his mug. 'Here's to the Doyle family,' he said. 'And the Doyle family farm.'

'Hear, hear.' George drank deeply, then filled his mug again. He pulled out his chair and sagged into it. 'I can't tell you how relieved I am.'

'Oh, I think I have a fair idea. Now, tell me, how did this all come about?'

'Rokeby-Taylor.'

To steady himself, Aubrey sat on the bed. 'Of all the

things I thought you were going to say, that wasn't one of them.'

'Well, once we alerted the authorities to Rokeby-Taylor's involvement in Tremaine's schemes, it was shock all round, it seems. It turns out that the bank that had our loan was one of his, and the manager was one of his underlings. Through some shifty business he brought things to a head, after actually organising the landslip in the first place. A bit of water magic, apparently.'

'I could have discovered that,' Aubrey said. 'Some poking around, a few questions here and there.'

'And I'm glad you didn't, old man, having given your word and all that.'

Aubrey had nothing to say. He didn't deserve such gratitude for doing nothing. But on the other hand, he had done something: he'd kept his word, even though it ran against all his instincts. 'And now,' he said, 'we have an exhibition opening to go to.'

George glanced at his watch, an action that caused Aubrey a pang over the fate of his own. 'Half an hour. Plenty of time to freshen up.' He stood and dusted crumbs from his chest. 'What is Mrs Hepworth's show about this time? Any sort of theme or title or such?'

'"The Frontier of the New", which doesn't say much, I suppose. I'm going with an open mind.'

'As you should.'

THE EXHIBITION WAS AT THE GREYTHORN GALLERY IN THE town. This was a blocky new building, two-storeyed, with many windows. Looking at it, Aubrey imagined that the county would now be overrun with retired glaziers looking for something to spend their money on.

On their walk to the gallery, Aubrey was still puzzling over Rokeby-Taylor's part in the plot against George's father. George had no further light to shed on it. They walked up the stairs and into the entrance hall of the gallery, only to run into the unexpected pair of Tallis and Craddock. *Sounds like a pair music hall of music hall performers*, Aubrey thought. *Put your hands together for Tallis and Craddock – a song, a joke and some questionable interrogation methods!* He didn't give them a chance to speak.

'Rokeby-Taylor,' he said without any preliminaries. 'Why would he want to ruin George's father?'

To give Craddock his due, he played an immaculate forward defence. 'That's where the personal becomes the political.'

Tallis nodded, hands behind his back. 'It was part of a larger plan.'

And when is anything not, these days? Aubrey thought.

A stream of people came up the stairs, chattering and oblivious to the discreet meeting that was being held in the entrance hall. Society's finest disappeared through the glass doors into the exhibition room, ready to explore the Frontier of the New, while sipping champagne and nibbling on carefully constructed canapés.

Tallis eyed these art lovers with suspicion, but went on. 'Rokeby-Taylor was trying to get at the Prime Minister through those close to him. At least, that's what the bank manager claimed during interrogation. It was all a plot to divert the Prime Minister, burden him with worries, to affect his judgement, his decision-making.'

George muttered a series of colourful oaths. Aubrey felt they were too mild.

This was the third plot that was directly aimed at people around Aubrey's father. First came the attempts on his mother's life, then her near abduction on the high seas, and now this. While it may have looked like sound strategy – distracting the Prime Minister made good, if distasteful, sense – Aubrey had a feeling that it was more personal than that. Added to that the fact that Dr Tremaine had once kidnapped his father and was on the verge of doing him physical harm before thwarted, Aubrey was starting to wonder if Dr Tremaine's interest in his father had a special edge.

'A very subtle plan,' Craddock said. 'Tell me, did Rokeby-Taylor strike either of you as a subtle man?'

'Quite the opposite.' Aubrey leaned against one of the half-pillars that decorated the walls.

'Since your report on Rokeby-Taylor's demise,' Tallis said, 'we've done considerable checking into the man's affairs. It seems that he had a manager who was the business mind, taking care of all financial matters while Rokeby-Taylor swanned around, making contacts and greasing up to people. Interestingly, this Mr Ingles studied business in Holmland.'

'And so I'd say he won't see the outside of one of His Majesty's prisons for some time,' Craddock said. 'We can continue our chats with him there.'

'And this plan to ruin George's family?' Aubrey asked.

'Who do you think could invent such a scheme, if Rokeby-Taylor was incapable of it?' Craddock asked.

'Dr Tremaine.'

'So it would appear,' Craddock said.

'One thing that still puzzles me,' Aubrey said.

'And what is that?' Craddock asked. Tallis eyed him suspiciously.

'Why are you two here?'

'In Greythorn?' Tallis said.

'At this exhibition.'

'A number of reasons,' Craddock said, after several significant glances were shared between the two men. 'We were invited, for one. We've both known Ophelia Hepworth for years.'

'Superb artist,' Tallis growled, 'not afraid to experiment with space and perspective.'

So unexpected was the artistic insight, for an instant Aubrey was sure that Tallis had vanished and an alien had taken his place.

Craddock went on. 'And Professor Mansfield is another reason. We're wondering why she left so suddenly for Aigyptos, so visiting Greythorn was a useful start.'

Aubrey drew on his years of amateur dramatics and constructed the best puzzled face of all time. 'Aigyptos?'

'We know she's been there before,' Tallis said, 'and is friends with the Sultan, so it's no real surprise. The haste was, though. Sudden leave of absence, mid-term?'

The silence that stretched out after this observation was not embarrassed, nor awkward. It was more like a challenge.

Aubrey was surprised when Craddock cracked first. 'I'm keen to get in to see the paintings,' he said. 'Rumours are that Ophelia has done something extraordinary with light.' He glanced at Aubrey. 'Did you hear that the Rashid Stone was stolen from the Museum?'

'Rashid Stone? Museum?' Aubrey said.

'Stolen?' George supplied, to round out the set.

'Well, if that display doesn't convince us that you know nothing about it, I don't know what would,' Craddock said dryly.

'The gang of thieves that was rounded up at the museum were quite forthcoming,' Tallis said. 'They claimed they'd been hired to steal the Rashid Stone, but had been prevented by magical defences. They couldn't tell us who contracted them either. A mysterious man, was all they could provide, and they were being most helpful by that time.' He studied Aubrey. 'Your information that Rokeby-Taylor was involved with this scheme tallies with this perfectly.'

'I had some of my best operatives search the workshop for magical residue,' Craddock said, 'but we'd waited too long and couldn't find a thing.'

Aubrey's heart restarted. 'Pity.'

'So we seem to have a mystery here, which shouldn't surprise us,' Craddock said, 'mysteries being the order of the day, lately.'

'Lovely,' George said, but his attention seemed to be on the people entering rather than fully on the conversation. 'But you haven't really answered Aubrey's question. Why are you both here? Why didn't you just abduct us if you wanted a chat?'

Again, Craddock and Tallis shared a look.

Tallis cleared his throat. 'Apparently one of Tremaine's plans was to sow discord between our two services. Futile, obviously, but it was felt that a united front may be the best thing to present for a few months. In public, most particularly.'

'You're on your best behaviour!' George said, delighted. 'You've been scolded and now you have to put your best foot forward!'

Both men looked as if they'd sucked on a lemon apiece. 'That's a rather simple view,' Craddock said.

'But not incorrect,' George said.

Aubrey kept a straight face. He could only think of one person who could bring about such a rapprochement between the two men. He hoped his reports had been of assistance to his father in this matter.

'Some other news we thought you'd like to know,' Tallis said. 'Count Brandt and his people have all been arrested.'

'You've taken them into custody? What for?'

'Ah. You haven't heard?' Tallis said. '*We* didn't arrest them.'

'At their request, Count Brandt and a number of his most influential people were conveyed to a remote part of the Holmland coast in a submersible, in order to arrive undetected,' Craddock said. 'The Rokeby-Taylor experimental submersible.'

'The *Electra*? How on earth did they organise that?'

'Rokeby-Taylor,' Tallis said. 'Before his demise and exposure, he still had influence. He had an audience with the King and apparently explained how brave and noble Brandt and his crowd were. With royal backing, Rokeby-Taylor was able to convince the navy that Brandt should have the blasted thing.'

'Their plan was to meet with the leaders of this Circle, the secret opposition group in Holmland,' Tallis said. 'Arriving undetected was vital, so they could spend time gathering their strength, meeting key people, planning and so on.'

Aubrey had that most useless of premonitions – one that happens just a split-second before the event. He knew what Craddock was about to say.

'The Circle was a hoax. It was carefully constructed by a branch of the Holmland intelligence services to appear like a real, functioning dissident group. It meant that they were able to know exactly what Count Brandt and his crowd were up to, and move in on them as appropriate. They've been taken and the experimental submersible captured.'

Aubrey's heart sank. All those innovations, financed by Albion, built by the best Albion minds, now in the hands of Holmland. He now saw that the first attempt on Count Brandt's life – the thunderstorm spell – was just a way of nudging Count Brandt into action. Nothing like a deadly attack to make someone feel their foes meant business – and that they needed counter-attacking.

Craddock nodded. 'I have a suspicion that the whole business with Count Brandt and the Circle was really a ruse to get hold of the submersible. First, they tried to destroy it, but someone must have suggested this complex plan to steal it.'

'Complex plan. That's a synonym for "Dr Tremaine", isn't it?' Aubrey rubbed his temples. 'How were Count Brandt and his people captured?'

Tallis glowered with, it appeared, some pleasure. 'The Great Manfred was with them. He promised to introduce them to key members of the Circle, but instead he handed them over. He'd been in constant contact with a branch of their intelligence agencies.'

Aubrey's head spun. 'Wait. Manfred was one of ours. A counter-spy.'

'So we thought,' Tallis said. He glanced at Craddock. 'It seemed he was playing a double game.'

'A double-double game,' Aubrey corrected absently, as his mind raced through the implications. He felt suddenly chill when he remembered how Manfred was eager to get him to Fisherberg.

Perhaps there were four plans to get at the Prime Minister through those closest to him.

George snorted. 'I don't know what the world's coming to. If you can't trust a counter-spy, who can you trust?'

'Brandt was sending money to the Circle,' Aubrey said. 'With the best intentions.'

Tallis and Craddock both looked pained. 'A great deal of money,' Craddock said. 'It was a superb scheme.'

'All's not lost. The money we've been pouring into the Holmland treasury this way will be balanced neatly by the fairy gold the *Imperator* is taking over there,' Tallis said.

'The *Imperator* is on its way?' Aubrey said.

'A lovely birthday present for the Elektor,' Craddock said.

'What about Count Brandt?' George asked. 'What about his people?'

'They're in Harsgard Prison,' Tallis said bleakly.

Aubrey knew that Harsgard Prison was notorious for 'incidents'. Many who went into the place never left.

Craddock took out a notebook. 'On more magical matters – if you'll excuse us, Tallis – you haven't had any more thoughts on the nature of the magic Dr Tremaine was wielding?'

It had also been the Magisterium who'd freed

Maggie's Crew. After painstaking, meticulous work, they were removed from the array through a combination of careful stabilising magic and delicate engineering, but their recovery needed long-term treatment. They were still in the care of the specialised team at St Michael's Hospital, but the latest outlook was positive.

Other squads of Magisterium operatives had spread through the under-city, mapping Tremaine's tunnels and beginning the work of disconnecting his underground web. Trinovant had experienced more than the usual number of disruptions to trains, water and electricity, but in a city where grumbling was as natural as breathing, it simply made everyone feel vaguely satisfied that they had a hard lot.

'On urbomancy?' Aubrey said. 'I want to do some more research. It might be important, it might be nothing. I'll need more time.' *And the assistance of Professor Mansfield, when she gets back after her little job.*

Professor Mansfield had been only too happy to return the Rashid Stone to her good friend the Sultan, especially after Aubrey showed her the mysterious fragment. She was just as fervent in her desire to return the stone to its rightful owners as Lady Rose was.

'I see,' Craddock said. 'And your status as irregular operative, you're happy with that?'

Aubrey thought for a moment. 'I wouldn't mind some more training and some access to the Magisterium's resources.'

'I'll see what I can do.'

At that moment, a hubbub broke out from the direction of the street. Aubrey was automatically alert, but he relaxed when he saw his parents mounting the stairs.

Sir Darius greeted Craddock and Tallis as if he had expected them to be there. On reflection, Aubrey thought that was probably the case.

'Hello, Mother,' he said. He kissed her cheek. 'Interested in seeing experiments with space and perspective?'

'Hello, Aubrey. Are you eating properly? I heard you were ill and had to miss some classes this week.'

'Three times a day, as prescribed. Feeling much better.'

'Is this true, George?'

George blushed, as was his wont when in the presence of Lady Rose. 'True? Rather. Three meals, one after the other. Made him ox-like in the health stakes.'

Lady Rose looked sceptically at both of them. 'Then you need more vegetables, Aubrey. See to it.' She leaned close. 'Your father has told me about your latest exploit. I'm proud, and he is too.'

'He is?'

'He may tell you. He may not. Sometimes he thinks that too much praise is not helpful for a young person. I argue that unearned praise is the problem, but credit where credit is due is my policy.'

Sir Darius offered his arm to his wife. 'To the paintings?'

'Of course. That's what we're here for.' She smiled. 'Among other things.'

Tallis and Craddock followed Sir Darius and Lady Rose. Aubrey and George were left alone. 'Shall we go?' Aubrey said.

'You go, old man. I'm waiting for someone. Ah, here she is.'

A pretty, diminutive young woman hurried up the stairs. Her golden curls peeped out from under a small, excessively stylish bonnet. She smiled widely when she saw George.

'Sophie!' he cried and dashed across the entrance hall. He took both her hands. 'Aubrey, do you remember Sophie Delroy from Lutetia?'

'Of course I do. Hello, Sophie.'

'Hello, Aubrey. What progress has your father made with women's suffrage in your country?' She took a notebook and pencil out of her bag and waited for his answer.

'Not now, Sophie,' George said. 'You're here to report on Ophelia Hepworth's exhibition first. Politics after.'

'Politics always come first, George,' she said. Her accent made his name sound like Zhorzhe. Aubrey had an inkling that George enjoyed it.

George offered Sophie his arm. 'To the paintings?'

She frowned. 'Haven't you forgotten something?'

George reached into his jacket and took out a notebook of his own. 'Ready.'

This time, Aubrey was left alone. He was happy George had such a kindred spirit to enjoy the exhibition with. They were a fine couple and he wished them happiness.

A familiar voice interrupted his thoughts. 'I saw Craddock and Tallis in the exhibition. What on earth are they doing here?'

Caroline was wearing something vaguely oriental, high-waisted, in a combination of shimmering silver and crimson. She had a small hat with a feather in it.

Aubrey swallowed, tried to hide it, nearly choked.

Caroline sighed. 'If you're going to keep reacting like that, I'm going to stop dressing up.'

Red-faced, Aubrey waved a hand frantically. 'No, no, don't do that. Last thing I want. Something just got caught in my throat. A fly. Beetle. Something.'

She crossed her arms. 'So tell me about Craddock and Tallis.'

When he'd finished, Caroline glanced toward the exhibition area. 'They don't suspect that you gave the Rashid Stone to Professor Mansfield?'

'I think Craddock might. But he didn't press the point. The Sultan may have more friends than he realises.'

'It's a pity that Mr Ravi didn't have a chance to investigate the stone. From what you've told me, his insights could have been vital.'

Aubrey – and the entire university – had been shocked at the news of Lanka Ravi's death. The brilliant theoretician had abruptly sailed for home, but died on the voyage, of an unspecified disease. It was a loss that would be felt for years, but many were already clamouring to be allowed access to the numerous notebooks Ravi had left behind. Rumours were abounding about the contents of the notebooks – brilliant, difficult insights that would need much close attention. Aubrey hoped that he'd be allowed to see them some day.

'And with all that's happened, where does that leave us?' Caroline said and Aubrey was nearly lost in the heady import of her words.

Where indeed? A thousand scenarios played out in his mind.

'Sorry,' he said when he realised Caroline was staring at him. 'It's getting a touch stuffy in here.'

'I agree. You need some fresh air.'

'I haven't seen the exhibition.'

'I've seen it. I'll tell you about it while we walk.'

'We? Walk? We?'

'If you're just going to mumble nonsense rhymes, I'm going alone.'

THEY WALKED IN SILENCE FOR SOME TIME, TOWARD Whitsun College. They crossed the lawn of the courtyard, out the Bannister Gate and along the well-populated river bank. In the early evening, the luncheon picnics that had become afternoon teas were well on their way to becoming supper, with groups of languid students enjoying the last vestiges of the day.

Aubrey, as always, sought for things to say that wouldn't make him sound stupid, or crass, or anything else she wouldn't like. After some internal struggle, he decided on a novel approach: he chose to remain silent.

They passed tennis courts. The sound of tennis balls on racquets reminded Aubrey of a chain of bubbles bursting, very slowly.

Eventually, it was Caroline who broke the silence, as they rounded the last of the courts and headed towards the town. 'Are you unwell?'

Aubrey considered this. 'You mean, apart from my condition?'

'I'll get to that. It's just that you're unusually quiet.'

'Ah. I was being mysterious.'

'Is that what it was? I thought you might have indigestion.'

So much for mysterious, he thought. 'You're back into your studies?'

A tennis ball came sailing over the fence. Caroline caught it in one hand and lobbed it back. 'Of course. I have some catching up to do.'

'It gets like that, sometimes.'

'What does?'

'This adventuring business. Exciting stuff, but eventually day-to-day life has to be taken care of. It's lucky you're a quick study.'

'Yes.' She wrinkled her brow. 'You've managed it, adventuring then catching up?'

'Not without some late nights and close squeaks. Sometimes the adventure is the easy part, and catching up the hard part.'

They wandered by the Botanic Garden, where cactuses and succulents seemed to be making a determined bid to take over the perennials bed.

'Speaking of your condition,' Caroline said. 'How is it?'

'Precarious. Unstable. Fragile.' He sighed. 'No change, in other words.'

'And what are you doing about it?'

Aubrey would have appreciated some sympathy, but Caroline's matter-of-fact confidence that he would have matters in hand – or at least have some sort of plan – was oddly cheering. 'Well, the Rashid Stone and the Roman fragment look promising. I'm hoping that when Professor Mansfield gets back we can really start to crack that ancient script. It might hold some clues.'

'Or it might not.'

Aubrey glanced sharply at her, but she touched him on the arm. 'I don't mean to be harsh. But your state is too serious not to have an alternative plan, just in case your first is fruitless.'

'I'm in the right place for research. An answer could be waiting for me in a book, on a parchment, something. I just have to find it.'

'If it's there at all,' Caroline said and once again she touched his arm to remove the sting from her words.

Aubrey didn't mind. The balm was worth the hurt.

'Or there is Dr Tremaine,' Aubrey said cautiously. 'He might know something.'

Caroline's face set hard. They walked in silence past the red brick of the Music Faculty and turned a corner toward the centre of town.

'Then you want to find Tremaine as much as I do,' she said eventually.

'Oh yes. As well as his knowledge, there is a matter of the Brayshire Ruby. I haven't told Father yet . . .'

'As you thought you'd get it back before he noticed it was gone.'

'Yes.' Aubrey shrugged. 'He's dangerous, Tremaine.'

'Which is why he should be found.'

'And brought to justice.'

'Anything to stop him.'

Aubrey bought ice-cream for them from a roadside vendor, even though he wasn't hungry. It dripped, and he imagined someone following his vanilla trail along the street.

He hadn't yet made a fool of himself so, according to precedent, he was about to. Rather than leave it to happen haphazardly, he decided to take matters into his own hands. 'And what about us, then?'

Caroline's face clouded. 'I don't know.'

'That's unusual. You're usually quite certain about things.'

'Yes. It's important to be certain.'

She finished her ice-cream, thoughtfully. To Aubrey, she looked unbearably sweet and impossible. At that moment, with her as perfectly charming, wise, fascinating and lovely as she was, he realised how things were, and how things had to be.

He cleared his throat and gave the last of his ice-cream to a hungry-looking dog that was waiting outside a pub. 'I was thinking that things were going well,' he said, every word a stab in his heart. 'I mean, going well as they are. I enjoy your company, and you're more than handy, adventure-wise. Vital, even, when it comes to saving the country. Not that anyone would know because our exploits are secret. But there you have it.'

What have I done? he thought, but he knew. He'd made sure that any hopes he'd had were dashed.

'Babbling, Aubrey,' she said. This time she glanced at him. 'And babbling very kindly.' It was her time to clear her throat. Aubrey had enough perspicacity to look away when she touched the corner of her eyes with a knuckle. 'I won't be so ungrateful, so gauche as to contradict you, dear Aubrey. So I'll agree. Yes, I think things have been going well between us.'

'Perfectly manageable,' his traitor mouth said as they walked side by side, not looking at each other.

'Perfectly manageable,' she repeated softly.

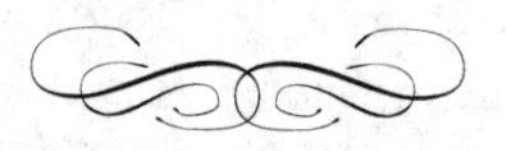

Aubrey and Caroline wandered back to the gallery through an evening that was warm and drowsy. Honeysuckle scented the air.

George dashed down the gallery stairs, towing Sophie and waving a newspaper. 'Look! I'm in *Luna*!'

He thrust it in front of Aubrey and Caroline. Submersibles. Stage magic. Underground tunnels. Traitors. Exploding thunderclouds.

'I don't remember any bronze giants,' Aubrey said.

'Nor armies of giant sloths,' Caroline added.

George beamed. 'I had to fiddle with the details a little.'

'A little? What's this about a hot air balloon in an underground chamber?'

'License, license.' George waved a hand. 'It's the sort of thing my readers love. Brave John Hope, useful Arthur St Clair and the lovely Charlotte Henderson. The Adventurers Three.'

Caroline raised an eyebrow. 'Lovely Charlotte Henderson?'

Aubrey opened and closed his mouth a few times. '*Useful* Arthur St Clair?'

'Imagination is a wonderful tool, isn't it?'

'But it's not true.'

'Fiction isn't meant to be true.' George grinned at their expressions. 'Since all this is secret, I had to say it was all made up. They loved it.'

Aubrey, Caroline and Sophie laughed. George looked offended for a moment, but couldn't keep it up. He joined in, until people looked out of windows to see what all the jollity was about.

The mysterious Beccaria Cage could be the cure for Aubrey's condition: a way to reunite his body and soul. But could its usefulness hide something more sinister?

After Aubrey narrowly escapes the worst fate he can imagine, he realises there is only one thing to do: he must confront his nemesis. With George and Caroline at his side, he travels to Holmland – the home of Dr Tremaine and the heart of hostile territory – only to face magical conundrums, near-death experiences, ghosts, brigands and enemies on their own ground.

Fisherberg is a city on a knife edge. Can Aubrey solve its mysteries before Dr Tremaine's warmongering tips the world into chaos?

Out now!

About the Author

Michael Pryor has published more than twenty fantasy books and over forty short stories, from literary fiction to science fiction to slapstick humour.. Michael has been shortlisted six times for the Aurealis Awards (including for *Blaze of Glory* and *Heart of Gold*), has been nominated for a Ditmar award and longlisted for the Gold Inky award, and five of his books have been Children's Book Council of Australia Notable Books (including *Word of Honour* and *Time of Trial*). He is currently writing the final book in the Laws of Magic series. For more information about Michael and his books, please visit www.michaelpryor.com.au